DADDY IN COWBOY BOOTS

LAYLAH ROBERTS

Laylah Roberts

Daddy in Cowboy Boots.

© 2020, Laylah Roberts

Laylah.roberts@gmail.com

laylahroberts.com

Cover Design by: Allycat's Creations

Editing: Celeste Jones

❀ Created with Vellum

LET'S KEEP IN TOUCH!

Don't miss a new release, sign up to my newsletter for sneak peeks, deleted scenes and giveaways: https://landing.mailerlite.com/web-forms/landing/p7l6g0

You can also join my Facebook readers group here: https://www.facebook.com/groups/386830425069911/

BOOKS BY LAYLAH ROBERTS

Doms of Decadence

Just for You, Sir

Forever Yours, Sir

For the Love of Sir

Sinfully Yours, Sir

Make me, Sir

A Taste of Sir

To Save Sir

Sir's Redemption

Reveal Me, Sir

Montana Daddies

Daddy Bear

Daddy's Little Darling

Daddy's Naughty Darling Novella

Daddy's Sweet Girl

Daddy's Lost Love

A Montana Daddies Christmas

Daring Daddy

Warrior Daddy

Daddy's Angel

Heal Me, Daddy

Daddy in Cowboy Boots

MC Daddies

Motorcycle Daddy

Hero Daddy

Protector Daddy

Haven, Texas Series

Lila's Loves

Laken's Surrender

Saving Savannah

Molly's Man

Saxon's Soul

Mastered by Malone

How West was Won

Cole's Mistake

Jardin's Gamble

Men of Orion

Worlds Apart

Cavan Gang

Rectify

Redemption

Redemption Valley

Audra's Awakening

Old-Fashioned Series

An Old-Fashioned Man

Two Old-Fashioned Men

Her Old-Fashioned Husband

Her Old-Fashioned Boss

His Old-Fashioned Love

An Old-Fashioned Christmas

Bad Boys of Wildeside

Wilde

Sinclair

Luke

1

L inc felt like a creeper.

But he couldn't help but be drawn to the giggles drifting out of the open window from Charlie and Clint's living room. He stood in the shadows on the porch, staring in as they danced around.

Yep, definite stalker vibes.

Sadness filled him. He was happy so many of the men on Sanctuary Ranch had found their other half, but he couldn't help but feel lonely.

As Ari moved away from the couch, he spotted a woman with gleaming dark hair pulled up into a high ponytail kneeling by Charlie. Who was she? She moved her head, smiling up at Charlie.

Dear Lord, she was beautiful. His heart started beating faster.

Easy, man. You don't even know her.

Something told him, though, that this girl was special. He watched as she gracefully stood. She was petite but with an abundance of curves he longed to run his hands over. Her gaze dipped down as Ari gave her some money.

Shy?

He watched as she walked out of the room, her arms precariously filled with two large containers. Well now, that wouldn't do. Tiny thing like her shouldn't be carrying around anything heavy.

She could hurt herself.

Walking around the porch, he headed to the front door, making it there just in time to see her heading towards the steps. The tubs in her arms covered her face and he watched as she stumbled, misjudging the step. The containers went flying through the air and he leapt forward to catch her as she cried out.

Wrapping an arm around her waist, he set her down on the porch. Her scent drifted towards him. Cinnamon and apples. Yum. Made him wonder how she would taste.

Not wanting to let go, he held her a bit longer than was appropriate before he stepped away. Hopefully, she'd just think he was making certain she was steady on her feet. Damn though, he wished he had the right to sweep her up into his arms. To feel all that softness pressed against him.

Easy, man.

She was staring up at him, her lips parted slightly.

"You all right, sweetheart?" he asked.

"Oh...oh yes. I'm fine." Her voice was slightly husky. Fuck. Him. How could someone so sweet looking have such a sexy-sounding voice?

"What are you doing carrying around all that stuff? You should have asked someone to help you," he scolded her gently.

"That's okay, I'm used to carrying it on my own. I just misjudged where the step was. It's not the first time it's happened. You saved me from another skinned knee, thank you."

"You're welcome. But I don't like the idea of you hurting yourself. Next time, you get someone to help you, okay? Little bit like you doesn't need to be carrying such heavy stuff."

"It's not that heavy." Her gaze went down, her shoulders curving in.

Fuck. What had he said? Was he pushing too hard?

Ease up.

"Hey, everything okay?" he asked.

"Oh yes." She laughed nervously. "I better pick everything up. I hope nothing's broken."

She turned away from him and he had to fight his instincts to pull her back, to press her against him. To admonish her that she shouldn't be walking down steps without holding his hand.

Yeah, that would go over well. She'd likely run a mile, trying to get away from the crazy dude. He followed her down the steps.

"I'm Linc by the way. What's your name?"

"Marisol."

Marisol. Pretty.

"Nice to meet you, Marisol." He stacked the containers on top of one another before she could do it. "Now, where am I taking these?"

"Oh, you don't have to carry them for me."

He was silent. Did she seriously think he was going to just stand here and let her carry them? What kind of men was she used to? His nana would have whipped his ass for letting a woman carry something when he had two able arms.

Eventually, she caved. "Uh, if you could carry them over to my car for me, that would be great. Thank you."

"You're welcome."

"You, uhh, you work here?" she asked.

She sounded so uncertain and he could have kicked himself. Here she was, alone in the dark with a strange man who hadn't even bothered to introduce himself properly.

"I do. I'm the ranch manager."

She stopped beside a small, beat-up car. Even with just the security light to guide the way, he could tell it was a heap of junk.

It wasn't a car he would ever allow his woman to drive. If she had to drive somewhere without him, then she'd be in something safe.

Not a tiny death trap that looked like it should have been scrapped years ago.

"This is what you drive?" He couldn't keep the disapproval from his voice.

"Yes," she said quietly. She opened the trunk and he stuck the containers inside. He was aware that her shoulders had slumped again.

"Hey, I didn't mean to insult you. It's just that even in the dark I can tell this car needs some work." He ran a hand along the side of it, feeling the dents and scratches. Had someone used it as a damn rally car?

"It's my aunt's," she confessed. "I'm just borrowing it."

Her aunt let her drive this?

"Thanks for carrying my stuff and for, uhh, rescuing me before."

"No problem," he replied easily. "You ever need a knight in shining armor. Or a hero in cowboy boots, you know where to find me."

She laughed. She obviously thought he was joking.

If only she knew, he was very serious.

Miss Marisol hadn't seen the last of him.

MARISOL HAD a new hero to fill her dreams. She still couldn't believe that he'd come to her rescue the way he had, sweeping her up as though she was a lightweight when she definitely was not.

The man had to have muscles on muscles. He'd definitely felt very firm. Of course if she was actually dreaming, he wouldn't just let her drive off. He'd flip her over his shoulder and carry her away to his cabin in the woods, lock the door and ravish her. Then spank her ass. Then cuddle her.

And repeat.

A sigh escaped her lips. A girl was entitled to dream, right?

Of white knights and damsels in distress.

Or maybe a hero in cowboy boots and a curvy nail technician?

"Urgh, Marisol, you have no chance with that guy," she muttered to herself as she pulled out of the driveway of Sanctuary Ranch.

Her aunt had been thrilled when she'd been asked to come out here for Charlie's bridal shower. Sanctuary Ranch was owned by the Jensen family. Apparently, they were a big deal around here. Wealthy. Connected.

Marisol had been worried that the women tonight would all be stuck-up snobs. Sometimes she found that she was treated less as a professional and more like a maid at these sorts of parties. She was there to do nails and facials, not serve food or clean.

But the women tonight had all been lovely. Fun. Friendly.

A pang of loneliness hit her. What would it be like to have friends like that? Who would dance and laugh and be there to support you?

Marisol had always been painfully shy at school, it had been hard for her to make friends. She'd been looked down on. The poor orphan. Pitied. Ridiculed.

But Charlie and her friends hadn't been like that tonight. She'd spent the evening painting nails and doing facials after a full day of working at her aunt's day spa and as fun as it had been, she was exhausted.

All she wanted to do was go home, shower then curl up with one of her Daddy Dom books in bed. She had a new one from CJ Bennett she was dying to dive into. Pretty much all of the small wage her aunt paid her went to buying books.

They were her escape.

Only, she knew she wouldn't be dreaming about any of the heroes in her books tonight. Nope, she'd be dreaming about a broad-shouldered cowboy with a voice like sin. A voice that had made her insides dance, even when he scolded her.

Oh, who are you kidding? Especially when he scolded you. Like you haven't dreamed of a man who was protective, loving and sometimes stern.

The way he'd scolded her for carrying those tubs on her own had made her insides tighten. Heck, she didn't know who he thought would carry them for her. But it was sweet that he'd cared. After all, she was a complete stranger to him.

And she'd likely never see him again. She didn't have any reason to go back out to Sanctuary Ranch. He definitely didn't have any reason to come to the spa where she worked. It wasn't like she ever really went anywhere else. Most of her time was spent working or at home, doing the housework.

Any free time she had was spent reading and daydreaming about handsome, sweet, sexy, bossy Daddies.

In cowboy boots.

Oh, yes, please.

She caught a glimpse of the time on the dash of the old car and swore under her breath.

Shit! If she didn't get home soon, her aunt was going to have a fit. She pushed down on the accelerator, taking a corner fast. A smile lit up her face. She loved driving fast. And while this old rust bucket of a car might not have a working heater or decent suspension—she bounced with each hole in the road—it did have a bit of horsepower.

Turning another corner, she let out a giggle at the rush of adrenaline. She shot down the straight road. Headlights headed towards her on the other side of the road, and she dimmed her lights, but didn't slow down. She had a good speed going now.

"Go, baby, go," she cheered.

Then her good mood plummeted as she heard a siren go off behind her.

Mierda! No.

Not good. Not good.

The other car had turned around and was heading back her way. She hadn't even noticed that it was a cop car.

Drat. Damn it. Her aunt would kill her if she got a speeding ticket. She slowed and put on her indicator, driving off to the side of the road.

The cop car pulled up behind her, the headlights flooding her car with light. Nerves filled her stomach. *It's all right. It's not him. Not all cops are bad.*

Rosalind had filled Marisol's head with stories of corrupt police officers. Of how all cops were to be feared. Were evil. Once she was older, she realized her aunt had done that on purpose, that she'd likely made most of those stories up in order to make Marisol mistrustful of the police.

Then when she was ten, her aunt had been arrested and Marisol had been questioned by a police officer on a power trip before social services arrived. He'd yelled at her, threatened her, terrified her. But she'd never said a word to him. Or anyone since about what happened. Still, it had further ingrained a fear of the authorities.

You have nothing to be afraid of. Just take the ticket and drive away. Nothing to be scared of.

It wasn't like she hadn't gotten speeding tickets before. Just never at nighttime. On such a quiet road.

He could do anything to you and no one would ever know.

Okay, she had to stop.

What was a cop doing out here at this time of night anyway? There was a knock at her window and she jumped, letting out a cry.

Shit! She held her hand to her heart. He'd scared her half to death. What did he think he was doing?

He's probably trying to get you to wind down your window so he can talk to you . . . idiot.

"Right, right," she muttered to herself as she reached over and wound down the window.

"Evening," a friendly voice said.

Even psychopaths can sound friendly. Assassins can sound friendly. School principals can sound friendly.

But they all have the potential to make your life a living hell.

"Miss? You okay? Miss? Are you hyperventilating?"

"I'm really sorry for speeding, I won't do it again. I promise. I mean, I wasn't going that fast, right?"

"You were going ten miles over the speed limit."

Crap. Crap. "Is that bad? That's bad, right? Please don't take me to jail and lock me up in a cell with some scary woman doing time for cutting off her husband's penis. Because if she could cut off a penis then what could she do to me? I have no self-defense skills. None. My only skills are nails and facials and I don't think that's going to help me against someone who can turn a bar of soap into a shank."

"Can you turn a bar of soap into a shank?" the cop asked curiously.

"Yep, I saw it on one of those real-life crime shows. Or was it a fictional crime show? I'm not sure. Do prisoners get bars of soap?"

"Well, we do let them wash themselves. We're not completely heartless."

"I'm doomed."

"Okay, someone has been watching way too much TV." The voice still sounded calm, even amused.

"Sorry," she muttered. She clenched her hands into fists, trying to calm herself down. The last thing she needed was for him to think she was on something.

"So do you do this a lot?"

"Ramble on about penises and shanks?" She gaped up at him.

He's not him. He's not him.

He cleared his throat. She got the feeling he might be trying not to burst into laughter. She didn't know why he would be laughing. None of this was funny.

If she didn't end up in a cell then her aunt was going to kill her for getting a speeding ticket.

"Ah no, I meant speeding. Since you seem to have this fear that I'm about to drag you away to a jail cell I wondered if that meant you had a whole ream of unpaid speeding fines."

"Oh no, I always pay my speeding fines. I mean, I don't get that many. At least, not in Montana. Those sorts of things don't follow you from other states, do they?"

The policeman made a strangled noise and she finally dared to look up at him.

All right, he was tall. But then she was sitting down so it was kind of hard to tell for sure. Broad shoulders. Like Linc.

But this guy was a cop.

Easy, Marisol.

It's not him. This isn't the same. Not all cops are corrupt assholes with enormous egos who think they can threaten little girls.

She couldn't tell much else about him considering it was dark and his headlights cast his features into shadow.

"License and registration please."

"Huh?"

"License and registration."

"Oh right. Should have thought of that. I'm just gonna get them from my glove box."

"That would be good, thank you," he said politely.

Okay, so far, he was blowing all her preconceptions about cops into pieces. Her hand still shook slightly as she passed over the bits of paper.

"Ma'am, are you okay? Have you been drinking tonight?"

"I had a few sips of a pink lemonade. Oh no, I never asked if it had alcohol in it. What if it had alcohol in it? No, I don't think it did. I would have been able to tell, right?"

There was a beat of silence and she went back over what she'd just said. Right. He wouldn't know if it had alcohol in it, because he wasn't there. He didn't have a pink lemonade.

"Jesus, Marisol. Get a grip," she muttered.

"Pardon?" he asked as he shone his flashlight down onto her credentials.

"Nothing, sorry. I'm rambling. I talk a lot when I'm nervous."

"I make you nervous?"

"Yes. But don't take offense," she said hastily. "All cops make me nervous."

"Yeah? There a reason for that?"

"An over-active imagination," she said meekly. No way was she telling him the truth. Cops stuck together. Even when they lived in different states.

"Okay. You need to stick to the speed limit while driving, young lady."

Young lady?

"I'm sorry, sir." He just had that kind of voice that commanded respect, even though he wasn't being harsh. His tone was a mix of firm and kind.

Weird as that sounded.

She wondered again what he looked like. He had a nice voice. But he was likely old. Wrinkled. Maybe with a hairy nose and ears.

"Where have you been tonight?"

"At Sanctuary Ranch, I work for the spa in town. I was hired to do nails and facials for a bridal shower."

"Ahh, Charlie's bridal shower? Heard she's been ill."

"Um, yeah. That's why I came out here. Because they couldn't come in earlier. Charlie has really pretty nails now."

"I'm sure she does," he said warmly. "Right, Marisol. Here's what's going to happen—"

"I'm going to jail."

"Okay, you need to stop thinking that I'm going to put you in jail. You're giving me a complex."

"But you're a police officer. Isn't that what you do?" she asked nervously.

"Funnily enough, there is more to my job than taking people to jail. It would be rather full if I did that to everyone I met."

Right. Of course. Stop being a twit.

"So, what's going to happen is that you, young lady, are going to drive home at the speed limit or less the entire way. From now on, there is to be no more speeding or the next time you're caught I'm not going to be so lenient. Understand?" His voice was very stern now.

But strangely, it didn't do things to her like Linc's voice had. Maybe it was because she'd felt more at ease with Linc. He wasn't a dirty cop, after all.

Jeez, Marisol, this guy likely isn't a dirty cop either. He hasn't done anything but be nice to you.

"Yes, sir, I understand. Sorry. It really won't happen again."

At least, she hoped if it did, that she didn't get caught.

He handed the papers back through the window to her.

"You're really not giving me a ticket?" she asked in a small voice.

"I'm really not."

She let out a relieved sigh. That would save her from her aunt's wrath.

"Everything okay, sweetheart?" he asked. "Are you all right driving home alone?"

"Oh yes, I'm fine."

"You've got a cell phone? It's charged?"

These were weird questions for a cop to ask, right? Maybe it was a country thing. She'd only ever lived in cities before now.

"Ah, yes, I do." Her aunt had given her one of her old cell phones. But it only had a small amount of credit on it. Her aunt liked her to have it on her so she could call her when she needed her. It was a wonder she hadn't already called to see where Marisol was.

"Good. You shouldn't be driving around at night alone without a phone. Keep the doors locked and drive straight home, understand?"

"Yes, sir." It slipped out automatically even as she tried to work out why he cared.

"Good girl. Good night, Marisol."

"Good night, sir."

"Call me Ed. Nice to meet you. I'm sure I'll be seeing you around."

Lord, she really hoped not.

2

—————

Marisol pulled up around the back of her aunt's house with a sigh of relief.

She never thought she'd be happy to get home. Not that this was her home. It was Rosalind's house. Never hers. Which was just as well since this house was butt ugly.

It was enormous. Way too much space for just the two of them. Although she was grateful that it had just been the two of them lately. The last place they'd lived in, her aunt's boyfriend had been around a lot. As had his friends. When that happened, Marisol usually hid in her bedroom with the dresser across the door and her headphones on, losing herself in a book.

The next morning, she'd wake up to a mess she was expected to clean up. Because God forbid that Rosalind ever tidy up her own mess.

That would never happen.

Her stomach dropped as she walked through the garage and saw the big black truck with red flames along the side sitting there.

Mierda!

Saber was here.

Stupid ass name for a total asshole. Her aunt's longtime boyfriend. So longtime that she'd been seeing him throughout her past two marriages. Rosalind was a serial trophy wife. She liked them old and super-rich. The man she'd been married to when Marisol first came to live with her had been her favorite. Harrison.

Unfortunately, he'd divorced Rosalind when Marisol was only seven. She wished she could have stayed with him. She'd begged her aunt to leave her with him, she'd cried for him every night for weeks. He'd been the only father she'd ever known. Her own father had abandoned them before she was even born. And her mama had died when she was four.

Harry had always been there for her. When it was her first day of school, he'd taken her. When she broke her arm falling out of a tree, he'd rushed her to the emergency room. When he'd learned one of the girls at school was bullying her, he'd marched down to the school and taken care of it.

Life would have been much different if Rosalind had stayed with Harry. Or left Marisol with him.

But after Harry, Rosalind had moved onto greener pastures. Each time, she'd gotten a divorce or her husband died, she'd ended up richer. Which is why Marisol had been surprised when Rosalind told her she was opening a beauty spa. Rosalind didn't exactly like to work. Now she had five beauty spas in four different states.

Not that she worked anyway. No, she liked to sit and direct. They'd moved around a lot these past few years. From Texas to Arizona to California and now they were here. In Montana. But weirdly, Rosalind hadn't chosen a big city this time. Her aunt wasn't a country sort of person. She liked to be somewhere she could flaunt her wealth.

There were no expensive shops or snooty restaurants here in Wishingbone.

Which Marisol actually loved. Wishingbone was still big

enough to have everything but it still retained that small-town feel. Still, she didn't understand it. Her aunt liked attention. Case in point, buying the most expensive, ostentatious house she could find.

It was so ugly, it hurt Marisol's eyes.

But it showed her aunt for what she was. Totally classless and clueless. Rosalind thought money bought her respect and power. Marisol doubted it would impress the people in this town. The Jensen's house was slightly smaller, but far nicer. You could tell they had money but it wasn't pushed in your face.

They didn't scream *look at me.*

Marisol had been hoping that Saber wouldn't turn up here. She was certain small-town Montana wasn't his thing either.

She should have known better than to think her aunt was done with him. There had to be some reason Rosalind moved here and she would bet it had everything to do with Saber and his gang of goons.

Marisol glared at his truck. She wasn't allowed to put her car in the garage, she had to drive it around the back, even though she lived here. Wouldn't do to let the neighbors see it. She hadn't bothered to point out that they could easily spot her coming and going in it. She'd learned it wasn't worth standing up to Rosalind. She held all the power.

Sometimes Marisol thought about just leaving. Walking away. There had to be a life out there for her, right?

There was just one problem. Money.

She had none. The small amount she'd managed to squirrel away might get her a bus ticket out of here and a few weeks in a cheap motel.

But it wouldn't be enough to get her into even a cheap apartment.

And it definitely wouldn't be enough to pay for her medication.

So here she was, stuck. Did she know her aunt was exploiting her? Course she did. Did she know that how she treated her was illegal? You bet. She wasn't dumb. But what could she do? Report her? And where would that get her?

Homeless and on the streets. That's where.

At least with her aunt, she had a house to live in, books to read and access to the medicine she needed.

Kind of important things.

She slid into the mudroom then out into the kitchen, listening carefully. Some thumps and moans came from the direction of the living room. Christ, she knew exactly what those sounds were. You didn't grow up with Rosalind without hearing them plenty.

Why couldn't they take things into the bedroom? Why did they have to fuck out in the open where anyone could see?

She was pretty certain her aunt was an exhibitionist. But, eww, the last thing she wanted was to see her aunt naked.

Or even worse, Saber.

Sure, he was okay looking for an older guy. In shape. But yuck, she really didn't want to see his willy.

Willy. She whacked her hand over her mouth so she didn't giggle. She'd been reading this romance written by a woman who lived in the UK and had seen the word. It made her laugh every time. She knew that was childish, but she needed something to lighten the tension flooding her.

She had three choices. She could go back outside and wait in the car until they were finished. That was problematic because if her aunt caught her walking in later, she was likely to get mad at her for being late.

Choice number two, wait in the kitchen until they'd finished. But that was basically as bad as waiting in the car, only she could hear them fucking in here.

Bang. Bang. Bang.

Something smashed. Great. She was going to have to clean

that up before her aunt got up in the morning. While her aunt might like to hump all over the house, without a care to being caught, she hated when things got broken. Usually because they cost a disgusting amount of money.

With a sigh, Marisol knew which choice she was going to go with. She would have to sneak past the living area to the stairs and hope they didn't catch sight of her.

Right, Marisol, you can do this. You know how to move quietly when you want.

Yep. She'd had lots of practice.

Graceful and light. Two things she'd never be.

Exhaustion came over her in a wave and her stomach growled, reminding her that it had been a while since she'd eaten. Not good. She grabbed some cheese and crackers from the kitchen, stuffing it all in her handbag to eat in her room.

Sweat broke out along her skin as she tiptoed along the passage towards the stairs. Just as she'd guessed, the living room doors were wide open, inviting anyone who walked past to peer in.

Gross.

She snuck a peek. Not because she wanted to see them fucking, but because she wanted to gauge whether either of them were facing her way. She immediately regretted it when she saw Saber's naked ass as he pounded into her aunt who was lying stomach down over the back of the horrid floral couch.

Please don't let them stain it.

Also, note to self, don't sit on that couch ever again.

Wishing she could erase her memory or burn her eyes, either would suffice, she made her way around the banister and started climbing the stairs. Her aunt was making these weird keening noises while Saber grunted like an animal.

Too late, she remembered the stair that creaked. She cringed as she stepped on it. Like a deer caught in headlights, she froze.

Then she glanced over to make sure that her aunt hadn't heard her.

She hadn't. But Saber had.

His dark gaze caught her. A shiver of dread went through her.

Then he smiled.

Goosebumps crossed her skin and she thought she might vomit. She rushed up the stairs as he let out a deep roar. Her aunt's cry following.

Jesus. Jesus. So gross.

She flung herself into her bedroom, and quickly turning, locked it. The lock was pretty flimsy and she didn't really trust it. She should move the dresser.

She spun around, heaving out a breath of relief.

And realized that in her haste, she'd failed to pay proper attention to her surroundings. Her heart beat sped up, her stomach dropping as she took in the heavily-tattooed man lying on her bed.

"Hello, Marisol. Long time, no see."

3

Marisol froze.

She stared.

"Have you got no greeting for your brother?" he said with a purr.

"You're not my brother." The idea of it was ridiculous. And horrifying.

"When our parents get married, I will be."

"She's not my mother," she spat at him. Married? Oh God. Please don't tell her that Rosalind was marrying Saber?

He narrowed his gaze at her. Those green eyes turned dark. They were so like his father's that another shiver worked its way through her. "What's wrong, Marisol? Don't like the idea of being my sister? It won't stop us from becoming more intimately acquainted. It's not incest, after all. But it does add a certain taste of the forbidden, don't you think?"

What she thought was that she was about to throw up.

She needed to get this asshole out of her bedroom.

Why hadn't she thought about the fact that Tiger would be with his father? He might be twenty-four, but he'd been raised in his father's gang. He was being groomed as his Saber's right-hand man.

And he seemed to believe that he had some claim on her.

Not. Happening.

She'd rather take her chances on the street than end up under this man. No, boy. Linc was a man. Tiger was a spoiled little boy who didn't like hearing the word 'no.'

Actually, her telling him 'no' seemed to make him dig in his feet. It seemed to be some sort of challenge to him. A game. He couldn't seem to comprehend that she didn't actually want him.

Sure, under other circumstances, if he was a guy just walking down the street, she might have thought he was cute. But because she knew him, knew what he was capable of . . .

He was ugly.

"I've been having to entertain myself until you got home." It was then that he held up the thing in his hand. Too late, she realized what it was. Her heart beat sped up.

"That's mine."

Her precious eReader. The only thing that kept her sane. If she didn't have her books, she didn't know what she would do. The characters in those stories were her friends.

Her only friends. Her only escape.

"Give it back."

"Some very interesting stories in here. These are some very kinky desires that you've been hiding, Marisol. Tell me, does your aunt know about the stuff you read?"

Her entire body shook. She didn't know if it was in reaction to his words or her blood sugar levels getting too low. A mix of both, she was betting.

He stood, moving with the elegance of a coiled snake waiting to pounce. She watched him, barely breathing. He grew closer and her fear grew. If he wanted to hurt her, he could. There was no one here to stop him. She doubted her aunt would care and his father would probably cheer him on.

Now she was wishing that the sheriff had taken her to jail and locked her up. She'd take her chances with that soap shank.

"What was it you called me last time I saw you? Depraved?"

"You suggested I have a threesome with you and your dad!"

"You should have been flattered." He started to circle around her and it was all she could do to stand there. To not follow him, not show how afraid she really was.

How terrified.

"F-flattered? He's my aunt's boyfriend!"

"So? She could have watched."

"Eww."

Too late, she realized she should have guarded her words better as he grabbed her wrist, dragging her towards him. He squeezed her wrist until she cried out in pain.

"You want to be very careful about the way you treat me, Marisol. You think you're better than the whores who hang around me and my dad, trying to get their hands on our cocks? You're not. And very soon, my old man and I are gonna be your family. Then I'm going to be in charge of you."

She forced herself to stay still, hoping if she didn't fight back that he'd release her. Eventually, he loosened his hold, shoving her hand away. She cradled her arm against her chest.

"I'm twenty-three, I don't need anyone to take charge of me."

"Actually, I think you need very close watching. I don't think I'm going to let you out of my sight for a good long while. Or should that be, out of my bedroom." He moved in front of her, running a finger along the base of her neck. "These books you read just gave me an insight into what you need, Marisol. You need someone strong to take charge of you. You're looking for an alpha male, someone to dominate you, fuck you, punish you. I'm the man you need."

Only if she was looking for an egotistical psychopathic creep.

Thankfully, she didn't say that out loud. But something in her face must have clued him in. His face filled with anger again. She stepped back, staring at him fearfully. Just as he was reaching for her, a knock came on the door.

"What?" Tiger snapped, still glaring at her.

Was it her aunt? Was she going to do the decent thing for once and try to help her? Hope filled her chest. Only to come crashing down.

"Tiger! We've got to fucking go!" Saber said impatiently.

"Can it wait five fucking minutes, kind of busy."

"No, it can't fucking wait. This is more fucking important than you getting your dick wet. Shit has gone down. Jackal and Falcon are dead."

"What the fuck?" Tiger strode over to the door, unlocking and flinging it open.

She didn't know who Jackal and Falcon were. And she knew it was wrong, but she was really glad they were dead right then.

That's kind of an awful thing to think, Marisol.

Yeah, but then if they were friends of Saber, they were hardly going to be nice people.

Saber moved his gaze from Tiger to her. His gaze felt so filthy that she wanted to immediately jump in the shower. And still, she didn't think she'd get that oily feel off her skin.

"Your aunt has some good news for you, Marisol," Saber told her with an evil grin. "We'll be seeing you real soon."

He turned and strode away. Tiger grabbed hold of her sore wrist, making her cry out. He dragged her against him. "I'll be back, Marisol. And you better be fucking prepared to kneel."

At the doorway, he turned back and threw her eReader towards the bed. Only he had shit aim and it smashed against her bedside drawers.

No. No. No.

Tiger left and she fled over to where her eReader lay on the floor. *Please let it be all right. Please.*

She turned it over, tears dripping down her cheeks as she took in its cracked surface. It had taken her so long to save up for it on the measly allowance her aunt gave her.

"What are you doing sitting on the floor, sniveling?"

She looked over at her aunt's spiteful voice. She guessed Rosalind was a beautiful woman. If you judged her on her outside appearance alone. She was forty-five, but looked ten years younger. People often mistook them for sisters. Rosalind loved that. With long, shiny dark hair, big hazel eyes and a tiny waist with her generous boobs, she was gorgeous. But Marisol could see under the surface. And all she saw was darkness. Rosalind was mean. Spiteful. Petty.

But surely, she wouldn't let her be abused? A spark of hope lit inside her. If she told her about Tiger would she keep him away from Marisol?

Or would she not care?

"Tiger broke my eReader," she explained.

A wave of nausea came over her. She really needed to eat something.

"So? You've always got your face in that damn thing. You have more important things to do. He did you a favor."

"A favor?" she whispered, anger stirring inside her. "He was talking like he ... like he wanted to ..."

"What, Marisol?" Her aunt brought a cigarette up to her mouth and puffed on it. She only smoked the things post-sex. It made Marisol shudder at the memory of Saber pounding into her.

She now wore a black silk negligee and gown over the top. Marisol hoped she wasn't expecting Saber to come back.

"Spit it out. I don't have all night. You're late."

"He wants to have sex with me." She knew she was bright red as she spat the words out.

"And? So what? You should do what he wants."

Marisol's mouth dropped open. She knew she should have expected it. Her aunt had never once shown any sort of affection or care.

"I don't want him!"

"So? Jesus, Marisol, grow up. Sometimes you just have to do things even if you don't want to. Do you think I wanted to marry any of those old farts? That I enjoyed having their wrinkly, cold hands on me? Course I didn't. But I let them touch me because I wanted something from them. And they never complained."

She just stared at Rosalind. She knew the other woman hadn't married any of her husbands for love. Still to just hear her say it out loud like that was disturbing.

"I'm not letting Tiger touch me."

Rosalind sneered. "Get off your high fucking horse. You have to lose your virginity at some time. You could do much worse than Tiger. He's gonna be somebody. Don't you realize how powerful Saber is? He's not just the leader of a branch of the Devil's Sinners, he's the leader of all of them. I don't know why Tiger wants you, but you should be flattered as hell that he does. Just open your legs and make a few noises. Get him off and he'll be happy. Likely that will get you out of his system once he realizes you're a cold fish. Then he might want a real woman." She smiled smugly.

"You can't mean . . . you?" She let out a startled laugh without thinking.

Rosalind stepped forward and slapped her. Hard.

Marisol's eyes watered, her cheek throbbing. It wasn't the first time Rosalind had hit her, of course. Not by a long shot. Didn't mean that it hurt any less. Every time.

You can't stay here, Marisol. She really needed to work on an escape plan. Because remaining here wasn't going to be possible. She had some money stashed away she'd managed to keep hidden from her aunt. She'd have to figure out a way to make that work.

She had to leave. Soon.

"You think he couldn't want me? I'm a thousand times the woman you are. I'm not some mousy, fat, bookworm with no life. I know how to take care of a man. Here's what's going to happen, Marisol, if you want to stay under my roof, where I pay for everything including your medication. You're going to do whatever Tiger and Saber want. They're more important than you. And soon they're going to be family."

Her aunt waved a huge, diamond ring in her face. "Saber asked me to marry him and I said yes. So very soon, Tiger and Saber are gonna be around here a lot more. Get used to it. Now where are the fucking tips from tonight?" Her aunt held out her hand.

Marisol reached into her pocket and drew out five twenties, handing them over.

"That's it? Thought they would have been more generous."

Don't react. Don't react.

"Typical. The rich ones are always tight with their cash. There's a mess downstairs to clean up. Then get to bed, you look like shit. Honestly, I have no clue what Tiger sees in you." Her aunt gave her a disgusted look. "Oh and you're opening in the morning."

"But I'm not on tomorrow and I thought Eileen was opening."

"She called in sick. You need to cover her clients too."

What? Seriously. She ground her teeth together to stop herself from going off. She was exhausted. Rosalind had told her she could take the day off tomorrow. She should have known better than to trust her word.

After her aunt left, she quickly locked the door. If only she had some way of locking the door to keep people out when she wasn't here. With her entire body shaking, she climbed into the closet and drew out her blanket and doll. She kept them hidden in here so her aunt didn't find it. The blanket was a mix of pastel colors, while the doll had dark hair and wore a princess tiara.

She'd had it since she was a little girl, so it was getting worn in places. She didn't dare wash it, worried it might start falling apart.

Sitting on the floor of the closet, she lifted up one corner of her snuggly, rubbing it under her nose to soothe herself. Then she slipped her thumb into her mouth.

Shivers ran through her. She knew she should eat and go to bed. Everyone was gone. The door was locked. But she couldn't make herself leave the safety of the closet. It felt safe in here. Like no one could hurt her.

What was she going to do? She sat back against the wall of the closet and just tried to settle her heartbeat.

First, she had to hide the rest of the tip she'd gotten tonight. It was always a risk, holding back some of her tips from her aunt. She didn't tend to do it with her regulars, afraid her aunt would catch on. But when someone tipped a lot then she kept some of it back.

She wished she had enough that she could just leave. But she needed to be careful about this. Running was only going to work if she had some sort of plan in place.

Living here with Tiger and Saber wasn't an option, though. Feeling ill, she drew out the hundred dollars she'd kept back and slid it into the trinket box she kept in the hole under the floor-boards. It was the only thing she had left of her mother. The lining inside the box was loose. With hands that still shook, she tucked her money in there and hid the box again.

She knew exactly how much was in there. One thousand and forty-eight dollars. That was the result of years of scrimping. If she'd saved what her aunt gave her for working at the spa, she'd have more. However, after her aunt took out money for room and board, there wasn't much left. Just enough to buy some eBooks to read and occasionally some clothes from Goodwill.

She'd protested once that she deserved more pay. Her aunt had slapped her and called her ungrateful. She'd gone into a rage that had terrified Marisol enough that she hadn't said anything again. What choice did she really have? Stay and be treated like shit but have a job, a roof over her head and the medicine she needed. Or leave and be all alone, maybe end up on the streets.

She just needed a bit more time and a few more tips.

Disappointment flooded her. She actually liked it here. Living in a big city was hard for her. All the people and the noise. She liked the peace and quiet here.

But it was becoming more and more obvious that she had to go. Thankfully, it sounded like Saber and Tiger had their hands full for a bit longer.

Crawling out of the closet, she stood and grabbed the worn black bag that held her diabetic supplies out of her handbag. Carrying it into the bathroom, she washed her hands. All the bedrooms in this monstrous house had their own bathrooms. A prick of her finger to draw blood and the blood glucose meter told her what she'd suspected. It was low. She'd gone too long without eating.

She'd had Type One diabetes since she was thirteen. Managing her blood sugar levels would be much easier if she had a CPM monitor, but her aunt claimed her insurance wouldn't pay for it. She grabbed a few glucose tabs from her bag and unwrapped them, popping them into her mouth.

Walking back into her bedroom, she sat on the bed, staring down at the eReader in her hand. Sadness flooded her. It felt like she'd lost an old friend. She wiped away a few tears. Today, she'd feel sorry for herself.

Tomorrow, she needed to figure out a way of saving herself.

4

Linc was cursing himself for not getting her number.

Or not giving her his. But then that had seemed too pushy. He hadn't wanted her to think he was some weirdo. Even if he was at times.

You know where she works.

Right, I'm sure it's every day that a cowboy strolls on in and asks for a manicure.

Idiot.

A cool wind whipped down the street. Shit. He hoped it was warmer for Clint and Charlie's wedding tomorrow. He strode towards the diner, thinking he'd get some lunch before he attempted some shopping.

Gah. Shopping.

Up ahead he saw a small figure dressed only in a pair of black pants and a black shirt nearly collide with a lamp post. She pulled away at the last second, only to start tumbling back, tripping over her own feet. He quickly raced forward, and managed to grab hold of her before she landed on her butt, setting her on her feet.

"Whoa, there. You okay?" He turned her around, surprise filling him as he saw it was her.

He hadn't recognized her in the shapeless, black clothing. Which he now realized was obviously a work uniform. There was an emblem on the top right-hand corner of the shirt.

"Marisol? Hey."

Wow. That was smooth. Really smooth.

"It's Linc," he added when she didn't say anything. "From last night. At Sanctuary Ranch."

Okay, it kind of hurt that he hadn't been able to stop thinking about her and she couldn't even remember him.

"This is kind of déjà vu, huh?"

She was just staring up at him, her cheeks flushed, her lips parted.

"Only this time there's no containers in your arms, blocking your view so how did you nearly walk into that lamp post?" he demanded.

Ease up, man. You don't need to go all Daddy on her.

"Oh. . . umm. . .oh . . ."

"Marisol? Are you okay?" He reached out and placed his hand over her forehead. She didn't feel warm. In fact, she was kind of cold. Another breeze worked its way up the street and she shivered.

"Where's your coat, Mari? Gloves? Hat?"

"Umm, the sun was out so I didn't think I needed any."

"The sun might be out but there's a cold breeze. Where are you from?"

"Originally? Texas. But we move around a lot. I've been living in California most recently."

"That explains it." He took off his jacket and wrapped it around her, noticing the book in her hand. "Were you reading while you were walking? Is that why you nearly hit that poor lamp post?"

"Yes." Red filled her cheeks as she closed the book and placed it in her oversized handbag. "You should take your coat back, you'll get cold."

"I'm acclimatized to it. Besides, I'm a lot bigger than you. Reading while walking isn't a very safe thing to do. What if you'd stepped off the sidewalk and in front of a car? Or if you hadn't seen that lamp post and hit your head?"

"I often read and walk at the same time. I hardly ever get hurt."

He didn't like the sound of that 'hardly ever' part.

"I don't want you doing that anymore, okay? You could get seriously hurt."

She gave him a surprised look but nodded.

"Are you on your lunch break? Considering how late you worked last night, I thought you might have had the day off." She looked tired. Pale.

He didn't like it. At all.

"Unfortunately someone called in sick and I had to cover for them. I have to be back in an hour."

"I was on my way to the diner. Come have lunch with me."

"Oh, umm . . ." She looked away.

Jesus, you idiot. She obviously doesn't want to have lunch with you.

"Or not," he said coolly, the rejection cutting even as he tried not to let it get to him. "It's fine. Take the jacket, I'll come grab it from the spa on my way home."

"It's not that I don't want to," she whispered so quietly he almost didn't hear her. "I just don't have any money on me." Her gaze was low, her shoulders slumped, her embarrassment clear.

Fuck. He needed his ass kicked.

Rejection was a trigger for him. But he didn't need to act like an ass and make her feel ashamed or embarrassed.

"I'm sorry, Mari. I jumped to the conclusion that you didn't want to have lunch with me. Which, even if you didn't, I don't need to react like an ass. Would you like to eat with me? I'm paying."

"I couldn't ask you to—"

"You didn't ask, though, did you? And just so you know, I'd pay even if you did have some cash on you. My view is if a man asks a woman out to eat, then he pays."

"Really?" She gave him a surprised look.

"I've got some old-fashioned manners. And views. My nana would whip my ass if I did otherwise."

"Does she live here?"

"No, she died a few years ago now."

"I'm so sorry."

He could see the sincerity in her eyes. "So, lunch?" He held out his elbow to her.

"If you're sure," she said, but she was sliding her hand into the crook of his elbow as she said it.

"I'm definitely sure," he said firmly as he led her towards the diner.

"Another old-fashioned gesture?" she asked, pointing to where her hand rested on his arm.

He grinned down at her. "Nah, this is just to make sure you don't run into any more lamp posts."

Her mouth dropped open then to his delight she burst into laughter. "I only walk into things when I'm distracted."

"Why, ma'am, are you saying that I'm not a distraction? I'll have to work on my game. I'll have you know that my ass is an excellent distraction."

Humor twinkled in her eyes. "I wouldn't know. I haven't looked."

"We'll have to remedy that."

He slid his arm free, immediately missing her touch. Then he strode down the footpath in front of her, putting some strut into his stride. It was worth it, to hear her laugh again. She had a sweet laugh.

He winked at a couple of older ladies strolling past. They

smiled back. He turned and held his arms out as Marisol moved towards him. "How did I do?"

"Well, I didn't walk into any lamp posts, however you're right. Your ass is most definitely a distraction."

"That's what I wanted to hear," he said huskily, taking her hand back in his elbow when she reached him. "So tell me, how much experience do you have with weddings?"

SHE GAPED up at him as they reached the diner. True to his word, he showed some more of those manners by reaching out and opening the door for her.

Marisol didn't have much experience with men. This was the first time she'd gone out for a meal with a man who wasn't one of her aunt's conquests. And even those meals were rare. Although she remembered Harry taking them often. Her aunt would complain, because instead of an upscale restaurant, they'd go to a family restaurant.

And he would always open the door too.

Was Linc like Harry? A decent man? She hoped he was what he seemed to be. Funny, kind, generous. But too often someone hid their true colors. She'd have to be careful.

It's not like you're going to get involved with him, even if that is something he wants.

"Marisol? Did I shock you into silence?" he asked as he led them towards a booth at the back.

People called out to him and he waved with a smile. Obviously, he was well liked around here, which eased something inside her. She couldn't imagine people treating Saber or Tiger like this.

"Oh, I'm so sorry. Sometimes I get caught up in what's going on in my head."

He raised his eyebrows as he waited for her to slide into the booth. To her shock, rather than sitting across from her he moved in beside her.

"Anything wrong?"

She carefully adjusted her sleeves, making certain to cover the bandage on her wrist. She'd figured it was the easiest way to cover the bruise. If anyone asked, she'd just tell them she'd burned it. Easier to explain than the bruise that wrapped around her wrist.

"No, of course not. What were you saying about weddings?"

Was he trying to ask her if she was married?

"Ahh, well, see I still have to get Clint and Charlie a wedding gift."

"Isn't their wedding tomorrow?" She gaped at him.

"Yep."

She couldn't stop the startled laughter from escaping.

"Do you usually leave things to the last minute?"

"No, I'm usually very organized. If this was a work thing, I would be all over it. But this is a shopping thing. I hate shopping." He batted his eyelids. "Help me. Please."

"And what makes you think I'm any good at shopping, huh?"

"You're a girl, aren't you?" He grinned to let her know he was joking.

She gave a mock-growl. "That's very sexist. Just because I'm a girl, doesn't mean I like shopping."

"You're quite right. I do apologize." He placed his hand on his heart, with a sad sigh.

"Do they have a gift registry?" she asked.

"No, they said no gifts."

"Umm." She didn't know how to point out the obvious.

"I know they said no gifts, but I want to get them something. Even something small. Clint has been good to me over the years. He hired me on when I had very little experience, taught me everything he knows and now he trusts me to manage his ranch."

She loved the hint of vulnerability in his gaze. Linc wasn't a man who was afraid of showing his emotions. Of admitting when he was wrong. Or doing something silly to make her laugh, like strutting his stuff along the street.

"Hmm, that's a tough one."

A waitress came along, looking slightly harried. "Sorry. We're a waitress down today. What can I get you to drink?"

"I'll take a sweet tea," Linc said, looking at her expectantly.

"The same please." She nearly winced. Drat. She didn't know why she said that. She hated tea.

The waitress nodded and headed away. Linc passed her a menu. "I already know what I want," he told her a bit sheepishly.

"Eat here often?" she teased. She could hardly believe that she was sitting here, eating lunch with a gorgeous man. And that she dared to tease him. This was the closest she'd ever gotten to a date. She thought she'd be shy and jittery.

But Linc was different. There was something about him that put her at ease.

"Well, whenever I get into town, I do. They make the best burgers here, though."

"Ooh. That sounds nice."

"Good, two hamburgers with fries it is then, please, Sally," he said to the waitress as she brought their drinks back.

"Oh, but . . ." she said as the waitress left. She'd been going to see what was cheapest on the menu. She didn't want to take advantage of his generosity.

"Sorry. You didn't want the burger." He winced. "I jumped the gun. I'll call her back."

"No, no." She didn't want to make a fuss. Especially not when the diner was so busy. "That's fine. I just need to go to the bathroom first."

"Of course." He slid out then held his hand towards her. She reached up to grab his hand, realizing too late that her sleeve had ridden up.

He froze as he stared at her wrist. Then his gaze met hers. "What is this?"

5

L inc stared down at the bandage. Had she had that last night? He thought back. He hadn't noticed it, but it could have been easy to miss in the dark.

"Marisol," he said in a deep, commanding voice that had her staring at him in shock. This was the firmest he'd been with her, so her surprise was understandable.

"Oh that," she said with a nervous laugh. He could already tell that she was going to lie and it made him grind his teeth in anger and frustration. "It's nothing. I was dealing with hot wax at work and burned myself."

"Can I see the burn?"

"Oh no. It's fine. I put cream on it." She couldn't meet his gaze as she spoke. "Could I get up now?"

He nodded, unable to answer her without demanding the truth. As she disappeared into the bathroom, he slid into the booth and tried to decide what path he wanted to take.

If he didn't intend to see her again, to take this further, then he could just let this go. It worried him that she had to lie to explain the bandage, though. Made him wonder about what really happened.

But if he decided that he did want to know her better, then he'd need to make it clear that she'd crossed a line with him. One that she shouldn't cross again. At least not without consequences.

Okay, bringing up consequences might be going a step too far. One step at a time.

He glanced over at the bathroom door, she'd been gone a while. He hoped she was okay. Just then, she walked out and came towards him. He slid out.

"Oh, you didn't have to move," she said.

He shook his head. "Safer for you to go in first."

She blinked at him in confusion.

"Wall on one side. Me on the other," he said in clipped sentences.

"Right," she replied, giving him a small, worried smile. "Are you all right?"

He tapped his fingers against the table then turned to her. "I know you just lied to me."

Her face paled. Those expressive caramel-colored eyes stared up at him, trying to get a read on him. There was an anxious air around her. He instantly wanted to soothe her. To reassure her that no harm would come to her. That she was all right. They were all right.

But he knew that he had to start as he meant to continue on. Allowing her this one lie could bleed into more lies. Bigger ones. And he couldn't allow that. Lies and rejection were big triggers for him. So she needed to know this now.

And if he was too much for her, then he needed to know that too.

Maybe it was crazy to be so interested in someone this quickly. But Linc had watched so many of his friends find their other halves recently and it made him impatient and yeah, a bit lonely. He wanted someone of his own. Someone to come home to at night, share dinner with, laugh or commiserate with over their days. Someone to curl up around in bed and wake up to in the morning.

And he was drawn to her.

So yeah, maybe he should make this clear from the start.

"Lying is something I can't ever tolerate, Marisol," he told her firmly. Her breath hitched, her eyes widening even further. "I get that maybe you don't feel comfortable telling me the truth since we don't know each other that well. But that doesn't mean you need to lie. If I ask you something that makes you uncomfortable, that you don't feel you can answer honestly, then you tell me that. Don't make something up, okay?"

"Okay," she whispered. "But what if there's something going on and I can't talk about it, then won't you be mad at me for not telling you?"

Their food arrived and he took a moment to answer. "We don't know each other so I get there might be things you don't want to tell me. As we get to know each other and you come to trust me, I would hope you would confide in me, tell me what's going on."

"I'm not used to trusting in people," she told him.

"It can be tough. But when you find the right people, it can also be the easiest thing in the world. I'm here if you want to tell me something. Anything. All right?"

"All right."

He picked up his burger and took a bite, noticing the way she just stared at her food, looking sad.

Fuck. This wasn't the conversation he'd meant to have. This wasn't even a proper date and things had taken on a very serious tone.

"Hey." He reached out and lightly touched her hand which was resting on her thigh.

She jumped with a gasp, flinching back.

Mierda!

"Sorry, Mari. Didn't mean to scare you."

"Sorry, my mind was a million miles away."

He heaved out a sigh. "I've messed this date up completely, haven't I?" He hated that sad, confused look in her eyes.

"This is a date?" she asked, looking surprised.

"Well, I was hoping it was." He still held onto her hand. "But if you're not interested in me like that, it can just be two friends sharing a meal."

She gazed away from him. "It's not that I'm not interested. I am. You're gorgeous. But I . . ." She cleared her throat and he frowned slightly wondering what she'd been about to say about herself. He got the feeling he wouldn't have liked it. "But my life is a bit of a mess right now. I'm not sure I can offer you anything."

"All right, then we'll be two friends sharing a meal. Of course, you actually have to eat for that to be the case."

Disappointment filled him, but he forced himself to push it deep. This wasn't rejection. She said she wanted more. That things were complicated.

He just needed to remove all the complications.

"Anything I can do to help?"

She shook her head. "No, but thank you."

"Come on, eat something for me. Here." He picked up a fry and held it to her lips. She opened her mouth and took it. Something moved inside him. A possessive beast that wanted to claim her.

Mine.

Christ, slow down, man.

Her tongue came out and licked the salt from her lips. He nearly groaned.

"Are you okay?" she asked him.

He grinned at her. "Yeah, I'll be fine. I'm sorry if I got a bit intense just now."

"It's okay, I understand. I'm just not used to anyone, well, caring about me I guess." She shrugged as if it was no big deal. But it hurt him to think of no one caring for this girl.

"I care, Mari."

SHE LIKED THE NICKNAME. It made her feel special.

She wasn't sure why he cared when he barely knew her, but it filled her with warmth. She turned back to her food to hide her confusion. Even though she wasn't hungry, she knew she had to eat. She drank some sweet tea, barely holding in a grimace at the taste.

"Don't you like sweet tea?" he asked.

"Umm." What to say? He'd just told her not to lie. She sighed. "Not really."

He raised an eyebrow. "Then why'd you order it?"

"I don't know," she sighed. "I guess because you did. I get flustered sometimes. Say the wrong thing."

"Okay, so what would you like to drink?"

"Diet coke."

He raised his hand to the waitress.

"Oh, but she's so busy. It's okay, I'll drink it." She reached out again for the sweet tea.

"Mari, put the sweet tea down and back away." It was said jokingly but there was an undercurrent of command in his voice.

She slid her hand back under the table as he ordered a diet coke. Reaching out, he slid a few strands of hair behind her ear. "From now on, if you're given or accidentally order something you don't like then tell me, yeah?"

She couldn't imagine this situation coming up again but she nodded in reply.

"You're such a sweet, little thing, aren't you?"

Marisol wasn't used to someone talking to her this way. It made her feel flustered. And special. Definitely special.

"I'm making you feel awkward, huh?" he asked.

"Just not used to people talking to me like this."

"You don't like it? Want me to stop?"

"No, I do," she said hastily.

He leaned in towards her. "Good. Because I like it too." He glanced back down at her plate. "You need to eat a bit more."

She took another bite of her burger. She'd never had someone encourage her to eat. Her aunt was always telling her that she ate too much. Of course, she lived on air and alcohol so . . .

"Tell you what, eat three more bites of that burger and I'll buy you an ice cream sundae. They're pretty good here."

Ooh yum.

Although she wasn't sure what was more delicious. The thought of the sundae, or the way he spoke to her. He reminded her of one of the Daddies in CJ Bennet's books. And he was a cowboy.

Double delicious.

Chill, girl. You barely know him.

Even though she didn't intend to order the sundae, she took three hasty bites and he laughed at her. She blushed as she realized what she'd done. Seems her self-control was shot.

"That was cute. Although make sure you chew all that, I don't want you to choke on such a big mouthful."

Urgh. That was so not attractive, Marisol. Way to act like a sophisticated grown-up.

As she was chewing, her phone beeped and she pulled it out of her bag. She sighed as she realized it was nearly time to head back. She swallowed and drank down some of her diet coke.

Yum.

"That was my alarm. I have to get back to work," she explained as she slid the phone away.

"You set an alarm as a reminder?"

"Otherwise I tend to forget. One day, I was three hours late getting back because I got caught up in a book. My aunt was very unhappy with me."

"She owns the spa, right?"

She nodded as he raised his hand to the waitress to ask for the bill.

"Next time, I'll get you that sundae."

She didn't say anything. She doubted there would be a next time, but it was nice that he was thinking about it. She wished she could offer to pay. It seemed like that would be more polite.

"Next time it's my turn to pay," she blurted out as the waitress dropped the bill and moved away to another table.

He turned and gave her a firm look. "Definitely not. Old-fashioned views, remember?"

She bit her lip. It didn't feel right somehow.

"Tell you what, you can repay me by giving me your phone number."

"You want my phone number?" Was he serious?

"I do. That a problem? I was joking about you having to give it to me as payment for lunch. You don't have to do anything you don't feel comfortable doing."

"Oh no, it's not that. It's just. I thought maybe . . . never mind. Here . . ." She opened the contacts in her phone and he tapped something in before giving it back to her.

"I sent myself a text so I'd have your number." He winked at her.

She popped it into her bag without looking at it.

"Now, I need you to give me some wedding gift ideas as I escort you back to the spa."

"You don't have to do that," she said as he moved from the booth then helped her out. He still frowned slightly as he looked at the bandage. Thank God he couldn't see the bruise underneath.

He led her through the diner and held open the door then he walked on the road side of the footpath next to her. She kind of wished he'd offer her his arm again, but he didn't.

"So what do you think I can buy on short notice here?"

"Hmm, let me think."

"Oh, and remember that Clint is loaded so he basically has everything he could ever want."

"You're not making this easy on me."

He shook his head. "No, it's Clint who isn't making this easy on me. What about a mug that says, *Richer than Croesus but not nearly as handsome.*"

She burst into laughter. "That's terrible."

"Not a good wedding gift?" he asked with a grin.

"Not a good anytime gift. Especially not if you want to keep your job."

He waggled a finger at her. "You make a good point, Mari-girl."

They reached the spa after he'd given her a few other silly suggestions and she was practically bent in two with tears streaming down her face.

"Marisol," a cold voice snapped out.

She looked over and winced as she saw her aunt climbing out of her BMW. Shoot, how had she missed her? Her aunt closed the door with a slam and strode over to them.

Dressed in a red skirt that just covered her ass, a matching jacket and a black silk shirt with black high heels, she looked like she'd just stepped out of a meeting with the devil.

Marisol wouldn't be surprised if that was the case.

"Who is this?" her aunt purred as she grew closer. She looked Linc up and down.

"This is Linc. This is my aunt, Rosalind."

"Hello, Linc." Rosalind held out her hand.

Linc reached over and shook it. "Pleased to meet you."

"Not as pleased as I am to meet you."

Gah. Gross. She wondered what Saber would think to learn that her aunt flirted with everyone with a dick in a five-mile radius.

"Aunt Rosalind just got engaged last night," she told Linc.

"Congratulations," he said while her aunt shot her an angry look.

"Aren't you supposed to be back at work by now, Marisol?" Rosalind snapped. "You don't want to keep the clients waiting. Marisol can be extremely forgetful. A bit flighty."

Marisol ground her teeth together.

"Really? She doesn't seem flighty to me at all. The fact that she worked late last night then came in to work so early today tells me that she is quite a hard worker."

Her aunt's gaze narrowed. Uh-oh. "Yes. Quite. I have to get inside. I have things to do. Marisol, don't linger. And for goodness sake, straighten your shoulders, you're slumping."

Shame filled her but she forced herself to turn to Linc. "Sorry about that."

He raised his eyebrows. "She seems like a fun person."

"Yeah. You could say that. Good luck with the wedding gift shopping."

He grimaced. "Thanks, I'm going to need it. I'll text you later. Oh, what days do you have off?"

"Sundays. The spa is shut."

He frowned. "Only Sundays?"

"Yes. But it's fine. I like work," she said quickly.

"Okay. If you're free Sunday would you like to do something?"

She sucked in a breath. She should say no. She wasn't planning on sticking around. But God, she really wanted to say yes. When had she ever done anything for herself?

"As friends, of course," he added.

Oh. Of course he just meant as friends. And she shouldn't feel a stab of disappointment, because being a friend was all she could offer. She wasn't sure she'd make a good friend, but she'd try.

"All right. I'd like that. As friends."

As she walked away, she was aware of his gaze burning into her back. She tried to straighten her posture not wanting to slump as Rosalind had accused her of doing. When she got inside, she quickly moved into the bathroom and washed her hands before checking her blood sugar levels.

They were good. Maybe hanging around Linc was good for her.

If only she'd met him in a different time. A different place. With a sigh, she moved into the employee backroom and stashed her handbag in her locker. Then she headed down the passage towards the front of the spa.

The sound of a news report made her stop and she poked her head into her aunt's office. Her aunt was staring at the television mounted on the wall with a frown. Marisol turned to see what she was staring at. Surprise filled her to see a news report. There were images of a burning building.

"The police can't say for certain what happened here. But it looks to have been some sort of gang war. The building behind me was the reported headquarters of a gang trying to get a foothold in the city. The Devil's Sinners have connections to the Devil's Kings, a gang based in Texas and Arizona. Police are currently searching for anyone who saw anything. They'd also like to hear from anyone who saw or had contact with these two men that night."

Mugshots of two men popped up on screen.

Jeremy 'Falcon' James and Matthew 'Jackal' James. What had Saber said last night to Tiger? That Falcon and Jackal were dead. Holy shit.

At least this meant they were likely to be tied up for longer, right? It could give her some breathing room.

"What are you doing just staring at that TV?" her aunt

snapped. "Shouldn't you be working? Do I pay you to stand around gawking?"

She didn't pay her at all. At least, not enough.

Marisol turned around.

"Oh, and Marisol, stay away from that cowboy. I didn't like him."

She meant that she didn't like that Linc hadn't fawned all over her. Marisol didn't say that though. And her aunt's demand only made her more determined to see Linc again. Right now, he was the only bright spot in her life.

She strode quickly into the main reception area and smiled at her two o'clock appointment. Mrs. Long was usually Eileen's client. The older woman was a terrible gossip. And a bit mean too.

"You're late," Mrs. Long snapped, rising.

By one minute.

Marisol grit her teeth and smiled. "My apologies." She led the woman to one of the nail booths. Two other booths were already filled by some of Mrs. Long's friends. They liked to get their nails done at the same time so they could gossip together.

"Was that Linc Johnson I saw you with out there, dear?" Mrs. Olsen asked. Her question sounded innocent enough but she sensed all the women's eyes turn to her.

"That's right."

"You two looked cozy," Mrs. Olsen said slyly.

"He's a friend."

"You want to be careful about associating with the people on Sanctuary Ranch," Mrs. Randall told her.

Don't ask. Don't ask.

"Have you heard the rumors about them?" Mrs. Long asked in a loud voice.

"I don't listen to gossip," she replied. She knew she had to be polite. They were the clients after all. Still, she hated the glee in their voices. They were enjoying this too much.

"Well," Mrs. Olsen sniffed. "Just thought you might like to know how they treat the women out there."

She stiffened.

"She might be into that sort of thing," Mrs. Long sneered.

"It's sick, it is," Mrs. Randall said. "Not natural. And now I hear that two of them are seeing the one woman. At the same time. They all live together in the same house. It's just not right."

"It's abuse," Mrs. Long added. "I reported it to the sheriff. I told him that Madison told me that she heard the men all spank the women and won't allow them to do anything without their permission. I wanted the sheriff to investigate and he refused. He told me to stop making up stories. So rude."

"He's so incompetent," Mrs. Randall said.

Good for the sheriff. She thought of the cop from last night. He'd actually been nice. And concerned for her. As they changed their topic to some woman who was having an affair with her best friend's husband, Marisol's mind wandered to what the women had said about Sanctuary Ranch. She didn't believe that any of those women were abused. They were all so happy and sweet. She knew what it was like to be stuck. To be scared.

Those women seemed secure and healthy.

And Linc definitely didn't strike her as the sort of man to hurt a woman. No, she dismissed those accusations and her mind instead turned to the news report she'd just seen. It reminded her that even though she might have some more time to plan, she still needed a way out of here.

For good.

6

M arisol grabbed some food from the kitchen and moved quickly up to her bedroom. The house was quiet and her aunt's vehicle wasn't in the garage, but that still didn't make her feel any happier. She was exhausted.

At least tomorrow was going to be a bit quieter with so many people at the wedding.

She opened her door cautiously, part of her expecting to see Tiger lounging on her bed. It was empty. Breathing out a sigh of relief, she walked in, put her food down then locked the door and pulled her dresser across it for good luck. By the time she'd done that, she was feeling sweaty and slightly light headed.

Shoot.

She didn't know if she was just tired or her blood sugar was low again. Honestly, sometimes it felt like she could never rest. It was a constant worry in the back of her head. Trying to figure out what she'd eaten that day. What her symptoms meant, if anything.

She just wanted to be carefree. To have nothing to worry about. It wasn't possible, of course. Not with her life.

But after checking her blood sugar, she was pleased to see it was all right. Must just be tired. After a shower and dinner, which consisted of a peanut butter sandwich and some yogurt, she grabbed her snuggly and Princess Nana, her doll, from the closet. As she rubbed her snuggly against her nose, her thumb found its way into her mouth and she just lay on the bed, trying calm herself.

This was the closest she ever got to being able to relax and let things go. She never fully let her Little side out. She didn't feel like she had a safe space to do so. There was no way she wanted her aunt discovering her. So she usually just lost herself in the stories she read.

But there were times, like now, when she just needed the extra comfort. If she closed her eyes, she could almost feel a man curling up around her, holding her tight, telling her that every-thing would be okay.

Daddy will take care of you, Little girl. You don't have to ever worry while you're in Daddy's arms.

Her imaginary Daddy was usually faceless so she was startled to realize that tonight he had a face. Linc smiled down at her, crooning to her, comforting her.

He gave her definite Daddy vibes. She could picture him taking care of her if she stubbed her toe, being gentle and caring. But also stern when he needed to be. She wondered what it would be like to be taken over his knee and spanked. She'd had a bit of a spanking fetish for years. Even though she'd never once been spanked. Her aunt preferred to verbally abuse her. Or lock her in her room. That was usually her go-to when Marisol was a child. Once she'd locked Marisol in her room all day. She'd had a seizure and knocked herself out. By the time she'd been found, she was nearly in a diabetic coma. She spent a week in the hospital.

Her aunt had stopped locking her up after that.

She started sucking on her thumb harder as she felt her

anxiety grow. She wished her snuggly was big enough to wrap around her.

She hugged Princess Nana tight. Thank God, Tiger hadn't found her. Harry had won Princess Nana for her at the fair. That was the only fair she'd ever been to. Her aunt had tried to make her leave the doll behind when they'd left Harry. But Marisol had managed to sneak it into her bag. Eventually, Rosalind forgot where the doll came from.

Her phone beeped then and she closed her eyes. Seemed reality was hell-bent on interrupting her me time. Some people took baths, others got their nails or hair done.

She sucked her thumb and pretended she had a Daddy who cared. A Daddy who wanted a big Little girl. Like the ones in CJ Bennett's books. That's what she wanted.

The phone beeped again. She sighed and heaved herself out of bed. She felt so heavy-limbed. As though she was moving through quicksand. A yawn caught her by surprise. She wished she could watch some mindless TV until she fell asleep. But that would involve going downstairs. And she didn't want to risk seeing her aunt. Or falling asleep on the couch.

She could read, but she'd finished the paperback she had already. She needed to go to the secondhand bookstore and get some more, since her eReader was gone. But she hadn't had time to get there today.

Maybe she should read one of the books she already owned. That could be fun, like returning to see old friends. Grabbing her phone, she rested back against the headboard. Only a few people had her number and so she was expecting it to be from her aunt or someone at the spa.

She nearly fell over in shock as she saw the name pop up.

Sexy Cowboy.

She let out a shocked laugh. That's what he'd typed his contact in as? She rolled her eyes as she eagerly opened his message.

Hi, Mari-girl, just checking to make sure you got home safe. What are you having for dinner?

Oh. That was sweet. She'd never had anyone check in on her. Sure, her aunt didn't like her out late, but that was a control thing. Not because she actually cared.

Hello, sexy cowboy.

Okay, she sent that before thinking it through.

*Why, Mari-girl, thank you for the compliment. *blushes**

She grinned. He was so silly.

I had a sandwich for dinner. You?

No veggies? Tut-tut. That's naughty. I had pot roast with all the trimmings. I even ate the beans.

Ick. Beans. I like most veggie. But even if I could cook, there's not much point for just me.

Your aunt isn't home?

She hesitated before replying. Was it wise to tell him that she was here alone? But she had never once gotten a vibe from him that he might hurt her.

No. Don't know where she is.

You've always lived with her?

Since I was four when my mama died.

Oh baby girl, I'm so sorry.

Tears reached her eyes. Jeez, she felt like she was on the edge of an emotional breakdown and one push would send her over.

It was a long time ago but thank you.

I still miss my nana. She raised me. Taught me all those old-fashioned values.

She sounds like a wonderful person.

She was.

This was different, she'd never had a friend she could text. Suddenly, her phone rang in her hand. His name popped up.

"Hello," she said shyly.

"My fingers were getting sore. Not used to all this texting," he joked.

"I was just thinking the same thing."

"Young thing like you? Didn't you spend most of your teenage years texting?"

"You have to have someone to text," she said jokingly. But his silence told her that he heard the truth in her words.

"You didn't have friends, Mari-girl?"

Christ. There went those tears again. She blinked rapidly.

"We moved around a lot. There wasn't much point in making friends."

"Must have been hard."

"It was. And then I mostly attended schools in wealthy areas, and well, I wasn't rich. I just went there because my aunt has a thing for rich men and we lived in those neighborhoods. Most of the other kids just saw me as a poor relative."

"Oh, Mari, I'm so sorry."

"It's okay. Being a teenager is never easy, right?"

"Nope. Try being a teenage boy being raised by your grandmother. I was fifteen before she sat me down to have the birds and the bees talk. I didn't have the heart to tell her I'd already taken sex ed at school and that there was a reason I went through so many socks."

She choked on her laughter.

"Oh, you think that's funny, do you?" he said, a laugh leaking through. "She caught me going for it once. I had just come home from a date with Carly-Sue Anderson. She was the prettiest girl in our class. We spent half the night making out in the back of my car. When I get home, I thought my balls were gonna explode. High-tailed it up to my room without even checking in with Nana. I was in my room, pounding away when in she walks to ask how my date went."

She burst into gales of laughter, holding her stomach as tears streamed down her face. "That did not happen."

"Oh, it did. We had an unspoken agreement to never speak of it." He started laughing. "Being a teenager was definitely hard."

She giggled. "I can't believe you told me that."

"Hey, friends share their embarrassing teenage moments with friends. Haven't you got any to tell me?"

Well, she could tell him that right now she was lying with her snuggly and hugging her doll. But nope.

"That's okay," he said quietly, letting her off the hook.

They talked for ages, him telling her about growing up with his nana. She told him stories about some of her previous clients. About an hour passed before she started yawning.

"I'm so sorry," she apologized. "It's not the company."

"You must be exhausted from working late last night then getting up this morning to open. And you've got work tomorrow."

"And you have a wedding to go to. Did you get a gift?"

"Sure did. Charlie really likes photography and Clint likes fishing. So I got them this fish photo frame. It's like in the shape of a fish and you set the photos into the body. What do you think?"

"You didn't."

He was joking, right?

"Uh, I did. Is it no good? I can take it back."

"No, no, I'm sure it's fine," she said, managing to sound somewhat convincing. She hoped. "I'm sure they'll love it."

Oh shoot. Did that count as a lie? Well, it's not like she knew them. Maybe they would like it.

"Are you free Sunday?"

"Oh. Yes, I suppose so."

"You suppose so?"

"Sorry. I just . . . sometimes my aunt springs things on me."

"Ah, right. I was hoping you might come on a picnic with me. But if you think you'll be busy . . ."

"I'll make it work," she blurted out.

She should say no. It would be better for both of them. But how could she say no when she knew she would regret it? She'd spend all of Sunday sitting around, wishing she'd said yes. As long as she got up early and cleaned the house then left before her aunt got out of bed, which was never usually before midday, she should be fine.

"Good. I'll pick you up around eleven?"

"Actually, could we meet in town? Maybe outside the diner or something?"

There was a beat of silence.

"Of course, Mari-girl."

She let out a silent sigh of relief. She'd been worried he'd want to know why she didn't want to be picked up at the house. But she wasn't going to take the risk of her aunt seeing her with him again.

There was silence.

"I don't want to hang up," she confessed, feeling herself blush. She hoped that didn't sound too clingy.

"Me either," he confessed. "All right, how about this? I'm going to put you to bed."

Put her to bed? What did that mean?

"That all right?" he asked.

"Yes, that's all right," she agreed.

"Why don't you put the phone down and go brush your teeth, pee, and then when you're ready, climb back into bed and pick up the phone again."

"Okay," she said kind of breathily.

She threw the phone and it slid off the bedside table and fell to the floor.

"*Mierda!* God damn freaking crap!" She grabbed the phone picking it up to check that she hadn't accidentally ended the call. "Are you still there?"

"Yes. Interesting language you have there, Mari-girl."

Whoops.

"Sorry, the phone fell off the table and I thought I'd lost you."

"I'm right here, teeny," he said in a low croon that sent a shiver through her blood. "And if you'd lost me you know how to find me again, huh?"

Right. She sure did. She just panicked.

"Right. Sorry." And teeny? Where had that come from?

"It's okay. Go to the bathroom. I promise, I'm not going anywhere."

Wow. He knew just what to say to make her knees go weak.

You met him yesterday. You've known him twenty-four hours. Sure, it felt like it had been longer. They'd just talked for over an hour and it had seemed like five minutes. It felt natural and right. But she had to remember that this was a temporary thing. She had to leave.

She brushed her teeth, washed her face and used the toilet. She took her blood sugar level again.

It definitely seemed like being around him was a good thing for her body and her emotions.

After climbing back into bed, she reached for the phone. "I'm in bed."

"Good girl. Teeth brushed?"

"Yes." She blushed a bit at the question. It was something a Daddy might ask.

Don't think about that right now. Last thing she wanted to do was blurt something out inadvertently.

Wouldn't that be embarrassing?

"The light's off? You got everything you need for bed?"

Her snuggly? Check. Princess Nana? Check. Nightlight? Check. She turned off the bedside lamp.

"Yes. I've got everything I need. And the light is off."

"Good girl. Is there anything else you usually do before bed?"

"I read."

"Hmm, well, I don't have any stories here to read to you. I might have to make one up, that okay?"

"Yes." *Daddy.*

Christ, that was close. She bit her lip. She really had to watch herself.

"What's your favorite animal?"

"Dragons."

"Dragons?"

Her eyes popped wide open and she groaned. Idiot.

"Hmm, you do realize that dragons aren't real, don't you?"

"Well, they could be," she defended herself. "Just because you haven't seen one doesn't mean it's not real."

Oh dear Lord, Marisol. What are you even saying?

"You're quite right. Dragons could very well be real."

She let out a sigh. "I know I sound like an idiot."

"Hey," he said in a firm voice. "I don't like you calling yourself names, understand?"

She chewed worriedly at her lip. This was something new to her as well. She'd gotten so used to others putting her down, it seemed almost natural to do it to herself. "I understand."

"Okay, snuggle in. And just listen." He started to tell her a story over the phone. It involved a prince, a princess and a dragon. He had such a nice voice that she soon found her eyes drifting shut.

And she didn't find out the end of the story, unfortunately.

She hoped it had a happy-ever-after.

7

Marisol strode towards the diner.

She was early, but she thought it was best to get out of the house in case her aunt woke up. Although Rosalind hadn't come in until the wee hours of the morning, so it was doubtful.

She drew out a new paperback she'd bought on her break yesterday. As she strolled along, she read it. She was chewing on a piece of gum, blowing out bubbles with it.

Suddenly, she slammed into something solid. Her book dropped as she attempted to step back and catch her balance. She sucked in her breath, forgetting about the bubblegum and started choking.

Firm hands clasped her forearms before she was turned, one arm was pressed under her breasts as a large hand whacked her between her shoulder blades. She wasn't sure if it was the harsh smacks of his hand or just the sheer shock of being manhandled, but the gum shot back up her throat and into her mouth.

"Breathe. That's it. Breathe," he commanded in a low voice that wasn't to be disobeyed.

Oh hell. She knew that voice.

He placed a large paw under her mouth. "Spit it out."

She shook her head. Nuh-uh. No way.

"Marisol," he said firmly. "Spit."

She spat the gum into his hand. That was truly, truly gross. He moved away from her, throwing the gum in the trash can before he opened the door to the truck parked alongside the sidewalk. Shit. How had she missed him? She'd walked right into him.

How embarrassing.

He drew out a napkin from out of the truck. He quickly wiped his hand before leaning in and grabbing a bottle of water. He held it out to her.

"You're not wrinkly and hairy."

"Um, thanks, I think?" He gave her a strange look.

You're talking out loud, Marisol.

"Here." He wiggled the drink in his hand.

"Ahh, no thanks."

"It's new. I just bought it. Drink."

"Oh no, I couldn't. You'll need it."

"Marisol," he said in a commanding voice.

"Besides, I'm fine. Not thirsty at all." Except her voice was all raspy from her choking fit and that bottle of water was looking mighty tempting.

"Are you always this stubborn?" he asked with a hint of exasperation.

Her eyes widened at the accusation. "I'm not stubborn. I'm very easy-going. I never make waves at all."

"Not from what I've seen."

She put her hands on her hips. "Look. Just because I don't want a drink of water doesn't make me stubborn."

"It does when you're refusing on principle not because you're not thirsty. I promise, it doesn't come with strings attached."

"I didn't think it did." She snatched the bottle of water from him, grumbling to herself as she took a few long sips. She was only drinking it because she wanted to, not because he'd goaded her into it.

She tried to hand it back but he shook his head. "Keep it. Drink it. Now, where are you headed to?"

"Umm..."

She was saved from having to answer him by a big red truck pulling up. Out climbed Linc and she sighed in relief.

"Morning, Linc," Ed called out. Obviously, he wasn't on duty today. He was dressed casually in a shirt, jeans and black jacket.

"Morning, Ed," Linc replied with a nod of his head before turning his attention to her. "Morning, Mari-girl. Everything okay?"

"Fine." She smiled at him widely.

"We just had a collision," Ed countered.

Really? Did he have to make it sound so bad?

"A collision? Are you all right? What happened? Was it in that crap piece of car of yours?" Linc asked with concern as he gently ran his hands over her arms and down her body. "Where does it hurt?" He turned to Ed. "Why haven't you taken her to the hospital?"

"I'm fine. It wasn't a collision." She glared at Ed. Why did he have to make it sound like that?

"It didn't happen while we were driving. She walked straight into me." Ed bent down and picked up her book, looking at the cover.

Which had a half-naked, muscular man on the front. She wished she had her eReader. Nobody could see what she was reading then. Truth was, Ed wasn't the first person she'd banged into while she was reading and walking.

Once, the man she'd bumped into had shoved her aside and she'd ended up on her ass on the road in a puddle.

That had been humiliating.

"Can I please have that back?" She reached for the book, snatching it from Ed's hand. He grinned at her.

"Wait. Was she reading while walking again?" Linc turned to her with a frown.

"Again?" Ed asked. "This happens often?"

"She nearly ran into a lamp post day before yesterday." Linc crossed his arms over his chest.

"Hmm, that so?" Ed replied.

"Yep. And I seem to recall telling her then that I didn't want her walking around with her head in a book again."

She gaped at Linc. What? Had he actually been serious about that? She could feel the blush rising in her cheeks as she stared from Linc to Ed then back again.

"Never thought I'd have to instigate a no-reading-while-walking rule." Ed shook his head.

"What? You can't just make up rules!" She turned to Linc. "He can't, can he?"

"Well, let's see. He is the sheriff."

Her mouth dropped open. "You're the sheriff?" She gulped.

Ed nodded and she took a longer look at him. He was about an inch taller than Linc and just as broad with dark hair and gray eyes. He filled out that shirt of his nicely. She couldn't believe she'd just thought that.

He's a cop. The goddamn sheriff.

But he wasn't in uniform right now, which made it easier to be around him.

"Even the sheriff can't just make up rules like that."

"Well, I was hired to protect the people of this town, including you, little miss. And this is the second time you've been in trouble, isn't it?"

"Second time?" Linc asked in a low voice.

Uh-oh.

"We have to get going, don't we, Linc? Sorry I crashed into you,

Sheriff. It won't happen again. Bye!" She slipped her hand into Linc's arm and tried to move him.

It was like attempting to shift a mountain. The man was made of solid muscle. She let out a frustrated noise. "You could've just let me steer you away."

"I could have," he agreed.

The sheriff raised his eyebrows and turned to Linc. "The two of you are headed somewhere?"

"Going on a picnic by the river," Linc explained.

"Ahh. I see."

Something flashed over Ed's face. She wasn't sure what it was, but it looked almost like regret. That made no sense, though.

"Laid a claim, have you?" Ed asked.

"I'm trying," Linc said.

Huh? A claim on what? What were they talking about?

"Sorry. If I'd known that I would have told you about pulling her over the other night for speeding."

"What night was this?" Linc asked quietly. Staring down at her.

She had to stop herself from shuffling her feet in guilt.

"When she was at Sanctuary Ranch for Charlie's bridal shower. Surprised you didn't have her stay over. It was late for her to be driving home alone on that road."

"We only just met that night," Linc said, his eyes narrowing as he scowled at the sheriff, obviously not liking the rebuke in his voice.

She glared at the sheriff as well. She could look after herself, thank you very much.

Well, not really. But still. His words were worthy of a glare in her opinion.

"You move fast," Ed observed.

"When I find something I want, I know I need to move quickly before someone else steps in and snatches it up."

Ed nodded slowly. "Wise call."

Okay, she was really confused.

"We best go. You ready, Mari-girl?"

"Yep." Relief flooded her. She'd spent enough time around the sheriff. Even though he didn't seem a bad sort. For a cop.

"All right. I'll leave you to your picnic." Ed gave a tight smile that seemed forced. He turned to her. "No more walking around while you're reading, Miss Marisol. You could have hurt yourself or someone else. And you could have been in real trouble choking like that."

"I was only choking because I crashed into you."

"And you crashed into me because you weren't watching where you were going." Ed gave them both a nod before turning and walking away.

Linc spun her carefully to face him, but the gentleness of his hands was at odds with the fierce frown on his face.

"What does he mean you were choking?"

Linc checked her over again for injuries.

What was she thinking? Speeding? And hadn't they just talked about her habit of walking around with her nose in a book? Obviously, he should have been firmer.

Easy. She only wants to be friends.

Ahh. But that wasn't what he wanted. He admitted he was hoping to change her mind. Anyway, friends could still be protective, right? Hopefully, she'd eventually trust him with whatever was going on in her life.

He knew it was a risk, showing his cards now. But yesterday, as he'd watched Clint and Charlie declare their love for each other, all he could think of was Marisol. And he knew that was what he wanted with her.

He'd demanded honesty from her, shouldn't he give it back?

But maybe he'd take her on the picnic first. If she was going to reject him, he'd at least like it to happen on a full stomach.

"What was he talking about, you choking?" he asked.

"He was exaggerating. Seems to be something he does a lot of." She scowled.

"Marisol, tell me."

"It's really nothing. I was chewing on some bubble gum and when I crashed into the sheriff, I kind of just sucked it in. I started to choke. But I was fine. It was just gum."

He gave her a look and she had the grace to appear somewhat guilty.

"What am I going to do with you, Mari-girl?" he murmured.

"Take me on a picnic?"

He cupped her face between his wide hands. Damn, her skin was smooth. And her cinnamon and apple scent swirled around him, tempting him. He had to fight the urge to kiss her, to see if she tasted as sweet as she smelled.

Slowly.

"I can do that. But we're gonna be having a chat about all this."

Her eyes widened at his stern tone. "I'm in trouble?" Her voice was smaller, the words almost childish sounding.

He swallowed heavily. God, she sounded like a Little. He wondered if she knew about age play and Daddy Doms.

He tapped her nose. "How about you tell me? Do you think it was wise to speed? It's dangerous. It puts you at risk. It puts the other people on the road at risk. Have you had your brakes checked lately? Would they even work that well if something jumped out in front of you?"

She sighed, dropping her gaze down. "You're right."

He tipped up her chin. "I just want you to be safe, Mari-girl."

"I know. And I get it. I've always had a bit of a lead foot. And I tend to get distracted."

"And I made myself clear about not wanting you to walk around with your head in a book, right?"

She nodded, blushing slightly.

He ran his thumb across her cheek. "You're precious, Mari-girl. I just don't want something happening to you. As your friend, I'm asking you to take better care of yourself. Okay?"

"Okay."

8

You're precious, Mari-girl.

She could barely contain her smile as she followed him around to the passenger side of his truck. She'd never been precious to anyone before. Not that she could remember anyway.

Careful. Don't let it go to your head. You barely know him, remember?

Linc opened the door and she stared up into the high cab. What happened to running boards? Obviously, they hadn't made this vehicle with the vertically challenged in mind.

Before she could attempt to climb up, big hands wrapped around her waist and lifted her into the air, placing her on the seat.

Whoa. She'd had a demonstration of his strength the other night when he'd grabbed her, but it still took her by surprise. As she was trying to gather her wits, he took hold of her seatbelt then leaned across her to buckle her in. His chest pressed up against hers.

Her nipples instantly hardened. She bit her lip. Holy shit. He was muscular. The feel of him sent her senses into overdrive.

All too quickly, she was belted in and he was moving away from her.

Calm, girl.

She'd never reacted to a man like this before. Mind you, she hadn't been around that many men. Just her aunt's husbands, and most of them ignored her. Which was a good thing. Then there was Saber, Tiger and their friends.

She definitely didn't want their attention. Being around Linc was completely different. Instead of scaring her, he actually made her feel safe.

She snuck glimpses over at him as he hopped into the truck and started it up. Those hands of his were enormous. What would it be like if he touched her? Cupped her breast, ran his hand down her stomach to touch her . . .

"Mari-girl? Marisol? You okay?"

"What?" She stared at him. *Mierda!* Had he been talking to her? *Good work, Marisol.*

"Are you all right?"

"Oh yes, I'm fine. Sorry. I just zoned out a bit." She winced. Great. Now she made it sound like she was bored or something. "Sorry. It's not the company. I tend to spend a lot of time in my own head."

He drove them out of town. She hadn't done much exploring around. Her aunt usually only liked her going out in the car if it was for work or to run errands for her, so she was stuck on foot.

"That so?" he murmured thoughtfully. As though he saw much more than she wanted him to. She licked her lips.

"We're going to the river?"

"Yep. We're headed to a nice spot I know of."

"Did you have a good time at the wedding?" she asked, kicking her feet back and forth. They didn't even touch the floor and she couldn't see out the front window.

"I did. Charlie made a beautiful bride. And Clint could barely take his eyes or hands off her all night."

She glanced down at her lap to hide her sadness. How amazing would it be to meet someone who loved her like that? To have the wedding of her dreams? She couldn't see that in her future.

Linc parked the truck and she looked around in interest. They seemed to be in the middle of nowhere. Where was the river?

"Stay there. I'll come round and help you down."

Before she could answer, he was out of the truck, moving around with long strides. The sun glinted off his dark hair. God, he really was gorgeous.

What was he doing here with her?

She didn't know. Right then, she didn't much care, either. Maybe it was selfish. But she wanted this experience. The memory would keep her going for a long time. She didn't know where she would be next month, but she could always have this.

He opened the door and reached across to undo her seatbelt. Whoops. She could have done that herself.

But then he wouldn't have brushed his arm over her breasts.

Sliding his hands around her waist, he lifted her down. She was wearing a pair of jeans and a flowy, floral top with long sleeves and a high neck.

"We have a small walk. I should have warned you." He glanced down at her feet. She was wearing a pair of old tan sandals. "Can you walk all right in those?"

"Oh yeah, I walk everywhere in these, I'll be fine."

They were pretty old though and they didn't give much support. If she'd known, she would have worn sneakers.

"Are you sure? This is my fault. We can go back to town and have a picnic in the park."

"No, this is fine, honestly. Please, a picnic by the river sounds like just what I need right now."

"All right. But tell me if you're having problems. Understand?" There went that note of sternness again. There was something wrong with her that she found that so hot.

Just friends, remember?

He drew a picnic basket out of the back of the truck. It came complete with a red and black picnic blanket rolled up and attached to the side by straps. Then he grabbed a jacket.

"Have you got a sweater or hoodie in your bag, Mari-girl?"

She glanced down at her large handbag. "Ah no, I didn't bring one. The sun is out today."

"But it could get cooler. Next time we go on a picnic, I'm sending you a list of things to wear," he teased.

If only there was going to be a next time.

Reaching into the truck, he grabbed a hoodie. "It will be a bit big, but I haven't worn it much." He handed it to her and she tied it around her waist.

"I'm sorry. This is the first picnic I've been on."

He froze. "What? It can't be."

She frowned. It couldn't?

"Why not? I mean, I might have been on one when I was younger, before Mama died. But I can't remember so I guess it doesn't count, right?"

"Your aunt . . ."

"Isn't really into children. Or me. Oh, wait! I lie!" She clapped her hands together. "Harry took me on a picnic once."

How could she have forgotten that?

"Harry?" There was a funny note in Linc's voice but she didn't pay any attention to it.

"Yes, he's one of my aunt's ex-husbands. Actually, she was married to him the longest. I came to live with her and Harry after mama died. He took me on a picnic in the park by our house. I had fairy bread and orange soda."

"Fairy bread?"

"It's white bread with butter and sprinkles on it. Harry was born in New Zealand. After his dad died, they moved to Texas where his mom was from. He told me on special occasions like birthdays, they'd have fairy bread. I think he was trying to cheer me up. I'd had a hard night."

"You liked him."

"Yeah. I was really sad when he and Rosalind split up. He was my favorite of all her husbands."

"There's been a lot?"

"A few," she said vaguely, suddenly aware of how much talking she'd been doing. They were still standing by the truck.

Linc gave her that knowing look again. *You're showing him too much, Marisol.*

"Let's go." He held out his hand to her and she clasped hold, following behind him.

For a start it wasn't too bad. They walked across a flat paddock. But at the end of it, they had to walk down an incline which had lots of rocks. She kept a tight hold of his hand. He was right, these sandals weren't the best. He stopped in several spots to guide her down. By the time they reached the river bed, she was ready to sit down and rest.

She followed behind him to a shady spot under a huge willow tree.

"Wow, it's beautiful here."

"I like to come here for some peace and quiet sometimes. Don't get a lot of free time in my job. But this rejuvenates me."

He shrugged, almost looking embarrassed. She smiled at him.

"I know exactly what you mean. Moving here seems to have recharged me a bit. Living in the city was tiring. Everybody was always in a rush, they all had somewhere to be. And well, I've always moved at a different pace from everyone else."

"Isn't anything wrong with that, Mari-girl."

He laid out the blanket and gestured to her. "Have a seat. I'll get everything laid out."

"Can I help you?"

"No, teeny, you just rest."

Had he noticed that she'd gotten a bit winded on the walk here? How embarrassing. Which reminded her, she really needed to take her blood sugar levels before she ate. She bit her lip. Where to do it?

"I'm just going to go test the water," she told him, deciding to wash her hands in the river. She undid the hoodie that was tied around her waist and left it by his jacket.

"All right, but it's cold, so just dip your fingers in, nothing else," he warned.

Was he like this with everyone? She waited until she was facing away from him to roll her eyes. He seemed to think she was made of glass. It was endearing at times, frustrating at others.

"I'll be fine." She walked along the side of the river for a bit. Then she took off her sandals and stepped into the water.

Whoa. Cold. Bending down, she quickly pushed her hands under the water. A smooth stone caught her attention and she picked it up. Then moving out of the chilly water, she threw it up into the air. She giggled as it made a plopping sound.

"That looks like fun," he said.

She turned with surprise. She hadn't even heard him approach. "Oh, you gave me a fright."

"Sorry, Mari-girl." He was glancing around then bent down and picked up a round, smooth stone. "Ooh, here's a good one. Can you skip stones?"

"Skip stones? What's that?"

"Your childhood is sadly lacking." He shook his head. "City

dwellers."

"Hey," she protested, making herself grin. It wasn't being raised in the city that was at fault, but rather that she hadn't had much of a childhood.

He turned side-on then flung his arm back then forward, letting the stone go. It skipped along the water.

"Eight skips, not bad," he commented.

"That was awesome. I want to try."

She picked up a stone and tried to imitate what he'd done. The stone flung into the water and sank. Her lower lip dropped out. "Something was wrong with my stone."

He let out a bark of laughter. "I think it might have had something to do with technique as well."

She huffed, crossing her arms over her chest.

"Here, find a stone that's nice and flat. Like this one. Now hold it like this." He taught her how to hold it. "Turn side-on and pull your arm back and use your wrist to fling it."

She let the stone go. It sank.

With a sigh, she turned away dejectedly. "Hey, where are you going?" He caught hold of her arm, stopping her.

"Back to the picnic blanket. I'm obviously no good at this." Like most things.

"You just need to practice, teeny," he soothed. "Let me help you. Here's another stone." Instead of directing her verbally this time, he stepped in close behind her. Taking hold of her arm, he pulled it back. She had to repress a shiver of arousal as he stood so close that she could feel his hard body, his warmth. She longed to lean back, to give him her weight as he grasped hold of her.

"You listening, Mari-girl? Or are you away with the fairies?"

"I'm listening. I'm listening." She wasn't daydreaming about him touching her. Nope. Not her.

He went through the movement of her arm a few times then stepped away. She immediately missed his touch. She let the stone go and it skipped across the water four times. She jumped up and down with a squeal. "Yes!"

"Good job! High five!"

She slammed her palm against his.

"Well done, little one. I knew you could do it."

"Again," she demanded. Five stones later and she could now get up to ten skips across the water. Mastered it. She started searching around for another one.

"Come on, now. Come eat."

"One more," she said absentmindedly.

"You can throw some more after lunch. You must be hungry."

Her stomach chose that moment to growl. She blushed. Whoops. Maybe she was a bit hungry.

"Think we better get some food into you." He took her hand and she snatched up her sandals before he led her back to the blanket. She stared in amazement at the abundance of food he had laid out. Sitting, she laid her sandals next to her.

There was pasta salad, egg salad sandwiches, cut up carrot and cucumber with ranch dip. And some cupcakes with chocolate icing that looked absolutely delicious.

"Yum, this looks great!"

"Good. I wasn't sure what you'd like."

"Did you make this?" she asked.

"Ahh, I did."

She gaped at him.

He grinned. "What? You didn't think cowboys could bake and cook?"

"What? No, that's not it," she said hastily.

His grin widened.

"Okay, maybe I did think that. Sorry."

He shrugged and grabbed a plate, putting a sandwich, some salad and some of the sliced veggies on it. Then he handed it over to her. She took hold of it.

"My nana taught me how to cook and bake. I don't always have much time for it, but I enjoy it."

"But you must have gotten up early to make all this?"

He shrugged. "I'm an early riser."

Even after being at a wedding the night before? The thought of him making all this for her flooded her with happiness. If he was willing to do this for a friend, what would he do for a girlfriend? He filled his own plate then nodded to her. "Eat."

"Oh, I can't."

"What? Why not?" He frowned.

"I have to umm, do something, first."

Shoot.

Just tell him. You have no reason to be ashamed.

But when she'd told people in the past, she'd had mixed reactions. From people telling her that she needed to cut all sugar from her diet, to explaining that she should exercise more. On the other side of the coin, there were people that were completely uninterested.

"Do something first?" His face cleared. "You've got to pee? You'll have to go behind a bush."

"What?" Pee? Oh crap. She hadn't thought about that. There were no toilets out here. And now that he'd mentioned it . . .

Nope. No way. Not happening. She wasn't peeing behind a bush. That sounded horrible.

You are a total city person, aren't you?

One worry at a time.

"No, I don't have to pee. Thank God."

"Then what's wrong?" His eyebrows rose. "Do you have to—"

"I'm gonna stop you right there because I'm not sure what other bodily function you're going to come up with next. No, uh, here's the thing. I have to check my blood sugar level. I can just turn my back so you don't see me do it."

"Your blood sugar level? You're diabetic?"

"Yep, Type One."

"Why didn't you say anything? Check it. Wait, why would you turn your back?"

"Some people don't like to watch when I prick my finger."

"A bit of blood doesn't worry me," he told her dryly. Although he was frowning slightly. She wasn't sure what to make of that. Was he upset that she was a diabetic?

She took out the monitor and lancet device. She pricked her finger then placed the drop of blood on the new test strip in the blood glucose monitor.

"What did it say?" he asked.

"Oh, it's good."

"I don't know much about diabetes," he admitted. "I hope you don't mind me asking you questions."

"No, I don't mind," she said quietly. Questions were good. At least he wasn't immediately telling her what she should do or making assumptions about her life. "I need to take my insulin."

"Right, by injection, yes? Where do you do it?"

"Usually in my stomach or thigh, sometimes my arm."

"Can't you get like a pump or something?"

"Yeah, you can. But my insurance doesn't cover it," she told him as she cleaned her hands with a wipe then prepared the syringe. "You can get pens too which are easier, but my insurance doesn't fully cover them either." She cleaned her skin with an alcoholic wipe then injected the insulin into her tummy. "It's okay, I'm normally pretty good at keeping it under control. It's just sometimes I'll forget to eat."

She tidied up, putting the needle in a plastic container she'd brought with her so she could get rid of it later.

"Well, we'll have to see what we can do to stop that," he muttered. "Why didn't you tell me?"

She shrugged. "Some people react weirdly. Some act as though it's my fault almost. If I just did this or ate that, then I could miraculously cure it."

"That's ridiculous," he stated, making her insides go warm.

"I didn't want it to come between us."

"Nothing is coming between us." He reached over and took her hand. Then he cleared his throat awkwardly as though just realizing what he'd said. He let her hand go. "Is there anything I should know? Signs to look for if your blood sugars are dipping or spiking?"

"Oh well, signs of it spiking are usually a headache or I'll need to pee and drink a lot and be really tired. When it dips too low, I often feel light-headed and tired. Sometimes I get irritable and anxious."

He frowned. "I need a list of what to look for and what to do to help you. Will you give me that?"

"Sure," she told him. "I can do that." She dropped her head, feeling like she was being a nuisance.

He moved closer, setting his finger under her chin and raising her face up. "Hey, don't be embarrassed. You do whatever you need to do to be healthy. That's what is important."

She bit her lip shyly but nodded. "Thank you."

"You don't have to thank me for being understanding about your health. I never want you to hide anything that might put your health at risk, understand me? No matter what we are doing or where we are, you stop and you tell me. Got it?"

"Got it."

"I'm very serious about this, Mari-girl. I will not be happy if your health is put in jeopardy because you didn't tell me about something."

"Yes." Wow. He made her feel so special and cared for. It nearly brought tears to her eyes.

"How long have you been diabetic?" he asked.

"Since I was thirteen. It was hard in the beginning, there was so much to learn and remember."

"Was your aunt much help?"

Help? Rosalind?

"I'm going to take your answer as a no," he said dryly.

She shrugged. "No, she wasn't much interested in helping." She reached for a sandwich and took a bite. "Thanks for waiting for me. You didn't have to."

His eyes widened. "My nana would have whipped me good if I'd started eating first."

She swallowed a mouthful of egg salad sandwich. "She would have?"

"Absolutely." He winked at her.

The food was all delicious. A man who could cook and bake. Now, he was a keeper.

"I wish I knew how to cook," she told him.

"So you don't know how to cook at all?" he asked.

"Not unless you consider heating up a frozen meal cooking."

He grinned. "No. Can't say that I do. I could teach you."

Teach her?

An image of them kissing, of him touching her, of her wrapping her mouth around his cock filled her mind.

"Marisol?"

"What?" she asked absentmindedly.

"Do I want to know what you're thinking about?" he inquired, lifting an eyebrow.

Oh. Nope. He really didn't.

His eyes danced. "Would you like me to teach you? How to cook that is."

"I'd like that," she said shyly. "Only . . ."

"Only what?"

"I don't know if I'd have the time." Or if she was sticking around long enough. She felt so bad for not telling him that she might be leaving soon. She didn't want him to feel like he had to help her. Plus, she knew better than to talk about Tiger and Saber with anyone. They were dangerous guys. You didn't go around talking about them to people and live long.

No, she couldn't put him at risk. And they were just friends. This wasn't his problem. It was hers.

"You work a lot. I hope your aunt appreciates it."

She shrugged, feeling uncomfortable talking about it. "She took me in when Mama died. I don't know who my dad was, he left before I was born. If she hadn't taken me then my only other options were going into a foster home or having to go to Venezuela to live with a grandmother I'd never met. A grandmother who, according to my aunt, is the devil in a floral dress. Rosalind never wanted a child. But she saved me from that so I do owe her."

He frowned and shook his head. "Way I see it, you were just a child. You don't owe her your life."

"No, I don't owe her that," she said thinking of Tiger.

After finishing her lunch, she lay back with a groan. "I'm so full. That was so good." She placed her hands over her stomach as she looked up at the branches of the willow tree above her.

"Do you need to test your blood sugars again?" he asked.

"Not for a couple of hours."

"All right, I'll set an alarm on my phone."

That was sweet of him. As she lay there, her bladder protested, telling her that she really needed to pee. She sat up, pressing her thighs together.

"You okay, teeny?"

"Why do you call me that?"

"Because you're teeny-tiny."

Oh, because she was short? "I'm not that small."

"You seem very little to me." There was an emphasis on the word little and a strange sort of warmth filled her. Could he be . . . no . . .

She shook her head at her musings.

"There's something I wanted to talk to you about."

"What's that?" she asked as she helped him pack everything away.

"I know we haven't known each other long, Mari-girl, but I like you."

"I like you too." Guilt flooded her. As well as longing.

He opened his mouth and suddenly, she didn't want to know what he was going to say. She couldn't bear it. She wasn't sure if she was dreading him telling her that he liked her but as a friend. Or that he liked her and wanted more.

Shoot. Saying yes to this picnic was definitely a bad idea.

"I have to pee," she said suddenly.

Oh God, Marisol. Couldn't you have told him something else? Anything else?

She jumped to her feet and looked around as though she thought a toilet might magically appear out of thin air.

Idiot.

"Are you all right? Do you want me to drive you back to town?"

"No. No, I got this," she muttered. She really didn't. She thought she might be losing her mind to be quite frank. But she stomped her way behind a bush. *You are such a fool, Marisol.* After a quick look around to make sure she was alone, she pulled her pants down and got on with things.

Okay, how did one go about doing this? Did you sit? Crouch?

"Mari-girl? You okay?" Linc called out.

All right, even if he had been about to tell her that he wanted something more, she was guessing she'd likely turned him off by now. This wasn't sexy or attractive. It was more than a bit embarrassing.

"I'm fine."

"You ever peed behind a bush before?"

"Who hasn't? I mean, I'm an old hand at it."

"Are you lying to me, little one?" he asked.

"I wouldn't call it lying."

"Then what would you call it?"

"Totally humiliated babbling," she spat out. "This isn't exactly something I'm comfortable with."

"Teeny, there's nothing to be embarrassed about." His voice was so soft and sweet that she felt her insides melt.

Why did she have to meet him now? When everything was up in the air? When it was all a complete mess?

Because fate hated her. She was certain of it.

"Just squat right down so your hips are lower than your knees. If you can't squat easily, we can find you a tree to lean against."

"No, I'm fine squatting." She was not going to go on a hunt for a tree to pee against with him. How would that even go? What sort of tree qualified as a peeing tree? Nope. There had to be somewhere where she drew the line and that was it. No searching together for good spots to squat.

Oh dear Lord.

"Try to keep your clothes and feet out of the way so you don't pee on them." How could he sound so normal? Was this something he did every day? Coached someone on how to pee outside? And here she thought moving to the country, the only things she'd need to worry about were the different sorts of critters. She froze in a crouching position.

"What if there's a snake?" she asked in a high voice.

"There's a snake?" Now alarm filled his voice.

"Not that I can see!" She glanced around frantically. "But what if one appears?"

"Okay, Mari-girl. Calm down. I can hear you panicking from here."

Well. Yeah. She was freaking out. Peeing outdoors. Have snakes slither up on her while her pants were down. These were all new experiences and none of them good.

"Snakes are more scared of you than you are of them."

"I really don't think that's possible." Her thighs were starting to burn. She needed to start an exercise routine. Pronto.

Not that she ever intended on repeating this experience again.

Nope. Not happening. She should have just held on and risked peeing her pants.

"Snakes aren't really active this time of year, it's too cold for them. But if you want, I can come keep watch for you?"

"No! In fact, you should step away. Far away."

Last thing she needed was for him to hear her pee.

"I'm not going too far away in case you need me. Just let go, Mari-girl. I'm not embarrassed. You shouldn't be either."

Easy for him to say. He wasn't the one peeing behind a bush and making a fool of themselves.

Finally, knowing she couldn't crouch here much longer or she'd risk falling over, she forced herself to relax. She could hear Linc singing in the background as though he was trying to help her relax. What was he singing?

Whatever it was, it did the trick. She finished up and then stood behind the bush, trying to wait for the embarrassment on her cheeks to fade.

Come on, Marisol. You can do this.

"Are you singing?" she asked as she walked back towards him.

"Thought it might help," he told her.

"Well, it did. So thank you," she replied quietly.

Suddenly, something sharp pierced her foot and she let out a cry. Falling onto her ass, she grabbed at her foot, tears dripping down her face.

"What is it? What happened?" he demanded.

"I . . . I don't k-know!" she wailed. He crouched and grabbed her foot, looking around.

"Oh shit, you stood on a bee, teeny."

She sniffed, her foot was hot, burning. He turned it over and there was a red welt on her foot. Already it was starting to swell. He flicked the stinger away.

"Ow. Ow. Owie."

"Oh, baby," he crooned in sympathy. "Are you allergic?"

She shook her head. "I don't think so."

"Come on, let's get your foot into the water. The cold will help."

Linc stood and she expected him to hold out a hand to help her up. Getting to the truck was going to be a pain in the ass. Instead, he reached down and pulled her up, bridal style, into his arms. She squeaked in surprise. But he carried her down to the river and then he let her feet drop. He held her around the waist as she stood on her good foot and let the other one float in the water.

Oh, that was definitely better.

"I have a first-aid kit in my truck. After I get you out of the water, I'll run back and get it. It's got some calamine lotion in it."

"Thank you," she whispered quietly. She couldn't believe how caring he was.

Linc picked her up and carried her back to the picnic rug.

"You don't have to carry me," she told him.

"You can't walk on that foot," he pointed out. "Besides, I like carrying you."

He did?

He grabbed some clean napkins and wet them in the river then came back and placed them on the bottom of her foot. Ahh, that felt so good.

"Stay here, okay? Don't move." He gave her a warning look and she nodded.

She definitely didn't feel like moving anywhere right now. She held the wad of napkins against her foot as he grabbed the picnic basket and quickly disappeared.

Way to make a complete mess of things, Marisol.

inc made his way quickly back to the truck. He'd brought the basket with him because he wouldn't be able to carry Marisol and it at the same time. He grabbed the first aid supplies he needed.

This picnic wasn't exactly shaping up how he thought it would.

When he got back to her, she was where he'd left her. That was surprising. He had the feeling she wasn't always the best at following orders.

If she agreed to be his, they'd have to address that, as well as her lead foot.

He had to do some research into diabetes. He could ask Doc for some information. He didn't want to do anything to put her health in jeopardy. And there might be things he could do to help her.

He hated the fact that she didn't have everything she might need because she couldn't afford it. He'd look into that as well. Even though he knew she wasn't likely to let him help her financially, there had to be something that could be done.

Not for the first time, he wondered how much her aunt was paying her. She drove a crappy car that was on its last legs. Her sandals looked like they were close to falling apart and her clothes weren't in much better condition. She didn't seem to have anything appropriate for the cooler climate here.

There was something going on. Something he didn't like. But he knew he had to tread carefully. Family could be a tricky thing to discuss. And he knew that she felt an obligation to her aunt for taking her in.

He sat next to her and opened the first-aid kit. "Okay, let's see what Doctor Linc has here to fix your boo-boos."

She sniffled sweetly and he drew out a pocket pack of tissues that he'd found in the glove box of his truck. He reached over and wiped her cheeks gently.

"Oh." She froze as he cleaned her up.

"All good, Mari-girl?"

"Yes, thank you." She gave him a shy look.

He wiped her nose and she reared back. "Linc!"

"What? Do you need to blow?"

"No." She gave him a disgruntled look. "Can I have another tissue please?"

He hid a smile. He'd get her comfortable enough with him eventually that she'd let him take care of her in all ways.

Well, hopefully. If she reacted well to what he had to tell her. He grabbed an antihistamine and some of the bottled water he'd brought with him. "You're okay to take some antihistamines?"

"Yes, thank you." She swallowed them down as he gently grasped hold of her foot.

"Oh, poor darling, it's really swollen, isn't it?"

She whimpered as he ran some cream over the red patch. "Does that hurt?"

"Just a little bit," she sniffled. "I'm sorry."

"Why are you sorry, little one?"

"I kind of ruined the picnic, didn't I?"

"Hey." Moving on instinct, he pulled her onto his lap. She tensed. "You didn't ruin anything." He ran his hand up and down her back. "If anyone is at fault, it's me for letting you walk around without your sandals on. From now on, you wear shoes when you're outside."

"This is hardly your fault and you didn't let me do anything. I make my own decisions."

"Of course," he agreed. "But I'm the kind of guy who likes to take care of people who are special to him."

"Your old-fashioned views?" she asked, losing some of her tension and leaning against his chest with a sigh.

"Sort of. I want to ask you a question. You don't have to answer it, but you mustn't lie. All right?"

"Yes, okay."

"Do any of those books you like to read have BDSM in them?"

"Um, yes." She squirmed around and he had to hold her still before it became obvious just how much he enjoyed having her on his lap.

"Is there any aspect of BDSM that you particularly enjoy reading about?"

"I . . . I guess so."

She didn't elaborate. He decided to tread softly. The last thing he wanted was to send her running.

"You don't have to be embarrassed to tell me what you like, Marisol. I'd like to know everything about you."

"Why?" she breathed out. "I thought we were just friends?"

"We are. And I know you said you couldn't be anything more than friends. But I'm attracted to you. And I think you might feel the same way about me?" He pulled her back so he could look down into her face.

She bit her lip but gave a small nod. "I don't think there's a woman alive who wouldn't be attracted to you. There's something about you. You can be sweet and funny, but also commanding and protective. I like the way you look after me. That you're not trying to be someone you're not. You can make fun of yourself. I think you like to be in control but you're not a dick about it."

"I certainly hope I'm not," he told her. "And if I ever am, you can tell me."

"I heard some gossip the other day at the spa."

"Oh." Was she trying to change the subject? "Gossip?"

She wiggled again. Christ, was she trying to kill him? He held her steady.

"I don't usually listen, but I was covering for Eileen who was sick. Mrs. Long and her friends were talking about the ranch. I didn't put much credence in what they were saying."

"And what were they saying?" He knew Wilma Long and her friends. A bunch of narrow-minded women who made it their business to know everything that went on in Wishingbone. They weren't nice people and he didn't like Marisol being around them.

Easy, man.

"About how the men on the ranch are . . . well, that they spank the women."

Damn. It was hard to keep things that happened on the ranch completely quiet but he hadn't realized anyone had discovered any details about how the people at Sanctuary lived.

"Also that one woman lives with two men. I didn't really believe that. I mean, that doesn't happen in real life, right?"

Oh, it did. Caley lived with the two docs and she was very happy with both of them. What she didn't need, though, was to be gossiped about. She was a private person. They all were.

"Are you okay? Should I not have mentioned it?" she asked worriedly, staring up at him in concern.

"Did you tell anyone?" he asked sharply.

Her eyes widened. "What? No, of course not. Who would I tell? I wouldn't say anything anyway," she told him with a frown. "It's none of my business. But they did say they'd gone to the sheriff about it."

"What?" he snapped.

"Yeah. Oh, Ed is the sheriff, isn't he? Huh, guess he's not such a bad guy. For a cop, that is."

"They went to Ed about a rumor they'd heard?"

"Yeah. But don't worry, he told them to mind their own business and stop making up stories."

Well, there was that at least. But Ed should have told him. Or Clint anyway. Maybe he hadn't wanted to bother him while he was getting ready for his wedding. Linc would talk to Kent though, just to give him a heads up.

It wasn't like any of them cared what some small-minded people thought. But none of them would allow the women on Sanctuary to be slighted or upset.

Maybe, for the foreseeable future, the women shouldn't go into town without one of the men with them. It wasn't like they often went in on their own so it shouldn't be too much of a problem.

"Linc? I really didn't believe it. I enjoyed going to Sanctuary and meeting everyone the other evening. And Eden is one of my best customers."

Marisol looked worried as she stared up at him, chewing on her lip. Crap. He hadn't reacted well. Of course she wouldn't gossip, she wasn't like those other women.

"Shh, it's okay. Sorry if I was a bit harsh. I just don't want any of the women on Sanctuary to be hurt by rumors."

"That's really sweet of you. I don't want that either."

"Mrs. Long and her friends can be kind of . . ."

"Judgmental? Mean?" she supplied.

"Yes."

"Don't worry, I've seen it. She's narrow-minded about a lot of things."

"Has she said something to you?" He frowned, not liking that.

She shrugged. "First time she came into the spa, she wanted to know if I had papers to work here legally."

"That old bitch." Anger flooded him. At least the women on Sanctuary had protection, but who did Marisol have? An aunt who frankly, seemed to be a complete bitch.

"It's okay. I've met plenty of people like that."

"That doesn't make it all right. I don't want you around that old bitch and her friends again."

"Like I said, they're Eileen's customers. I don't have to deal with them much."

She shouldn't have to deal with them at all. Linc glanced down at her, seeing her pale worried face. He needed to get her home. And talk to Kent.

"Come on. Let's get you home so you can sit with that foot up."

10

She wished she'd never brought up that old bat, Mrs. Long. Linc had been quiet ever since. Did he now regret telling her that he was attracted to her? And how crazy was that? Why had he asked about whether her books had BDSM in them? And whether she liked any aspects?

Was it because he was a Dom? She could totally see it. But if that was what he'd been about to confess, he'd obviously changed his mind because he hadn't said a word about it since.

"You moved into the Stanford place, right?" he asked as he drove through town.

Oh shit.

She couldn't have him drop her off at home. Not when her aunt was likely to be around.

"Um, yes, but just drop me back at the diner."

He gave her an incredulous look. "I can't drop you at the diner. You can't walk on your foot. You can't even get your sandal back on it."

She looked down at her swollen foot

"Maybe I should take you to Doc. I don't like how swollen it is."

A doctor? No way was she going to a doctor for a bee sting. Besides, she'd already been away from the house long enough. Rosalind would be starting to wonder where she was.

"It will be fine. No need for a doctor. You can just drop me off at the end of the driveway."

He gave her a strange look. "Not want to be seen with me, Mari-girl?"

Her mouth dropped open. "Uh, no! That's not the issue at all. Sheesh, how could you think that? Look at you. Then look at me. You could go into a competition for the Worlds Sexiest Cowboy and win. While I—"

"I'm going to stop you right there, Mari-girl," he said in a deep, commanding voice as he pulled onto her street. "Because I am pretty certain I am not going to like what was about to come out of your mouth."

She pressed her lips together as he turned into her driveway. Well, her aunt's driveway. This wasn't her home. She was given room and board and she should be grateful.

Except she deserved more. She didn't owe her aunt her life.

"Mari-girl? Marisol? Are you all right?"

She glanced over to find Linc had already stopped the truck and was reaching for her. He undid his seatbelt then reached over to grab her hand. He placed his fingers over her wrist. What was he doing?

Taking your pulse.

"Your pulse is fast. Damn it. I knew I should have taken you to get checked over. We're driving to the clinic." He reached for the key to his truck.

"What! No! I'm fine! Really."

"You went all pale and your breathing picked up. Your pulse is going too fast. Are you feeling ill? Clammy? Hot? Cold?"

She undid her belt and leaned over to squeeze his hand. "Linc, I'm fine. I promise. I'm sorry for scaring you. I was thinking about something."

He frowned. "What?"

She shook her head, not wanting to lie to him. "I have to get inside. My aunt will be wondering where I am."

He studied her. "You're sure?"

"I'm sure."

"Mari-girl, you can tell me if there's something wrong, you know that, right?"

She sighed. "I can't talk about it. It's family stuff."

Understanding filled his face and he backed off with a nod. "Wait there. I'll come around to you."

She knew it was pointless to argue. Those old-fashioned manners of his. He opened her door and reaching down, grabbed her bag, putting it on her lap. That should have been her first clue. But she was still caught by surprise as he swung her up into his arms.

Marisol gasped. "What are you doing?"

"Carrying you inside," he replied in a matter-of-fact voice. "You shouldn't walk on that foot until the pain and swelling have gone down. Now which door should I take you in?"

"You really don't have to carry me in. It's just a bee sting, I'll be fine."

The look he gave her could have given a snowman the chills. "Marisol, I know we don't know each other well. I'm a pretty easy-going guy. But there are some lines you don't cross with me. And there are some things I don't bend on. This is one of those things. You're not walking on your foot until the swelling has gone down and it doesn't hurt. Now, either I carry you in here or I take you home with me."

Home with him?

God, it was tempting to say yes to that. She swallowed heavily.

"Here, please. My aunt, um, she isn't really keen on strangers in her house so she might be, umm. . ."

"It will be fine. Don't stress," he murmured to her reassuringly.

He hadn't been on the receiving end of her aunt's tirades or he wouldn't say that. Although, Linc didn't seem the kind of guy to take shit from anyone.

"Which door?"

Jesus, Marisol. Get it together. Don't just leave him standing here holding you.

"Through the garage is the best idea, if you don't mind." It was a bit further to carry her but she didn't have a key for the front door if it was locked. Which it likely was.

Unfortunately, she noticed her aunt's car sitting in the garage as Linc carried her through.

"Nice wheels. Where's your car?" he asked.

"I keep it around the back."

He just made a grunting noise. Probably regretting offering to carry her all this way.

"If you put me down in the kitchen, that will be fine," she told him as they moved through the mudroom and into the kitchen.

"Where's your bedroom?"

"Upstairs, but you really don't have to carry . . ." she sighed and stopped protesting. "I'm not sure why I'm wasting my breath."

"Neither am I," he replied, looking around. "Is this what the place looked like when you bought it?"

She studied the ornate hallway. The floors were marble and the lighting fixtures were all gold-colored. Everything screamed wealth but in the most ostentatious, showy way possible.

"Uh, yeah."

He started up the stairs.

"Oh no, what happened?" her aunt cried.

She barely contained a wince. Damn it. Too much to hope that they might have got up to her room without her coming across Rosalind.

"Marisol! Did you hurt yourself?" The words were said with fake caring. A show all for Linc. But she could hear the sharp note in her aunt's voice. She was annoyed. Whether it was about Linc being here or Marisol hurting herself or Marisol being carried by Linc, she wasn't sure. Probably a combination of all three.

She peered up at her aunt who was dressed in tight pair of jeans and a sheer white top. Oh, and she also had a red, lacy bra on that could clearly be seen through the shirt.

Jesus.

"I'm fine, Rosalind," Marisol told her. "Just a bee sting."

Rosalind threw back her head and laughed. "A bee sting? Are you serious?"

Marisol wasn't surprised at the laughter. It was a very Rosalind reaction to someone else's misfortune or pain.

"Of course she's serious. I don't see how it's something to laugh at," Linc said stiffly.

"Oh." Rosalind waved her hand through the air. "I know my reaction might seem callous, it's just that Marisol is always hurting herself or getting ill. She's a walking calamity. A bee sting is very minor to what I was imagining when I saw you carrying her."

Rosalind gave him an admiring glance, her gaze eating him up. Marisol clenched her teeth together in reaction. She didn't like Rosalind staring at him that way. Having a fiancé didn't seem to stop her from sleeping around.

"You must be very strong to carry Marisol. She's no lightweight. Why don't you put her down, I'm sure she can walk the rest of the way. I'll pour you a drink. You look like a scotch drinker."

"Actually, I'm going to carry Marisol up to her room and make sure she has everything she needs. Then I have to get going."

Rosalind sniffed, her face turning dark at the rejection. "Suit yourself. Try not to track dirt through my house." She sneered at him. "I don't want to be cleaning up after you."

Like she did any cleaning anyway. Wisely, Marisol didn't say anything. Linc dodged around her aunt and carried her up the stairs.

"My room is just down here." She pointed to the far end of the hallway.

He carried her to the closed door that she pointed to, shuffling her weight around as he opened the door. She wondered what he thought of her room as he looked around. It was pretty bare. A double bed and closet. A small bookcase. Luckily her snuggly and Princess Nana were hidden away. She didn't like leaving them out when she wasn't home.

"I expected more books," Linc teased. He set her on the bed and grabbed a pillow, waiting for her to get comfy before he set the pillow under her foot.

"We move around a lot so it's not easy to bring piles of books with us. I had an eReader, but it broke so I'm back to paperbacks. Which is fine. I like reading from actual books too."

Stop talking about reading, you're probably boring him to tears.

But when she looked up at him, all she could see on his face was warm concern. "What can I get you? Water? Snacks?"

"I've got some water here." She picked up the bottle of water she normally always kept on her nightstand. "And I have a couple of snacks in my bag." She set her bag down on the floor next to the bed.

"Will your aunt bring you up some dinner?"

Drat. How to answer that without lying?

"Never mind, I can tell by the look on your face that she won't. I should have just taken you with me to my place." He ran his hand through his hair, looking worried.

"I'll be fine, really. I'm sure the swelling will have gone down by dinnertime anyway."

He shook his head.

"Linc, I'll be fine. I promise."

"I don't like leaving you."

"I know. Thank you for caring."

He gave her a surprised look. "Of course I care. What time do you usually have dinner?"

"Around six."

"Fine. I'm going to text you at five-thirty to make sure the swelling has gone down. If it hasn't, I'll find a way to get some dinner to you. All right?"

She wasn't sure how he'd do that, but she nodded anyway.

"I can do that. I'll be fine. Thanks for the picnic. Sorry about all of this."

Sitting on the bed facing her, he leaned in and cupped the side of her face. Then to her shock, he brushed his lips against hers. Once. Twice. Small, soft brushes of his lips. But she felt his touch all the way down in her pussy. She pressed her legs together with a small moan as he deepened the kiss, sliding his tongue against hers, teasing her.

When he drew back, her breath was coming faster and his eyes looked heavy with lust.

"It was my pleasure," he told her. He brushed some hair behind her ear. "As I was trying to say earlier, I like you, Marisol. I know you said that things were complicated, but I want to do what I can to simplify them."

She opened her mouth and he placed a finger on her lips. "Just think about it, okay? With Clint away on his honeymoon, this is likely my last day off for a couple of weeks. So just take this time to think things over. I'm still going to be texting and calling. But just know, I want to take this further. I want you."

"Really?" When had anyone wanted her?

"Really. Think on it. And remember, I'm texting you at five-thirty. Make sure you answer, or I'll be back here checking on you. And you'll be in trouble."

Ooh. Was it wrong that the idea of being in trouble made her shiver in delight?

11

L inc was grateful not to encounter Marisol's aunt on the way out. That woman was a predator. He could handle that bitch staring at him like he was a snack and she was starving.

What he couldn't handle was Marisol having to deal with the unfeeling bitch day-in, day-out. He had a feeling there was more going on in that house than Marisol was letting on.

He didn't like it. Didn't like that he didn't know what was happening and that Marisol didn't yet trust him enough with the truth.

Soon.

He started his truck, feeling a curious wrenching in his chest. Something that told him not to leave. To go back there and gather Marisol in his arms, carry her down to his truck and take care of her.

He sighed. Unfortunately, with Clint leaving on his honeymoon, he wouldn't have a lot of free time over the next two weeks. Still, he was sure he could carve out some time for another date, maybe they could go into the city, take in a movie.

Do a bit of toy shopping.

She needs to know what you are, first. What you want. Need. And she may not want the same things. Perhaps she isn't a Little.

There had been a few signs, but he'd hoped for something more concrete today. Especially when he'd walked into her room. But there had been nothing to hint at a Little side. No toys, no stuffies, no coloring stuff. Not that that meant anything. She could have a Little side and not know. Or maybe her Little was older, or didn't like to play or . . . Christ, he didn't know.

He'd enjoyed himself today. She was fun. Sweet. Funny.

Turning into the driveway for Sanctuary Ranch, he headed up towards JSI headquarters and veered off to where Kent and Abby lived. Parking, he got out and walked towards the door. Laughter hit his ears as he knocked. Sounded like someone was having fun.

"Daddy, no! Put me down!"

There was a smacking noise that made his eyebrows rise and his lips twitch. The door opened and Kent stood there. There was a glob of something on his forehead that dripped down his face. And he held a wiggling Abby over his shoulder.

"Well, hello there, Kent. Miss Abby. You're looking beautiful today," he greeted them.

"Eek! Kent let me down!"

"Hmm. Let me think about that. How about no?" Kent smacked her ass as she tried to get down.

"Kent!" she cried, the embarrassment in her voice clear.

"Linc, come in," Kent told him, stepping backwards with Abby.

Walking in, Linc shut the door behind him. "Sorry to interrupt."

"Not at all. Abby here just thought it would be funny for me to wear the cookie dough rather than bake it."

"Pfft." Abby let out a breath of air in frustration. "You were teasing me first. Don't believe a word he says, Linc."

"Why, Little girl, do you think it's a good idea to call me a liar?"

Kent flipped her over once they were in the kitchen and set her on the benchtop. Then he placed both hands on the counter and leaned in with a stern look.

Though Linc thought he caught the other man's lips twitching. "Well? Hmm?"

Abby was bright red as she gazed from Kent then back to Linc. "No, Daddy."

Kent turned to look at him. "Linc, what can I do for you?"

"I just need a quick word. I can meet you in your office in ten?" Linc offered, trying to give them some privacy.

"No, stay," Abby said quickly. "Please. No need to go to Kent's office when you can talk here." She was a total sweetheart, even though he'd interrupted their Sunday together.

Abby looked a bit tired today. There was a paleness to her skin that he didn't like. And dark patches under her eyes.

"What do you say?" Kent asked her.

"Sorry, Daddy," she whispered.

Leaning in, he kissed her lightly. "Good girl." He stepped back and grabbed a towel to wipe off his face. "Linc, you want a drink or anything? Coffee? Something stronger? Beer?"

"Beer would be good."

Kent nodded and helped Abby down then he went to the fridge and pulled out a couple of beers. Abby moved to the sink where there was a pile of dirty dishes, obviously from their baking. Some cookies lay out on the tray, waiting to go in the oven.

Kent handed him a beer, then wrapped his arm around Abby's waist. "Leave these, sweet girl. I'll tidy up soon. You go on up and have a lie down for a bit, okay? I'll come in and check on you later."

She looked over at Linc then up at Kent. "Are you sure? I can get these done quick."

Kent shook his head then kissed her on the forehead. "I've got it. Off you go." He turned her around and with a soft pat on her ass, sent her off.

"Come into the living room. Take a seat."

Linc sat on one armchair while Kent sat opposite, both of them took a sip of beer.

"Abby okay?"

Kent nodded. "Yeah. Just tired. A nap and an early night and she should be fine."

"She's been busy lately, helping out with the wedding."

"Too busy for my liking. Everything okay with you?" Kent asked him. "Do you need something?"

"Ah. I'm fine." He tapped the cap of the beer against his leg. "Have you spoken to Ed lately?"

"Saw him at the wedding last night. Why?"

"You know the new spa in town?"

Kent nodded. "Eden likes going there. Abby said that the woman who came out and did their nails and facials from there was nice." Kent gave him a sly look. "Abby wondered if she could be a Little."

"Really?"

"Yeah. Charlie said the same thing. Course, they could be wrong. Said she was beautiful too."

"Marisol is beautiful. And sweet. Funny." His lips twitched.

"Oh yeah? Know her then, do you?" Interest filled Kent's face.

Linc made an irritated noise. "Are you taking lessons from your brother about sticking your nose into other people's business?"

Kent grinned, clearly not taking offense. "Hit a sore spot, did I?"

"I didn't come over here to gossip."

"Then what did you come here to talk about?" Kent asked.

"Marisol said that she was doing Mrs. Long's nails the other day."

Kent made a groaning noise. Yeah. Exactly.

"And she said that she'd heard rumors about what went on here at the ranch. About Caley living with the two Docs."

Kent's eyes narrowed.

"And about the women on the ranch being spanked if they misbehaved."

Kent's face darkened. "What the fuck? How did that become a rumor?"

"I guess something was bound to leak out. No matter how careful we were."

The people who lived and worked on the ranch were chosen because they were part of the lifestyle. Clint and Kent were very careful about protecting everyone on Sanctuary Ranch, but most particularly the women.

"Someone must have seen or heard something," Kent mused. "Clint won't be happy."

No, he wouldn't be. Clint was a giant mama bear. Gruff on the outside, marshmallow on the inside. But God help you if you threatened one of the people that he considered himself responsible for.

"But if it's Mrs. Long and her cronies spreading the rumor, people aren't likely to take too much notice," Kent mused. "She's a known gossip. They'll likely think she's making things up. And it's not like we're doing anything to be ashamed of."

"Yeah, well, that's the other thing. She went to Ed about it."

Kent straightened. "She what?"

"Yeah. Apparently, she wanted him to investigate you all for abuse. Because she heard that your women are spanked and have to ask permission to do anything."

"Fucking hell. That old bat. We're not doing anything illegal."

"So Ed didn't come to you or Clint? He didn't tell you about this?"

"No. He didn't. But he might have been waiting until after the wedding, so he didn't stress Clint out. I'll call him. Things are bound to slip. Especially now that we have more Littles living here, it's harder to keep everything secret. But the main thing is making certain that none of the women on the ranch are threatened or hurt by it."

"Might be best if they didn't go into town on their own for a while."

Kent sighed. "Eden will be thrilled by that. I'll let Zeke inform her."

Linc didn't envy Zeke that job. In a way, Eden was the most independent of all of them. Maybe it was because of the accident that had left her in a wheelchair, meaning she had to rely on people in other ways. Or maybe it was because she liked to drive fast and didn't want anyone around to witness that and report back to Zeke.

He knew someone else who liked to speed. Linc shook his head at the thought of Marisol driving that piece-of-shit car at high enough speeds to get pulled over by Ed. Meanwhile, her aunt was driving around in a car that cost more than some people made in a year.

He didn't like that.

Not. At. All.

12

W ith a yawn, Marisol turned down her driveway.
It was her late night at the spa, so she'd driven to work. Even her aunt didn't insist that she walk home in the dark and cold.

She was so tired that she nearly crashed into a car parked to the side of the driveway.

"*Mierda!*" She straightened the car, pulling it over into the middle of the driveway. "Shit. Shit. Shit."

There were several cars and motorbikes parked along the drive. Her aunt was having a party. Why hadn't she told her? Normally, she'd let Marisol know so she could either hide in her bedroom or make herself scarce. Her aunt didn't like her appearing at her parties.

Which suited Marisol just fine.

Now she'd have to find somewhere to spend the night.

Marisol's stomach tightened. What should she do? Usually, she'd sleep in the car or go to a late-night café. It was cold here at night and she didn't have a blanket or warmer clothing if she was going to sleep in the car. She tapped her fingers against the steering wheel as she thought.

Maybe you should ask Linc if you could stay with him?

She blushed at the thought. What would he say if she were to ask? Would he say yes?

What if he said no?

He'd told her that he liked her. That still made her smile. Until she remembered that she couldn't have anything with him. That she had to leave.

This is why she shouldn't let herself get close in the first place. She knew this already. Never get attached. People always left. Rosalind always moved them on to somewhere else. Only this time, she'd be moving on alone.

God, she was so scared.

Stop being a coward, Marisol.

She probably should have left already, but she wasn't ready to say goodbye to those evening calls, when he'd put her to bed. The funny texts he'd send her in the day. She'd just wanted to feel like she was special, like she was loved.

Silly, Marisol. He doesn't love you.

He was so sweet, though. One of the most caring men she'd ever met. The way he'd fussed over a simple bee sting, texting her to check on her that night. Wanting her to take the next day off and rest. She had reassured him that her foot was back to normal the next day. Which was sort of true. But he'd never know that she'd stretched the truth.

It hadn't taken long for the swelling to go down and the redness to fade and there was no way Rosalind would ever let her take the day off work because of a bee sting.

Hell, she'd have to be in hospital or half-dead for that to happen.

She couldn't call Linc. Telling him what was going on would just put him in danger.

She didn't know who was at the party. She sent up a prayer that it wasn't Saber and his guys. However, she didn't like her chances.

She needed to get her stuff. Her stash of money. Her extra insulin. Snuggly and Princess Nana. Which meant that she was going to have to sneak in.

Just get in, grab some stuff, then get out.

Simple.

After climbing out of the car, she slipped around into the garage. Carefully, she opened the door leading from the mud room into the kitchen. Nobody was in here. Okay. She took the opportunity to grab her extra insulin out of the fridge, stashing it in her handbag. There was music blasting through the house. As she stepped into the hallway, cigarette smoke assaulted her nose. She coughed a bit.

Great. How long had these people been here?

A loud scream made her jump in fright. Two men burst their way out of the living room. One punched the other in the face. His head flicked back, blood spurting from his nose.

Shit. Shit. Shit.

Her breath came in hard pants. One had long, straggly hair, the other's head was shaved nearly bald. They rolled around on the floor, fists flying, grunting and screaming.

Where was her aunt? Why was she letting this happen?

Maybe these people weren't here for a party. Maybe they'd broken in? Even now, her aunt could be tied up somewhere. *Mierda!* Perhaps she should call the cops.

The two men rolled into a side table and the vase on top smashed to the ground. A familiar screech reached her ears. Okay, so her aunt was here somewhere.

"What did you just do! Look at the mess!" Rosalind stomped her way into the foyer, her face filled with anger. So at least she wasn't tied up somewhere, being tortured.

The two men froze. Marisol watched on, her heart in her throat. These didn't look like the type of men who would take being told off by a woman well. Would one of them go for her aunt now? What would she do if they did? She couldn't let her be hurt.

"Babe, jeez, what's the problem?"

A familiar man stepped forward.

Oh shit. Fuck. It seemed she'd stupidly stayed too long. She should have gotten out when she could.

"The boys are just having fun. Letting off steam. They've had a tough few weeks. Leave them to it." Saber wrapped his arm around Rosalind's waist, leading her away. The two idiots got up and followed them, now laughing with each other as if sharing a huge joke. She let out a sigh of relief, grateful they'd slammed the door shut behind them. Music roared through the house, it practically rocked the house on its foundations.

She stepped forward, ready to fly upstairs when her wrist was grabbed. She let out a small cry as she was shoved back against the wall. Her other wrist was grabbed, her hands pushed above her head.

Oh no.

No. No. No.

He was here. One hand held both of her wrists while he ran a finger down her cheek, smiling evilly.

"Hello, Marisol. I've been waiting for you."

AFTER GETTING out of the shower and drying off, he checked his phone. Time to call Marisol and tuck her into bed.

He loved this time best. He tried to text her when he could. But his nighttime calls to put her to bed were the favorite part of his day.

However, it wasn't the same as having her with him. As seeing her sweet smile. Hearing her laughter.

Slipping on a pair of cotton pajama pants and a sleeveless T-shirt, he picked up his phone and headed into the living room. He hadn't pushed her for an answer about whether she wanted more than friendship. He thought that was best left until he could see her in person and use his powers of persuasion more fully.

With a grin, he pressed on her contact number. It rang then flipped to voicemail.

Huh. That was odd.

MARISOL'S BREATH sawed in and out of her lungs. Panic made her stomach revolt. She was close to vomiting or passing out. She wasn't sure what. She felt a vibration from where her handbag was pushed against her side. Her phone was ringing.

Linc.

Oh God. Linc. What she wouldn't give to have him walk through that door right now and save her. Because she sure as heck didn't know how to save herself.

She always felt safe around him. And she very much needed that right now.

"What's wrong? Haven't you got a greeting for your brother?"

"You're not my b-brother."

Stay strong, Marisol.

He wrapped his free hand around her neck, pressing against it until she could barely take in a breath.

Please stop. Please stop.

Tears filled her eyes as she tried to fight him, to free her hands. But he was too strong for her. If anything, her pathetic attempts to free herself seemed to stir him on.

He pressed his hard cock against her, grinding himself as he choked her. Finally, when dark spots danced in front of her eyes, he eased his hold around her neck.

She took in gulping breaths, her entire body shaking. She didn't think he was going to stop.

"Do you need a demonstration of my ability to control you, Marisol?"

Oh God. Oh God. Where was everyone? Why was no one walking past? Not that they'd probably help her. No, in all likelihood, they'd spur Tiger on.

"Get on your knees, babe. It's time to suck my cock. It's time to show you who is really in charge."

Tears leaked out of her eyes and she cried out again as he started to tug at his jeans. This wasn't happening. It couldn't be happening.

No one is coming to your rescue. Fight, Marisol! Fight!

By now he had his jeans and boxers down over his hips, his disgusting cock was bared, the tip gleaming with pre-cum. She was going to vomit.

He took a step back, loosening his hold on her hands. This was it. Her chance. Pulling her leg back, she drew it up, bending her knee as she slammed it into his dick. Hard.

For a moment she thought it hadn't done anything. Then he let out a noise like a pig squealing. He let go of her, both hands reaching down to cup his balls. Marisol didn't think. She ran. But instead of heading out the door, like she should have, she raced up the stairs.

She couldn't leave Princess Nana and snuggly behind. Racing into her bedroom, she locked the door behind her. Her hands shook so hard, that it took her longer than it should have.

Focus Marisol.

She flew to her closet and pulled out snuggly, Princess Nana and her trinket box with her savings, stuffing them into a bag. Out. She needed to get out of here.

There was a rattling at the door and she froze.

Oh no. Oh no.

"Marisol! Open this fucking door!" Tiger roared.

Mierda!

She stared at the door. That was all that stood between her and her nightmare.

"I'm going to fucking kill you!" He banged against the door. It wasn't going to take much more before he got through the door.

Out. Get out.

A sob broke free. What to do? She looked over to the double doors. There was a small balcony out there. She was still up on the second floor, but maybe she could climb over the railing and drop.

Damn it.

"Marisol! Let. Me. The. Fuck. In. Fucking cunt!"

She had to go.

She opened the door and climbed out onto the balcony, shivering in the cold. Her heart raced. Fear flooded her. She needed to calm herself. Closing the door, she moved to the railing and looked over. She was at the back of the house, but there didn't seem to be anyone out here who would see her climb over. She stuffed her handbag into her backpack then put it over her shoulders. Putting her leg over, she held onto the balustrade then moved one hand down to a bottom rung then the other and let herself drop.

Her arms burned as she dangled in the air. Oh God. What was the best way to fall?

She had no idea. So she just let herself drop before she could overthink it.

To her shock, she managed to land on her feet. Then she stumbled backwards a few steps, falling onto her ass. Graceful as always.

Getting up hastily, her legs shaking beneath her, she raced away from the house. She didn't know how long she had until

Tiger broke into her room. But after discovering she wasn't hidden anywhere inside, he'd likely figure out that she'd gone over the balcony.

She wanted to be long gone before that happened. She rushed towards the trees at the back of the property, breathing a bit easier once she was hidden amongst their depths.

There was just one problem now.

What was she going to do next? If she could, she'd take the car. But it would be a risky move to head back to the house. The car was parked out front with all the other vehicles. What if she ran into someone? What if she ran into Tiger?

She shuddered and leaned against a tree to catch her breath. Her body continued to shake, flooded with adrenaline.

Okay, options.

Reaching into her backpack, she drew her phone out of her handbag. She tried to turn it on.

Blank.

Oh no. No, no, no. She let out a sob, despair filling her.

Calm down, Marisol.

Calling anyone was out. She couldn't get to the car. She had her emergency stash of money, so the only thing to do was walk into town and hope she could get a room in the local motel.

Good. A plan. That was all she needed.

Making her legs work, she jogged towards the road. If she moved around the edge of the property she could head around the front, hopefully without running into anyone.

The sound of yelling from the house made her jump. She had no idea if it was another fight breaking out.

Or if Tiger was coming for her.

But she wasn't waiting around to find out. She wished she had a flashlight. The moon was out, giving her some light, but she was a city girl. Walking around the countryside in the dark wasn't her idea of a good time. Pushing away thoughts of wild animals, she made herself move.

She had to wonder what the neighbors thought of all the noise and yelling. Managing to stick to shadows, she quickly snuck her way around the front of the property.

She kept away from the driveway, staying close to the fence line. Once she made it to the road, she started breathing easier.

Moving briskly, her gaze roamed up and down the road. Would he come after her? God, she didn't know but she had a feeling that he might. Fear and cold had her teeth chattering as she wrapped her arms around herself. Noises in the shrubbery made her jump.

There's nothing there. Everything is fine. There's nothing there.

She could do this. Just keep putting one foot in front of the other.

She silently sung Christmas carols to herself to cheer herself up. Maybe it sounded silly, but singing *Jingle Bells* and *Grandma Got Run Over by a Reindeer* managed to keep her from completely losing it.

Christmas was magical, right? And right now, she could use a bit of magic. Or luck. Or something.

Lights shone in her face, headlights headed towards her. Instead of moving, she froze.

Marisol, dive.

The car was coming from the wrong direction, heading towards the house. So it wasn't Tiger searching for her. But that didn't mean it wasn't one of his buddies heading to the party. Her heart pounded, blood rushing to her head.

Please don't stop. Please don't stop.

The car slowed and came to a stop. She was hidden behind a tree, too scared to go further into the forest but terrified to reveal herself in case it was one of Tiger's friends. A car door opened. Footsteps crunched on gravel.

Go away. Please, go away.

She was going to throw up or pass out. *Calm down, Marisol.*

"Hello? Is someone there?"

Her legs gave out beneath her as she recognized the voice.

"Hello?"

"H-hello, sheriff?"

13

"Marisol? Is that you?"

The footsteps drew closer. She forced herself to move out from behind the tree and stumbled as she made her way towards him, her legs nearly giving out on her.

"Whoa there, honey. Are you okay?" Ed leaped towards her, grabbing her around the waist to hold her steady.

"Y-yes," she managed to say through her chattering teeth.

"Shit. You're shaking. What happened? Did someone hurt you? Marisol? Can you tell me what's happened?"

She opened her mouth and tried to speak but nothing came out.

"Okay, honey. Take a deep breath in. Let it out slowly. In. Out. You're okay. I'm here. You're safe. That's it. Nice slow, deep breaths. Good girl. That's a good girl. Come on, come sit in the car and let's get you warmed up. You're freezing. And in shock, I'm thinking." As he spoke, he led her around to the passenger side of his vehicle as one might lead a frightened child.

His voice as he spoke was low and soothing. No sudden movements. He opened the door and then helped settle her in so she was sitting side on, facing him. Crouching in front of her, he studied her under the car's inside light.

"You're a bit pale and shaky. I have a blanket in the trunk of the car, but first I need you to tell me whether you're hurt anywhere."

"No, I'm not hurt anywhere."

"You wouldn't lie to me, would you, Marisol?"

She shook her head, trying to hide her wince as the movement pulled at her sore neck. Shit would that bruise? "I'm not lying, I promise. I'm not hurt. I just . . . I had a fright and it made me feel shaky and scared. Then I was walking in the dark along the road and I'm not used to all the noises in the forest. I'm fine. Really."

"All right, I'm going to go get the blanket. Don't move, hear me?"

She nodded shakily, not wanting him to leave her sight.

You're safe.

He returned quickly with a blanket. "I'm just going to put this around you then I'll take your pulse, all right?" He continued to talk in that soothing voice. The blanket was tucked in around her lap. She didn't even jump as he took hold of her hand and placed his fingers over her pulse.

His touch didn't do anything to her like Linc's did. But she did feel calmer now that she was with him.

And safely away from Tiger.

"Good girl. You're doing so well. Your pulse is a bit fast. Ready to tell me what's going on yet?"

She shook her head, and took a shuddering breath.

"I can't help you if I don't know what's happened, Marisol. That's my job. To help the people living in my town."

She huffed out a breath. "That h-hasn't been my experience w-with cops."

"I'm really sorry to hear that. I take everyone's safety in my town seriously. If someone hurt you or scared you, then I need to know so I can take steps to protect you. And to stop that from happening to someone else."

"I'm okay," she replied. She didn't think anything good would come from her telling him about Tiger. Ed was just one guy. There had to be thirty or so Devil's Sinners members at the house. He didn't stand a chance on his own. And she wasn't sure if they'd care that he was the sheriff.

"Right. Well, I was headed out to your aunt's place. We received a noise complaint. Do you want me to drive you there?"

"No. No, please, I can't go back there." She tried to stand, in a panic at the thought. He placed his hands on her legs, holding her to the seat.

"Easy, honey. You don't have to go anywhere you don't want to."

Right. Right. Her heartbeat started to slow as she took in his words.

"I don't want to go back there."

"Then you won't. Slide around. I'll shut the door and turn the heat up to keep you warm. Don't want you catching a cold, do we? Then I'll take you back to my office while I get someone else out here to deal with the noise complaint."

"Sorry. I don't mean to be a hassle." She bit her lower lip worriedly.

"You couldn't ever be a hassle, Marisol. Okay? Now put your legs in for me, sweetheart."

She shuffled around in her seat.

"Want to take your backpack off?"

She shook her head.

"You can hold onto it, but you shouldn't wear it with your seatbelt. It's not safe."

It wasn't? She frowned but it seemed he wasn't budging so she shrugged off the backpack and let him fasten her seatbelt. Under normal circumstances, she'd likely have protested him treating her like a child.

But right now, it was nice to give over control to someone else. To not have to think. It would be even nicer if it was Linc who she was giving all her control over to.

He closed her door then walked around to the front of the car.

Maybe you should tell Ed the truth. He seems like a good guy. But he was still a cop. And she had trouble trusting him.

Ed opened the door and climbed into the driver's side. He grabbed his radio and called for someone to go to her aunt's place to talk to them about the noise control.

"Don't let them go alone," she said suddenly.

"What?" he asked, looking over at her with worry.

"Your deputy shouldn't go to the house alone. They should take back-up. Maybe. I don't know. They wouldn't hurt a cop. They wouldn't be that stupid, right? No, I'm sure they wouldn't. Forget I said that."

"Marisol, look at me please."

She glanced over in surprise at the firm note in his voice.

"What's going on over there?" he asked.

She licked her dry lips. "There's a party."

"Right. Gathered that from the neighbors' complaints. Who is there?"

"My aunt's boyfriend," she told him quietly.

"And?"

"And his son."

"That's all?" he asked.

"No," she whispered. "You've heard of the Devil's Sinners?"

She felt rather than saw him tense. "Yeah, I have. You saying that members of the Devil's Sinners are at your aunt's place?"

She couldn't let his deputies go in blind. "Yes."

"How many?"

"Not sure. But if I take into account all the cars and bikes, then I'm guessing maybe thirty? More?"

"Jesus Christ. And you've been there tonight? Did you know they were coming?"

"No, I was working late. They were there when I got home. I can't go back there again." She was on her own. Oh God, what was she going to do? Why hadn't she worked harder to get a plan set up?

Because she didn't want to leave this town. To leave Linc.

"Can we go? I don't really want to stick around here." She looked around nervously.

"Yeah, honey. But I think you're right. In this case, back-up might well be necessary."

She blocked out what he was saying into the radio unit. She knew she was trembling but she couldn't seem to stop. When the car started up, she jumped.

"Easy, sweetheart," he murmured. "Let's get you back to the department. I have some really bad coffee there. If you're really good, there might even be some creamer."

"That sounds . . . so appealing," she murmured.

"Doesn't it? Tell you what, if you're a good girl for me I'll find Kiesha's secret stash of hot chocolate and break it out. Of course, I'll have to swear you to secrecy. Because if she discovers me raiding it, I'm dead."

"Kiesha?"

"Our dispatcher."

"Do you always work so late?" she asked as he drove. "I thought the sheriff would finish early."

"I like to do patrol work. There's just me and four deputies to cover a large area. It's all hands on deck. Besides, wouldn't be much of a boss if I asked other people to do what I wasn't willing to."

She gave him a surprised look. She'd never thought about it that way. Then again, she'd never had a decent boss, had she? She'd only ever worked for Rosalind and she preferred to get everyone else to work while she went shopping or lounged around at home.

She hadn't expected for someone like Ed to feel that way. But then, so far, he hadn't acted at all like she'd thought he might. He'd been nothing but kind, understanding and even protective. Maybe it was time to stop painting all cops with the same brush. Just because she'd had an experience with one bad cop didn't make them all bad.

Way to stereotype, Marisol.

"Marisol? You okay?"

"I don't like cops."

"Right. Got that. You've had a bad experience in the past?"

"Yeah. I was ten. They came to our house with a warrant for my aunt's arrest. Rosalind always told me these stories about the cops back in Venezuela. How corrupt and terrifying they were. She said an officer killed her uncle for no good reason. So I was already scared of them. And then, this one cop, he . . ."

"Did he hurt you?" Ed asked in a voice that was darker than she'd ever heard from him.

"He didn't touch me." She let out a shuddering breath. "He didn't have to. Not when his words terrified me so much. He kept telling me how I was headed to jail unless I told him everything I knew. That nobody would be around to protect me. That I'd likely be beaten and abused. As he was yelling, his arms were moving around and spittle flew from his mouth. Even though I knew I wouldn't go to jail, his words scared me enough into believing him. Plus, I have a pretty good imagination."

"Yes, I remember how you thought you were going to end up in jail and shanked by a piece of soap."

"Oh yeah, sorry for overreacting."

"Seems like you had a good reason for reacting the way you did," he murmured calmly. "What happened?"

"He seemed like this terrifying monster to me. I curled myself into a ball in the corner of our living room. Even if I had known anything, which I didn't, there was no way I could have told him."

"Where the fuck were the other cops?"

"I think he was in charge. I don't know. I only remember him. Until she came in."

"Who?"

"The child services lady. She . . . she was amazing. She raced in the door, heard him screaming at me and she just ripped into him. She tore him to pieces. Told him all the things she was going to do to him. I can't really remember now what she said, but I knew that even in my terrified state, she was on my side. Then he stepped towards her. I thought for sure he was going to hit her. I remember this next part. She said, 'Do it, I'm not a helpless child. Hit me and I'll have the proof I need to take you down and make you suffer'."

"Jesus fucking Christ."

"I don't know if she was happy or sad that he didn't hurt her. But he turned and left and she rushed over to me. She didn't touch me. Just crouched down in front of me and started talking to me. She was my hero."

"It sounds like she was. What happened after that? Did you go into child protective services?"

"The social worker, her name was Violet, she asked me if I had any family. I wasn't thinking clearly. I gave her the name of our last housekeeper. Rosalind had fired her a month before. Nobody lasted long working for Rosalind. She usually found some fault with them and fired them or they quit. Violet must have known Ana wasn't family, but somehow I was allowed to live with Ana and her family for a week."

She rubbed at her forehead. "It was one of the best weeks of my life. Ana had four sons but no daughter. They treated me like I was family. Ana had only been with us for a year. My aunt treated her like trash, yet she took me in and took care of me. I was devastated when I had to leave. I cried the whole way home in the car."

"What happened with your aunt?"

"I'm not sure. But whatever they'd arrested her for, they obviously couldn't make it stick. We moved soon after to a new city. My aunt found another rich old man to marry. I never saw Ana again."

"I'm so sorry, Marisol. Do you happen to remember the name of the cop that scared you?"

"No," she said quietly.

"Where did this happen?"

"Why?" she asked suspiciously.

"Because I want to make sure this bastard isn't still out there terrorizing kids," he said in a cold, grim voice. Ed pulled up around the back of the police department and parked. There were a couple of other police cars back here.

She sucked in a breath. "I never thought of that. Oh no, all this time he could have been hurting other children that had no one to protect them."

"Hey, listen to me," he told her insistently. "Look at me."

She turned her gaze to him. The security lights out here made it possible to see the serious look on his handsome face. She wondered how old he was? He had to be in his early forties. A lot older than her. Not that she was interested in him like that.

An image of Linc's handsome face danced through her mind. She wished he was here right now.

"That isn't your worry. Whatever he has done, it's on him. Not you."

"If I'd just told . . ."

"No. Still not on you. You were a child. I don't want you worrying about this anymore. Understand? I'm sure his colleagues knew what he was like. And they were adults. You were a terrified kid. You're not taking this guilt on, Marisol."

She wondered if Ed was a Dom or if he was just simply an alpha guy. Either way, she felt his words move through her. She made an effort to let go of the guilt. It wouldn't be that simple, of course. But he was right. She was just a kid.

"Where were you when this happened, Marisol?"

"In Tucson," she murmured. "It was nearly thirteen years ago."

"Good girl," he praised. "Come on, let's get you inside. It's too cold to be sitting out here. I'll make you that hot chocolate."

She grabbed her backpack, her hands shaking as she reached for her seatbelt. He was at her door before she'd even noticed him leaving the car. He let her get out herself and she appreciated it. Even though she felt more comfortable with him, she wasn't prepared for touching him any more than was necessary.

Ed led the way to the back door, inputting a code into the pad and then opened it for her, stepping back.

She waited then followed him down a corridor, past a few doors until they ended up in the open front area. It was quiet. There were some lights on, and a woman was puttering around, watering indoor plants. She had a sucker in her mouth.

"Kiesha," Ed said with surprise. "What are you still doing here? Where's Steven?"

She pulled out the sucker. "He popped down to the diner to get some dinner. I said I would stay until he got back." Kiesha gave her an interested gaze. She was a stunning woman with black, straight hair that she had tied back in a ponytail and brown skin. Curves in all the right places.

Ed sighed. "You were supposed to be gone over an hour ago. If Steven wanted to leave, he should have waited for me. Get going home."

"Sure thing, boss." She snapped a salute at him.

Marisol's eyes widened and she looked up at Ed to see how he was taking the other woman's sarcasm. He just shook his head, the look on his face stern. Just that look alone would have had Marisol scrambling to obey him.

But then, she wasn't very brave. Not like this woman. Maybe if she were braver, she would have left her aunt a long time ago.

"Kiesha, can you stay with Marisol a moment while I check on Jace and Ranger?"

"Sure thing, boss man. I live to serve."

Ed gave the other woman an exasperated look then walked off, disappearing into a room that she figured was his office.

"Hi, I'm Kiesha." The other woman stepped up to her, holding her hand out.

Marisol shook it. "Marisol. Nice to meet you."

"Get you a drink or anything?" Kiesha asked. "Got a stash of cookies I keep hidden from the boys. Working with five guys, you learn to hide food quick."

"You work at that new spa in town, huh?"

"Oh. Yes." How did she know that?

"Gossip runs rampant in this town," Kiesha told her. "Not much happens that I don't know about."

"You know how I feel about gossip, Kiesha," Ed told her sternly as he returned.

Kiesha rolled her eyes. "Yeah, yeah, boss man. Heard it all before. Nice to meet you, Marisol. I'll come get my nails done on my next day off and we can have a proper chat without the boss man listening in."

Marisol watched her saunter away, confidence in her every step. What it must be like to be so sure of yourself, to not be afraid or measure each word. "Wow, she's . . ."

"A brat," Ed told her.

"Um, are you allowed to say that about an employee?"

He snorted. "I've known her for years. Our mothers were friends. She's never forgiven me for spanking her when she was sixteen and I caught her at a party, drinking."

"You . . . you spanked her?"

"Sure did. She deserved it. She was hanging with the wrong

crowd, getting into trouble, worrying her parents. So I stepped in and got her attention. Unfortunately, she's been pissed at me ever since."

Marisol took a step back, away from the sheriff. Just when she was starting to let her guard down with him, he went and said something like that.

Ed narrowed his gaze and held up his hands. "Whoa, sweetheart. Don't give me that look. I'm not about to start accosting you. Or anyone else for that matter. I apologize for scaring you. I've known Kiesha a long time and people around here know that the two of us can be like oil and water. I would never hit her or abuse her. This happened a long time ago, remember."

She swallowed heavily. "So you wouldn't spank her now?"

"No, I wouldn't." He eyed her curiously. "Being with Linc, I didn't think hearing about a spanking would worry you."

"What does that mean?" she asked, confused.

He ran his hand over his face. "I'm talking out of turn and you've been through enough tonight. Why don't you come sit down in my office and you can tell me what happened tonight to send you running in the dark and cold?"

She shook her head. "I want to go."

"And where are you gonna go?"

"I don't know. To the motel, I guess."

He glanced over at the clock. "The reception desk closed an hour ago, sweetheart."

What? Seriously? Damn it.

"I'll call a friend, get them to come get me," she lied.

He crossed his arms over his wide chest and gave her a rather formidable look as he leaned back against one of the desks. "Oh yeah? What friend is that?"

"Nobody you know," she snapped.

"Sweetheart, I know everyone in this town. And you would do

well not to lie to me. Until you have somewhere safe to go, I can't let you leave." His voice was gentle but firm.

"You can't just keep me here!" He couldn't, right?

He gave her a look that wasn't unsympathetic. "Come into my office. My deputies headed in and had a chat with your aunt. She was co-operative and turned the music down. But I've told them to wait on stand-by. I don't like this situation. However, I'd really like to know what happened tonight. The full truth."

She walked behind him in a daze. So many things had happened tonight and she wasn't certain how much more she could take. Where that point would be where it all became too much. "Your ride should be here soon, anyway."

"My . . . my ride?" What was he talking about? "You just said you wouldn't let me leave." Why was he contradicting himself? And who was her ride?

He pulled out a chair for her and she sat. Her legs were trembling so badly she didn't think they could hold her up anyway.

"I said you couldn't leave if you didn't have anywhere to go," he explained.

"Why do you care?"

"You live in my town. I look after the people who live here. And you're in my care right now. I couldn't let you leave without knowing you were going to be all right." He sat on the desk. "I wouldn't be able to sleep tonight from worrying about you."

"You're a strange man," she muttered. "Most men wouldn't care."

"Sweetheart, I think that the men you have known aren't the best examples of how a real man looks after those he cares about."

Maybe he was right. After all, she hadn't had the best role models when it came to men. Other than Harry. And she could barely remember him now. All she felt was this warmth in her tummy when she thought of him.

"Who is my ride then?" she asked, although she figured she knew. There could only be one man he would call.

Ed gave her a look. "Linc, of course. Did you really think I wouldn't call him?"

"I wish you hadn't. He's too busy at work to be bothered about this." She frowned up at Ed.

"I'm never too busy to be bothered by anything to do with you, Mari-girl," the deep voice came from the doorway.

She turned with a gasp. She hadn't even heard him enter the building, never mind walk up behind her. She must be more out of it than she'd realized.

Being attacked and having to jump off a balcony and run for your life will do that for you.

He was wearing a plaid shirt and dark blue jeans with a black jacket. There was a slight scruff on his cheeks as though he hadn't shaved for a day or so. It only added to his appeal. His gaze looked tired as he ran it over her, as though checking her for any harm.

"I'm so sorry you came all the way in, Linc." She glared up at Ed. "I had no idea that the sheriff called you."

Ed whistled. "Back to sheriff. Ouch."

Linc stared down at her with an unreadable look on his face. What was he thinking? That he couldn't believe how troublesome she was? That he wished he'd never met her?

He strode over to where she was still sitting, then he drew her up and straight into his arms.

"I'll give you two a minute," Ed said.

She didn't even notice the sheriff leaving. She was too engrossed in the feel of Linc holding her tight. He rocked her gently.

"Jesus, teeny. You scared the shit out of me."

Her eyebrows rose. It was unlike Linc to swear in front of her. But she could hear the fear in his voice. Now she felt even worse.

"You okay? Please tell me you're okay?"

She was glad for her high-necked sweater. She hadn't had time to check if there was any evidence of Tiger choking her.

"I'm fine. I promise."

You should tell him the truth.

"Mostly."

He growled, tightening his arms around her. "Damn it. Damn it." He gently let go of her then he arranged the chairs so they faced each other.

"Sit. Please."

He sat as well, his thighs on either side of hers, trapping her. But she didn't feel scared. A bit worried maybe. Definitely guilty.

"I'm so sorry, Linc. You shouldn't have come in. Really. I'm all right."

"I shouldn't have?" He raised both eyebrows.

"You look tired. I know you're busy. I'm so sorry you had to drive all the way in here."

"That so?" he drawled, giving none of his thoughts away.

"Yes." She licked her lips. Was he going to say anything more? "Are you okay?"

"Not sure. That's a loaded question. Tell me, did you have any intention of calling me?"

"Calling you?"

"Yes. Ed said he found you walking along the side of the road, in the dark, no jacket and a backpack on. He said that you were trembling, upset, that clearly something had happened."

Drat Ed anyway.

"He's a big old tattletale."

"Did you just call Ed a tattletale? Marisol, this isn't a joke. This is serious."

Oh, she didn't like him calling her by her full name.

He gave her a stern look. "What were you planning on doing if Ed wasn't there? Would you have called me then? Or were you planning on walking all the way into town, in the dark and cold?

Would you have called me when you got to town? The next morning? At all?"

His voice was cold. Hard. She'd never heard him sound like that. Or look this way. He could be firm. Even stern. But nothing like this.

"You're angry with me," she whispered, wringing her hands together. She didn't like that he was so upset with her. Unlike Rosalind, his anger ran icy cold rather than fiery hot.

She guessed at least he wasn't yelling at her. She wasn't sure what she would do if he did that.

"I'm upset with you. Do you know why?"

"Because I didn't call you? But I was going to call you. I tried to when I was walking towards the road, but my phone was dead."

He let out a sigh, leaning back in his chair. "Okay, that's something. I want you to know that you can always call me if you're in trouble. No matter what the time is or what I'm doing. I'll drop everything for you, Mari-girl."

Okay. Wow. That was unexpected.

"The entire drive here all I could think of was the ways you could have been hurt or harmed. It was torture."

"I'm sorry," she told him.

"What happened? What made you leave your aunt's house on foot at night?"

"I'd like to know that as well," Ed said, walking back into the room.

"She hasn't told you?" Linc asked him.

"Not exactly. She just keeps telling me that she's fine. Figured she'd tell you, though."

Linc leaned forward, staring at her sternly. "You're going to tell me, aren't you, Mari-girl?"

. . .

LINC STUDIED MARISOL. She looked nervous, unsure, frightened. There were some dirt stains on the high-necked sweater she wore. Flyaway bits of hair had escaped from her ponytail. He wanted nothing more than to pull her onto his lap and reassure her that everything would be all right.

However, he needed her to tell him what the hell was going on. Why she'd been wandering along the road at night. Once he got some answers, he could comfort her.

Then he planned on taking her home and never letting her leave.

Mine.

Deep breath, man. You can't go scaring her with your possessiveness.

Marisol would learn to lean on him. Rely on him. He would be the first person she would call when she was hurt. He didn't care if it was something serious or a goddamned stubbed toe.

He. Would. Know.

He wasn't letting her get away from him. And she was going to be grounded for the next year anyway so . . .

Okay, man, ease up. She doesn't even know what you are yet. Or about any of this. And she didn't agree to any of your punishments or rules.

But still . . . the thought of keeping her ass inside his house for the next year was all that was stopping him from losing it. He was usually much more even-tempered. He couldn't remember the last time he'd skated the edge of control like this.

Then again, he couldn't remember the last time he'd cared about someone as much as he did her.

She was precious. And she needed to know that.

Marisol took a small breath. Her eyes were wide. Filled with fear. What the fuck?

"Marisol? You okay, sweetheart?" Ed asked as he sat across from them.

Linc shot him a look. He'd seen the way Ed watched her. Knew the other man was interested in her, even though Linc had made it clear to Ed that she was his.

No way would he lose Marisol to someone else. That wouldn't happen again.

He liked Ed. But he'd take that fucker down if he tried to move in on what belonged to Linc.

"Teeny, look at me. Teeny," he repeated firmly when she lowered her gaze to her lap.

She raised her eyes to his.

"Good girl," he praised her, watching as some of the tension in her shoulders drifted away. "Hold my hands." She reached out with trembling hands. He took them in his. "That's it. Now take a nice, slow deep breath for me. That's it. Slowly in. Squeeze my hands if you need to. Good girl. Calm, deep breaths. Nothing is going to hurt you. I'm here. Nothing is getting past me to you. I promise."

He kept his voice firm but calm. She needed calm right now. He knew that deep down she was strong. She might not see it, but he did. In the way she coped with her diabetes, with her aunt, the constant moves and upheaval. She was obviously shy, found it hard to be around a lot of people yet she got up every morning and did her job.

He hated that he had no idea of what had happened tonight. Even though things were busy with Clint away, he should have made more time for her. Phone calls and text messages were obviously not enough.

"You can't promise that. You don't know what they're like," she told them both. She slid her hands from Linc's and he immediately felt the loss of her skin pressed against his. Warming him from the inside out.

"The Devil's Sinners?" Ed asked. "Did one of them threaten you? Hurt you?"

"The Devil's Sinners?" Linc said sharply. "They were just on the news, right? All that shit with some of their leaders going missing and their headquarters set on fire?"

"Yeah, that's right." Ed rubbed his chin. "I was headed to Marisol's aunt's house because of a noise complaint. There's a gathering of Devil's Sinners members at her aunt's house."

"Fuck! Did one of them hurt you?"

She shook her head, looking pale and scared. He fucking hated it.

"When I got home from work tonight, the driveway was filled with cars and motorcycles. My aunt usually warns me when they're coming around so I can make myself scarce. Or hide in my room. Generally I try to leave though. Sticking around isn't safe."

Linc ground his teeth together. Jesus. Fucking. Christ. What was her aunt thinking?

"Why isn't it safe, Marisol?" Ed asked in a calm voice.

Do not lose it. Calm. Be calm. She needs you calm now. You can't lose it on her.

"They're not good people."

He hated that. So much. Hated that she'd been exposed to them.

"You said she normally warns you. This happens often?" Ed asked.

"The parties? No, not that often, thank God. But her boyfriend comes around a lot. She's been with him for years. Even through her last two marriages. They're getting married now. His son told me that he'd now be my brother. That he was going to be . . . to be in charge of me." Her voice broke on a sob.

"What the fuck?" Linc spat out, hating how pale she'd grown. In charge of her? Who was this prick? Linc fought the urge to drive out to her aunt's place and hunt this fucker down.

The fear on her face gutted him.

"Marisol? Did he hurt you? Is that what happened tonight?" Ed leaned forward again.

Linc held himself very still. He wasn't sure what he would do if she said that somebody had harmed her.

Kill them all.

Jesus. He'd never felt like this at all in his life. Not even when he learned of Jessica and Jon's betrayal. Sure, he'd been fucking furious. But he hadn't wanted to tear Jon to pieces and then roast his limbs on a firepit.

"Linc? Are you okay?" she asked.

He stared down at her in amazement. She was worried about him right now?

You're not taking care of her the way she needs.

Leaning in, he cupped the side of her face. "Hey, you don't need to be worrying about me right now."

She bit her lower lip and he reached down and freed it from her teeth then rubbed his thumb along her full bottom lip. Shit. If Ed wasn't in the room, if she wasn't so upset, he'd likely feed her his thumb and order her to suck. Then he'd take her mouth with his.

But Ed is here. So he drew his thumb away from her mouth.

"You seem really upset."

"I am. But that's not your concern. It's not your worry. Your job right now is to tell me what happened so I know best how to protect you."

And protect her he would.

Ed cleared his throat. "Tell *us* what happened so *we* can protect you."

Linc shot him another look. He should know that Linc was riding the edge of his temper. He didn't want to push him over. "She's mine to protect."

Ed held up his hands. "Not arguing that point. Just saying, I do wear the badge in this room. My job is literally to protect. You wanna let me do that?"

If he had to.

Linc gave a nod. He turned to Marisol who was watching them with wide eyes. "Don't worry about me, teeny. Just answer our questions honestly, okay? Give it all to me . . . to us, we'll take care of you."

She swallowed heavily. "Okay."

"Marisol, what happened to make you run?" Ed asked.

14

M arisol took in a deep breath. She didn't want to talk about this. Her head was pounding. She just wanted to curl up with her snuggly and Princess Nana and sleep.

Although the likelihood of her sleeping tonight wasn't good.

"Um, I guess I have to start further back than tonight. Back to that same night as when I went out to the ranch for Charlie's bridal shower. And you caught me speeding." She blushed as she looked at Ed.

Linc let out a low growl. "That won't be happening again."

She had to admit, she kind of liked this dominant, bossy side of him. She wouldn't want it all the time. Sometimes she needed softness. But she liked knowing that someone cared whether she was hurt or not.

"When I got home, I noticed his truck in the garage, my aunt's boyfriend." She rubbed at her temples.

"Do you need a drink? Some pain medication?" Ed asked with concern.

"Um, no."

"Get her some water," Linc demanded.

Ed just stared at him. They got into some alpha male stare down and she held her breath.

"Please," Linc bit out but didn't let his gaze drop. Ed nodded and rose, leaving the room.

Linc took her hand in his, placing his fingers over her pulse. "Are you okay? Have you eaten recently? Do you need to take your blood sugar levels?"

She looked at the clock.

"I checked my blood sugar before I left work. I usually have a snack before bed."

He nodded. "I'll make sure you have something before bed tonight."

She could take care of herself. She'd been doing it for years. Pretty much from the day that Harry told Rosalind to get out.

But she didn't argue with him. She was tired. Exhausted. It was so hard to constantly be on guard. To never know when the person who was meant to love her might turn on her. Rosalind's emotions were up and down on a good day. On a bad day. . . well, it was hard to live with someone when you never knew how they might react. Unpredictable was her norm. And then there were the other dangers lurking. Saber and Tiger. The Devil's Sinners.

Ed returned with a bottle of water for each of them. Her hands shook as she tried to open hers. Without a word, Linc reached out and took it, unscrewing the top for her.

"Thank you," she said quietly as she sipped from it.

Both men waited for her to finish but she knew they had to be getting impatient. She had to get this out. Now.

"Like I said, my aunt has been with her boyfriend for the past few years. He's a creep. But a smart creep. Cold. Calculating."

She shivered as though cold. Linc pulled off his jacket immediately and put it around her.

"We need to get you a jacket, teeny," he told her.

"I've been meaning to go to Goodwill to get one."

Linc muttered something she couldn't hear.

Ed cleared his throat. "What happened, sweetheart?"

Linc glared at him, and she was unsure why. But it didn't matter. There was a lot she didn't understand. Especially when it came to men.

"That night, I came home and found my aunt and him in the house, and they were, um . . ." She could feel herself blushing at the memory. "Anyway, I wasn't paying enough attention. I walked into my bedroom and there *he* was, sitting on my bed, holding my eReader." She swallowed hard, her heartbeat speeding up. "He seems to take delight in terrifying me. I've had run-ins with him a few times. But never in my room. He . . . he was saying how my aunt marrying his dad would mean that I was under his control. That when that happened, he wasn't going to let me out of his bedroom for a good long time."

"Fucking hell. That fucking asshole." Linc stood suddenly, making her shy back. He took a deep breath and let it out slowly. His hands, which had been clenched into fists at his sides, gradually loosened and he stared down at her with regret. "Sorry, teeny. I didn't mean to scare you. I hope you know that I would never hurt you."

He reached out to touch her face then pulled back before touching her. She hated that. That she'd made him hesitate. Quickly, she grabbed hold of his hand, holding on tight.

"I know you wouldn't. Sorry, I didn't mean to flinch. It's just that talking about this has brought it all up. It's close to the surface and I just reacted without thinking."

"I get it. Christ. Please tell me he didn't touch you," he begged.

She ran a shaky hand over her hair, tugging at her ponytail. "Not like that. He grabbed my wrist. Hard."

"The bandage, that's what it was covering?" He glanced down

at her wrist. The bruises had finally healed. "Why didn't you tell me the truth?"

"I didn't know you that well, and then once I did know you better and I realized how protective you are . . . he's dangerous, Linc."

"You didn't think I could protect you?" He almost sounded hurt and she flinched.

"I don't know what he's capable of. And I didn't want you to feel like you had to protect me."

"Damn it, Marisol."

"I've never had a friend before," she whispered. "I didn't want to scare you off."

"What sort of friend would I be if I ran at the first sign of trouble?" he countered.

Ed cleared his throat. "Can you keep going, Marisol?"

"Yes. I'm not sure what would have happened if we weren't interrupted by his dad banging on my bedroom door." She took in a shuddering breath. "They had to go because there was some trouble with some of their guys. He threw my eReader that's how it broke. Then he said he would be back."

Linc started pacing up and down the office. She stared at him for a moment then over at Ed.

"You didn't think to report this?" Ed asked.

"All he did was bruise my wrist and make some vague threats. It wasn't anything his lawyer couldn't argue against," she told him dully. Her head was really thumping now. And she was worried about Linc's reaction. "Besides, you know how I feel about cops."

"So I take it they were at the party?"

"Yeah, they were. That was my mistake . . . I should have left before now."

"Left?" Linc strode over and sat back in his chair. "What do you mean? That you should have left your aunt's? You certainly should have. Christ, I can't believe you stayed there when they could turn back up at any time."

"I stayed because of you," she cried.

"Me? What do you mean?"

"I'm sorry. I didn't mean that the way it sounded. It wasn't just you. It's this town. I like it here. It's so peaceful. Most of the people are nice. Then there's you. I've never had a friend or a boyfriend." She blushed slightly. "Your texts and calls are the highlight of my day. I didn't want to leave you."

"So you were planning on leaving town?" Ed asked.

"What choice do I have? I can't stick around with him here." Especially not now.

"If you don't mind my asking, why haven't you left before now? Why stay with your aunt?" Ed asked.

She ran a hand over her face, feeling ashamed. "Money. I have diabetes. If I left, I wouldn't have any insurance. I don't have much in savings. I don't have any other family. So I guess I was too scared. Worried I would end up homeless and alone. without anyone to help me. She might not be much, but she's the only family I have."

"Did you tell her about any of this?" Ed asked.

"Yeah." She sniffled. "She told me to give him whatever he wanted."

"That fucking bitch," Linc snapped.

She flinched and Ed held up a hand. "Linc, easy."

"I've known for a long time that she doesn't feel much towards me. I'm a convenient maid. Someone she can use, I barely get paid anything. She takes it all for room and board. The only reason I have any money saved is from when I've been given a big tip and managed to hide some of it from her."

"That fucking bitch. She told you to give him what he wanted. Your own aunt fucking said that." Linc's body was practically vibrating with rage.

She ran her hand over his shoulder and arm, trying to soothe him. "It's okay. I'm all right."

He gave her an incredulous look. "I can't believe you're trying to reassure me right now." He shook his head. "That's my job."

"You seem to need it more than me."

"And tonight? He was there?" Ed asked.

Linc scowled at him, but she nodded. "Like I said, I drove up and saw there was a party going on. I needed some things from my room. My money, my insulin." She didn't mention Princess Nana or her snuggly. Some things they didn't need to know about.

"I got inside and there was a fight. I hid while it was going on. Then I was about to run upstairs when he grabbed me. I was trying to resist him and he pinned me to the wall. He put his hand around my neck, he was strangling me. Then he . . . he was undoing his pants, threatening to make me . . ." she let out a sob.

She could hear Linc swearing. A long string of words she'd never imagined she'd hear out of his mouth. Then he reached over and grabbed the tissue box that Ed held out. But instead of handing them to her, he shocked her by gently picking her up and lifting her into his lap.

She stiffened. She still wasn't used to being held on someone's lap. He drew her in close, and tilted up her chin, wiping her face gently.

"It's okay, little one. You're safe. He can't hurt you. I have you. I'll never let him touch you again."

She slumped against Linc, unable to hold herself up. She was exhausted. He rubbed his hands soothingly up and down her back. A feeling of safety stole over her. She should probably move, no doubt she was squishing him.

But she just couldn't move.

"Are you bruised?" Linc pushed aside the neck of her sweater, hissing in a breath.

"What?" she asked.

"You're all red there," Ed explained, his eyes narrowed, jaw clenched. "Likely gonna bruise."

"Motherfucker," Linc snarled. "I'm going to fucking kill him."

"You won't," Ed warned. "You'll leave this to the authorities."

"He threatened her! He likely would have raped her!"

"And he'll be taken care of. He won't get away with this," Ed reassured him.

"Yeah, cause he's going to end up in a six-foot hole," Linc replied.

"Jesus, Linc. You can't threaten to murder someone in front of a cop."

"Be one less criminal on the streets. You should—"

"I'm not pressing charges," she interjected.

The silence in the room was ominous. She suddenly found it hard to take a decent breath. Both men were staring at her. She looked down at her hands, unable to take their intense gazes.

"You want to say that again, Mari-girl?" Linc asked.

Not really. She kind of wished she hadn't said it in the first place. But she had. And it was the right decision. At least she hoped it was.

She squirmed on his lap, but he held her steady. Then he gently cupped her chin in his hand, raising her head so she couldn't hide.

"Why wouldn't you press charges?" Linc asked.

"If you're scared that he'll hurt you, I can protect you," Ed added.

Linc's gaze narrowed dangerously. "Mari doesn't need your protection, because she knows that I will protect her. Don't you, Mari-girl?"

Uh-oh. That tone in his voice told her that she better answer him the right way.

"You can't go up against him."

"Linc can't. But I can," Ed said firmly.

She shook her head. "If I press charges, they'll be after my blood."

"And so you want to do nothing and let him do this to someone else?" Ed asked.

She gasped, feeling like she'd been punched in the stomach. Linc stood, setting her on the chair and then leaning over the desk he got in Ed's face. "Don't you ever speak to her like that again. Do not put this on her. This isn't her fault. And you know what she says is true."

Ed and Linc glared at each other. Marisol wrapped her arms around herself. Should she pursue charges? If she didn't do anything, would he just do this to someone else?

"You're right," Ed conceded. He looked over at her, regret in his eyes. "I'm sorry, Marisol. I shouldn't have said that to you. I'm just upset that this happened to you while you were living in my town. I had no call to say that."

"Maybe you're right. I should stop being a coward." She lowered her gaze, ashamed of herself.

"Hey, nobody called you a coward." Linc turned to her, pulling her close and hugging her gently. "It took a lot of courage to do what you did tonight, to get away from him."

Had it? She'd been running on adrenaline and fear. She hadn't felt very brave.

Linc sat back in the chair, pulling her onto his lap. At least the two men were no longer glaring at each other.

"You're not a coward, sweetheart. At all. Why don't you tell us the rest? Then we'll know how to proceed. How did you get away?" Ed asked.

"I kneed him in the balls then I raced upstairs. I locked my door, grabbed what I needed and then I . . . I climbed out over the balcony."

"What?" Linc snapped.

"I'm okay, it wasn't that far to jump. I ran towards the road then Ed found me. That's all."

"That's all," Linc repeated, dropping his head back. "Lord help me. That's all."

"I can't stay here. If I do, he'll find me. And he'll hurt anyone who helps me."

"LIKE FUCK you're going anywhere, teeny," Linc snapped. Not now. Not ever. Not that he said that out loud. But she wasn't leaving. He couldn't believe she thought he would just let her go. Had she even intended to tell him she was leaving?

"The way he talked about me, he really thinks I'm his possession."

"What's his name, Marisol?" Ed asked. "Don't think I haven't noticed that you deliberately haven't said his name or his father's."

She sighed forlornly. "It's Tiger."

"Tiger? Tiger Mason?" Ed snapped.

"Yes." She winced. "So you have heard of him?"

Ed closed his eyes for a moment, looking pained. "Are you saying that your aunt's boyfriend is Saber Mason?"

"Saber and Tiger? Really?" Linc asked.

"After they go through initiation, they're given a new name," Ed explained. "For the higher up guys, it's related to an animal."

"The guys were on the news. The ones that turned up murdered. They were called Jackal and Falcon," she told Linc.

"And Saber Mason is the top of the chain," Ed said grimly. "He's the leader of all the branches. Fuck. Why did your aunt come here? Because of them?"

"I don't know. Maybe. We move around a lot. Texas, Arizona, California. Then here. Saber used to travel between Washington and Texas and Arizona a lot. My aunt would go visit him in Seattle too."

"The Devil's Kings run Texas and Arizona. Saber's brother is their leader," Ed said.

"I didn't know that," she said quietly. She felt so tiny in Linc's arms. So defenseless. He wanted to wrap her up in layers of safety and never let her go.

He kissed the top of her head.

"I've tried to keep my distance from them. Saber has always creeped me out. Tiger has only been around the last year. I think maybe I heard something about him being with his uncle."

"Probably training with the Devil's Kings," Ed said. "Shit. Marisol, I really wish you'd change your mind about pressing charges."

"I . . . I don't know. It's my word against his."

"At least let me take photos of your neck. Just in case you change your mind."

"All right. I suppose we should do that."

"I don't want him coming after her," Linc stated. "I want them gone from town." And far away from Marisol. The sooner this bastard forgot about her, the better.

"You and me both," Ed replied dryly. "I'll go out there, my deputies are still hanging close by so they can go in with me. I'll have a word. Make Tiger and Saber see that leaving town for good would be the best possible idea."

"They'll know I talked to you," Marisol said worriedly.

"Don't worry, I won't mention your name. Your aunt has been with him for a long time?"

"Yes."

"And she owns several spas, yes?" Ed asked.

"Uh, yes. She's opened a number across the country. Why?"

"Places where the Devil's Sinners have set up branches?" Ed asked her.

"Well. I don't always pay attention, but yeah, I guess so. The last one she opened was in Seattle, but I never worked at that one. I stayed back in San Diego."

She shivered in Linc's arms and he tightened his hold on her. "He will not harm you. You're coming home with me and I will keep you safe."

Leaning back, she stared up at him with those big hazel eyes. "And who will protect you?"

"That's not something you need to take on your shoulders," he told her.

"But it is. Because if something happens to you, it will be my fault. And I'll never forgive myself."

He cupped the side of her face. "Nothing is going to happen to me. I live on a ranch with the best security in the state. Every man on the ranch will watch out for and protect you. You wouldn't be safer anywhere else."

"He's right, Marisol," Ed told her, standing. "You need to go home with Linc and stay with him. Sanctuary Ranch really is the safest place for you right now. I'll get Steven to take those photos of your neck so I can get out there. Excuse me." He left the room.

Linc stood and reached out his hand. "Come home with me, Marisol. Let me take care of you."

"Why would you want to? My life is such a mess. Shouldn't you want to see the back of me?" she whispered forlornly.

"I want to because I care about you. Yeah, we've got some stuff to talk about, to work through. But I'm not going to just let you walk away. I can take care of you. All you need to do is trust me."

To his relief, he felt her little hand slide into his.

Thank. Fuck.

15

Her hand was firmly engulfed in his. As though he was worried she might run unless she was tethered to him.

That was probably a valid concern. She was still concerned about putting him in danger. Tiger had made his claim on her. And while she had no intentions of ever being with that asshole, she knew that he didn't care about her thoughts on the matter.

She also had a feeling that Tiger wasn't used to women kneeing him in the balls and running from him. She shivered.

No, she was pretty sure none of this ended well for her.

Linc led her outside after Steven had taken the photos of her neck. She shivered slightly, even with his jacket still wrapped around her. Silently, he led her to his truck. He opened the door. He already had her backpack in his other hand, he'd refused to let her carry it herself.

"I think you need to start carrying a stepladder around," she grumbled.

He placed the backpack down in the truck then wrapped his

hands around her waist. "You don't need a stepladder when you have me."

Aww, that was sweet.

He set her down on the seat then reached across her to do up her seatbelt.

"Well, what if you're not around? How will I get in?"

"If I'm not around why would you be trying to get into my truck?" He closed her door and walked around to the driver's side. Climbing in, he started the truck, turning on the heater and aiming it her way.

"What if I had to drive it somewhere? Then I'd need some way of getting in it, wouldn't I?" She wasn't sure why she was so focused on his truck. Maybe because it was taking her mind off the mess her life was in.

"Teeny, you aren't ever going to drive my truck."

She crossed her arms over her chest with a pout. "Why? Because I'm a girl?"

"No," he replied calmly. "Because you're not even five feet tall. You can't see over the dashboard. You probably couldn't even reach the pedals."

Okay, those were valid reasons, but she wasn't giving in.

"I'm sure I can drive this just fine." No. She wasn't.

"Uh-huh, sure you can. Tell you what, tomorrow you can sit in the driver's seat. If you can see over the dashboard and reach the pedals then if there is ever a time that you need to drive my truck, you can."

"All right then."

"But if you can't reach the pedals and see over the dashboard, then you're going to agree to using a booster seat."

"What? No way!" Was he kidding?

"Yep."

She scowled. "Linc, I don't need a booster seat."

"Someone as small as you, it's got to be safer. Wouldn't you rather be able to see out the window properly anyway?"

"I can see out the window." Just not the front window. "I'm not sitting in a booster seat."

"We'll see."

"I'm short, not a child."

There was a beat of silence. Her nerves started to get to her again. Linc fell silent. Guilt ate away at her. She knew he wouldn't be happy about her keeping things from him.

"Linc, I—"

"Were you ever going to tell me? About Tiger?"

Oh God. That guilt increased. "I . . . I don't know." She didn't know what to say to make everything better. They both fell silent again as he turned his truck into Sanctuary Ranch's driveway. The big gates opened automatically and his truck started forward. She took a deep breath in and let it out slowly. She was going to Linc's house. Where would she sleep? She hadn't even asked if he had a spare bedroom. Was he expecting something more from her? Sex? She'd never had sex. She didn't have a clue what she was doing.

Oh hell. Why had she said yes to coming home with him?

Because you didn't want to say goodbye.

"What if I put everyone here in danger?" she whispered.

"Did you meet Clint? When you were out here?"

"Umm, yes." Clint Jensen was a big, blunt man. Kind of scary. But it was clear to see his adoration for his now-wife.

"Well, his brother, Kent owns Jensen Security International. And their base of operations is the ranch. Most of the guys working for him live here. They're mostly all ex-military. They're highly trained. This ranch has the best security you can get. We take the safety of all the women very seriously. You'll be safe here. They're safe here. Stop worrying so much. It's all going to be okay."

All right. That made her feel better. And she remembered

someone mentioning JSI in the spa, she just hadn't realized what exactly it was.

"Sometimes it's easier for me to think about what could go wrong, then I can prepare myself. If I think everything will be all right and then it all unravels, well, then it's much harder to pick myself back up."

"I hate that you've had to teach yourself to think that way. You should be filled with hope for the future, not expecting everything to go to shit. Excuse my language."

She had to smile at that as they pulled up outside a quaint log cabin that was surrounded by tall trees. "You don't have to worry about your language."

"Still shouldn't be swearing in front of you. Nana would have my hide for how I've been talking around you tonight. Wait there."

She thought it was kind of cute that he worried about what he said with her around. She undid her seatbelt as he opened the door. Reaching up, he lifted her down and grabbed her backpack.

"Pretty sure I can get down on my own," she told him. "It's getting up that's the issue."

"You might hurt yourself jumping down, especially when the ground is uneven."

"I jumped from a far higher height tonight without a problem," she commented without thinking as she followed him up onto the porch.

"You could have hurt yourself. What if you'd broken your arm? Or your foot?"

Well, she guessed she wouldn't be here right now since she was sure that Tiger would have found her. But she didn't say that. She wasn't silly.

He opened the door to the house and ushered her in.

"You don't lock your door?" she said with surprise.

"I left in a hurry."

To rush into town to help her.

"I'm so sorry. You must be so tired. I didn't know Ed was going to call you."

"Which just makes things worse. Since you should have demanded he call me the minute he picked you up." He toed off his cowboy boots and she did the same with her sneakers. Grabbing them both, he set them in the coat closet. She noted it was neat as a pin.

"Sorry," she whispered.

Reaching out, he grasped hold of her chin. "I don't care what time it is, how much I've been working or what is going on, if you're in trouble, if you're hurt, you call me. Understand?"

"I understand."

He took hold of her hand and led her into a tidy living room with a cathedral ceiling, making the room feel cavernous. She looked up, seeing gable windows. There was a fireplace that had already been lit. She rushed forward but he kept hold of her hand, not letting her get close.

"Be careful around the fire, okay? Don't stand too close."

She thought about pointing out that she wasn't an idiot, but he'd already shown that he was on protective overdrive tonight. So she just nodded.

"You can have a snack while I set up your room." He looked her over with a frown. "Or do you want a shower first?"

She did feel kind of sweaty and gross. "That would be great."

"All right." He grabbed her hand again. A shiver worked its way up her skin at the feel of him touching her.

The man was potent.

He pointed to a room off the living area. "Through there is the kitchen and dining." They walked down a short hallway. "My room." He nodded at the door across from his room. "The bathroom and your room are down there." He opened the bathroom door and walked to the shower, turning it on. Again, everything was neat and clean. Weren't men living alone meant to be messy? "You got PJs in here? Toothbrush?"

"No, I didn't have time to grab any."

"I'll get you one of my T-shirts."

He opened the cupboard and rustled around, pulling out a toothbrush in its packaging as well as a razor. "Here you are. Help yourself to anything you want. Clean towels are in here." He pointed to another cupboard. "I'll grab that T-shirt. When you're clean and dressed head back out to the living area."

She nodded. He quickly returned with a red T-shirt. After showering, a wave of exhaustion washed over her and she had to sit on the toilet lid for a moment. She only had one pair of panties so she'd gone without. She'd have to wash them now so she could wear them tomorrow.

Tears filled her eyes.

She knew she was just tired. That she had to get up and keep moving. Nobody was going to do this stuff for her. She'd been taking care of herself for a long time. Sometimes, though, it would be nice to let go of all the worries. To let someone else shoulder some of the decisions. Take care of her.

Linc takes care of you.

Yes. But she couldn't get used to it. She wasn't sure if he was taking care of her because he still wanted her. Or because he felt like he had to because she had nowhere else to go.

And she didn't want to ask.

A knock at the door startled her and she realized she'd actually fallen asleep on the toilet. Yikes. That was embarrassing.

"Um, yes?"

"You okay?" he asked.

"Oh, yeah, coming." As soon as she found some energy.

"You dressed?"

"Yep."

The door suddenly opened without warning and she let out a

startled cry. Okay she hadn't been expecting him to just walk in. Thank God she hadn't been lying about being dressed.

Walking forward, he crouched in front of her, resting his hands on her thighs.

Oh shit. She was all too aware of her bare pussy. Her clit throbbed as she pressed her thighs together.

"You're all done in, aren't you?" he crooned.

She sniffled. "Sorry. I just need a minute."

"I don't think a minute will help. You're spent. You need a good night's sleep."

She wasn't sure if that would be happening tonight. She wasn't a very good sleeper anyway. And with everything that had happened tonight, plus being in a strange place, she was pretty sure sleep would elude her.

He brushed a thumb over her cheek. "Right. Let's do what we have to in order to get you tucked up in bed. Any talk can wait for tomorrow. Do you need to pee?"

Her bladder just made itself known. Crap. Why did she have to have such a small bladder?

"Urgh, yes."

"I'm guessing you won't be comfortable with me staying while you go?" he asked.

Was he serious?

"You would guess right."

He rolled his eyes at her. "Don't know why. It's just peeing."

"I bet you wouldn't want me watching you pee," she countered.

He grinned. "Wouldn't worry me. Just a bodily function. We all do it."

Yeah, but that didn't mean she wanted him around while she went. Sheesh. He stood and held out his hands, helping her stand. Thankfully, she was so short that his T-shirt reached mid-thigh.

"Right. You can pee on your own. But I'm going to leave the door cracked open. If you have any problems, call out."

"I've been peeing on my own for a long time," she told him dryly.

"I know. But you're under my care now. You're exhausted and trembling. I don't want you falling and hurting yourself, okay? So just humor me."

"Don't stand out there listening to me," she ordered.

He leaned in, brushing his lips across her cheek. "One day, you will be completely comfortable with me in the room when you pee then you'll learn you're worrying over nothing. I'll take these and put them in the wash." He picked up all her dirty clothes before she could say anything and left the bathroom.

Yeah. She didn't see that day coming anytime soon.

Some things just didn't need to be shared. Mumbling to herself, she peed and washed her hands then grabbed her backpack and made her way out into the hallway.

He was standing there, waiting. Which didn't surprise her. Her dirty clothes were gone so he must have chucked them in the wash.

"I could have washed my clothes."

He raised his eyebrows. "Of course you could have. I didn't take them because you're not capable. I put them in the wash because I want to help you."

"Oh." *Way to sound ungrateful, Marisol.* "Sorry, I'm not used to people, uh, helping me."

He frowned slightly. "I figured that. Your aunt isn't the motherly type."

She let out a small bark of laughter. "No, definitely not."

"Gonna need to put an extra blanket on your bed. Don't want you getting cold."

He seemed to have an obsession about keeping her warm. It was kind of cute.

"Come on, I have a snack ready in your bedroom."

She made to follow him, but her legs seemed to have a mind of their own. She stumbled as she tried to walk, falling into the wall.

"Bad legs. Do as you're told," she muttered to herself.

Linc turned and grabbed her by the waist. "Whoa there. You're not supposed to walk into the walls. And did you just tell your legs off?"

He drew her up into his arms, holding her against his chest.

"They're not listening to me."

"Hmm. I know what that feels like." He gave her a pointed look.

"What does that mean? I listen to you."

"Right. You just don't always do what I say."

"You're not in charge of me."

He set her down on a comfy, large bed. The covers had already been pulled back and a lamp was on beside the bed, giving the room a soft glow.

"Not yet. But tomorrow, you're gonna learn that in this house, in this relationship, baby, I'm the boss."

16

I*n this house, in this relationship, baby, I'm the boss.*

Those words wouldn't stop swimming through her head.

She rolled over, barely suppressing a groan. This bed was super comfortable. The room was lovely. Not only had Linc made her a snack, but he'd produced an ice pack for her neck, fussing over her in a way no one had before. After she'd eaten and checked her blood sugar level, he'd tucked her in tight, then sat with her to tell her one of his stories. She'd closed her eyes and pretended to fall asleep, knowing he likely wouldn't leave until she did.

He'd left the door cracked open with the hall light on. She'd waited until he was out of the room to climb from the bed and turn the lamp on then shut the door. Luckily, the lamp had a dim setting so it wasn't too bright.

It had taken her a while to get out from under the covers. The man sure did know how to tuck a girl in tight.

The door didn't have a lock, but she had to hope he wouldn't just walk in. Going to her bag, she'd grabbed snuggly and Princess Nana.

Now here she was, her thumb in her mouth, snuggly rubbing back and forth under her nose as she tried to get to sleep.

It was so quiet here.

And when she closed her eyes, the events from tonight just kept running through her brain on repeat.

Not to mention her body felt like she'd been run over by a train. Seemed jumping from a second story balcony wasn't a great idea.

Who knew?

There was also a part of her that was somewhat disappointed she wasn't sleeping in Linc's bed. She knew that was crazy. If he'd wanted her to sleep with him, she'd likely have freaked out. But now she was worrying that he didn't want her like that.

She knew he was upset with her and she understood why. She just didn't know how to fix things.

Knowing she wasn't going to sleep, she pushed the blankets back and stood. A groan escaped as her body protested. Maybe she should have taken a bath. It was too late now, she didn't want to wake Linc up. He'd told her that he would get up early and go do a few jobs then be back around eight. He definitely needed sleep more than she needed a bath.

Grabbing the bedding off the bed, she knew there was only one place she'd feel safe enough to maybe sleep. Opening the closet door, she made a bed for herself on the floor. Then she dragged in Princess Nana and her snuggly.

With a yawn, she snuggled into her makeshift bed. Wishing she had her eReader, she lay there until her eyelids eventually grew heavy. Exhausted, she finally slipped into sleep.

LINC MOVED QUIETLY through his cabin, Marisol's clean clothes in his arms. He'd been up for a few hours working, clearing some time so he could come back and see Mari. He'd also spoke to Kent about her situation. Kent had assured him he'd put everyone on alert, and that whatever Linc needed, he was there for him. He wished he'd checked in on her this morning before he'd left. Actually, he wished he'd insisted that she sleep with him. In his bed.

But he figured that was pushing things too far too fast. He didn't want to scare her off. Plus, he'd needed some time to process things. He wasn't happy about everything that she'd kept from him. But he also had to realize that they hadn't known each other long. If she'd done this after they'd been in a relationship for a few months, their chat would go very differently from the one he intended to have with her.

He wasn't surprised that she was still sleeping, she'd been exhausted last night. But he was wondering if he should wake her. He'd had a chat with Doc about type one diabetes and Doc had suggested sticking to set times for eating. He wasn't sure when she usually ate breakfast and it was now after eight. Although she did have a midnight snack, so maybe he shouldn't worry so much.

Opening up her door, he peeked in. He frowned when he saw the stripped bed.

What the hell? Where was she? Why had she taken the top sheet and blankets off the bed?

He strode in, worry flooding him. Had she left? But no, there was no way she could have. She didn't have any clothes or a way off the ranch.

Setting her clean clothes on the dresser, he crouched down to check under the bed. Not there. He turned to the closet door and opened it.

His heart nearly stopped as he found her. It was a walk-in closet, and she was so short that she didn't even look scrunched up. She was lying on her front with one leg cocked up. His T-shirt, that she was wearing, had ridden up just enough to show him the curve of a plump buttock and a hint of her pussy lips.

Fuck. Shit.

Immediately, his cock hardened and he felt like a pervy asshole.

Crouching down, he flicked the blanket over her naked backside. He noticed that she had a princess doll tucked into her bent arm. And in her hand, she held the corner of a pastel-colored blanket. She was sucking on her thumb and rubbing the blanket under her nose.

Fuck. That was adorable.

And another sign that his gut was right.

That she was a Little.

Affection filled him as he watched her. He wondered how long she'd had the blankie. It looked a bit old and worn in places. Should she be sucking her thumb? Maybe a pacifier would be better. He wondered if she'd ever tried one.

Suddenly her eyes opened. She looked up at him.

Then she screamed.

MARISOL SCRAMBLED BACKWARDS QUICKLY HITTING a wall as she tried to get away from the man looming over her.

There was a man in her room. A man in her room.

Tiger!

"Marisol."

She whimpered. Why hadn't she locked the door? Idiot!

"Marisol!" He reached for her and she slapped at his hands. Tiger coming for her. Tiger grabbing her, forcing her to her knees.

"No! No!" she screamed.

"Marisol, it's me. It's Linc."

"No. Noo! Tiger, no!"

"Oh jeez, baby girl. Teeny, it's me. Shh, you're killing me here. It's me. It's Linc."

"Stay away. Stay away."

"I'm not going to touch you. Just breathe, teeny. Look around you. You're not with Tiger. You're with me. Linc."

The calmness of his voice combined with the fact that he wasn't trying to touch her finally got through to her.

"L-Linc?"

"That's right, Mari-girl. It's Linc. Can you open your eyes up and look at me?"

Shudders worked their way through her body as her breath heaved in and out of her lungs. She looked up at him, taking him in.

Relief flooded her body. Linc. She was at his house. Nowhere near her aunt's place or Tiger.

"Oh God. I'm so sorry." She wiped at her cheeks as she realized she was crying. "I was dreaming about... about what happened and then I woke up and saw you there. Sorry. I didn't hurt you, did I? I'm so sorry."

"Hush," he told her gently as he sat on the floor. Then she realized she was in the closet. Crap.

"Come on. Come out of there." He stood and held out his hand, helping her out. Then he led her to the bed. When she was sitting on the mattress, he grabbed some tissues from the box on the nightstand. Kneeling on the floor in front of her, he grasped hold of her chin and wiped her face free of tears with an expert touch. "Of course you didn't hurt me. And it was my fault for standing over you like that. No wonder you woke up screaming."

She drew back and he let her go, studying her intently.

"Wait. What are you doing in here? Were you watching me sleep?"

Red tinged his cheeks. Was he embarrassed? Wow. She hadn't thought someone as confident and together as Linc would blush.

That was sexy.

"I came in to check on you and you weren't in your bed so I went looking for you. Sorry."

"Oh God. Please don't tell me I was doing anything embarrassing," she moaned.

He raised his eyebrows. "What could you possibly do that would be so embarrassing?"

Any number of things. Drooling. Talking in her sleep. Sucking her thumb.

"I was worried that you might be sleeping too long. Why were you in the closet?"

She shrugged. "I often did that as a kid. I guess it feels safer to me somehow."

He frowned. "You feel unsafe here?"

"No, no I don't. It's just . . . with everything that happened, I suppose I was feeling anxious. So I crawled in there."

"No more sleeping in the closet," he commanded.

"I was fine in there. It was comfy."

"Not happening. Remember, I'm the boss."

Oh yeah. She wasn't forgetting him telling her that anytime soon.

He studied her. "You still look tired. You might need a nap later."

She didn't know why, but him telling her she might need a nap made her want to squirm. It also made her want to pout like a three-year-old who was certain that they definitely didn't want a nap. No matter how tired they were.

You're not three. You're an adult. Act like it.

"Did you have any other nightmares?"

"Ah, no, I don't remember them if I did." She let out a shuddering breath. "I actually slept pretty well considering. Sometimes I have trouble sleeping."

"Not a shock you had one about that asshole. I'm going to call Ed soon and see what happened last night. You hungry?"

She nodded.

"Doc said it might be a good idea to stick to regular times for snacks and meals for your diabetes, is that what you do?"

Wow. He'd talked to a doctor about her? That was sweet. "Ahh. I try. Sometimes I forget though.

"I'll go make some breakfast. Scrambled eggs on toast okay?"

"Sorry to be so much hassle." She glanced down.

"Hey, look at me." He waited until she raised her face. "You're never a hassle, understand me?"

She nodded. But she didn't believe it. She'd been a hassle her entire life. And things didn't seem to be changing anytime soon.

"Oh, your clean clothes are on the dresser. We're going to need to get you some new things, though. As cute as you are wearing one of my T-shirts, I don't think you want to wear them all the time." He winked at her and then left.

Crap! How had she forgotten that all she was wearing was his T-shirt? Yikes. How easily she could have flashed him.

After checking her blood sugar levels, she got dressed and pulled her hair back into a ponytail. She made the bed. She tucked her snuggly and Princess Nana back in the backpack. He hadn't said anything about them. Maybe he hadn't noticed them? Or maybe he thought she was a weirdo. If he'd seen her sucking her thumb, no doubt he already thought that.

Just get out there and eat breakfast.

She injected some insulin. Then, heart sinking, lead in her stomach, she practically dragged her feet into the kitchen and dining area.

Linc looked up from where he was setting two big plates of food on the small kitchen table. He gave her an inquisitive look.

"I know my cooking isn't cordon bleu, but people don't usually come to the dinner table like it's their last supper, either."

Oh jeez, Marisol. Way to be ungrateful.

"I'm so sorry, it's not the food. I guess I'm just feeling a bit down right now." Was it okay to admit that? People didn't like to be around people who were feeling low, right? Maybe she shouldn't have said it.

Urgh. She just wasn't good at this crap. And by crap, she meant anything to do with other people.

"Shoot. Sorry. I just keep mucking up."

"Hey." He took her face between his hands, raising it so he could stare down into her eyes. "It's completely understandable that you're feeling a bit off. Okay? You never have to apologize for your feelings."

"I don't want you to think I don't appreciate everything you've done."

"Far as I can tell, I haven't done much at all."

"You came out in the middle of the night because I was in trouble. Brought me back here. Washed my clothes. Gave me yours to wear. And you just made me breakfast. I can't remember the last time someone helped me this much. I don't think anyone has made me breakfast in years. Not since Ana."

"Ana?"

"She was our housekeeper for a while when I was younger, she was from Venezuela. When my aunt wasn't home, Ana would make me all sorts of goodies like *arepas* and *cachitos*. I was telling Ed about Ana last night. She was our housekeeper for about a year until my aunt came home one day and discovered her teaching me Spanish. She fired Ana and forbid me from ever speaking the language. The only bits of Spanish I know is a few swear words I've picked up here and there. Then about a month later, my aunt was arrested and this lovely social worker let me stay with Ana and her family. That week that I stayed with Ana, well, I actually felt like part of a family."

"God, teeny," he said with sympathy. "That aunt of yours has got a lot to answer for."

She shrugged. "She is what she is."

"Well, I don't like that you weren't cared for the way you

should have been. That won't happen while you're here. How is your neck this morning?"

She raised her hand to touch the still-sore skin. "It feels all right. Hopefully, it won't bruise too badly."

He scowled. "That bastard. Excuse my language. I won't let him hurt you again, I promise."

"What about my job? How will I work?"

"You're not going back there, Marisol. It's not safe. You're going to need to stay here on the ranch for me until we figure out whether Tiger is going to come for you. Hopefully Ed can scare him away, although I have my doubts."

So did she. She nibbled at her lip.

"Were you happy at that job? Did you like it?"

"No," she whispered. "I only did it because that's what my aunt wanted. But I'm kind of an introvert. Being around people all day exhausted me."

"Then it's no big loss to go back."

"I just feel bad about leaving everyone in the lurch."

"Your aunt could always cover for you."

Right. That would never happen.

He pulled out a chair for her, pushing her in. The chair must have been made for a damn giant because her feet didn't even touch the ground when she was seated on it. She had to scoot forward to the edge and even then, the table was kind of high.

So embarrassing.

"This won't do. You could use a highchair."

Umm. She had to have heard him wrong. Right?

"Did you say a higher chair?" she asked. "Any higher and I will need a stepladder to get on it. Is all your furniture made for giants?"

He opened his mouth, a twinkle in his eyes.

"And no short jokes," she told him sternly, holding up a single finger.

To her shock, he leaned over and took her finger into his mouth, sucking on it strongly. Holy. Shit. That sent an answering shockwave down to her clit.

He let go of her finger with a small plop. "No pointing your finger at me."

Her heart was beating too rapidly for her to answer. For her to do anything but stare at him. "I'll go get something for you to sit on." He turned away, walking towards the door. Then he turned back, giving her a cheeky grin.

Uh-oh.

"And no, I didn't say a higher chair. I said highchair. I'm sure the same place that does booster seats can make those too."

She just sat there, staring after him. Even when he walked back in, cushion in hand, she was still staring.

"Stand."

After she stood, he set the cushion down on the seat. She sat and he pushed her chair in for her. Sitting across from her, he reached over and tapped her plate. "You need to eat."

She ate a couple of mouthfuls. Guilt swirled in her stomach, making it hard to swallow. He was taking such good care of her. It just made her feel worse.

"I'm sorry I didn't tell you what was going on," she blurted out, needing to apologize again. "And that I lied about my wrist."

He gave her a firm look. "You know how I felt about lies."

She nodded miserably. "I know."

"And I hate knowing that I had no idea of what you went through. Of how bad things were for you. Keeping something that big from me, it can't happen again, Marisol."

"It won't."

"I also know that we haven't known each other long and that trust can take time. So I'm not mad at you, Mari-girl. Okay? Just a bit disappointed."

Jeez. She thought that might be worse. In fact, she was sure it was. What could she do to make things better?

You could ask him to punish you.

Okay, that might be taking things a step too far. She wasn't even sure that he wanted her anymore. Or that he wanted that sort of a relationship. Even though he'd asked her whether she read books with BDSM in them, he'd never said that he was into it. Or really mentioned it again.

She forced herself to eat some more. "I'm just not used to relying on other people. For anything. We moved around so much that I never put down roots anywhere. I was always the hanger-on. The extra. The poor relative. To be pitied and picked-on at school. Ignored or yelled at when at home. Nobody stuck around. None of my aunt's husbands or boyfriends, except for Saber. None of our staff. The only person I can ever remember caring about me was Harry. And Ana."

"Harry was your aunt's ex? The guy who took you on your only picnic?"

"Yeah. He was kind to me. I was devastated when he kicked Rosalind out. I begged her to let me stay with him. She told me that I was the reason he was divorcing her. That I was too needy and annoying and that he couldn't be bothered with me anymore."

"What the fuck?" he snapped. "Sorry for my language."

That was so cute.

"I'm not sure if she was telling the truth. She likely said it to shut me up or hurt me. But I can't help thinking that if he'd cared for me at all, he would have tried to see me again. Or contact me." She shrugged, trying to play off the pain. But it was still there. Even after all these years.

"Maybe she wouldn't let him." He reached across the table and took hold of her hand. She'd eaten as much as she could. "That sounds like the sort of thing she'd do."

"Yeah, you're likely right. I'm used to people leaving me, Linc. Or being forced to leave them. People don't want to stick around."

"Look at me, Marisol."

She stared into his intense gaze. "I'm not going anywhere. I brought you back here with me because I care about you. My feelings for you haven't changed. I still want a relationship with you."

"You do? You still want me?"

"Yes," he said firmly. "I'm attracted to you. I want you. I think you're gorgeous, smart, funny and kind. I can't get too upset with you for holding back because I've been doing the same. I haven't been upfront about exactly who I am and what sort of relationship I want."

She frowned at that. "Did you lie to me?"

He shook his head. "I never lied. I was just waiting to see if there were signs you wanted this sort of relationship too. And I think you do. But that talk can wait a bit until you're settled in. Besides, I don't have the time right now. But I need you to trust me enough to let me protect you."

"I do trust you," she said. "That's not why I never said anything about Tiger. I just wanted to protect you."

"Which is sweet. But remember I'm an old-fashioned guy. I protect you. I have the means to protect you. But to do that, I need you to open up with me. Right. I've got to get back to work. Your phone is dead, right?"

"Yes, I don't have the charger. I don't think I should use it anyway. It's my aunt's old phone and she still pays the bill. She might be able to track it. Should I contact her? Let her know that I'm safe?"

"I suppose that's up to you. But I want to be here when you call her. Why don't you take some time to think about it today?"

"Yeah, okay." Even though her relationship with her aunt wasn't great, she felt like maybe she owed it to her to let her know she was safe.

Then again, she had told her to give Tiger whatever he wanted. So maybe she owed her nothing. And it wasn't like she would report her missing. Rosalind hated the police.

"Help yourself to anything you want while I'm gone. Call me if you need me. I'll write down my phone number. I'd also like that list you were going to write me about anything I need to watch out for with your diabetes and what to do. I've done a bit of research already, but there might be something I've missed. I'll check on you throughout the day. Let's get you settled on the sofa with the TV remote. Today, you're doing nothing but resting and taking care of yourself. Understand me?"

So bossy.

"Okay," she whispered.

"That's my good girl."

SHE SET the mop aside and looked down at the clean floors with satisfaction. She'd sat and watched TV for about an hour before she'd started to get antsy. She wasn't used to sitting around for long periods of time. Well, not unless she'd lost herself in a good book. Then the whole day could go by with her barely noticing.

She also felt guilty that she was relaxing while Linc was out working. With all that he was doing for her, the least she could do was clean his house. Not that it needed much cleaning. The man was very tidy.

He even kept lists for God's sake. There was a to-do list on his fridge as well as a shopping list.

Now, if only she could manage to make something for dinner. But her cooking skills were non-existent.

A knock on the door had her frowning, her heart racing. *Mierda!* Linc hadn't told her what to do if someone came to the door. Surely, if he'd been expecting someone, he would have told her. He'd already called her to check on her.

Another knock. It couldn't be Tiger, anyway. He wouldn't knock. But was it a good idea for anyone to know she was here? Was Linc telling people? Shit. Why hadn't she asked any of this stuff?

Knock. Knock. Crap. She was just going to answer it. Racing to the door, she took a deep breath then opened it carefully.

To find Abby standing on the other side, a smile on her face and a large casserole dish by her feet. Mari's eyes widened. "Abby?"

"Marisol! I was starting to wonder if you were here. I mean, Kent said you were and I didn't think you could go anywhere. Unless you went down to the stables, I guess. Or for a walk."

Marisol just stared at her.

"Urgh, I'm sorry. I'm babbling. Kent told me you were staying with Linc, so I thought I'd do the neighborly thing and bring you some shepherd's pie." She crouched down and picked up the dish.

"Shepherd's pie?"

"Yes. Oh no, you do like it, don't you? You're not vegetarian? Oh no, you're vegetarian and I brought you meat. Shoot, I knew I should have gone for cookies. Everyone likes cookies."

"Actually, I'm not a vegetarian so shepherd's pie is great."

"So I did good?" Abby's face filled with relief.

"Would you like to come in?" It felt a bit awkward to invite someone else into Linc's house but she couldn't leave her standing out there after she'd brought over food.

"Oh yes. I can't stay long, though. I just told Kent I was going to bring this down and come straight home. He's in a meeting so I have a few minutes to spare. But if my butt isn't home and lying down within the next forty minutes, I'm in trouble."

Abby followed Marisol through the house into the kitchen. She set the casserole dish on the counter with a sigh.

"Trouble?" Marisol questioned worriedly.

"Yes. Kent's very protective. All the men on the ranch are. He thinks I exhausted myself helping with the wedding and now I'm supposed to take afternoon naps until my energy is back. He's worried about me."

"Oh. That's actually quite sweet."

"Isn't it?" Abby said with a sigh. "I mean, sometimes his over-protectiveness will make you want to slap him with a wet sock in the face while he's sleeping, but mostly it just makes me all gooey inside."

Marisol grinned. She got it.

"Of course, you'll find that out for yourself now that you're living with Linc. He's just as bad as the rest of them." Abby gave her an interested look.

Marisol found herself blushing. "It's not like that. I'm staying here because Linc is protecting me. There's this asshole who thinks I'm his. We're not sure whether he's going to try and find me."

"Oh, Marisol." Abby came forward and to her shock, took Marisol's hand in hers. "I'm so sorry you're going through that."

Her too. It kept coming back to her during the day, catching her by surprise, the memory of his threatening her, strangling her had threatened to make her panic. She'd reached for the phone so many times to call Linc then pulled back.

He was working. She shouldn't bother him.

That was part of the reason she'd taken to cleaning the house as well, to keep her mind busy.

"I'm glad you're here then. Kent didn't have time to tell me much of what was going on. He just said that you were here, and that I wasn't to say anything to anyone off the ranch. Which I wouldn't. Kent and his guys are the best in the business. And I know Linc will take good care of you."

"He already is."

Abby looked around, obviously spotting the mop. "You've been cleaning? Was it a mess in here? Do you need a hand with anything?"

"Oh no. It was actually rather tidy. I just thought I'd make myself useful and clean. Linc wanted me to rest, but I can't sit around all day."

"Uh-oh."

"Uh-oh, what?"

"Well, these guys can be rather alpha. They like to be in control. If he said to rest then that's what he expects you to do. Just like I'm supposed to be in bed right now. I best go. But Marisol, I'm glad you're here and that Linc's keeping you safe. If you need anything, call me. Bye!"

She watched with a smile as Abby left as quickly as she arrived. Coming here might have been the best thing to ever happen to her.

17

Exhaustion filled him as he pulled up outside his cabin later that night.

He'd worked hard today in order to get enough work done so he could take tomorrow off to spend with Marisol. He hadn't liked leaving her on her own today. He called her a few times on the house phone.

They had a few things they needed to deal with. Her lack of clothing. Her health. He wanted to take her to see Doc. He was prepared to help get her whatever she required to make it easier to manage her diabetes.

Thankfully, he'd managed to get some things for her today. Climbing from his truck, he reached into the back and dragged out the few bags he had stashed in there.

Linc thought he was starting to understand Marisol better. She'd never had someone she could rely on for any length of time. Her aunt might have been around, but she was verbally abusive. Neglectful. Marisol had been moved from place to place. Being somewhat introverted, that must have been so hard for her. The one person she'd formed an attachment to, she'd been made to leave and had never seen or heard from again. It was no wonder she didn't trust that he'd stick around. Or that he'd want her to stay with him.

But he was prepared to do whatever was necessary in order to make her feel more secure. She'd spent most of her life tiptoeing around her aunt, that she'd never had a chance to be a child. To be carefree.

He wondered how she would feel if he offered her a way to just be, without all the stress, the fear. To have him take all that on so she could damn well relax.

To him, that was the ultimate. For her to trust him enough to give him complete control.

Walking inside, the smell of food hit him, making his stomach rumble. He frowned. Hadn't she said she couldn't cook? He'd been intending to make something quick for dinner. He hoped that she hadn't been working hard all afternoon when he'd wanted her to rest.

Strolling into the kitchen, he saw her crouched in front of the oven, peering into the window.

"Mari girl? Everything okay?"

She let out a screech and fell on her bottom.

"Oh, baby. Are you okay?" He dropped the bags in his hands and leapt forward, helping her stand. Tears had filled her eyes and he felt like a complete ass.

"Jesus, I deserve my butt whipped for that. I thought you would have heard me come in the door. I didn't mean to frighten you. Is your bottom sore?"

Holding her to his chest with one arm around her lower back, he rubbed her bottom gently, hearing her moan. She sagged against him and her moans turned to whimpers. Noises that were filled with need.

Liked that, did she?

He filed that away for further thought later.

"I'm so sorry, teeny. Are you all right?"

She sniffled. "Oh yes. I'm fine. Sorry, I just got a fright."

"Understandable. Is your bottom all right?"

"What? Hmm. Oh yes. Yes, I guess so."

Was that a note of disappointment in her voice? Did she want him to keep touching her?

"What were you doing? Did you make dinner? I thought you couldn't cook?"

"I was watching the oven. I didn't. And I can't."

He drew back to peer down at her quizzically. She blushed slightly. "Abby dropped by with a shepherd's pie. She said just to heat it up in the oven. But I wasn't sure what temperature to put it on or how long it should be in there for. And I couldn't Google it because I don't have my phone."

Oh crap. That reminded him of the bags he'd dropped as he'd rushed to get to her. He'd check them soon. If the phone was broken then it was broken.

"You didn't ask Abby?"

She looked down. "I didn't want her to think I was an idiot."

"Hey." He grabbed her chin, tilting her face up. "Nobody would think you are an idiot, least of all Abby. She's one of the sweetest people I know."

"I know. I just feel stupid for not knowing something so simple."

"If you've never had to do it and haven't had anyone to teach you then how are you supposed to know?" he said simply. "Ellie can't cook to save her life, but nobody thinks anything less of her. Now, that's the last time I want to hear you refer to yourself as an idiot, understand me?"

"Yes, sir."

Oh, he liked the sound of that. But he'd like to hear her call him Daddy more.

"Good girl. Now, I'll figure out what's going on with the shepherd's pie. Have you had your insulin?"

"No."

"Why don't you go get your bag?"

"Okay." She disappeared and he glanced around. Were the floors shinier than they had been?

He drew out the shepherd's pie and checked it. Bit crispy on top but otherwise it was fine. He'd let it rest for a few moments.

When Marisol returned, he grabbed her hand and drew her towards him.

"I spoke to Ed today," he told her gently.

She tensed up. "What did he say? Did he see Tiger? What happened?"

"By the time he got to your aunt's place last night, most of the Devil's Sinners were gone. However, he had a chat with your aunt and Saber. Told them he was looking for Tiger."

"Did he say why?" Fear thrummed through her.

"No, Mari-girl. But Saber told him that Tiger wasn't even in the state. That he was in Seattle. And that if his son was being accused of something, he'd like to know because he was certain his son had plenty of alibis."

"Oh God, Saber doesn't even know what he's done and already he's setting Tiger up with alibis."

Yeah. The fucking asshole.

"They wouldn't let Ed take a look around, so there is no way of knowing if he's there or not. Not unless you want to press charges."

"I . . . I . . . they'll all come after me."

He nodded. "That's my gut feeling too. I told Ed I didn't think you would change your mind. Hopefully, the bastard is gone."

But his gut said that even if he had, he'd be back. But Linc had no intentions of letting him harm Marisol.

"How long is he going to be a threat to me?" she whispered.

He drew her against his chest. "You're safe here, Mari-girl.

Nobody will get to you. All of Kent's guys are on high alert, and I've spoken to the ranch hands. Everyone knows not to mention your presence here. But they'll also be on alert for him. Kent said he'd send Zander to track him down if necessary."

"But even if we manage to find him, then what?"

"Well, I've never felt that Ed warning him would be enough. So maybe we send a warning of our own."

"No. These guys are dangerous. You can't." She shook her head.

He rubbed her back. But in the back of his mind, he kept that as a possibility. He wouldn't have her always worrying about this asshole. And if that meant sending a strong message to Tiger that Marisol wasn't his, well, that's what he'd do.

"Take your insulin then set the table for dinner. You need to eat."

She slipped out of his hold, but she still looked worried.

"Did you rest this afternoon?" he asked, trying to shift her mind off Tiger

"Um, yes," she said. But she couldn't look at him.

"Really? Because these floors look cleaner than they did this morning," he chided.

"I might have done a bit of cleaning," she admitted as she got her insulin ready then injected it into her tummy.

Then she started setting the table. She'd obviously acquainted herself with where things were in the kitchen.

He liked this. The two of them working together to make dinner. This felt right. It was all he'd ever wanted. Someone to share his life with.

He started to dish up two servings of the shepherd's pie. He'd have to remember to thank Abby for this.

As she walked over with the plates, she was setting down a beer for him and a glass of water for her. He placed the plates down on the table then leaned in and kissed the top of her head.

"Thanks, Mari-girl."

"I didn't do anything," she said with a small blush. "Abby made it."

"Thank you for your company then. It's nice having someone to come home to. Even someone who was naughty today."

Her mouth dropped open. "I'm not naughty."

"What did I tell you to do when I left this morning?"

She bit her lower lip as he took a bite of the shepherd's pie. Delicious. "Rest."

"And what did you do?" he asked sternly.

"I rested for most of the day," she protested. "It was just a bit of cleaning. I felt bad being lazy all day. It also kept my mind off other things."

"What happened with Tiger," he guessed.

"Yes. It kept sort of sneaking into my mind. If I kept busy there was less time for me to think."

"I shouldn't have left you alone today." He frowned.

"It's not up to you to babysit me."

"I don't consider it babysitting when you're my Little one. And it's not being lazy. It's called self-care. Well, actually, it's Linc-care. I wanted you to take it easy because you're exhausted. You had a bad scare last night and then you slept in a damn closet," which wouldn't happen again, "so you needed rest. Did you take a nap?"

She shook her head, looking a bit embarrassed. "No."

"Then it's early to bed for you, little girl." Without thinking, he reached over and tapped her nose with his finger.

Marisol froze, staring at him. "Are you . . . are you a Daddy Dom?"

HER STOMACH DROPPED as he froze. Damn it. Why had she just come out with it like that? Why hadn't she waited for him to tell her? Maybe he didn't want her to know?

But he was the one going on about booster seats and high-chairs. And the way he'd just spoken to her . . .

Maybe that's just the way he is, Marisol.

Now she felt ill. Like he was going to get insulted or tell her that was ridiculous.

"I am."

Linc was a Daddy Dom.

Holy. Shit.

"I thought they were a myth. Like sasquatch. Or unicorns," she muttered, staring at her food without really seeing it.

"You thought that Daddy Doms were a myth?" he asked in his deep voice.

"Um. Yeah, I guess. I mean, I've never met one."

"That you know of," he pointed out. "They don't make us carry around badges. Or T-shirts that say, I'm a Daddy Dom."

"It would be really helpful if they did," she muttered.

"And what about the other way around?" he questioned.

"What do you mean?"

"Should Littles have a way of being identified? What would you wear if you wanted me to know that you are a Little?"

"You think I'm a Little?"

"You trying to tell me that you're not?" he asked.

She licked her dry lips. "I don't know . . . I mean, how do you know?"

"What do you know about Daddy Doms and Littles?" he countered.

"I have no real-life experience. I only know what I've read in books."

"So you have read books with age play in them?"

"Umm. Yes." They were only her favorite sort of books to read.

"And how did they make you feel? When you first read them, what did you think?"

"I thought that it was all fiction. That it couldn't be real. But at the same time, I guess I hoped it was real because then that might mean that one day, I'd meet a Daddy Dom." She kept her gaze on her food, which she'd barely touched. It sounded silly when she said it out loud.

But then again, she had met Linc, hadn't she? So perhaps not such a foolish hope after all.

"I'm beginning to see that conversations while you're eating should be kept light," he said. Then he tapped her plate with his fork. "Eat up. Let's talk about this after."

She ate for a few minutes, everything she'd learned running through her head. Hadn't Abby hinted at this earlier this afternoon. And the way she'd talked about Kent . . .

"Is Abby a Little?" She glanced up at him.

Linc narrowed his gaze. Shoot. Had she messed up?

"Sorry," she said quickly. "Should I not ask those sorts of questions?"

"It's not that you shouldn't ask them. But it's not something we would talk about with people who don't live on the ranch. You've heard the rumors going around about the ranch from Mrs. Long."

Oh. About the men spanking women on the ranch and not letting them do anything without permission.

"Abby seems really happy here. Not like she's being held against her will or anything. Although she did say she was going to get in trouble if she didn't get home and rest. Does that mean Kent would spank her?"

He'd just taken a sip of beer and he started to choke.

"Are you okay?" She jumped off her chair and rushed into the kitchen to pour him a glass of water. She handed him the glass, lightly patting his back as he sipped it. He placed it down then pushed his chair back. To her shock, he grabbed hold of her, bringing her onto his lap.

"Right. You need to eat. Or it won't be Abby who has a red bottom."

Her mouth dropped open at his words. "You'd spank me?"

He forked up some shepherd's pie, feeding her. He didn't answer until she ate it.

"First, answer a few questions for me. Are you a Little, Marisol?"

He'd answered her question. She couldn't do any less, right? "I think so. But I've never had a Daddy. I don't really know how it all works in real life. Or what I'll like or dislike. Reading about something doesn't mean I want to do it."

He fed her again. "I get that. What do you like to read about?"

"I guess I've always loved books with protective men. It didn't have to be a love interest. Books where the older brother or a friend took charge or protected the heroine has always been my thing. When I was fifteen, my aunt was reading this really sexy book. I remember being surprised because she didn't read much."

She looked away with a blush. "Turns out, she was using the book to get ideas for seducing husband number three or was it four? No, I think it was four. I'm not sure that number three could still, umm, get an erection."

By now her face was flaming red, but he was listening attentively.

"Anyway, when she was done with the book, I decided to read it. She didn't care. It had a lot of sex in it. Elements of power exchange. And spanking." She looked down at the table. "I've kind of had an obsession with alpha heroes and spankings and punishments since."

Marisol snuck a glimpse at him to see how he was taking this. But he didn't say anything. His face didn't change. "Then a few years ago, I found age play books. It finally clicked with me. I loved the more nurturing side of the power exchange. And I also identified with the submissive. The Little."

She ate another mouthful. "I didn't have much of a childhood. There were no stable, long-term influences in my life. I can't remember my mom. My dad left before I was born. There are times when I feel like I have always been an adult."

She pinched the top of her nose.

"Headache?" he asked.

"A little bit."

"You need rehydrating." Placing the fork down, he reached across the table and grabbed her glass of water. But instead of handing it to her, he held the glass to her lips.

It was the sort of thing that she thought she shouldn't like, but did. Him taking care of her in small ways. After she'd drunk her full, he drew the glass away and set it down.

"We need to watch that you're drinking enough," he muttered almost to himself. "Do you need some painkillers?"

"No. I think I'm just a bit tense." She glanced away, thinking. "I don't remember a time where I didn't have something to worry about. Where I could be carefree. Where I could give over decisions and worries, even if just for a short time, to someone else. The idea of watching cartoons while eating cookies and crafting, it seems bizarre to some, I'm sure. To me it sounds like heaven. Having someone that I could actually rely on, who I could trust. Who would care about me, my best interests. I've never had that. Not for any length of time, since Harry."

"What about giving someone else control? Having rules to follow? Consequences if you don't? Do you want that as well?" he asked.

"I think so," she whispered. "It's not just that I've never been in an age play relationship. I've never been in any sort of relationship. I'm not good with people. I'll probably mess it up."

"Nobody said that," he told her sternly. "Did your aunt have rules for you?"

"I'm to work for her. I'm to keep the house tidy. And I'm not supposed to take the car without permission. As a child, I just had to stay quiet and out of her way. Not complain."

He fed her until she couldn't eat any more. Then he started eating his own food. "What happened if you broke the rules?"

"When I was younger, she'd usually lock me in my room. Often without food. This was before I was diagnosed with diabetes. Although once, after I was diagnosed, she forgot and locked me up. My blood sugar got so low I nearly went into a diabetic coma. I nearly died."

"How old were you?" he asked in an oddly calm voice.

"Fourteen. After that, she punished me in other ways."

"Like what?"

She chewed at her bottom lip, worriedly. "I don't know if I should tell you."

While he sounded and looked calm, she could see a tic going by his right eye. He wasn't as calm as he was attempting to pretend to be.

"Oh, that means you should very much tell me."

"She'd get mad. Stop giving me money for my books."

"That's not all of it, though, is it?"

"No," she said quietly.

"What did she do when she was upset with you, Mari-girl?"

"She'd yell. Call me names."

"That all?"

She shook her head. She really didn't think she should tell him.

"What else, teeny?" he pressed.

"She'd slap me sometimes," she whispered.

He went still. She'd kind of expected for him to get angry. Lose his temper. But he'd almost turned to stone under her lap.

Finally, he let out a breath, closing his eyes as he pressed his lips together.

"Are you okay?" she asked.

"Okay?" he repeated. "No, pretty sure I'm not okay. You were given into your aunt's care. By what you've said, she's been neglectful as well as emotionally and physically abusive."

"She's never really hit me," she protested.

He opened his eyes and stared at her incredulously. "What do you call slapping you?"

Damn it. It didn't matter how she tried to deny it, he was right.

"She basically told you to give Tiger whatever he wanted."

"I know," she whispered. "I guess it's just hard to know that the one person you have left, your only family, cares nothing about you. I think that's part of the reason I stuck around. I told myself it was because of my diabetes and not wanting to be without insurance. But I also think it's because she's all I have. What would I do if I left? Where would I go? I have no money. I have no one. I don't know how to make friends. I don't have family. I was scared."

"Oh, baby." His face softened.

He wrapped his arms around her, holding her securely. "You're not alone anymore, little one. You don't have to put up with that bitch anymore. I'm here. If you want me, I'll be here for you as your man and your Daddy. Do you think that's something you might want? Are you interested in more than friendship with me?"

18

L inc held his breath as he waited for her reply.

He didn't know what he would do if she said she wasn't interested in taking things further. He'd still protect her, but it would be hell to come home to her every night and not touch her, kiss her, hug her.

But it needed to be her choice.

"I do want more. I've wanted it since you first mentioned being interested in me. I couldn't believe that you would want me. Boring, mousy Marisol."

"I'm going to stop you right there," he said sternly even as relief flooded him. She wanted him too. "You are not ever to call yourself boring or mousy again. Or an idiot. I won't have that. Understand? That's a very firm rule."

"We're talking about rules already?"

"Yep. This is important. I want you to see yourself how I see you. Gorgeous. Kind. Funny."

She stared up at him in amazement. "Really?"

"It kills me that you don't know your own self-worth. That you don't see that you're a freaking queen and that's how you should be treated." He leaned in and brushed his lips against her ear. "Unless you're being a naughty little princess. Then you'll receive a different sort of treatment. Have you thought about being turned over my knee?"

A shudder worked through her. Oh, he was going to take that as a yes. Still, she had to tell him herself.

"Do I have to answer?"

"Yes," he said firmly. "And remember how I feel about being lied to."

She squirmed on his lap.

"Marisol," he warned. He wasn't letting her get away without answering. He had to know.

"I don't like when you call me by my name."

"What?" he asked, confused. What did she mean?

"Usually you call me Mari or Mari-girl or teeny. When you call me Marisol it's usually because you're upset or annoyed."

Really? Huh. He hadn't actually realized that, but she could be right.

"Tell me, Mari-girl."

"Yes," she blurted out.

"Good girl. That wasn't so hard, was it?"

"For you, maybe," she muttered.

Oh, one part of him definitely got hard thinking about turning her over his knee and spanking that naughty bottom.

"Have you imagined me doing anything else to you?" he asked in a husky voice. "Me kissing you?"

"Yes," she said breathily as he placed one hand on her upper thigh.

"Me too. Every night since we went on our picnic, I've gotten myself off while thinking of you. Have you done the same?"

"What?" She went rigid.

Maybe he was pushing too far too fast. But he wanted her to know how much he desired her. Despite the fact that he was exhausted at the end of the day, he'd still get hard thinking about her in the shower and he'd jerk himself off thinking about her.

He drew a pattern on her thigh with his finger, moving closer and closer to her pussy. She widened her thighs without him saying anything. He heard her breath hitch.

"I wonder if I slipped my finger under your panties and ran it along your lips whether I'd find them slick with arousal? Would I, Mari-girl? Are you turned on? Do you need to come?"

"Linc," she groaned.

Gently, he cupped her pussy. "Don't ever doubt how much I want you. I can think of nothing else but you. My concentration has been shot. Whenever I'd call you and hear your voice, I would go instantly hard. I haven't fucking played with myself this much since I was a teenager."

"Linc!" She let out a startled giggle.

He grinned. That had been his intention. To make her smile. To hear that cheeky laugh. To break some of the tension. Leaning down, he pressed a kiss to her neck.

"I want you, Mari-girl. I hope you want me too."

"I do."

"Thank fuck." He kissed her, his lips soft but then the kiss grew harder, his tongue slipping between her lips. She whimpered as he drew back, staring down at her.

He cupped the side of her face with his hand. "I'm taking tomorrow off. I'll be on call if anyone needs me. But I want to spend some time with you. We can talk about your rules. Your expectations and mine. I want you to think about what you might want or need from me. It isn't just about play or discipline. I can help you in other ways. If there's something you're struggling with or worried about. For tonight, I want us just to get comfortable with each other. We'll bundle up on the sofa and watch some television before bed. But I do want you in my bed."

He felt her tense and knew what she was thinking.

"Not for sex. Although I want that almost more than I can tell you. But because I need to hold you in my arms. I want to make sure you can sleep without having to get into the closet. All right?"

She bit her lip, looking worried.

"What is it?" he asked, rubbing his thumb along her lower lip. "You can tell me anything, teeny. If you've got cramps, if you feel ill or unsure or horny. Anything at all, but especially that last one."

He winked and she laughed.

"I sleep with Princess Nana and my snuggly," she blurted out.

"Princess Nana? Your doll? That's an interesting name."

"I had an obsession with bananas when I was a kid."

"You saw her?"

"This morning, you had your thumb in your mouth and you were holding onto Princess Nana and your blanket."

"Oh God," she groaned.

"You looked so cute. Sleeping with your blanket and toy isn't a problem, Mari-girl. Although I am going to have one rule about sleep time."

"What's that?"

He moved his finger to her thigh, drawing more patterns. Her breath left her in a whoosh.

"This morning, all you were wearing was my T-shirt. And you were on your tummy, with one leg bent and up. The T-shirt wasn't covering you properly, so I got a good view at the curves of that delicious bottom. And also, that nice, plump pussy."

"Oh my God, Linc!" She whacked his chest, trying to move off his lap.

Nope, he wasn't having that. "Do not move. You're not to get off Daddy's lap without his permission."

Now she gaped up at him. "I thought . . . I thought we weren't doing anything tonight . . ."

"We aren't. But you're being naughty and I think you need to know some rules now. If you're on Daddy's lap, there's no getting off unless he gives permission. And I don't care where we are or who is around. Understand?"

"I understand."

"I understand, Daddy," he told her firmly.

"I understand, Daddy," she repeated.

"Good girl."

A small smile lit up her face. That was better.

"If Daddy takes hold of your hand you must not let go until he gives permission, understand?"

"Yes, Daddy."

"Now, the rule for sleep time is this. You are not allowed any panties unless you're ill or it's that time of the month. You can wear lingerie or one of my T-shirts. Some cute pjs if you're Little. But no panties. Understand?"

"Yes."

"What do you call me?"

"Yes, Daddy."

"Very good, Mari-girl. You never did answer me earlier. Did you make yourself come while thinking about me?"

She squirmed on his lap. "Yes, Daddy."

"Yes, Daddy what?"

He heard her breath hitch. Oh, he would bet she was soaking through those pretty panties right now.

"Yes, Daddy, I made myself come thinking about you."

"How did you do it?"

"What . . . what do you mean?"

"I mean did you use your fingers on your clit? Maybe twist your nipple? Were you in bed on your back? Or in the shower? Bath? Or did you use a vibrator? Another toy?"

"I don't . . . I don't have any toys."

"We'll remedy that."

He loved the way she looked so shocked. Maybe she didn't expect him to speak openly about sex. Or perhaps she didn't expect he would insist she take part in the conversation. He wasn't sure.

But he did have to remember not to push too hard and risk her running from him.

After kissing her forehead, he set her back on her chair.

He got up and grabbed their plates carrying them to the dishwasher. "See those bags over there." He nodded to the bags he'd dropped earlier. "There's some new underwear and clothes for you in there. As well as a new phone."

"You bought me clothes and a phone?" She got up and moved to the bags, looking inside them.

"And panties." He grinned. "Not that I really think you need to wear them. Bear and Ellie went into Russell today, so I asked them to get you some things. Think I got the sizes right. They didn't get a jacket or boots because I thought you might want to pick those, plus I wasn't sure I'd get your shoe size right."

"You didn't have to buy me anything. Let me get you some money to pay you back."

"You will not," he said firmly.

"But you shouldn't have spent your money on me."

"Why not?" He turned and leaned against the counter.

She looked confused at the question. "Well, because, you shouldn't have to support me."

"What if I want to?"

"But ... but ..."

"You can't work at the moment, Mari-girl. Your aunt hasn't even been paying you properly. I have plenty of money. Not like my expenses here are high. I could buy you a thousand pairs of panties and not blink. If it makes me happy to buy you things, to provide for you, then are you really going to say that I can't?"

"No," she said quietly. "I guess I'm not. This is just weird for me. I can't remember the last time someone bought anything for me."

"Well, let me remind you of what to say." He walked over and grabbed her hand in his. "The proper thing to say is 'thank you, Daddy—'"

"Thank you, Daddy."

"I hadn't finished," he told her.

She stared up at him with wide eyes.

"You say, 'thank you, Daddy. You're the most handsome, sexy, smart Daddy in the whole entire world'."

Marisol laughed. And his heart lightened.

This was exactly what he'd always dreamed of having.

19

M arisol sat on the sofa as Linc grabbed the remote and sat down on his big recliner. She expected him to put on some sort of sports game that she wouldn't understand. But she wouldn't say anything. This was his house. He'd worked hard all day.

She wished he'd let her help clean up, but he'd insisted that Little girls didn't do jobs like wash dishes. He had let her clear the table. She'd tried to point out that she wasn't in Little space at the moment, but he'd just given her a stern look that told her she'd best be quiet and do what she was told.

The more commanding and bossy he got, the more aroused she seemed to become. As she sat on the sofa, she was all too aware of her wet panties. She pressed her thighs together.

To her surprise, he settled on a romantic-comedy. "Come here. You're too far away."

"I thought I might go take a shower." And deal with the need still flooding her.

"After." He patted his lap.

"Umm. Okay." She stood.

"Grab that blanket, would you?" He pointed to the blanket on the end of the sofa. She picked it up and walked over to him. Linc kept the house toasty warm so the blanket wasn't necessary for warmth.

She moved next to his chair. He took the blanket from her.

"Would you like to get more comfortable before you sit down?" he asked her.

"Comfortable?"

"I know women often like to take off their bra at night. Thought you might like to do that first."

"Oh, umm." She would love to take off her bra. It was pretty much the best feeling in the world. Nearly as good as an orgasm.

Sometimes better.

"You can take off your pants as well."

Her mouth dropped open and he grinned up at her.

"I think my pants are just fine on," she said primly. "But I'll just go take off my bra—"

"No need to go anywhere." He placed his hands over his eyes. "I promise not to peek."

Oh, she just bet.

Nobody ever died because they needed an orgasm, Marisol.

No. It just felt like it sometimes.

"Uh-huh, I believe that."

"Why, teeny, are you calling Daddy a liar?" His voice was a soft croon that had made her shiver with pleasure.

"Of course not, Daddy," she managed to squeak out.

"I thought not. That would be very naughty."

Oh shoot. Her pussy clenched at hearing him call her naughty.

She turned around and managed to wrangle her bra off without having to take off her sweater or T-shirt. It was only after she had it off that she thought about the fact that she was going to be braless around him.

This was not going to help her arousal issue. She turned back around to see he was indeed peeking between his fingers at her.

"Daddy!"

"What? I have to keep an eye on my Little one. Means you get into far less trouble. Hand me the bra."

"Why?"

He raised his eyebrows as though to tell her that he didn't need a reason. With a reluctant sigh, she handed it over and he tucked it down the side of the recliner.

"Come here."

She walked over, wondering how she was going to fit on there with him. Reaching out, he picked her up and plonked her down on his lap. She was resting with her back against his front, her head on his shoulder.

Then he arranged the blanket over them.

"Comfy?" he asked in her ear.

No. Not at all. How did he expect her to be comfortable when he surrounded her? His scent teased her. He smelled like the fresh outdoors with a hint of smoke from when he'd lit the fire.

Earthy. Outdoorsy. His strong arm was wrapped around her middle, just under her breasts. She shifted slightly, trying to get more comfortable. Trying to put some space between them. Her erect nipples brushed against her T-shirt.

That was a bad, bad idea.

"Stay still, Mari-girl. Moving around isn't a good idea."

"Sorry," she said. But she didn't last long until he was moving around again. Especially when he shifted his arm, and brushed it against her hard nipples.

"Linc," she groaned.

"What do you call me," he growled.

"Daddy."

"What's wrong? You're all squirmy."

"N-nothing."

He slid his hand lower, close to the top of her pussy.

"You sure about that? You wouldn't be lying to me, would you, Mari-girl? Because lying means you get an immediate punishment."

"Punishment?"

"Yep, I'd have to have you strip off your pants then lie over my lap. Then I'd lower your panties and smack your little bottom until it was rosy red."

"Oh God," she groaned. Was he trying to kill her?

"Does that turn you on, Mari-girl?"

She was already turned on. Hearing him talk to her that way just made it worse.

"Is that what the heroes in your books would do? Would they spank the heroine for lying?"

"Y-yes," she replied.

"Is that what you want? To feel my hand smack against your bottom?"

"I . . . I . . ."

"Or do you want something else?" he murmured to her. She closed her eyes as his finger reached lower, just pressing against her clit. He just left it there, not moving. She made a frustrated noise, trying to thrust up against his finger.

"Uh-uh. No trying to get your own pleasure." He kissed her cheek. "Weren't we supposed to be just watching a movie and relaxing? Seems my naughty girl has other ideas. Tell me, why did you really want to go have a shower? Were you going to play with yourself? Make yourself come?"

There was no way she was telling him. Nuh-uh.

"You don't have to tell me, of course. But if you don't, then I won't know there's a problem that needs taking care of, will I? We'll just have to sit here, with you wriggling around on my lap because you won't tell Daddy what you need. Like today, when you didn't tell Daddy that you were struggling. That was very naughty."

"I can't say the words!"

"No? Why not?"

"I'm a virgin," she blurted it out. A twenty-three-year-old virgin. That had to be an odd thing in this day and age, right?

"I figured you were," he said very matter-of-factly.

She slumped against him. "You did?"

"Yep. We don't have to do anything you don't want to. If I take things too far, if I push too hard, you can say your safeword and I'll stop. No matter what."

"A safeword? Like for BDSM play?"

"Uh-huh. But this safeword can be used at any time. We'll stop whatever is going on and talk. Okay?"

All right. That actually made her feel much better. She slumped back against him. "Yes, Sir."

"Good girl. You know I'm an old-fashioned guy. I'm not into casual sex. I've had other partners, yes. But only those I've been in a relationship with."

She did not want to hear about his other sexual partners.

"And I haven't felt for them a fraction of what I feel for you."

Thank God. Warmth flooded her.

"I'm not going to fully take you until you're absolutely sure you're mine. Because that would be the last part of me claiming you. Fully. Right now, this is all new to you. You're inexperienced when it comes to sex, to men, to being a Little. My Little. And I need you to be sure, because it would break me if I gave you everything and you left."

"I don't want to break you," she whispered.

"And I don't want to break you either. So we'll play, we'll get to know each other. And then when I'm sure you're in this for good, I'll claim all of you. Now, would you like me to help you relax? Or do you just want to sit and watch the movie? Just know that while

I'm giving you this choice tonight, you won't often have it. Sometimes, I'll order you to sit on my lap and spread your legs so I can play with your clit. Other times, I might have you kneel between my legs and suck my cock. Would you like that, Mari-girl?"

God, would she ever. She squirmed again, pressing her thighs together as her clit throbbed. It seemed like he knew exactly what to say to her to push her arousal higher.

"Yes, Daddy."

"You know what, baby? I think you were made for me. My perfect little angel sent from heaven. Dirty and hot. Sweet and playful. Hmm? Don't you think?"

"Yes, Daddy," she cried out and he moved his finger against her clit.

Oh thank God. That felt so good. Yet it still wasn't enough. Because she wanted to feel his finger against the tight nub. Wanted to feel it rubbing back and forth along her slick lips.

She couldn't believe she was doing this. She'd gone from zero to a hundred. From having no one other than the characters in her stories, to having a gorgeous, sexy, dirty-talking cowboy. One who wasn't afraid to act silly to make her laugh, but could switch on his rough, dominant voice and turn her into a pile of goo in two seconds flat.

It was insane. Maybe she should take a moment to breathe. To think. But then, where had thinking gotten her? She'd spent her life overthinking.

This was the time to live. If he ever left her—and that worry was still at the back of her mind despite his reassurances that he wouldn't—at least she'd have these memories.

"Tell me, Mari-girl. What would you like me to do? Do you want me to help you relax? Or remove my finger and behave myself? I should warn you, though. I've never been good at behaving myself."

"I can tell," she said dryly.

"You're not very good at that either. Too bad for you, when you misbehave, you end up with a red bottom."

She whimpered. Those words, they just did something to her. She'd had an obsession with spanking for so long. The more she read, the more she desired that sort of relationship. And now to have found someone who would be willing to discipline her when needed. To fuck her like she desired. And to treat her like a treasured little princess. Or a queen.

Damn. It was like a fairytale come to life.

"Mari-girl?"

"I want you to help me relax," she burst out.

"Good girl for telling me what you need. I want you to know that you can always come to me with what you need. I might not always grant it, although I am a rather indulgent Daddy, so barring anything that might endanger you, I'm thinking there is little I would deny you."

Oh boy.

"I feel especially indulgent when my good little girl does exactly as I tell her to. Do you understand?"

"Yes, Daddy."

"I want you to stand up and take your pants and your sweater off. You can leave your T-shirt and panties on."

Thank goodness for that.

"I know you're probably still feeling quite shy and I'm not going to push you to show me all of you. Yet. Be warned though, that will come."

He helped her stand, holding onto her hand until she was steady. With hands that shook from anticipation and arousal, she pulled off her sweater. Then she reached for the button of her pants.

"Slowly," he told her. "That's it. Good girl. Let them drop. Okay, now turn around and bend over to pick them up. Show me that delicious ass of yours. Baby, that is a beautiful sight."

Marisol could feel herself blushing at the heat in his voice. But she could hear how turned on he was. Aroused by her. It filled her with a confidence she'd very rarely felt and she bent to grab her pants, folding them and placing them with her sweater on the couch.

"Come here, Mari-girl." He held out his hand and helped her sit back in the same position, with her back to his front.

She was grateful for this position, she wasn't sure she could look at him while he . . . while he touched her.

Holy. Shit.

Lincoln Johnson. The gorgeous, funny foreman of Sanctuary Ranch was going to touch her. Was this really happening? She was afraid to pinch herself and wake up.

"Spread your legs apart and put them on either side of mine."

She widened, feeling her heart beat race. Crap she hoped she didn't pass out from excitement. That would be embarrassing.

"What's your safeword going to be?"

Did she really need one? Nerves flooded her. Maybe this wasn't such a good idea. He arranged the blanket over her again, making her feel more secure. He seemed to be so in-tune with her. As though he knew when something pushed the boundary of what she was comfortable with. Pushing her, but not too much.

"Mari-girl? You can use red if you like. Easy to remember."

"Yes . . . I . . . red is good," she managed to get out.

"Good. Remember, you can use it at any time. If you're scared, worried, unhappy or feel ill. Okay?"

"Yes, Sir."

"Unless I say otherwise, you're to keep your legs exactly where they are. Your hands are to remain at your sides. And your eyes are to stay on the movie. Understand me?"

"Yes."

"What do you call me?"

She blushed. "Yes, Daddy."

She gasped as he cupped her right breast. His other hand moved lower, his finger running along her slick lips, still covered by her red panties.

He rolled her nipple between his finger and thumb. "My, these panties are very soaked, aren't they? You should have told me. I'd have had you remove them. They must be so uncomfortable. Are you uncomfortable?"

She groaned at his words. Who knew he'd like to talk during sex? Then again, he didn't seem afraid to talk about anything so why wouldn't he talk to her like this?

"Mari-girl?" He paused and she knew he wasn't going to continue until she answered him.

"Yes, I'm uncomfortable," she told him.

"Well, we can't have that. Take them off. You can keep the blanket over you."

Without a word, she slipped her panties down over her hips and managed to get them completely off without revealing anything.

Oh hell. There was something much more wicked about lying on top of him with her bottom half bare.

"Now, isn't that better?"

"Yes."

"And it means I have better access to all of my girl. Now, keep watching the movie, while I have a play. I need to see what you like and don't like."

He ran his finger up and down her slick lips. "So turned on. Do you like me talking to you? Telling you what to do?"

"Yes," she groaned as he circled her clit. He suddenly gave her pussy a sharp slap that had her crying out.

"What a plump, swollen clit you have. It needs to be touched, doesn't it? When you touched yourself would you circle it like this?" His actions followed his words as he circled her clit slowly.

"Or would you flick it like this." She groaned as he flicked the needy nub.

"Like that," she told him, barely able to keep her gaze ahead. She had no idea what was going on in the movie, her attention was totally on what he was doing to her pussy. What his fingers were doing to her nipple.

"I can tell you like that. And what about these nipples? Would you play with them?" He brought both hands up to her breasts. He toyed with her hard nipples through her T-shirt. Plucking at her nipples.

She took in a sharp breath as he tugged at them far harder than she'd ever dared to. But the slight pain sent an answering shot of arousal through her blood, down to her clit which throbbed in reaction.

"Oh. Ohhh."

"You do like that, don't you? What about this?" He lightly flicked them with his fingers and her breathing grew harsher, faster.

"Please. Please."

She tried to put her legs together, but he grabbed hold of her thighs.

"Naughty girl, were you given permission to close your legs?"

"No."

"That's going to earn you some punishment isn't it?" He gave the inside of her thighs two hard smacks each. Smacks that had her crying out in shock at the pain. And the pleasure.

"Now keep your legs there. I say when you get to move." He kissed the shell of her ear. "Just like I get to say when you come. Just so you know, there is no coming without my permission. If I ever discover that you've disobeyed me, I'm going to tie you to my bed and bring you to the point of orgasm again and again without letting you come. Then the next day, you'll wear a clit tickler. Only

I'll have the remote so I decide when you come and when you don't. Understand?"

"Yes, Sir." The sir slipped out, but he didn't correct her.

"Good girl. But for tonight, you can come as often as you want."

"I'll only come once."

"Sorry?"

She squirmed, feeling embarrassed. "I've never been able to come more than once in one session. I can't."

"Oh, baby. Don't you know better than to throw down a challenge like that when I'm trying to be good?" he crooned.

This was him trying to be good?

Wait. What did he mean by a challenge? That wasn't a challenge.

"Now, I'm always going to make sure that you come several times."

She shook her head. No way.

"Yes." He reached up and grabbed her chin, turning her face around so he could kiss her. The angle was a bit awkward, but that didn't stop her body from turning to goo.

"Back to watching the movie." He moved both hands down to her pussy. "Place your legs over the arms of the recliner."

She moved them so she was spread obscenely wide. Who knew this was where her day was going to end up when she'd woken up this morning?

Not her.

"Tell me," he asked as he flicked at her clit while circling her entrance. "Have you ever played with your bottom hole while you made yourself come?"

Oh God.

"O-once."

"Only once." The finger at her clit began to move faster. She was growing closer and closer to that peak. "Didn't you like it?"

"It was weird."

"Hmm, weird good or weird bad?"

"I . . . I don't know." One finger thrust very shallowly into her pussy, not pushing against the barrier of her hymen. Another finger joined that one, stretching her. "Good, but wrong at the same time."

"I get it. But if it brings pleasure and it doesn't hurt anyone, then how can it be bad?"

She'd often wondered if her desire to be Little was weird or wrong. She wasn't hurting anyone though. And even though she hadn't been convinced that people really lived like this, she knew she wasn't the only one who liked to read about it. CJ Bennett's books did well enough to prove that people enjoyed age play stories.

Now it seemed that people really did live like this. She wondered again if Abby was a Little. And what about the other women who lived on the ranch? Maybe he wasn't ready to tell her yet. It made sense that they would guard their privacy.

"You are so gorgeous. So sexy. So hot. My girl."

"Oh. Ohhh." It was enough to send her over the edge. She shuddered in his arms as he held her tight. He patted her clit gently, bringing her down slowly.

"That feel good?"

"Yes, Daddy." She slumped against him. Exhausted. Sated. She was going to sleep well tonight.

"Good. Then it's time for round two."

Oh hell.

M arisol laid her head back against Linc's chest.

Three. Three orgasms.

She'd never had three orgasms in a day. Never mind one after the other like that.

Linc turned her so her back was cradled by his right arm. His other hand lay possessively at the top of her thigh.

"How you feeling, Mari-girl?"

"Like I'll never walk again." Suddenly it was too much effort to even hold her head up. She let it flop against his chest, her eyes drifting halfway closed. She'd never felt so relaxed. It was like everything going on in her head, all the voices whispering doubts and fears, had closed up shop for the night.

"It's so peaceful," she whispered.

"What's that?" he asked quietly

"In my head. It's so quiet. It's never been so quiet. I'm always thinking about something. But right now, I feel like I could just drift off."

"Good. That's what I want for you. I want to be that safe place where you can just be you. Where you don't have to worry about what's going to happen. Or what you have to do or say. Because you can give that all to me. Just let it all go. Just be."

She let out a contented sigh, burying her face into his chest. "Thank you."

"No need to thank me. It was my pleasure. You'll find Little space like that too. Once you trust me enough to let go and fully show me your Little. No, don't tense up. Not saying you have to do that right now. We have time. You're not going anywhere."

Marisol let it sink in that she really didn't have to go anywhere. He wanted her here.

"Right now, though, it's time for my Little girl to go to bed. Especially since she didn't rest properly like Daddy told her to," he lightly scolded. He tilted her towards him and rubbed her bottom cheek lightly. A warning. "Tomorrow we'll discuss those rules."

She wiggled at the thought. He groaned, and she stilled as his hard cock pressed against her thigh. "Jesus, baby. Keep moving like that and I'm going to do something I haven't done since I was a teenager and come in my pants."

"Linc!"

"What?" He gave her a devilish grin. "It's just the truth. Playing with your sweet pussy, touching those luscious breasts, listening to those moans and whimpers as I pleasured you, I'm surprised I haven't come already."

He stood with her in his arms. Shit, he was strong. She tried to reach for the bottom of her T-shirt to pull it over her bare ass.

"Linc!"

"What do you call me?" he asked her.

"Daddy."

"That's right. In these walls, I'm Daddy. Or Sir if you're more comfortable calling me that while we're playing around." He wiggled his eyebrows at her, to let her know what kind of play he was talking about.

Like she hadn't gotten it already.

"Outside these walls, you can call me Linc. If that's what you want."

He strode towards his bedroom and set her down on his bed. She'd peeked in here earlier. It was neat as a pin. A king-sized bed with a wooden slat headboard. Plain, dark-blue cover. Two wooden nightstands and one dresser.

"There's two spare drawers in the dresser for you. Your side of the bed is the one closest to the wall." He pointed at her side of the bed. "It's safer for you."

Mr. Protective strikes again. It filled her with warmth. He was so caring.

"There's plenty of room in the closet, once we get you some more clothes."

"Okay," she said, her mind spinning.

He crouched down, his hands on her thighs. She had them pressed together to keep herself somewhat covered.

"I know this is a lot to take in. But I'm here to help, all right? Whatever you need, you only have to ask."

"All right," she whispered.

"Good girl. Do you want to shower on your own or do you want Daddy to bathe you?"

She swallowed hard. Her legs definitely felt like jelly. But she wasn't sure if she was ready for him to see her completely naked.

"I know I've pushed you a lot tonight, so I'm giving you the choice. But soon, I'm going to see all of you. There won't be a part of you that I haven't kissed, touched, studied."

Her breath hitched. Jesus. She couldn't be turned on again, could she? Her gaze went lower to the bulge in his jeans. "Do you want me to help you with that?"

Oh no. Did she just say that? What was she going to do? She knew nothing about cocks.

All right. That's not entirely true. You know what you've read in books. You could use that as an instructional manual, right?

She just needed to reread all those scenes with blow jobs. Damn, she wished she had her eReader. But maybe she could find some free books to download onto her new phone.

"Did I lose you, Mari-girl?"

"What? No! Sorry." She knew she was bright red.

He grinned. It was a wicked grin that made his eyes dance. She braced herself for what was about to come out of his mouth.

"Did you just offer to give me a blow job?"

"What? I-I-I . . . what?"

He waited patiently for her to finish stumbling over her words.

"I think so," she said lamely.

He threw back his head and laughed. "Well, when you know so, then you can give me one. What you can do is part your legs and let me have a small taste of your pussy before I go take care of this."

Her eyes widened. He wanted to taste her? Wait. He was going to take care of things himself?

Holy shit was her first thought.

Can I watch? was her second.

Jeez, Marisol. When did you become a voyeur?

Linc ran his hands up along the inside of her thighs, slowly parting them until she was completely on display for him. As soon as she realized what he'd done, she put her hand down to cover herself.

"Uh-uh, hands on your thighs and keep them there. This is my reward."

"Reward for what?" she asked, removing her hand and placing her palms on her thighs. God, it was hard. What did he think? Did he think she was pretty? Was she funny looking? Oh man, she wished he'd say something.

"Reward for not ordering you to strip off, lie back on the bed so I can have my way with you. It's taking a lot of restraint. You should let me have my reward."

"I don't know if I can . . . I'm so sensitive down there."

"Who said you were going to get to come? This is my reward. I want a taste. Naughty girl."

Her mouth opened then shut. Then he ginned at her and winked.

She growled at him. Actually growled. She was shocked at herself.

"Of course I did say you could come as often as you wanted to tonight. So I'm just gonna have my reward and whether you want to come or not is up to you. If it's sore or too sensitive, though, you tell me and I'll stop."

He started kissing his way up her thigh.

What if she smelled awful? She was still slick from the orgasms he'd given her. What if she didn't taste nice? How mortifying would that be?

"Red!" she called out before she could think about it. Immediately, he sat back on his heels, giving her a surprised look.

He withdrew his hands and she wanted to put them back on her legs, feeling bereft without his touch.

Mierda!

She'd made a mistake.

"Okay, I wasn't expecting that. I'm sorry. I pushed too much, didn't I? Of course you're too sensitive. What was I thinking?" He was frowning, berating himself and she couldn't stand it.

"I'm sorry!" she burst out.

He blinked, looking confused. "What are you sorry for, baby? I'm the one who pushed too hard. I should have backed off when you said you were sensitive. You're just so gorgeous, it's hard to keep my hands off you. Do you need some space? Maybe a warm cloth between your legs will help."

He made to stand and she lurched forward, wrapping her arms around his neck.

"Hey, what's this?" He patted her back. "It's okay. Shit, you're shaking. I deserve a whipping for upsetting you. Hey. Hey." He sat next to her, pulling her onto his lap and rocking her. "It's all right. Nothing happens that you don't want to happen. Did I scare you? Mari-girl, you have to talk to me!"

"I took away your reward," she wailed.

He tensed. "What? That's why you're upset? Baby . . ."

"I just, I've never had a man's mouth there . . . well, obviously I haven't. I've never done anything. What if you didn't like it? What if I taste weird? What if—"

He placed his hand over her mouth. "Gonna stop you right there, Mari-girl. You're worrying far too much about something you shouldn't. Like I told you, there's not a part of your body I won't know. I want all of you. You're the most gorgeous, sexy, sweetest person I've ever met."

She still didn't know how he could think that.

"All I have to do is think of you and I get hard. Parts of sex are messy and sometimes strange, but it's all about what we both enjoy. You're not going to know if you enjoy it until you try it. Try oral sex, don't like it, then maybe we put it on the back burner to try another day. Try a certain position, don't like it, same thing. Okay? There's no right or wrong. But just so you know, you smell delicious and you're going to taste even better. The only problem will be how badly I get addicted to the taste of you."

Oh dear Lord.

He leaned back to look into her face. "You good now?"

She nodded. "Sorry for overreacting. I panicked and then when you stopped touching me, I panicked some more."

He frowned with a nod. "You took me withdrawing touch as rejection or punishment?"

"Kind of."

"I pulled back because you said your safeword and I thought it was what you wanted. I won't do that again, all right?"

"All right."

"I think you've had enough for the night. You're exhausted. Do you want a snack before bed?"

She nodded. "Just a small one, maybe."

"I'll grab you something. Want me to run you a bath or you just want a shower?"

"I thought you wanted your reward?" she whispered quietly.

"There will be plenty of time for that. Right now, you need sleep more than anything else. Now, shower or bath?"

"Shower please."

"All right. Stand up and show me you're steady enough to shower on your own."

She stood, managing to get her legs to work.

"Good enough. You can eat your snack then take a short shower only. Don't put the water on too hot and leave the door open so I can hear you if anything happens."

"I've been showering on my own for a while now," she told him dryly.

He stood and kissed her lightly. "Not anymore. From now on, Daddy will take care of you. In all ways."

Gulp.

21

Marisol was nervous as she entered Linc's bedroom. He'd insisted she take one of his T-shirts to put on after her shower.

She immediately noticed all of the bags he'd had earlier sitting on the bed. She could hear his shower still going. She wished she was brave enough to take a peek at him. She wondered if he was touching himself.

Holy shit.

Instead, she forced herself to go over to the bed. Grabbing a bag, she drew out some panties. She bit her lip. They were all lacy but soft. The tags had all been pulled off so she didn't know how much he'd spent.

All lacy and in various shades of colors. There were even matching bras. Jeez, how had he gotten her size right? That was a skill right there. A few T-shirts, two pairs of yoga pants and a teal hoodie with the picture of a cat on the front.

It was seriously cute. And soft. She ran her fingers over it. Oh wow. She couldn't wait to wear this. She found the empty drawer and put everything away.

She grabbed the other bag, pulling out a brand-new iPhone. Yikes. These things cost a bomb. And then her heart stopped, a little gasp leaving her as she pulled out an eReader. He'd bought her an eReader?

"Is it the right kind?"

His voice startled her and she glanced over to see him walking in, dressed in just a pair of black, cotton pajama pants. Damn, He was ripped. Gorgeous. He'd taken a shower and the ends of his hair were still a bit wet. She couldn't help but drop her gaze to his crotch. Which was no longer thick and hard. Had he taken care of that in the shower?

Crap. Maybe she should have asked to watch.

Too late, she realized he was standing in front of her. And she'd just been caught staring at his crotch.

Whoops.

"Mari-girl? That the right kind? Bear said they didn't have a lot of choice. We can take it back if it's not." He touched the eReader in her hand.

"It's . . . it's perfect. You shouldn't—"

He placed a finger on her lips. "What did I tell you to say when I give you something?"

Oh. Right.

He removed his hand. "Thank you, Daddy. But still—"

"Nope." His hand went back over her mouth. "You just need to stop after thank you, Daddy. I don't want to hear how I shouldn't have. I wanted to do it. Besides, you're gonna be stuck here on the ranch for a bit and unfortunately, I can't take much time off to keep you entertained. This will help keep you from getting into trouble."

"I don't get into trouble." She pouted.

He snorted. "Right. Sure. Your life is safe and boring."

"It usually is! I'm never in trouble. I'm not interesting enough to get into trouble."

"Careful," he warned. "That sounds suspiciously like putting yourself down and you know how I feel about that."

She bit her lip worriedly. He ran his thumb over her bottom lip, freeing it. Then he shocked her by leaning down and running his tongue across it. "I don't want my baby getting bored. When she gets bored, she does naughty things like clean when she should be resting. So I've got to make sure she's got plenty to keep her entertained. Tomorrow we'll get you some more clothes and some toys and set you up a play area. That will help."

Play area. Toys.

Holy. Hell. Where did she start with all that?

It was like she'd entered some alternate reality. Where she was no longer a boring bookworm and she'd become someone to be treasured and desired.

She had to say, she liked it. A lot.

"Where are Princess Nana and your blanket?" he asked.

In the other room. Because she hadn't been certain that he'd really meant it when he said he didn't mind her sleeping with them.

"In my bedroom."

"This is your bedroom now. I want all of your stuff in here. Go get them. I'll grab you a bottle of water."

"Oh, you don't need to—"

"I want to. Go."

She practically scurried out of the room, grabbed snuggly, Princess Nana and her bag she used to carry around her diabetic supplies. She'd already checked her blood sugar levels so she hopped back into Linc's bed. The sheets were smooth and fresh. The bed was enormous. She felt tiny sitting in it.

He walked back in with two bottles of water, one of which he set on his nightstand. He undid the lid of the other one and handed it to her. She took just a few sips.

"Drink some more, Mari-girl. I'm not convinced you drink enough. I'll ask Doc about that."

She took a few more sips to appease him. But she thought she drank plenty of water.

"We're really going to see a doctor tomorrow?"

"The ranch doctor. Technically, he works for Kent. But he looks after everyone who lives on the ranch."

"Umm, what about insurance? My aunt is bound to take me off hers."

"That's all covered. If you need anything he can't give, you'll be under the ranch's insurance."

"Really?" But she didn't work here. She didn't contribute anything.

"Yep, I'll set it up tomorrow. Don't worry. If Clint was here, he would insist on it. Now, Doc can be a complete grouch, but you'll get used to him. He's softened up some since Caley came to live with him."

"She seemed really nice when I was doing her nails for Charlie's bridal shower."

"She is. She lives with Doc and his brother, Archer."

"Two men? Really?" Caley lived with two men? She'd thought Mrs. Long had that wrong.

"That a problem?"

"With me? No. It doesn't worry me. I mean, I've read plenty of menage and reverse harem books. I just didn't realize that happened in real life."

He narrowed his gaze. "You better not think of starting your own harem. Because I don't share. Ever."

Her eyes went wide. "I can't even handle one man. How would I handle more?"

"You wouldn't. Because I'd kill them and punish you. This is a big ranch. There's lots of places to hide a body."

She nearly laughed. Until she realized he was completely serious. Yikes. No harems. Got it. Like that was really a concern.

She was a twenty-three-year-old virgin for cripe's sake.

"Are there any other relationships like that on the ranch?"

"Menages? No. But every man on the ranch including those
who work for JSI were chosen because they have similar views on
how a relationship should be."

"And how is that?"

"That there should be a head of the household. Someone who
takes control. That all the women are protected by all the men.
Most of the men here are Daddy Doms."

She thought that through. It made sense with everything she'd
seen and after talking to Abby. "And many of the women are
Littles?"

"Yep." He watched her carefully. "Most of the women who live
in the ranch are Littles."

"Wow. That actually makes things a lot easier."

He gave her a surprised look. "It does?"

"Yeah. Knowing others have the same desires and needs. That
I won't be ridiculed or made fun of for my needs." She dropped
her gaze.

Reaching over, he tilted her chin up. "Never. Nobody will ever
make fun of you here. And if anyone does, you're to tell me. I'll
take care of it."

She was sure he would. Linc seemed like he could take care of
anything.

"Time for sleep. Were you a good girl and did what I asked
you to?"

"Yes," she said quietly, remembering his order not to wear any
panties to bed.

"Hmm, I'm almost disappointed."

"What?"

"A nice spanking before bed could do wonders to help you relax."

Oh good Lord. She just glared at him, not bothering to even reply. He let out a small bark of laughter.

"You need a light on to sleep?"

"Yes. I um, left my nightlight behind."

He got out and turned on the bathroom light, leaving the door open just a few inches before turning off the lamp on his side of the bed.

"Okay?" he asked as he climbed into bed.

"Yes, thank you."

"We'll get you a new nightlight too. Lie down. Got Princess Nana and your blanket? Does it have a name?"

"I just call it my snuggly," she whispered, worried about what he might think.

But she need not have worried. Like everything else, he took it in stride.

"Snuggly, that's cute. Princess Nana and snuggly. Okay, Mari-girl. Get comfy."

She rolled onto her side, away from him, Princess Nana and her snuggly held tight. Expecting him to keep his distance.

Again, she should have known better.

Grabbing hold of her hip, he dragged her against him, so he was spooning her. His arm wrapped around her just under her breasts.

Oh hell. He had to be kidding her?

Then his leg went between hers, his thigh pressing up against her pussy. He wasn't really expecting her to sleep like this. Right?

She'd once read somewhere that being the big spoon meant you felt protective and possessive of the other person.

And well, if there were ever two words to describe Linc . . .

Oh and sexy, bossy and funny as well.

It was a killer combination.

"Relax, baby. Sleep time."

There was no way at all she was gonna sleep. Nope.

MARISOL WOKE up as she usually did, on her tummy with one leg hitched. With her thumb in her mouth, snuggly being rubbed under her nose.

Only this time something was different. There was something hot on her ass. Something that cupped and squeezed.

"Good morning, Mari-girl. Sleep well?"

She let out a small squeak and opened her eyes to find Linc staring at her. His hair was deliciously tousled. His eyes dark and smoky. What did they call them? Bedroom eyes? Holy hell. She totally got that description now. He ran his gaze over her, taking her in. His hand cupped her ass.

She tried to speak then realized that she still had her thumb in her mouth. Quickly, she withdrew it, blushing.

"Don't remove it on my account," he told her huskily. "You look so sweet, lying there with your snuggly and your dolly, sucking your thumb. Have you ever tried a pacifier?"

She shook her head.

"Would you like to?"

"I don't know," she whispered.

He studied her. "You've never thought about it?"

She bit her lip. She couldn't lie. And not answering would be like telling him anyway. "I have. I've just never gotten up the courage to buy one. I was worried my aunt would find it."

"Well, you don't have to worry about that anymore. What about a bottle?"

"Umm. Maybe," she replied. She'd definitely thought about it.

He rewarded her honesty with a warm smile. "We can try whatever you like, Mari-girl. This morning, we'll go online and buy some toys and supplies for your Little. As well as some toys for big Mari."

"W-what toys?" He continued to squeeze her ass. Her clit throbbed, wanting him to move his hand down lower to play with her slick lips, to flick her tight nub.

He'd corrupted her. There was no other explanation.

"Oh, we're going to need a clit tickler."

Her breath hitched. He couldn't seriously mean . . .

"We'll get you some anal plugs as well. Have you thought about me taking you there?" He moved one finger between her cheeks and she tensed.

"Umm . . ."

"Answer me honestly, Mari-girl, or we'll start the day by reddening your bottom."

She closed her eyes, unable to look at him as she answered. "Yes."

"Good girl." He squeezed her bottom gently. Dear Lord, who thought that a butt massage would be such a turn-on?

"Your honesty is going to get a reward very shortly. How sensitive are your nipples?"

"V-very."

"Hmm, are you ready to show me them? To show me all of you? Don't you think I deserve that?"

"I'm not sure you'll think of it as much of a reward," she muttered.

Smack! That same hand that had been playing with her, landed sharp on her bare ass.

"Ouch!"

She tried to reach down and cover the area but he flicked the blankets back, pulling her T-shirt up over her bottom. He gently rubbed the sore spot as her cheeks filled with red at the sight she knew she must make. She tried to push her T-shirt down, but he gave her a stern look.

"You just earned your first punishment."

She tensed. "What? Why?""

"You know very well what for," he replied. "But before we get to that, do you need to go potty? Check your blood sugars?"

"Um, yes." Anything to avoid punishment.

He landed another smack on her ass. "Go do that."

She scrambled out of bed, grateful for the reprieve.

"But don't take too long or Daddy will assume you need help and come in."

Crap. So much for that tactic.

She took care of matters then walked slowly back into the bedroom. Surely, he hadn't meant what he'd said.

He was sitting up in bed. When he caught sight of her, he crooked a finger then pointed at her side of the bed. She moved around and sat, facing him. She took a quick glance at the door then away.

Reaching out, he grasped hold of her chin. "We haven't talked about limits. I'm not planning on using anything but my hand until we do. Okay?"

Something settled inside her. "Okay."

"And you always have your safeword."

She nodded and he let her go then patted his lap. "Over you go for this conversation."

Oh holy hell.

"Are you sure?"

"Over. Now."

Gulp. That tone of voice meant business. She lay herself over his lap, squirming slightly at the feel of his hard thighs beneath her tummy. She pressed her thighs together as he raised her T-shirt above her ass.

"Uh-uh, relax and spread your legs slightly. This is a punishment spanking not a fun one. So there's no pressing your legs together and trying to pleasure yourself. Now, if this was a spanking for fun, I would get you off while spanking you." He sighed with exaggerated sadness. "Another time."

Damn him.

"Now, if you can tell me what you did that was naughty, your punishment will be short and quick. But if you deny that you were naughty, I'm not stopping until your bottom is bright red, understand?"

Her breath hitched.

Another smack landed. Ooh that stung. She pressed her legs together as her clit throbbed.

"Hey, I didn't answer!"

"You were taking too long." Another smack. "And keep those legs apart. I'll keep smacking this delicious ass until you answer me. And these spanks don't count towards your punishment."

"I was naughty," she cried out.

Another smack. She glared at him over her shoulder. Damn man just grinned at her unrepentantly.

Ooh. He was trouble.

"Why?" he asked. Smack!

"Because I put myself down?"

"You don't sound certain. Say, I was naughty because I put myself down."

"I was naughty because I put myself down."

"Better. Now it's a count of ten."

"What? You already spanked me!" she protested.

"And I told you that they didn't count. Now, remember you have your safeword if you need it. Maybe we need to get you a nice, fat punishment plug. So after your spanking, you can stand or sit in the corner with your legs spread wide so you can't give yourself any pleasure and a big plug inside your bottom. How does that sound?"

Like torture. And yet, she desperately wanted to try it.

"We could even find some ginger lube if you're especially bad. That would provide a nice sting."

Dear Lord, the man was going to kill her.

"Keep your legs spread and your arms out in front of you. If you move either, we start all over again. Count it out." He slapped his hand down on her already hot ass.

"O-one," she managed to call out.

Another smack.

"Two!"

He moved from cheek to cheek then back to the middle of her ass. By the time he got to ten, her bottom was warm and throbbing. He definitely hadn't held back. It had hurt more than she thought it would. And being made to keep her legs open felt almost worse. If she could have gotten some friction against her clit, she might have enjoyed it more.

But then that wasn't the point of this spanking, was it? She wasn't sure she'd like a harder spanking.

Well, you know how to avoid that.

He lay back and turned her so she was lying sprawled on his chest. He held her tight until her breathing grew more even.

Ooh. This part she really liked. He ran his hand up and down her back. "You're beautiful. So sexy. I wish you could see it. I'm dying to see all of you, to cover every inch with my lips, my tongue. I'll tell you as often as you need to hear it that you're a goddess."

Did he really mean that?

"My aunt's favorite insult is to call me a fat mouse."

He grew tense beneath her. "That woman has a lot to answer for. Mari-girl, she was putting you down, trying to make you feel small so she could feel big. People like that, they don't like anyone who is prettier than them, sweeter than them, smarter than them."

"But she's beautiful," she protested.

He rolled her onto her back and held her face between his hands. "No, baby. You are."

They looked at one another. And as she stared up into his eyes, it settled more deeply inside her. Was Rosalind jealous of her? It was hard to believe. Yet there was no mistaking the sincerity in Linc's eyes.

And to her shock, she found herself reaching for the bottom of her T-shirt. Linc moved away, kneeling beside her, watching. He didn't say anything. Didn't try to hurry her along. He just stared at her with a gaze that was equal parts hungry and thankful.

She drew his top off over her head and lay there, completely naked. It was hard. Really hard. And she had to work not to cover herself.

Linc just sat there, frozen.

"Aren't you going to say something?" she finally asked.

"I'm the luckiest guy in the world."

That hadn't been what she'd expect him to say. Yet at the same time, it was perfect.

She giggled.

"Nope. Make that the universe. Luckiest guy in the universe. Good lord, woman. How could you think you are anything but magnificent? Have you not looked at yourself in the mirror?"

"I try to avoid doing that."

"Baby, if I had your body, you wouldn't get me away from the mirror."

She burst into laughter, rolling to her side and holding her tummy. "I can just see you standing in the mirror, preening at yourself."

"Hey, I'll have you know that it's not preening." He climbed from the bed and struck a silly pose with his hand on one cocked hip the other hand behind his neck. "It's posing."

"So sorry. Very nice posing."

"I can do better. Wait there." He pointed a stern finger at her, his eyes twinkling.

He walked into his closet and when he returned, he had a

cowboy hat on. Damn, that was sexy. Her heart raced as he turned around then looked back over his shoulder at her, wiggling his eyebrows.

The man had a very fine ass. Too bad it was covered in pajama pants. She licked her lips and he turned, holding up his arms and bending them, flexing his biceps.

"Are you drooling, Mari-girl?"

She quickly swiped at her mouth as he laughed. She mock-glared at him. Then he tipped off his hat, holding it in front of his cock. "Would you like me to do a strip show for you tonight? You seem to like my posing."

"Why not now?" she asked huskily.

He knelt on the bed then tossed his hat aside. Too bad he wasn't naked underneath.

"Because if I do it now, then we're not leaving this bed until you're well fucked. And if we're late to our appointment with Doc, he'll throw a hissy fit. Plus, I need to feed you. And before that, I need a small taste."

She rolled onto her back as he came over her, his hands resting on the bed on either side of her as he dipped his mouth low and took her nipple into his mouth with a groan. He sucked on her nipple until she had to press her thighs together to ease the throbbing in her clit.

He let her nipple go with a plop.

"I'm going to wake up each morning and suckle on these breasts."

Dear Lord. Was it possible for her to blush any harder? The things he said were crazy.

"When we're at home alone you're not to wear any panties. I want easy access. Unless you're in Little space, then Daddy will dress you up like his princess ought to be dressed."

"Are these rules gonna be written down somewhere?" She groaned as he moved to her other nipple.

"Of course, Mari-girl."

Suddenly, he drew back and stood then pulled her up beside him. "Time for breakfast." He walked around and grabbed the T-shirt she'd been wearing last night and pulled it over her head. Then taking hold of her hand, he led her into the kitchen.

He wasn't serious. Did he expect her to eat when she was so turned on?

"But ... but ..."

"But what?" he asked as he reached the kitchen. Turning, he grasped her by the waist and lifted her onto the counter. She gasped at the feel of the cool, hard surface against her ass. The cold felt good. Sitting, not so much.

"What are you doing?"

"Putting you on the counter to keep you out of the way and out of trouble."

"I don't get into trouble," she insisted. "And I can't sit on the counter with a bare bottom." She tried to wriggle down but he placed a heavy hand on her shoulder.

"Uh-uh, when Daddy puts you somewhere, he expects you to stay there."

She felt her Little side rising up.

"And you do get into trouble when unsupervised." He placed his hands on either side of her. "You seem tense. What do you need?"

"I don't know." She squirmed.

"I think you do. Remember, you have to ask me for what you need. What is it that you need, Mari-girl?" He spoke into her ear, his breath brushing against her skin.

"I need ... I need ..."

"Yes, baby, tell me."

"I need to come."

"Good girl for telling me." He drew away from her and she let a small whimper escape. Then he drew off her top, leaving her sitting there naked. "Lie back. I'm going to make you breakfast and in between I'll pleasure you."

Holy, holy hell.

But she lay back and he spread her legs wide, he lay kisses up her thighs until he got to her pussy where he lapped at her. As she was squirming, he drew back and she heard him moving around the kitchen.

She wanted to beg, to plead, but she held back.

Then he returned to her. This time he used both hands to squeeze her nipples as he feasted from her, sucking on her clit as he turned her nipples into hardened nubs.

Then he left again. She could hear the coffee machine working. Something sizzled. The smell of bacon cooking made her stomach grumble.

But right then, she couldn't seem to care much.

Then he came back to her, pushing her legs even wider as he ran his tongue over her entrance. He dipped it in just slightly before moving it higher to flick at her clit. By now, she was wriggling on the counter, her cries filling the room. Her thighs were tense, her need to come like nothing she'd felt before.

When he moved away this time, she let out a cry of frustration. "No, no, please!"

"Please what?" He appeared next to her head, bending over her to lick at her nipple. "Please leave you alone? Please play with your nipples? Please kiss you? You must tell me what you want."

Right. She had to ask him. All she had to do was ask and he'd give it to her, right? As long as she wasn't in danger.

"Please make me come!" she blurted out.

Then he kissed her mouth. "All you had to do was say so."

Returning to the other side of the counter, he raised her legs so they were up over his shoulders then he feasted on her until she came with a scream, her orgasm so intense that tears actually leaked from her eyes.

And as he brought her down with light licks of his tongue, she felt the room spinning slightly. She was dazed. Boneless.

He drew back. A worried look filled his face. "Are you okay, Mari-girl?" He wiped away her tears.

"Yeah. Just really happy."

"Good." He kissed her gently. "Because so am I."

After putting the T-shirt back on her, Linc sent her off to take her insulin. When she returned, he insisted that she sit on his lap and let him feed her. He fed them both from the one plate. Small bites of egg and bacon. Bits of toast with butter.

Maybe she should have felt self-conscious being fed this way. Instead she leaned against his chest and felt . . .

Cherished.

She'd also become all too aware of the hard cock pressing against her throughout breakfast. That had to hurt, right? He'd gotten her off several times now and hadn't come himself. Well, except for taking himself in hand in the shower last night.

Damn, she still wished she'd seen that.

After breakfast, he wouldn't let her help clean up.

"Are you sure I can't do anything to help?"

"Help cook or help me?" he teased.

She blushed as she realized she'd been staring at his cock which was pressed against his pajama pants.

"Umm, both?" she managed to squeak out.

He laughed. "You are so precious." He leaned down and cupped her chin. "Thank you for offering, but Little girls stay out of the way in the kitchen unless they're given specific chores. And as for the other, well, as nice as the offer is, we have other things today and a hard-on never killed anyone. I hope." He winked, making her giggle.

"Now, you go take a shower and get dressed while I clean up. You can wear panties since we're going out to see Doc later."

He kissed her. It was a long, hard kiss that made her want to beg him to join her in the shower.

When had she turned into such a sex fiend?

It had to be him. There was just something about him . . . it put her into overdrive. Maybe she should make that shower a cold one.

22

When she entered the living room, he was already sitting on the sofa, tapping on a tablet. "There she is." He glanced up at her, running his gaze over her black yoga pants and the teal hoodie she was wearing.

She'd pulled her hair back in a ponytail.

"Sorry, were you waiting on me? I figured I'd better wash my hair. It can take a while to wash and dry. I'm thinking about cutting it, honestly." It was nearly down to her bottom

"Does it give you headaches?" he asked as he patted the seat beside him.

She sat. "Not really. It's just tiresome to take care of."

Leaning over, he ran his fingers through her hair. "Then it's now Daddy's job to take care of your hair. I'll wash it, dry it, braid it. You don't need to worry about it anymore."

She blinked at the finality of his words.

"You look shocked."

"You really want to do that?" she asked.

"Nothing gives me greater pleasure than to take care of my baby in all ways."

Wow.

"Here's the tablet. I want you to go through and pick out any clothes you want. I especially want to see some warmer things in the shopping cart. A couple of jackets, jeans, thermals and hoodies or sweaters. Whatever you like to wear. This site also has lingerie, order some things for at night. Then we'll get some things for your Little. Don't worry about your big girl toys. I've already ordered them."

Oh hell. She didn't want to think about what big girl toys he'd ordered. Or maybe she did and that was the problem.

"I'm going into my office to make a few calls. I have ranch stuff to deal with. When I come back, I'll pay for all this." He frowned slightly. "You'll need a credit card to order your online books, right?"

"Umm, yes."

"Grab your eReader and I'll add my number to your account."

She squirmed, hating that she had to use his money. But she knew he'd just argue that this was stuff she needed. And that he wanted to provide for her.

Fifteen minutes later, he returned and looked at her cart. He shook his head. "What am I going to do with you?"

She squirmed at the scolding tone of his voice. "This isn't acceptable. Let's see, we'll add some more sweaters. Another jacket. Do you like this one?" He pointed to a bright green one.

With a sigh, she pointed to a buttery yellow one she liked better.

"There's no lingerie in here. Let's add some of that." He picked out a few lacy gowns, as well as several snap-crotch teddies. Holy hell. "There we go."

By the time he was finished, the cart had three times as much stuff.

"Did you get your eReader?" he asked, after paying for the clothes.

"Oh no. I'll go grab it. If you're sure," she said shyly.

"Mari-girl, I don't usually say things I don't mean. But you're sweet for checking." He wrapped his hand around the back of her head and pulled her in for a kiss. "Now, go get your eReader. Get Princess Nana and snuggly too. You might need their help with choosing toys for your Little."

Jumping up, she ran and got her doll, snuggly and eReader. He quickly added his credit card to her account.

"Thank you." She hugged him and he ran his hand up and down her back.

"You're welcome, teeny. I'm curious, did you always want to work in a spa?"

She shook her head shyly. "No. Never. I don't really like being around lots of people or having to make small talk all day. I don't really know what I want to do, though."

"You're young. You don't have to know. While you're here, so I can keep you safe, you'll read your books, watch TV and when we get your toys, you'll have them to play with."

"I've never really played in Little space."

"Then that's something to look forward to. Choose some books now, please." While he had said please, she knew it was an order. So she chose several books she'd been dying to read. She'd deleted her aunt's credit card but kept her account so she didn't lose her books.

Then they moved on to an age play site. It was one she'd actually looked at a lot. While she'd planned to spend as little of his money as possible, she squealed when she saw the cutest set of pajamas. They were a shorts and cami set with pink hearts on them and lace along the hem of the shorts and the top part of the cami.

Linc snorted. "Well, guess they're going in the cart."

"Sorry, Daddy." Her Little had pushed towards the surface as soon as he'd clicked on the website, it seemed. Or maybe she'd started to come out when he'd ordered her to go get Princess Nana and snuggly. She brought snuggly up to her nose, rubbing the soft blanket back and forth in a nervous gesture.

"Why are you sorry, teeny?"

"For spending all your hard-earned money on me." She slipped her thumb into her mouth, unable to help herself. She thought he might get mad for her bringing up the money thing again. Maybe she should have stayed quiet.

Silly girl.

"Are Little girls supposed to worry about money, teeny?"

"Big girls are."

He shrugged. "Only if they need to. And Daddy has told you that you don't need to, hasn't he?"

She nodded.

Reaching out, he tilted up her chin and then gently pulled her thumb from her mouth. "Daddy would very much like for you to stop worrying about money. There are things you do for Daddy and things that Daddy does for you, understand? Things do not have to be equal and yet in the end, they often end up that way."

She wasn't so convinced. How could they be equal when he was contributing all the money?

"Do you have any idea of why I might like being a Daddy Dom?" he asked her.

"You enjoy being in control. You like ordering me around."

His lips twitched. "You answered that question quickly."

She bit her lip. Was she not meant to say any of that? "Sorry, Daddy."

"No, don't be sorry. That was just the truth. And you're right, I do like taking charge. But there's more to it than me just ordering you around. Although I do enjoy that." His smile grew. "However, I also have this deep need to take care of someone special, in all ways. You may have noticed that I'm rather protective."

"Oh yeah, Daddy. I've noticed."

"Hmm, I feel very protective of all the women on the ranch, but none more than you. I could become a bit overbearing. You'll tell me if it's too much, yeah?"

She nodded. Although, she rather liked his overprotectiveness. It was something she'd never had and always secretly craved. She'd had those silly dreams of a white knight appearing at her school to rescue her from all the tormenting bullies. Of her dad turning up to claim her, saying that he'd never meant to leave her, taking her away from Rosalind. But it had never happened, of course.

Until Linc.

"Although I'm not sure how I'd stop myself from being quite so protective and possessive of you. Not when I could have lost you. I still cannot believe that jerk had his hands on you, choking you. Harming what belongs to me."

Oh God. Maybe the words should have scared her. After all, how long had they known each other? Instead, she found herself leaning into his touch as he cupped her cheek. She turned her head and kissed the palm of his hand. His eyes darkened with arousal.

"Maybe you'll be as possessive of me as I am of you?" he asked her.

"Yes."

He grinned. "Good. Looking after you makes me feel complete, Mari-girl. I feel this deep contentment knowing that you're in my house, sleeping in my bed, being pleasured under my hands and tongue. But I also want more than that. Like I said, earlier. I want to be your safe place."

She was pretty certain he already was.

"And believe me, I'll get a lot of pleasure from bathing you, dressing you, doing your hair. From watching you play with things that I bought you. Eat things I made for you. Wear the marks on your bottom that I will give you when you break the rules."

"I'm not going to break the rules, Daddy. I is a good girl." Okay. Whoa. Where did that come from? It seemed that browsing things for baby girls while Daddy spoke of rules and punishment was bringing out her Little.

He smiled wide then kissed the top of her nose. "And there she is, my own sweet little baby girl. Of course you're a good girl. But even good girls break the rules sometimes. And I think you have a bit of a rebellious streak in you."

Her? She did not. "I always obey the rules." She was in no way rebellious. She was too shy and quiet to break the rules. Growing up as she had, she'd learned to do exactly as her aunt required. The consequences if she didn't were too harsh.

"Really? So that wasn't you that got pulled over by Ed the other night for speeding?" he asked sternly.

"I didn't notice I was speeding. I was thinking of something else. It doesn't happen that often."

"Is that so?" he drawled.

"Well, I guess it depends on what you classify as often," she muttered, shifting around uncomfortably.

"That won't be happening again. That's one of your rules."

"I really need that list," she muttered.

"We'll get to that soon. We haven't ordered nearly enough stuff." He went through the site, adding so many outfits it made her mind whirl. There was the sweetest little onesie that was white with lacy sleeves. Then it had an attached skirt of see-through lace so the onesie was visible underneath. Written on the front was *Daddy's Little Princess*. It had a snap crotch and more cute snaps at the shoulder to help get it more easily over her head.

"Daddy, I can't wear that!"

"Why not? It's adorable."

She chewed at her lip. It was. And she really wanted it. But wouldn't she look silly? She had boobs and hips and dimply thighs.

"You don't think I'll look silly?"

He placed the tablet aside and she tensed. Uh-oh. Was she in trouble? Her bottom was still sore from this morning. But he just gave her a calm, tender look. Then leaning down, he lightly kissed her lips. His thumb ran along her jaw.

"I know that letting go of your adult worries and insecurities is hard. Especially when your aunt has drummed into your head all these lies, so that you don't even know who you are. But I can tell you this, you would never look anything other than gorgeous and adorable in my eyes. I won't make you dress in things that make you feel awkward or uncomfortable. That defeats the point of everything. Little space is supposed to be fun, you're meant to be able to relax and be who you want to be. I want you free of cares and worries. Not stressing about what you look like. Do you want me to take it back out?"

"You'd like to see me wearing it?"

"You'd look adorable. But this isn't about me. Or not just about me." He winked at her. "I'm getting plenty out of having you here. You didn't think I brought you home with me out of the goodness of my heart, did you?" He gave her a look of mock-shock, placing his hand on his chest.

She giggled and shook her head. "Add it, Daddy."

"You're sure, baby girl?"

"I like it. I want to be your princess."

"You already are." He kissed the top of her head. "But a princess needs lots of outfits. I want you in skirts, I think. We'll keep it nice and warm in here. What do you think of these skirts with long socks?"

She gasped in shocked delight at the over-the-knee striped pink and white socks. They were awesome.

"Yes, please, Daddy!" She clapped her hands, bouncing up and down. She was going to look so super cute. She could picture it now. Her hair in pigtails, she'd need pretty hair ties. A pretty T-shirt, puffy skirt and those socks.

He chuckled. "Thought you might like them. We'll get those in several colors as well these pleated skirts and some tutus. Some of these shorts and overalls. You'll also need some jeans. Oh, and look at these T-shirts. This one even has a crown on it."

"Eek! It's too much! I'm dying!" She slid back against the sofa dramatically.

Linc shook his head. "No dying allowed. I didn't find you just to lose you over some socks and T-shirts."

She sat up with a gasp. "Not just any socks and T-shirts, Daddy. The best socks and T-shirts in the wooorrlldd." She threw her arms into the air as she sang the last word.

Leaning in, he kissed her gently. "You're adorable."

After going through the clothing then the accessories like hair ties and headbands and even some cute pink and blue shoes, he moved to the childish panties buying her some that were more like diaper covers. They were so ruffly at the back that she knew it would be easily seen if she bent over in the short skirts.

But instead of being embarrassed, she just felt excited. A little nervous, sure. But she knew that this was what Linc wanted. And she wanted to give him that. Because pleasing him made her feel happy. Light. And she knew if there was something she didn't want, she only had to say.

She'd never had that. Had someone listen to her.

"You want some diapers or pull-ups?" he asked casually.

Umm. "I don't want to . . . to . . ."

"Use them?" he supplied helpfully.

"No," she said in a strangled voice. She knew her cheeks were bright red. "I don't regress that far."

He stared at her thoughtfully. "This is all new, but nothing is set in stone. You want to revisit that at a later date, you can. But I am ordering you a booster seat for my truck, that's non-negotiable.

It's a safety issue and Daddy is in charge of safety and health. Those rules will be your strictest and will apply for big and Little Mari."

She nodded, wide-eyed at his stern tone. "Yes, Daddy."

"Hmm, what about a crib for nap-time or would you rather have a cute princess bed?"

"I . . . I don't need naps, Daddy. I is a big girl." Okay, this was really bringing out her Little.

"Not that big, baby girl. And you will definitely be having naps. At night you'll sleep in our bed, of course. But we can set the spare room up as your Little room, once we take that other bed out. So let's get you a cute princess bed with a canopy. Look this one has stars all around the top and fairy lights. We'll see how you do in a big girl bed. If you're naughty and don't sleep, then we might need a crib. And we'll get you a pacifier to try. What do you like? Ahh, here's a princess one."

She had to admit, it was really cute. It was purple with a crown on the front. But she wasn't sure about it.

"You're frowning, teeny. Don't want a pacifier?"

"I like my thumb."

"I know you do. But you might like a pacifier too. Let's get a bottle to try as well. Princess baby's bottle. Perfect. And princess cutlery and a bamboo plate."

Dear Lord.

"Ooh a princess ball pit. Would you like that?"

"Really?" She grasped hold of the tablet, making him laugh. "Oh wow. They make ball pits for my size!"

"You're just a tiny thing." He took the tablet back and added princess ball pit to the cart. That was going to be so fun.

"Coloring books? Pens?" he asked.

"Yes. And I love crafting!" she said enthusiastically.

"All right. So we'll add crafting things. Hm, not sure about you using scissors. We might need some of those safety ones. Glue.

Glitter. We'll need a mat to put down so you don't make a mess. Colored card stock. Stickers."

"Lots of stickers! And look at that pretty paper! Ooh."

Finally there was a cart filled with everything she could possibly dream of having. Not just a ball pit and crafting materials, but also some building blocks and a doll's crib for Princess Nana. A pale pink and white striped beanbag chair for her to read on. A white fluffy rug for the floor. A pretty white bookcase and a matching desk that Linc told her would be perfect for sitting at and writing lines. She didn't like the idea of that at all.

"Now, we need some naughty girl supplies. Ahh, here we go, a heart-shaped spanker. Perfect." It was a long black wand with a heart-shaped leather pad at the end. She couldn't even imagine being spanked with it.

"This is ingenious." He showed her another spanking imple-ment. This one had a thicker handle and was round at the end. It was pink and had a picture of a princess on one side. The handle had a hole at the end and a chain was threaded through. What was it though? As she was trying to work it out, Linc showed her an image on the website of a woman walking around with it hanging from her handbag.

She gaped. "I'm not walking around with that!"

"Nobody will know. They'll think it's some cute attachment. But if you're naughty, I can slip away with you to somewhere private, take it off your bag and turn your bottom nice and red. Let's get two."

The man was an evil genius.

And she thought she might well be falling in love with him.

"I'm never gonna be naughty when we're out."

"Oh, I'll hold you to that," he told her with a grin. Lastly, he ordered a time-out stool that was white with the word, 'time-out' painted along the top. And a booster seat that could attach to the dining chair or be used in his truck.

"I thought I only had to use a booster seat in your truck if I couldn't drive it?"

"I changed my mind. It will be safer for you with the seat, so you're going to have the seat. I might get a custom-made one with straps yet."

Yikes.

"Now, that's all ordered. Let's get your rules sorted and go through any limits before we visit Doc."

"I feel like it's Christmas," she said with wonder.

"You always get paddles for Christmas? Goodness, you must be on Santa's naughty list. Tut-tut. It's a wonder the big man hasn't taken you over his knee if that's the case. Now, wouldn't that make a good Christmas photo?"

"Daddy! I am *not* on Santa's naughty list."

He sighed, shaking his head. "We'll see."

"It's just that other than when we lived with Harry, I've never been spoiled like this."

She didn't even know how long she was staying for. Although now that she was here, she couldn't imagine ever leaving. The idea filled her with fear.

His sexy control, his careful attention and overprotectiveness, the indulgence and tenderness. And the laughter. She never would have imagined after what happened with Tiger that she'd feel like laughing.

When was the last time she'd even thought about Tiger and her aunt? She guessed that was his intention. To keep her mind off everything.

Linc drew her onto his lap. Then he tilted her face and kissed her gently, sliding his tongue in to dance with hers. When he drew back, he kissed the top of her nose. "You deserve to be spoiled. And that's just what I'm going to do."

He set her back on the sofa. "Now wait here while I go get something to help you with remembering the rules."

Damn it. How could he go from talking of spoiling her to speaking of rules? That was just wrong. He returned with a white-board and pen.

She gave him a suspicious look. "You just happened to have those on hand?"

He grinned. "I might have gotten Bear to grab them for me yesterday."

Marisol groaned. "Daddy! You didn't tell him what you wanted them for, did you?"

"Of course I did."

"Daddy!"

"What?" He gave her an innocent look. He wrote *Mari's Rules* on the top in surprisingly neat handwriting.

Yeah. Right. Innocent, her butt. The man knew exactly what he was doing.

"Before I do this, do you have any hard limits?"

"Um, like you mean things like blood play." She shuddered. She'd had enough of needles. It just didn't seem sexy to her at all.

"Yep. Exactly like that. Although I should tell you that while I will always try to give you whatever you want or need, blood play is definitely not my thing. I also don't go to BDSM clubs, not anymore. Not since I was younger." He appeared thoughtful. "They don't hold good memories for me."

"Why not?"

"Ahh, because that was where I met my ex. And also where she met her current husband, while still dating me."

"You mean she cheated on you?"

"Yes, exactly that."

"What an idiot."

He blinked then a wide smile crossed his face. "You think so, do you?"

"I know so. She obviously wasn't good enough for you, Daddy. Because she didn't realize what a catch you are."

"So you think I'm a catch, do you?" He put the whiteboard pen and board down and lunged for her, tickling her mercilessly.

She screamed, trying to get away, his fingers seeming to find every ticklish part of her. Finally, she cried mercy.

"Daddy, I'm gonna pee! I'm gonna pee!"

He drew back and lightly kissed her lips. "We can't have that."

"I think tickling is going to be one of my hard limits," she sulked as he stood.

He held out his hands to her. "Ah, now that one I don't think I can agree to. You're just too fun to tickle." Turning her, he landed a sharp slap on her ass.

She rubbed her cheek, frowning at him. "What was that for?"

"Distracting me."

"Daddy!" Distracting him? Really?

He grinned. "We're having a very serious conversation about rules and limits and then you made me tickle you."

"Made you tickle me? Daddy!" She stomped her foot on the floor in outrage. Then she looked down at her foot in shock. She didn't think she'd ever done that before.

"Did you just stomp your foot?"

"I think it acted on its own. I didn't tell it to do that." She put her hands behind to cover her bottom as though she expected him to start walloping her. Seemed her Little side was coming out more and more around him.

"A foot with a mind of its own. That sounds terrible."

"Oh. It is." She nodded solemnly.

"I'll have Doc look at it. Tell him it stomped all on its own."

"Daddy!" she complained. He wouldn't! Right?

"Well, I can't have it going around stomping on its own. The next time you stomp your foot I might think you're about to throw a temper tantrum and put you in timeout to cool down. You don't want to be punished for something your foot is doing all on its own."

"You're so silly, Daddy. But I really didn't mean to do it. I don't think I've ever stomped my foot before."

"Then maybe it's a good sign."

"It is?"

"Yeah, teeny. It means you're feeling more at ease with me. That you can be yourself. Now, go pee. Or do you need help?"

"No!" she squeaked. Shoot, she'd forgotten she needed to pee and now she really had to go.

After she'd taken care of her bladder's needs, she stood in front of the mirror in the bathroom. She looked different. She couldn't put her finger on it exactly. Her eyes were shining, her cheeks slightly flushed and she was smiling.

You're happy.

She pressed her fingers against her cheeks. Happy. Imagine that. It seemed like such a foreign concept and she realized just how downtrodden and miserable she had become. Yet, she'd been here with Linc for two nights and she felt lighter. So light, she wondered if she might float away.

Silly Mari-girl.

She grinned wider.

She flew out of the bathroom and plonked herself directly in his lap where he sat on the sofa. Even though she'd surprised him, he immediately wrapped his arms around her, holding her tight.

"Hello, there. What's this about?"

"Nothing. I'm just happy. You make me happy." She buried her face in his neck. "Thank you for taking care of me, for letting me stay here, for wanting me."

"You don't ever have to thank me for that. For any of it. But I do appreciate it."

"Your ex, was she your Little too?" she dared to ask.

"She was. And the man who she cheated on me with was a very close friend."

"Oh, Linc." She slipped her hands around his neck. "I'm so sorry."

"That's why I can't stand lies. They lied to me for so long. I felt stupid, duped. If Jessica had just told me that she no longer wanted to be with me, then I could have walked away without feeling like a fool. Instead it went on for months behind my back. I finally caught them. In our bed. I'd gone out to meet a business associate for dinner but forgot my wallet. Couldn't believe it when I walked into the house and found them . . . well, you don't need to know the details."

"What jerks," she said angrily.

"Well, at least there are positives."

"There are?"

"Hmm. Yes, it gave me the push I needed to give up my boring job and do something I had always wanted to do. I got a job here as a ranch hand and worked my way up. I decided that if I ever found someone I wanted, someone I thought could be mine forever, then I wouldn't hesitate, wouldn't wait. I'd tell her what I wanted and I'd make sure she knew she was mine." He kissed her. Hard. Hot. "You're who I want, Mari-girl. For always. I don't expect you to tell me the same. Not yet. But I have no doubts. You're gonna be mine."

There was something so safe in his confidence. There were doubts, she couldn't deny them. Worry that they hadn't known each other long. That the newness would rub off and he'd realize he didn't want her anymore. But for now, she felt special and cared for.

"All right. Enough procrastinating. Limits. We've already talked about anal play. So that's okay."

Eek. Talk about jumping right into it.

"Now I read that diabetes can give you nerve damage, so I think we'll skip any sort of bondage."

"I don't have any nerve damage. My diabetes is pretty well

controlled. There are times when I go too long without eating or get a bit stressed or when I'm ill that I can have problems. But we could just try tying my hands? And for a short amount of time?"

"We can talk to Doc about it."

"Talk to Doc? Do we have to?" she squeaked.

He grinned. "It won't be the weirdest question he's had, I promise you that. You gave me the list of everything to watch for and what to do. But what about any other injuries? Allergies?"

"No, nothing else."

He nodded. "We'll ease into things. I'll only use my hand and the small paddles we bought you today. Punishments will be short, not prolonged in any way and I'll check in with you often."

It was a relief how seriously he took her health. She knew that she could trust him with it. Which was amazing since she'd never had anyone she could rely on.

"You always have your safeword. Like I said before, I fear I could be too indulgent with you. Maybe I should just take you over my knee and spank you each evening to make up for my indulgence during the day, to cover any naughtiness I miss while I'm working."

"What! No!" That didn't sound fair at all.

"No? Oh, wait, I just had another good idea."

She was starting to see that his idea of good ideas and hers were vastly different.

"What?" she asked suspiciously.

"Each evening, after you've had dinner and gotten ready for bed, you can sit on Daddy's knee and tell him all the mischief that you got up to. Then we'll add ticks to your naughty girl chart."

"I don't have a naughty girl chart." And she didn't need one.

"I'm sure we can make you one. I'll get another whiteboard for it."

She groaned. "You're one of those people aren't you, Daddy?"

"One of what sort of people?"

"Someone who really loves their lists."

He raised his eyebrows. "You have something against lists? Isn't it good to be organized?"

She shook her head. "Organized. Lists. How did we ever become friends?"

"Must have been my irresistible charm." He grinned at her. "And yes, Mari-girl. I love lists. You're going to love them too."

Somehow, she doubted that.

"Any more limits?" he asked her

She dropped her gaze to her hands. "Just don't humiliate or call me names. I think that's the one thing I couldn't ever take."

"Never, baby. Never. My little princess will only ever hear how beautiful and lovely she is. I promise. Now, we're going to have to do your rules when we get home because we're meant to meet with Doc in fifteen. And that man is grouchier than a bear with a sore paw when he's kept waiting."

23

"I really don't think I need to go see the doctor," Mari whined as Linc had her hold onto his shoulders while he pulled on her old sneakers. She needed some winter boots. The shoes he'd bought her wouldn't be suitable for the snow and ice.

After tying them up, he stood and grabbed one of his old coats from the coat closet. It was miles too big for her, but it would keep her warm. When he put it on, she looked like a girl playing in Daddy's clothes.

Too damn cute for his peace of mind.

He did up the buttons, then rolled up the sleeves so they weren't hanging off the end of her arms.

"We need to check with him that you've been getting the best care up to now. Which I don't think you have. Didn't you say there was a pump you could use to keep watch on your blood sugar levels?"

"Yes, but they cost money."

"And I explained that's going to be covered." He cupped the side of her face. "Stop worrying. Let's meet with Doc and see what he says."

She chewed her lip. "I don't like doctors, they always make me feel stupid. I never understand what they're saying. And I always feel like I'm doing something wrong."

"Hey, Doc isn't going to make you feel like that," he told her in a kind voice. "Okay? Sure, he's grouchy and has a terrible bedside manner."

She frowned and he inwardly cursed himself. He wasn't doing the best job at soothing her.

"But he's not ever going to be mean or condescending. Doc will just want what's best for you, like I do."

"So he won't be mean to me?"

Damn it, why had no one taken care of this sweet girl? Well, none of that mattered now. He'd ensure that no one was ever mean to her again. "Do you really think I would ever let someone be mean to you?"

She shook her head. "No."

"That's right. Never. I would never let anyone harm you, Marigirl. Because you are precious to me. Even if I wasn't there, Doc wouldn't be mean. I promise you. Bossy, yes. Mean, never. Remember, he's got his own Little girl." He reached into the closet for a hat and scarf for her. "You might even have heard of her."

"Of course I've heard of her. I've met her, remember?" she said as he wrapped the scarf around her neck and then plonked the hat on her head, covering her eyes. "And is all this necessary? It's not that cold and we're driving."

He crouched down, searching through the basket at the bottom of the coat closet for some smaller gloves. "Can't have you getting a chill. I don't think I have any gloves that fit. Oh and I know you met Caley. I just meant you might have heard of her pen name. Caley is an author. She writes Daddy Dom books, she goes by the name CJ Bennett." He spotted a pair that he thought might do. They were too small for him. "Ah-huh, here's a pair!"

He turned, only to find she'd disappeared. What the hell?

What happened to her? He'd thought she was just a bit nervous about meeting with Doc? Had she become so scared that she'd run off?

"Mari-girl? Mari? Where are you?" He strode into the living room, through the kitchen and then into the bedroom. Finally, after calling for her and searching everywhere, he thought of the closet.

Opening the door, he found her crouched on the floor. He breathed out a sigh of relief. Logically, he knew that she hadn't been in danger. It wasn't like Tiger could have snuck in and snatched her out from under his nose.

But still that fear had held him by the throat for a moment.

"Mari-girl? What happened? Why did you run off?"

She put her hands over her eyes, taking deep, shaky breaths. What was going on? Was she scared?

"You're not really scared of going to see Doc, are you? I told you that Daddy would look after you. Mari?" he asked.

"No, it's not that! Why didn't you tell me that Caley is CJ Bennett?"

Huh? This was why she'd panicked and run off to hide in the closet?

He sat down. They were going to be late and Doc wouldn't let him hear the end of it for months to come, but he could hardly carry her there, kicking and screaming.

Well, he could. But he wouldn't.

"Mari-girl, come out here." He reached a hand out to her.

She stared at his hand. "I'm not going. I can't. Not like this. I have to . . . to . . . oh man. I can't meet her!"

With a deep sigh, he reached in and drew her out onto his lap. When she attempted to struggle, he gave her one sharp smack on her ass.

"Ow," she complained but she stilled in his arms. He knew it hadn't really hurt. It was more to get her attention and help her settle.

"Stay still, little girl," he warned. She needed a bit of firmness right now. And he was going to have to make it clear that she wasn't to run from him like she had. "Now, tell Daddy what the problem is."

"She's my favorite author!"

"And that's a problem because..."

"I . . . I . . . I don't know," she finished lamely. "I guess I got excited and scared and nervous and then it just all became too much."

"So you ran away from Daddy?"

Her mouth dropped open then she grimaced as though realizing she might just be in trouble.

"I wasn't running from you, Daddy. I just . . . I'm not sure why I ran in here. I was overwhelmed."

"Okay, I don't get why you're so scared to see Caley. I thought you'd be excited."

"It's just . . . I don't know . . . it's kind of like meeting the President or royalty or something."

He had to bite back his smile. "Right. You're nervous then."

She nodded her head.

"Got it. What I could have told you if you had mentioned all this instead of running off, is that Caley is extremely sweet. She likes her privacy which is why I didn't mention this before. But I know you wouldn't tell anyone what her pen name is. You've seen how gossip works in Wishingbone."

"Oh, I'd never say a word. Wait, she's got two daddies, right? Doc and his brother? Wow."

"That's right. She does. And remember, you've already met her, you know how nice she is."

She thunked the palm of her hand against her forehead. "I did CJ Bennett's nails." She spoke with wonder. He had to bite back another smile, because he wanted her to know that he was very serious about this next bit.

He set her on the floor so she was facing him and gently grasped hold of her chin. "I want you to listen to me now."

"Yes?"

"You're not to run from Daddy like that again, understand? Not when I don't know where you've gone or why. I was worried when I couldn't find you."

"I'm sorry, Daddy. I didn't mean to worry you."

"I know it was just instinct. And given some more time, Daddy is hoping that you run to him rather than the closet for safety. But if you keep doing it, then Daddy might just have to buy you one of those baby leads."

Her eyes went wide. "I won't, Daddy."

"All right, let's go. We're already late."

MARISOL STUDIED Doc as Linc pulled up outside his cabin. It was larger than Linc's place and it was clear that it had been added to.

"Doc has a clinic at JSI headquarters as well, but they just built this extension and he decided to add a clinic here too. I think he just doesn't like leaving Caley for long. They all have their own office."

That was a good set-up. She moved her gaze back to Doc, he didn't look happy. In fact, if he'd been a cartoon character, steam would be coming from his ears.

She leaned back in her seat, waiting for Linc to come get her. He opened her door, and then undid her seat belt, lifting her down. In truth, it was a relief to get out of the hot truck. She was wearing so many clothes and Linc had had the heater blasting as they'd driven here. She was starting to overheat.

"You're late," the other man barked. He was handsome, with dark-blond hair, a neatly-trimmed beard and piercing blue eyes.

"Sorry," Linc called out. "Bit of a delay. Mari panicked when I told her that Caley writes books as CJ Bennett."

Doc's eyes narrowed as he stared down at her. She huddled into Linc, her hand firmly wrapped in his.

"And why would that make you panic? Don't you like Caley's books?" he snapped.

"What? No!" Her eyes widened. "I love them. I love her. I can't believe I met her and I didn't even know."

"Ah, you're a fan?" Doc's face softened and she swore he nearly smiled. Maybe.

"Her biggest fan. I'm so nervous now."

"She's writing at the moment. She's having problems with a character, so if you hear someone occasionally yelling, just ignore it."

"Ohh."

"Come in. It's cold out. Although I see you're wrapped up for the arctic." Doc sent Linc a look as they followed him into what had to be the waiting room. It held a sofa, two armchairs and a coffee table with some magazines on it. There was an open door to her left that she saw opened into an exam room. There was another closed door to her right. She wondered if that led to Archer's office. And the wall directly ahead of her had another door that she thought must take you into the main part of the house.

Hot air assaulted her and she started to sweat. Gross. She tried to pull off her scarf. Linc helped her pull it off.

"Poor girl is sweating under all those layers," Doc told him.

"Didn't want her to catch a chill."

Linc drew off her coat then his and she let out a sigh of relief. He left everything in the waiting room before grabbing her hand again, urging her after Doc. She listened in vain for any yelling. How cool would it be to hear her favorite author at work?

They walked into a bright office that held an examination table, a wooden desk and some cabinets.

Doc sat behind the desk and picked up a pen. Linc led her to one of the two chairs sitting in front of the desk. She bit her lip nervously, her leg moving up and down.

Doc didn't look up. "You can sit on Linc's lap if that makes you less nervous. Although I promise not to bite."

"Oh, umm."

"Most Littles prefer to sit on their Daddy's lap when they come to see me," he told her conversationally. As though they were making small talk about the weather.

She felt herself going bright red. "Is it that obvious?"

This time, he did look up. "What?"

"That I'm a . . . Little?"

Suddenly, his face softened with a smile. "No, sweetie. Well, maybe if you're looking for it. But I asked Linc when he made the appointment and he said you were."

She glanced at Linc, not sure that she wanted people to know. Then again, didn't she know about the other Littles on the ranch? That Caley had two daddies?

"He only told me in case you wanted to slip into Little space while you're here," Doc told her in an almost gentle voice. "Some Littles prefer to come to the doctor in that headspace. Some don't. It's up to you."

"Doc, how come you're never this nice when I come to see you?" Linc grumbled.

"Because you're late," Doc snapped.

"This is the only time I've ever been late."

"No, you were late for your very first appointment with me."

Linc sighed. "Eight years ago. Jesus, Doc, you have to let things go."

"Why?"

She knew they were bantering back and forth to give her time to figure things out. Doc turned to her.

"Um, I think I'm too nervous to be in, uhh, Little headspace."

Doc just nodded. Then he started asking her a series of questions. Linc reached over and took her hand in his. She gave it a grateful squeeze, pleased she didn't have to do this all on her own. The questions were all straightforward, though.

Then he started asking her questions about her diabetes.

"So you don't use a continuous glucose monitor?" he asked.

"No, my aunt's insurance wouldn't fully cover the costs. Or at least that's what she told me." Who knew if it was really the truth? Maybe the insurance would cover the monitor and her aunt lied to her out of spite.

"So if I order a monitor along with a supply of sensors, you'll use it? And would you use an insulin pump?"

"Oh." She looked at Linc. "Well, yes. If that's okay?"

"Why wouldn't it be okay?" Doc gave her a bewildered look.

"She's worried about the cost, Doc," Linc told him.

"Why the hell would you worry about that? It's under Linc's insurance. Not your job to worry about it. Got me?"

"All right."

"Sounds like you're doing good with managing it. But this will make your life easier and ensure that we are taking good care of you. You can now get some that are incorporated with insulin pumps. You can personalize them to your lifestyle and can get your blood glucose levels sent to your phone and to Linc's and mine if you agree to that. It will better help us monitor your health."

"That sounds amazing."

"You talked through her health with her? Triggers? Concerns? Play?"

She blinked at him then realized he was talking to Linc. "We've talked about it. We've decided on limited bondage. We're going to ease into any play in the bedroom. During Little time, I'll have to keep a closer eye on her, of course."

"The CGM will help with that. You know the signs of low and high blood sugar?"

Linc rattled them off, much to her shock. She'd given him the list but she hadn't expected he'd have it all memorized.

"Good. And if you have any concerns, you call me right away."

"Don't worry, I will."

"So I talked to Linc about how meal timing can be important. You likely already do that?"

"Yeah, I try to stick to regular meal times as much as I can."

"Good."

"I have an idea of how to help with that too," Linc added.

"Okay. Linc, you need to make sure you have something close by that is high in glucose in case Marisol's blood glucose level dips. And it's a good idea to have something by the bed as well."

"Already got that covered." Linc drew out a couple of hard candies from his pocket. "Been carrying these in the pocket of whatever jeans I'm wearing since she told me."

He had? Damn, that was so sweet. It hit her then, full force just how serious he was about taking care of her.

And she knew there would be no leaving once any danger to her was over. No way she could ever walk away from him. Not that she'd been seriously contemplating it anyway.

"I usually have my bag beside the bed, it has glucose tabs in it," she told Doc.

"Good. Getting a good night's sleep is always important. For everyone. Do you get off to sleep okay?"

"Um, not really," she admitted. "I tend to read at night until I drop off to sleep from exhaustion."

"That's not good," Linc commented. "You didn't have to do that last night."

She blushed at the memory of how many times she'd come last night. He'd exhausted her.

Doc snorted, obviously figuring out what had happened. "That's one way to do it. Having a good bedtime routine will help you get to sleep. Go to bed at the same time each night. Dinner. Relaxing with TV or reading or however else you like to relax," he gave Linc a knowing look which had her biting her lip, "bath time, small snack, then to bed. No devices or working right before bed."

"Got it," Linc said.

"Right, Marisol. Can you hop up on the table for me, please? Linc will help you. It's kind of high."

Doc got up and washed and dried his hands. She rose, still holding Linc's hand as he led her to the table. Then he lifted her up so her legs dangled over the edge.

"Don't I have to put on one of those scratchy gowns?" she asked.

"I try to avoid making my patients wear scratchy gowns," Doc replied dryly. "Although Linc can wear one for his next examination. Punishment for being late."

Linc just rolled his eyes. Then she watched as he grabbed a blood glucose monitor. He loaded a new lancet into the finger pricking device. Then he set up the monitor with a new test strip. She took the lancet when he handed it over to prick her finger so he could test her blood glucose level.

"Good," he commented, putting everything away.

To her surprise, Linc didn't leave her side as Doc started his examination, feeling her glands and looking in her throat and ears.

"You could stand a few feet away," Doc told him with a glare.

Linc crossed his arms over his chest and took one step back. Doc started muttering under his breath about overbearing cowboys.

"Let's take your temperature now that you're no longer roasting under ten layers of clothing."

Linc just snorted.

Doc used an ear thermometer. It beeped and he looked at it. "It's good. You ever had your temperature taken with a rectal thermometer, Linc?"

"No," Linc growled.

Doc turned and grinned at him. "Something to look forward to then."

She gasped. But then Doc turned back to her and gave her a wink. She dropped her head to hide her smile.

"I usually only use them with sick Littles, but I think from now on whenever someone is late, they'll get them at their next check-up."

"If you think that scares me, you don't know me that well," Linc replied.

Doc finished up the rest of the exam. "Right, Marisol, everything looks good. But I want to take some blood. Okay?"

"All right."

Even though she was used to needles and pricking herself, she just hated having blood drawn. It was something about seeing the blood squirt into the tube.

"Hey, you've gone all pale," Linc crooned. "Want to sit on my lap while Doc takes your blood?"

She nodded.

Linc helped her down then led her to the chairs. He sat with her on his lap. Maybe she should have felt silly, being in this position. But as he guided her to bury her face in his neck, she just felt protected.

"That's it, teeny. Doc's just going to take a small bit of blood and then you'll get a Band-Aid."

"I've got different Band-Aids for each of my girls," Doc told her. Each of his girls? Did he mean all the Littles?

"Let me see, there's bumblebee ones for Caley. Bears for Ellie. Rabbit ones for Abby. Charlie has mermaid ones. Daisies for Daisy. Eden just likes pale blue ones and Ari has these pretty gold, glittery ones. We tried to find koala ones for Gigi, but that proved a bit hard. So she likes the princess ones. Want any of those?"

"I'd like the princess one please."

"Good. That's all done. Linc, hold that there for me and apply pressure."

She moved her face away from Linc's neck and looked down at her arm in amazement. "It's done? I didn't even feel it."

"All done."

Linc removed his hand as Doc put the Band-Aid on. She looked down at the princess Band-Aid with a smile. Doc moved back around his desk and sat.

"When are you going to come into the twenty-first century and use technology?" Linc teased Doc who wrote on a pad.

"Bite me," Doc replied.

"Now, Doc, I thought you'd never ask."

Doc shook his head. "All I get around here is insolence. I need to ask Kent for a raise. Anything else you want to mention, Marisol?"

"Umm, no, I don't think so."

"Linc, can you go get us some cookies from the kitchen?"

Linc sighed. "Why am I fetching cookies?"

"Don't you want any?" Doc replied.

"What flavor are they? They're not bran and raisin or something like that, are they?" Linc asked suspiciously.

"Chocolate chip. Go."

Linc turned to her. "That okay with you?"

She nodded. "It's fine."

"I'll bring her to you safe and sound in a few minutes." Doc waited until Linc deposited her in her own chair then got up and left, closing the door behind him.

"Chocolate chip cookies are my favorite," she said sadly.

"There aren't any."

"What?"

"There aren't any cookies. Well, not where he'll find them anyway. But I figured it would keep him busy for a few minutes. Wanted to talk to you alone."

"Oh. What about?"

"Just wanted to check there wasn't anything you wanted to talk to me about that you couldn't say in front of Linc. I know that you were attacked recently."

She swallowed heavily. Right. That's what he wanted to talk about.

"I noticed the bruises on your neck."

She raised her hand. "They're much better."

"Linc said he strangled you. Threatened you. He do anything else?" There was a softness to his face even if his words sounded abrupt.

"No."

He watched her for a long moment. "You wouldn't lie to me?"

She shook her head. "I'm not. Really. He didn't assault me or anything. He didn't get that chance."

"But he threatened to. That can be terrifying."

"It was."

"If you want someone to talk to, I know a passably good therapist."

"You're recommending a passably good therapist?" she asked with surprise.

"It's my brother. I can't give him too much praise. His head is big enough as it is and I have to live with him. For some reason, Caley loves him."

She had to bite back a grin. "Can I think about it?"

He gave an abrupt nod. "You're happy staying with Linc? I don't think he'd pressure you into anything . . ."

"He hasn't," she said quickly. "He'd never do that."

"Good," he said softly. "Is there anything else?"

"No, I don't think so."

"Are you on birth control? Would you like to talk about options?"

"I'm not . . . I haven't . . . yes, maybe," she changed direction quickly, thinking it over. It would be the sensible thing to do.

"Do you notice that your blood sugars fluctuate more around your period?"

She nodded.

"Let's talk through your options then you can have a think about it. All right?"

They spent the next ten minutes discussing everything.

"Any more questions?" Doc asked her.

"No. Thank you."

"Good. We're finished here," Doc said abruptly. He stood. "Let's go find Linc. Think he's gotten lost looking for imaginary cookies."

Oh, he was terrible.

He strode from the office but she took a bit longer and by the time she stepped out of the waiting room and into the hallway, he had disappeared.

"Urgh! This is so annoying!"

Marisol watched in shock as a gorgeous, blonde-haired woman stomped into the hallway. Recognizing her instantly, she froze.

CJ Bennett.

Okay, so she'd already met her. But she hadn't known who she was. This was her favorite author. Her idol. And she currently had her forehead pressed to the wall of the hallway, her fists slamming against the walls.

"It's a terrible story, with a horrible plot. Everyone is going to hate it! This is going to be the end of my career."

"I'm sure it's not," Marisol said quietly. She felt like she had to say something. How could Caley think her book would be terrible when Marisol devoured every word she wrote as though they were water drops and she was dying of thirst?

"What?" Caley whirled, her feet stumbling over nothing as her arms wind-milled in the air. "Ohh."

Marisol jumped for her, but it was too late, she fell to the floor with a thump.

"Ouch."

"Oh God! I'm so sorry. This is all my fault. I shouldn't have frightened you and made you fall. Are you hurt? What can I do?" Marisol crouched down beside her, her breath coming in sharp pants.

"Whoa. First of all, honey, take a breath. I'm fine. I just fell on my butt. Happens all the time. Basically a daily occurrence."

"It is," a deep voice agreed from behind Marisol. She turned to find a tall man with chestnut-colored hair had walked through the door from the waiting room and she hadn't even noticed. "What did you trip over this time, poppet?"

"My own feet," Caley said dryly. "As per usual. You're home early. Finished with your head doctoring?" The man stepped around Marisol then leaned down, effortlessly picked Caley up and set her on her feet.

Marisol scrambled up as well.

"Archer, this is Marisol. Remember, I told you about her, she came from the spa to do our nails for Charlie's bridal shower? And now she's staying with Linc."

"Ahh, yes. Nice to meet you, Marisol." Archer had kind eyes and a warm handshake. After he let her hand go, he glanced down at Caley. "How sore is your butt? Does it need a rub? Maybe a magic kiss? Perhaps I should inspect it and see."

Caley rolled her eyes. "Don't mind him, he thinks he's a comedian."

But she could see Archer was rubbing Caley's bottom for her. Caley sighed, leaning into him.

"You stopping for the day, poppet?" Archer asked.

"My book is terrible," Caley wailed. "I can't make any of it work. At this stage, I'm never going to get it ready in time to send it to Daisy. It's just one, giant crappy mess. I'm going to be up all night trying to fix it."

"You'll be going to bed at your usual time," a familiar bark came from down the hall. Marisol peered round to find Doc walking towards them with a frown. Linc was behind him. He sent her a wink.

"No cookies. Doc lied," he told her with a sigh.

"And now all the cookies are gone!" Caley wailed, throwing her hands up in the air. "Will the blows never stop coming?"

"Hush," Doc told her, walking close and grabbing one of her hands gently, looking it over. "There's still some cookies left. I just told Linc there were none because I didn't want him eating them all."

"Jeez, Doc. I feel so loved." Linc shook his head.

"You're not loved. I love Caley. She gets a cookie. You don't."

Archer sighed. "It's hard to be your brother sometimes."

"Just sometimes?" Linc asked dryly.

"What about Marisol? Does Marisol get a cookie?" Caley asked. "She looks like she could use one."

"I think I've got some sugar free ones she can have," Doc replied.

"You don't eat sugar, Marisol?" Caley asked with interest.

"I'm diabetic," Marisol explained shyly, wishing she could kind of disappear now. Even if it was fascinating watching Caley with her two Docs.

"Really? That's great!"

"Um, it is?"

"Argh, Caley, think about what you just said." Archer nodded over at Marisol.

"Oh no, I'm such an idiot." Caley reached for her with the hand that Doc wasn't holding. "I didn't mean it like that. I'm so sorry. It's just the character in my story has diabetes and I'm having trouble figuring everything out. I can't believe I said that. Forgive me?"

"It's okay," Marisol told her.

"Oh good. So would you mind?"

"Um, mind what?" It was hard to keep up with Caley.

"Would you mind answering some questions for me? Or maybe even reading through the story to make sure what I've written is accurate? Do you like reading?"

"M-mind? I would love to! I love your books. I've read all of them. Several times."

"She got nervous about coming here when I told her your pen name," Linc explained.

"Nervous? To meet me? You don't have to be nervous. I'm just Caley."

"Just Caley is beautiful and smart and sweet," Archer told her. Wow, he was so sweet.

"Your hands are swollen," Doc snapped. "You need to sit with some heat packs on. Have you not been using your dictation?"

And Doc was so grumbly. She guessed they evened each other out.

Caley looked instantly guilty. "The words aren't coming, so I switched to typing."

"Caley," Doc growled in a disapproving voice. "That's going on your chart."

With a sigh, Caley pouted up at Doc. "My characters aren't behaving. What was I supposed to do?"

"Once your hands start hurting, you're supposed to stop," he told her.

"You're not winning this one," Archer told her with a soft pat on her ass. "Come on, let's go find some cookies and get your heating pad ready. You can talk to Marisol while you sit."

Caley looked over at Marisol. "But I need to take notes."

"I can do that. I don't mind," Marisol offered. "Or I could write things out as I'm reading your story."

"Oh, I couldn't ask you to do that."

"Please. I'd love to help. I just . . . your books have helped me when things haven't been so great in my life. I'd lose myself in them. I've read them several times. To help you in any way, would be amazing."

"I think that's one of the nicest things anyone has ever said to me." Caley slipped her hand around Marisol's arm. "Marisol, I think you are my new best friend."

24

Marisol was riding a high as they drove home.

"Can you believe Caley wants my help? Mine? And she's sending her manuscript to me so I can beta read for her?" She jumped up and down in the seat.

"Whoa. No jumping around while I'm driving." Linc shot his arm out to hold her against the seat, shooting her a firm look.

She sighed at him. "Daddy, we're not even on the road. I don't even need to wear a seatbelt."

"You most certainly do. I catch you without one and you'll get a spanking every night for a week."

Uh-huh. She didn't think so. Linc could never spank her that much. And she could barely feel the one she'd had this morning.

"You think I won't do it? I will. And before you tell me that one this morning didn't hurt that bad, that was just a light reminder. It wasn't a proper spanking."

It wasn't?

Hmm.

"Sit in your seat. Seems I do need to order the full car seat for you."

"You do not!" Bad enough she was getting a booster, but a proper seat with harness was not going to happen. Was it? She shot him a sideways glance.

Damn, he looked pretty serious.

He parked outside their cabin. She couldn't believe how today had gone. Not only was she getting help with managing her diabetes, but she now got to beta read for CJ Bennett. She'd taken notes as Caley asked questions, both of them eating a cookie, hers was sugar-free, with milk while the men all drank coffee.

Linc jumped out then adjusted the front seat for some reason. "Time to do the 'is Mari too short to drive Daddy's truck' test. Although I still don't think I'm going to let you drive it anyway."

"Daddy," she sighed. It was all too easy to call him that now. In fact, she couldn't imagine calling him anything else. She might have to watch out in public that she didn't slip.

"Don't Daddy me." He waggled a finger at her. "It's too big for you."

He helped her out of the truck and led her around to his side, lifting her in.

Crap. She shifted forward in the seat, reaching for the pedals. There! She turned and gave Linc a triumphant look.

"See, Daddy? I can totally drive this."

"Sure, if you don't need to see where you're going," a deep voice said, startling her.

She gave a gasp, twisting to see a big man standing behind Linc. He was several inches taller than Linc and broader. Thick with muscle, he had blond hair and a fair complexion. His beard was blond interspersed with red. Blue eyes watched her coldly.

Linc turned. Obviously, he hadn't heard the other man approach either. "Zander!"

Zander? That name sounded vaguely familiar. He didn't look like a ranch hand. Could this guy even ride a horse without it collapsing beneath him? Although he'd probably just terrify the cattle into doing what he wanted anyway.

"You're not serious about her driving your truck, right?" Zander asked without greeting Linc.

"It's good to see you, man. It's been a while," Linc said. "And no, I think it's clear she can't safely drive it."

Zander grunted.

Linc turned and lifted her down, giving her a wink. She slipped her hand into his, feeling uncertain.

"Zander, this is Marisol. Mari-girl, Zander. He works for JSI."

Another noise came from Zander. She couldn't work out if he was agreeing with Linc or not. She held out her hand and Zander just stared at it.

"Um, Zander doesn't shake hands, teeny," Linc told her gently.

Okay.

Linc squeezed the hand he held in comfort.

"What's up? Do you need something?" Linc asked him.

"Heard you got trouble with the Devil's Sinners," Zander said.

"Ah, yeah. Kent spoke to you?"

Zander just crossed his arms over his chest and stared at Linc.

"How did you get here so quickly?" Linc asked.

"I'm superman," Zander said.

Wait. Was that a joke? She looked up at Linc, unsure. He appeared just as confused.

"I was also in the area when Kent called. Need to talk to him about increasing the security for the ranch. I snuck in without setting off any alarms."

"I'm sure he'll enjoy that conversation," Linc said dryly.

"Yes."

Was he serious? Did he not understand that Linc was being sarcastic? She just couldn't tell.

"And you have no security on your cabin. The door was unlocked."

She moved closer to Linc as Zander gave him a disapproving look.

Linc wrapped his arm around her shoulders. Zander tilted his head slightly as he studied her. "Are you scared of me?"

Okay. She hadn't expected him to ask her that outright. "You're a bit intimidating."

He just nodded. He didn't offer any reassurances. He was an odd guy.

Zander turned to Linc. "Are you inviting me in or are we having this conversation out here?"

"Conversation?" Linc asked.

"About what to do about the Devil's Sinners."

"Oh right. Yep. Come in. Ahh, Mari needs her lunch soon, though."

"Would you like to stay for lunch?" Marisol asked, thinking they should be polite since it sounded like he was here to help them.

Zander watched her as though confused by the offer. "No. Thank you. I like to prepare my own food. Less likelihood of being poisoned."

"Poisoned? You mean food poisoning?"

"That too."

That too? Who was this guy?

"This won't take long," Zander said.

"Sure. Come in, we'll talk in my office." Linc took her hand again, leading her into the house.

"Your doors should be locked," Zander lectured. "And you need an alarm system. Do you have a weapon?"

"I've got a rifle."

Zander shook his head, looking incredulous. "You need a weapon in every room. Loaded and hidden."

"I don't think that's necessary," Linc said. "And it would be dangerous with Mari around."

Zander glanced down at her. "Do you know how to use a gun?"

She shook her head as Linc stripped off her jacket, scarf and hat, putting them away. The foyer was already pretty small, with Zander in here, it felt tiny.

Marisol really didn't want to learn how to fire a gun.

"She should know how to use one. Everyone on the ranch should," Zander countered.

"The ranch is a safe place to live."

"Doesn't mean trouble won't come here. Always be prepared for the worst. I told Clint to build a safe room into each cabin. Didn't listen to me. I have one in each of my houses."

A safe room? Guns? Self-defense? One in each of his houses?

She looked at Linc in alarm. He smoothed back her hair. "Why don't you go rest for a while, teeny. Read Caley's book. I'll put some leftovers in the oven to heat. We'll eat in about forty-five minutes, okay?"

"Don't you need me for this meeting?"

"I've got it."

Zander gave her a nod. Linc led him into his office and she raced off gratefully. Even if she did feel a bit guilty about leaving Zander to Linc.

LINC LED Zander into his small office. "Take a seat."

"I don't like to sit," Zander replied, leaning against the back wall and staring out the window. Linc sat with a sigh. He hadn't had much to do with Zander, even though the other man had worked for JSI for years.

Blunt and eccentric, Zander didn't live here on the ranch. Nobody knew exactly where he lived most of the time. Doc had to go and help him a few months back when he was shot, but he said he'd been blindfolded before being driven to him.

Paranoid.

Rumors were he had his own small group of mercenaries that he led. Linc wasn't sure why he even continued to work for Kent.

Anyway, none of that mattered right now.

"Kent told me everything he knows. Can you go over it in case he missed anything," Zander said jumping straight into business. He didn't really do small talk.

Linc told him everything that had happened with Tiger and Marisol.

"You want him taken out?" Zander asked bluntly.

Yes. Fuck. He didn't want this asshole breathing the same air as his girl. But could he order his murder and live with that on his conscience? "I'd like to know where he is. Maybe deliver a message."

Zander just raised an eyebrow. "Guys like that, they don't usually take messages like that well."

"If we kill him then Saber will have all of his men gunning for us."

Zander frowned. "Saber needs to go, too."

"You know him?" It was weird Zander turning up like this. He never came to the ranch.

"Got some business with him."

"So this is personal?"

Zander just stared at him. "My guys and I will find Tiger. Figure things out from there. Deliver a message. Marisol needs to stay here, under close watch. We can't have them figuring out where she is. Gonna tell Kent to lock down everyone as much as possible. Nobody leaves the ranch alone."

"Do you think that's necessary?" Linc asked. "He doesn't know where she is."

"If he's obsessed with her, he'll be searching for her. And you've been seen with her recently. He might be a dumb fuck, but he's not that stupid."

Zander just grunted and opened the office door. Then he stilled. "You need a proper car seat for her."

Before Linc could answer, he was gone.

25

"So he's going to track down Tiger?"

Linc looked up from the whiteboard he was writing on to see that Marisol had barely touched her lunch. Shit. His fault. He knew better than to talk about anything upsetting when she was eating. Her mood affected her hunger.

"He is. And he's the best tracker there is. He'll find him."

"He's unusual," she said carefully.

"I know. But if he says he'll do something then he does it. Now, that's enough talk about that. Eat your lunch, please. Or would you like Daddy to feed you?"

She pulled a face but spooned up some lunch. "But—"

"Marisol, I'm serious. That's going down as a rule."

"What is?"

"No serious talk while eating. Now, after lunch we'll go through your rules then you can have a nap while I work. After your nap, would you like to read?"

She crossed her arms over her chest with a glare. "I don't need rules. I definitely don't need a rule about not talking about serious stuff while eating."

"Really? Because you don't seem to be eating."

"Maybe I'm just not hungry.

"Or maybe you need Daddy's help." He dragged her plate over towards him, stealing her fork.

"Hey! Daddy!"

"Since you're not eating, Daddy is going to help you." He spooned up some food. "Open wide like a tyrannosaurus rex."

"Daddy!" She laughed. "I'm not a dinosaur." But she opened her mouth obediently.

"That's it. Good girl."

"You're meant to say open up for the choo-choo train."

"I am? That doesn't seem nearly as exciting. What about here comes the princess's unicorn flying through the air, ready to land?"

She opened her mouth and he gave her another mouthful. "That's better, Daddy."

"You're a good girl to open your mouth so obediently for Daddy." He wiggled his eyebrows at her. "I'll have to remember that for later."

She blushed as he'd thought she would. "Daddy!"

"What?" he said with mock-innocence. "I was talking about for dinner. Dirty-minded girl. Here comes another unicorn!"

After she'd eaten enough to satisfy him, he sent her into the living room to read while he tidied up. He looked down at the whiteboard of rules he'd started creating. Picking it up, he walked into his office to grab another whiteboard as well as a spare notebook.

When he walked into the living room, she looked up, her gaze narrowing in on the whiteboards.

"It was a two-pack," he explained with a grin.

She rolled her eyes.

"Right, time to talk about rules. Put down your eReader, please."

"But I'm reading, Daddy."

"You can have ten minutes of reading time before your nap, but you need to put the eReader down and listen to Daddy."

"Don't wanna."

He had to bite back a smile at her show of rebellion. He took it as a sign that she was now more relaxed around him. Although he didn't intend to let her see how amused he was.

"Marisol. You have until the count of three to put the eReader down and listen to Daddy."

She didn't appear to even hear what he said.

"One."

She didn't look up.

"Two."

Nothing.

"Three."

He plucked the eReader out of her hands and turned it off. She sat up straight. "Hey, what do you think you're doing?"

"No more reading until after your nap."

"What? Noooo. That's not fair!"

"Daddy needs to talk to you about your rules. And you need to pay attention. Which you can't do with your eReader in your hands."

"Daddy. That's just mean."

"Daddy is very mean," he agreed, writing on the rules' whiteboard.

"And I don't need a nap."

"Sure you don't, teeny."

"I won't sleep. I'll just lie there, bored out of my mind."

"As long as you stay in bed for the whole hour, that's fine," he told her.

"A whole hour! This is cruel and unusual punishment."

"It's terrible," Linc agreed as he continued to write on the whiteboard. "Not sure how you put up with me. I figure you're only with me because of my looks."

"You're definitely good eye candy."

He put down the whiteboard and leapt towards her, tickling her until she begged for mercy.

"I have to pee."

He chuckled as she raced off to the toilet. Little brat. When she returned, he was looking down at his list of rules with satisfaction.

"There, I think we've got most of the rules. No doubt more will come up but I reckon that covers it for now. What do you think?" he asked her as she sat next to him, turning the board towards her.

Marisol gave him a skeptical look.

"What? You think I missed some? Let's see what we've got. Mari's list of rules. No lying. She must talk to Daddy if something is worrying or upsetting her—"

"Those rules apply to Daddy too, right," she interjected.

"Of course. Next rule. No going anywhere without Daddy's knowledge. That's not me being a controlling jerk. It's about safety. I simply want to know where you're going and when you think you'll be back. You can't leave the ranch until we've decided that it's safe. And until you're more knowledgeable of the ranch, I'd prefer that you didn't walk around on your own. If you want to visit one of the other Littles or go on a walk, tell me. I'll take you. I don't want you getting lost. Okay?"

"Yeah. That's probably a good idea."

"If someone like Abby comes to visit and asks you to go to her place or one of the other Littles' houses, just send me a text okay? Not trying to keep you locked up. But I would like to know where you are. Coming home and finding you gone would have me panicking and sending out a search party."

"All right, Daddy."

"Next rule. No walking while reading."

"Okay."

"You must always wear a seatbelt, no matter if you're on the road or the ranch."

She sighed dramatically. "Fine, Daddy."

"And if you ever are driving, you must drive safely, which means no speeding or using your phone while driving. And no driving my truck."

"I still think I could manage it."

"Teeny, you can't even see out the front window. I ever catch you trying to drive it and you're getting my belt. Breaking a health and safety rule will always result in you getting a hot ass. And those punishments will be done as soon as is safely possible."

Damn, she was cute when she pouted.

"Next rule. No talking down about yourself. That's very important. You've had a small punishment, but the next time you do this, the punishment will be much harder."

She nibbled at her lower lip nervously. "Okay, Daddy. Although for the record, I thought that punishment was plenty hard."

"Did you? No talking about serious topics while eating. No moving from Daddy's lap without his permission. When you are Little, you will not swear and you will address Daddy as the most wonderful, handsome Daddy in the world."

"What? Daddy, that's not in there!" She glared at him as he stared down at the list in mock-surprise.

"It's not? It should be!"

She rolled her eyes at him. Little brat.

"Fine. I won't put that in there. But you can feel free to call me that whenever you like."

"Thank you, Daddy. I'll keep that in mind," she said dryly.

"No doing anything that might put you in danger."

"That seems rather vague."

"Well, I couldn't put down every example. But anything that might put you at risk is a no. Understand?"

"Yes, Daddy."

"No panties unless Daddy puts them on you or grants permission."

She huffed out a breath but there was no real protest.

"Bedtime is nine-thirty."

"Nine-thirty!" she exclaimed. "But I can read in bed, right?"

"No way. Doc said no devices right before sleep."

"I'll get some paperbacks then."

"Nope."

"But what will I do? I can't go to sleep at nine-thirty."

"I can think of one or two things." He gave her a pointed look.

She blushed at his pointed look. "Oh."

Oh? Was that all she had to say? She was so cute sometimes.

"Now, in this notebook, I figured you might want to keep track of what you eat and when. We could leave it in the kitchen. What do you think?"

"I guess it would be a good idea. What if I forget to do it or write it down, though?"

"Well, I guess that depends on you. If you want my help, I can do that. But this is up to you. I want to help you be as healthy as possible because I don't like the idea of my baby ill or injured. Why don't we see how things go first, okay? When you're in Little headspace, I'll take more responsibility, but you need to tell me if something I'm doing is wrong or if you feel unwell. That's very important so I figure this will help me too."

"Okay, Daddy. That makes sense."

He wrote out breakfast, lunch and dinner as well as three snacks on the first page, leaving room for her to write next to each heading.

"You sure do love being organized, Daddy," she told him. Then she wrinkled her nose adorably as she saw what was going on the top of the next whiteboard.

Mari's Naughty Girl Chart.

"Daddy, we really don't need that."

"Oh, I think we do. This will help Daddy keep track of your behavior so he doesn't miss anything. Each evening we can count up how many ticks you have. I don't want to wait until the end of the week. I have a feeling there could be quite a few on there by then."

"Daddy. I is not naughty!"

"Uh-huh. We'll see. Now, health and safety rules get an immediate spanking and several ticks on the chart, just so you know."

He placed her rules and naughty girl chart on the mantel above the fireplace while she sulked.

"Hey." He crouched down in front of her, gently placing his hands on her thighs. "Is this too much? I mean, you haven't agreed to be totally mine so maybe I should have waited, huh? I think I got too excited. We can adjust the boards or even get rid of them if you'd prefer."

MARISOL SAW the wistfulness in Linc's gaze as he stood and took a step towards the boards.

"No." She reached up and grabbed hold of his hand.

He looked down at her.

She shook her head. "It's not too fast. I want . . . the boards. The truth is, the rules make me feel . . ."

Damn it. She couldn't believe she was going to admit this.

"They make me feel secure. Cared for." Loved. "My aunt never cared much about what I did as long as I kept the house tidy, did my work and kept out of her way. She never cared about my safety or health."

"You sure?"

"I'm sure. It's just a lot of changes. Living here. Being free to explore my Little side. Having you as my Daddy." She gave him a shy look. "I really like it here. With you." And she definitely never wanted to leave. She opened her mouth to tell him that, but the words wouldn't come. And she thought she knew why. Because despite his reassurances, there was still a worry in the back of her mind that he would leave her.

Like everyone else.

She knew it wasn't fair to Linc. He'd never treated her as disposable. But having so many people enter and leave her life, with not one of them trying to find her or contact her again, it had done something to her. And trust just didn't come easily. Already she was amazed by how she'd opened up to him. However, it was just that step further to reveal her heart to him.

"I love having you here, teeny. I hope you'll never leave."

She smiled, her heart opening just that bit more. "You say the nicest things."

"It's only the truth. Now, it's time for your nap."

She frowned. "Can't I read my book while lying on the sofa?"

"Nope. You're having a proper nap."

"But I haven't done anything all day."

"It's not just physical stress that can be tiring, mental stress can be even more exhausting and you've had plenty of that lately. Besides, you told Doc you often don't sleep well so you have plenty of catching up to do." He stood and held out his hand to her.

She took it with a loud sigh. But she let him lead her to the bedroom. He stopped by the bed. "Do you need to test your blood sugar?"

Nodding, she grabbed her bag off the bedside table and tested herself. While she did that, he grabbed one of his T-shirts, laying it on the bed. "Arms up," he commanded when she was finished.

She held up her arms and he took off her sweater then her T-shirt. Finally, he reached around and undid her bra. She clasped hold of the front of it as he drew it off.

"Daddy!"

"Let go. You can't sleep in your bra. And none of your body

should be off-limits to Daddy. All of him belongs to you and all of you belongs to Daddy. Understand?"

"Yes." She lowered her hands and he drew off her bra. Then he knelt between her legs and ran a finger down her breast, twirling it around her nipple.

"These tits are so beautiful. I wish I could play with them all day. Suck at them, squeeze them, bury my face in them."

So now she was turned on. Damn him. How was she going to sleep like this? Well, she guessed she could take care of it herself.

"Lie back," he urged. Once she was on her back, he slid off her yoga pants and panties. She placed her arm over her eyes, knowing she was completely on display.

"That's a beautiful sight. Part your legs for me."

"Linc."

A light smack on her pussy had her groaning. Why was that such a turn-on?

"What do you call me?"

"Daddy or Sir."

"That's right. Now part your legs. I want another taste and we both know that a few orgasms help you to relax. Last night after you came several times, you slept like a baby."

She whimpered, but she couldn't deny it. Last night was the best night's sleep she'd had in years. She found herself pushing her legs apart. She wasn't given time to worry about her taste or whether he'd like it. He placed his mouth immediately over her shaved pussy. Then his tongue slid along her lips, brushing briefly over her clit.

"Oh God!" she cried out.

He lapped at her, his hands kept her thighs from closing as he played with her, swirling his tongue around her clit over and over until she was at the edge then jabbing at her entrance with shallow thrusts that drove her insane.

She wanted him inside her.

Then he raised his hands to her breasts. He played with her nipples as he returned his tongue to her clit. She threw her head back as heat rushed over her. Her pussy clenched down. Her orgasm grew and grew until she screamed with her release.

Still, he lapped at her, licking at her folds as her breath came in sharp pants, her entire body shaking with reaction.

"That's my good girl," he told her, kissing up her tummy to suck on one nipple then the other. He cupped her pussy. "Such a sweet pussy." A kiss landed gently on her lips. Then reaching over, he grabbed the T-shirt.

"Sit up, teeny."

She felt kind of dazed and out of it as he dressed her in the T-shirt. He drew the covers down and helped her into bed. After making sure she had Princess Nana and her snuggly, he pulled the curtains. The curtains were black-out ones so he turned the light on in the bathroom. Then he kissed her forehead gently. "When you wake up, you're to come find me immediately. Once the baby monitor I ordered arrives, you'll be able to wait in bed for me to come to you. Do not get dressed, just come straight to the office, understand?"

"Yes, Daddy, but I won't sleep," she muttered as her eyes drifted shut and she fell asleep.

26

Linc looked up from his work as a Little girl appeared in his doorway. Her hair was a tangled mess from her nap and he made a note to braid it next time. She still wore his T-shirt and as she rubbed at her eyes, it rode up far enough to show him that she wasn't wearing panties.

What a good girl she was.

Maybe he should always have her come to him like this after her naps. It was freaking adorable. And it was making his already hard cock strain against his jeans. Damn, it was a wonder he could get any work done with all the blood pooling in his cock.

She still had Princess Nana and her snuggly in one arm. He wished that he had her playroom ready. But he'd set up a different sort of area for her this afternoon. He was still working through a pile of paperwork that had gotten neglected. No wonder Clint was so grouchy at times, having to deal with paperwork made him grumpy too.

Maybe what he needed was a reward for getting through this work.

"Come here, Mari-girl," he told her. "Daddy wants you to sit on his lap."

She walked forward with a yawn. "I can't believe I fell asleep."

"You've been asleep for two hours. I was about to come in and wake you. Didn't want you to sleep too long or you'd never get to sleep tonight. Although they do say you're not supposed to wake a sleeping baby."

"Daddy," she protested as he lifted her onto his lap so she was straddling his legs. "I'm not a baby."

"Ahh, but you're my baby, aren't you? Tell me you're my sweet Little baby girl."

She squirmed on his lap. "I'm your sweet Little baby girl."

"That you are. Now do you have to go potty?"

"Daddy!"

"What?"

"You not supposed to ask questions like that," she told him.

"Then how am I supposed to know whether you need to go or not? And you didn't answer me."

"Yes," she whispered. "I have to go."

He stood her on her feet. "Let's go then."

"I don't need any help," she muttered.

"I won't stay while you pee, not until you're more comfortable with me doing that."

"Can't see that ever happening."

Oh, it would.

He took Princess Nana and her snuggly from her, placing them on his desk. He led her into the bathroom, then drew the T-shirt up over her hips so she was bare as he guided her onto the toilet. He kissed her gently as she growled at him.

"I'll go make you a snack. Do what you need to then come straight back to the office. Understand?"

~

"SUCH A BOSSY DADDY," she grumbled to herself as she walked back into the office. He was sitting behind the desk again. She looked over in interest at what he'd done in the corner of the room. There were two chairs from the dining table set up with a blanket over them and pillows scattered underneath.

"Daddy! Is that a blanket fort?"

"It's a reading fort," he told her. "Until we get your bean bag chair, I thought you might like to read in it and then I can keep you close to me. What do you think?"

She jumped up and down with a squeal. "It's perfect."

"Good. I'm glad you like it. Thought you might want to keep reading Caley's story while I work."

"That sounds perfect." She couldn't believe he was thoughtful.

"First, come give Daddy some loves and then have your snack and some water. You tested your blood sugars?"

"Yep, it's good."

She ended up sitting on his lap and eating her snack while he made sure she drank plenty of water. She wondered what it would be like to curl up on his lap while he gave her a bottle. Maybe she'd find out in a few days. The idea made her feel warm inside.

"Shall I go get dressed?" she asked.

"You can stay in what you have on. We're not going anywhere."

When she was finished eating, he kissed the top of her head.

"Right, teeny. You can go to your reading fort. I put your eReader in there already. If you need anything, then call out for me, okay?"

She climbed off his lap.

"Okay, Daddy. Work hard." She waggled a finger at him, giving him a stern look. "No slacking off."

He whacked her ass as she darted away too slowly. She giggled then grabbed Princess Nana and her snuggly off the desk before settling into her reading fort.

IT WAS about an hour before he started to notice her squirming. He eyed her water bottle. Not much had gone down. She was lying on her front, facing away from him. Every so often, she'd go to tug the T-shirt down, but it kept riding up giving him a glimpse of that pert ass.

"Do you need to go potty, baby?" he asked casually.

"No!" she replied.

"Then why are you squirming around so much?"

"No reason," she said in a suspiciously tight voice.

He put down the invoice he was reading and looked over at her. Was she in pain? Discomfort?

Aroused?

"Is my baby turned on?" he asked huskily.

"Oh God."

"You know you don't get to come without my permission, don't you?"

Another groan. He felt safe grinning since she was facing away from him.

"Is Caley's book turning you on? Maybe you should read it out loud."

"No!"

Oh, that just made him more curious.

"Answer me, Mari-girl. Are you aroused?"

"I don't wanna."

"Well, I guess I'm just going to have to come over there and find out for myself."

She whirled onto her back, her legs coming together. "No, you don't!"

"Oh, I think I do. You're squirming around so much it's distracting me. Are you in pain?"

Her eyes darted around, looking everywhere but at him. "No."

"Are you bored?"

"Nooo," she groaned.

"Then what else could it be?"

"Okay, I'm turned on."

"Then why didn't you ask me to help you? I told you if you needed something you were to ask."

"I can't ask for that!" she told him.

"Sure you can. If my baby needs to come then I want to know and like I told you, I'm a very indulgent Daddy. Which is very lucky for you because it means I likely won't deny you an orgasm unless you've been naughty."

He walked over and knelt at her feet. "Part your legs, I want to see how wet this pussy is."

She moaned and he thought she might put up a protest, which would have been futile, but she surprised him by parting those gorgeous thighs and showing him how wet she was between her legs. Leaning in, he licked at the crease of her thighs, tasting her sweetness. He took his time, lapping her mound without going anywhere near her slit.

"Daddy, please."

"I want you to read to me while I'm eating you out."

"I can't!"

"I want you to try. You're going to read to me until I say you can come, then you can put it down. But if you stop before I give permission, then I'll stop and go back to my paperwork, leaving you unsatisfied."

"You wouldn't!"

"Try me."

"But you said you would give me whatever I needed, I just had to ask."

"But you didn't ask, did you? You made Daddy guess. If you'd asked me if you could come straight from the get-go then you'd already have come and Daddy would be cleaning you up."

"Damn it," she muttered.

"Read," he commanded.

"Dear Lord, can't believe I'm doing this."

He licked up along her thigh.

"Okay. Okay. Here goes." She cleared her throat.

"LEAN OVER THE HAY BALE," Jonty ordered.

Mars had already put a blanket over the hay. Always thoughtful.

Tase had brought the plug and lube. Yeah, that wasn't so thoughtful.

Jonty was the undisputed leader of their little family. Firm but fair. He always got the final say.

Tase was the disciplinarian. Quieter than the other two and more serious. She couldn't get away with much if Tase was around.

Mars was the sweetheart. The indulgent one. She had him wrapped around her little finger.

Although right now, he wasn't looking all that indulgent. His face was stern. His arms were crossed over his chest. She gave him a pleading look. Surely, he'd argue on her behalf. He'd done it before when it came to discipline. When he turned to Jonty, she felt the knot in her stomach unravel slightly. She really didn't want to feel the crop on her poor bottom.

"Should we plug her before she's disciplined?" Mars asked. "Or after?"

Disbelief filled her. He didn't just say that, right? He couldn't have.

"Let's plug her first. Tase, you can plug her. Mars would you like to be the one to discipline her since you're the one she disobeyed?" Jonty asked casually.

"Yes, I would."

Lily felt the cheeks of her bottom being drawn apart. Tase pressed a lubed finger inside her bottom, stretching her, getting her ready for the plug.

Finally, she realized how serious they were.

And that she was in deep, deep trouble.

"PUT THE EREADER DOWN, MARI-GIRL," he commanded. Gratefully, she dropped it to the side. She was scarcely able to read, she was so turned on.

Marisol started to whimper as her need grew. Her nipples were tight buds as Linc sucked on her clit, his finger moving from her pussy down to her asshole.

"Please I can't . . . I can't. . . ."

He pressed his finger against the puckered bud, and she came with a scream, her entire body shuddering from the explosions. He continued to lap at her, bringing her down from her high. Then he lifted himself up over her body, peering down at her with a grin. "That was fun."

Fun wasn't the word she would use.

"We'll have to do that again."

She groaned. It was official. He was trying to kill her with orgasms.

And are you complaining?

Hell. No.

27

M arisol looked at the packages longingly.

They were all stacked in the living room, waiting to be opened. They were calling to her.

Open me, Marisol. Open me.

How was she supposed to resist? She'd waited sooo long already. Honestly, it felt like Linc had been gone for days not hours. When was he coming home? It had to be soon, right?

She'd been here four nights now. A whole lot of packages had arrived this morning, but it had been easier to resist their pull when she was busy reading Caley's book.

But she'd just finished it. And she was on her own with nothing to do.

Surely opening one of them would be okay, right?

How long was it until Linc got home? Two hours. And then she'd have to eat lunch and have a nap before she was allowed to open anything.

That just wasn't fair.

She'd open one then rewrap it. He'd never know. Marisol tiptoed over to the packages, even though there was no one in the house other than her. She grabbed a small package. Opening it up, she let out a delighted cry as she saw the box of building blocks inside. She couldn't wait to build something.

Excitement flooded her. Maybe she should just peek at something else. She grabbed another package and opened it up. Ooh. It was her crafting stuff. This was so much fun. Look at all the glitter. She couldn't wait to create something with this.

This was even better than Christmas.

LINC CLIMBED out of his truck and stretched. Last night as his baby slept, he'd gotten all caught up on paperwork so he could spend the afternoon with her. After her nap, of course. He thought most of the stuff he'd ordered was here, so he'd unpack some while she was sleeping and set up her playroom.

He was looking forward to spending more time with her Little. He hadn't pushed her on it, wanting her to open up on her own. But he figured this would help her relax more and put her in the right headspace.

Tonight, he might also convince her to let him bathe her. He'd ordered some special toys for the bath. For her big and her Little.

He had to adjust himself before he entered the house. His cock seemed to be constantly hard. He dreamed about her sweet pussy. Christ, he couldn't think of her pussy right now or he'd have to go take a cold shower.

After taking off his jacket and boots, he walked into the living room. "Mari-girl? Where are you?"

He came to a complete stop.

Holy. Shit.

The living room was a mess of packaging, toys, clothes and flat-pack furniture. Marisol turned from where she was pouring glitter onto a piece of cardstock. But as she turned, the glitter continued to pour out.

Right onto the carpet.

Shit. Shit. Shit.

He closed his eyes for a moment. In. Out. In. Out.

"Daddy? Daddy, are you okay?"

In. Out. It was just a mess. It was easily tidied up. That glitter might be an issue but that was what vacuum cleaners were for.

"Daddy? Oh God, have I killed you?"

He opened his eyes and looked down into Marisol's concerned eyes. She was biting at her lip worriedly, shifting her weight from foot to foot. She was wearing a pair of yoga pants and her cute cat hoodie.

"Are you okay, Daddy?"

"Marisol, what did Daddy tell you about all the packages?" he asked in a low voice.

She looked down at her feet. "That I wasn't to open them until you got home."

"And so why have all the packages been opened? Why are you playing with your crafting stuff?"

"I'm sorry, Daddy. I finished Caley's story and then I got bored. And the packages were just sitting there, going, 'Open me, Marisol. Open me.' I swear, they spoke to me."

"The packages spoke to you?"

"Uh-huh."

"That's the excuse you're going with?"

"It's not an excuse. It's the honest truth."

"Honest. Truth." He placed his palm over her forehead. "You don't have a temperature. But if you're hearing voices, I think I best check properly."

"Properly?" she asked.

"Uh-huh. The only proper way to take a Little's temperature is to use a rectal thermometer. Take your pants off and bend over the couch, I'll be back in a moment."

"No! I don't have a temperature, the packages didn't talk to me. I made it up."

He crossed his arms over his chest. "You're in trouble, little girl."

Uh-oh.

"I'm sorry, Daddy. Once I got started, I just couldn't stop."

"You shouldn't have even started, should you?" he said sternly.

"No, Daddy. You're not going to punish me, are you?" she asked in a small voice.

"Do you think you deserve to be punished?"

Damn him. She couldn't lie. But answering honestly was going to land her in trouble.

What was a girl supposed to do?

She didn't want to be punished.

Don't you?

Crap. She was all messed up.

"You boxed me in neatly," she muttered.

He gave a huff of laughter. "Why, teeny, whatever do you mean?"

She gave him a dirty look and his eyebrows rose. "Uh-uh, watch out or the wind might change and your face will end up like that."

Marisol rolled her eyes, crossing her arms across her chest. "That's not true, Daddy."

"It is. Happened to a baby girl I knew. She was grouchy because her Daddy wouldn't buy her an ice cream. The wind changed and that poor girl now has a permanent frown."

"Daddyyy," she complained at his silliness. "That's not true."

"Do you really want to take that chance?"

She thought about that and shook her head. "No, Daddy."

"Now, you didn't answer me. Do you need to be punished for disobeying Daddy?"

She thought about it. She had disobeyed him. And she did feel guilty for opening all the packages.

"Do you know why I wanted you to wait?"

She shook her head.

"It wasn't so I could torture you. It was so I could see your face as you opened each package. I thought it would be like watching you on Christmas morning."

Oh God.

"Oh, now I feel awful," she wailed dramatically. "I'm the worst Little girl in the world." Tears filled her eyes.

"I wouldn't go that far," he soothed her.

"I am! I'm so naughty. And I feel so terrible. I'm so sorry, Daddy." As she sobbed, he drew her close, pressing her face against his chest.

"Shh, baby. Shh. It's not the end of the world. You weren't that naughty. Shh."

"I was. I deserve a spankin'."

"Yeah? And how many smacks should I give you?" he asked.

"Twenty!"

"A whole twenty, gosh. You are feeling guilty. Guilt isn't a good emotion to feel, is it?"

"No."

"A punishment can clear all of that away. Is that what you want? To be punished so you no longer feel guilty?"

"Yes, Daddy."

"All right. Then Daddy will punish you for disobeying him."

She sniffled. With a sigh, he moved her towards the couch. Sitting, he drew her onto his lap then reached over for some tissues, wiping her face gently.

"Easy, teeny. There's no need for so many tears. At least not until you actually get your spanking."

"Oh no, you're going to spank me?" she cried.

"You just told me you thought you deserved to get twenty smacks on your bottom."

"Yes, but . . . but . . . oh no."

"Oh no, indeed. Hush, now." He held the tissue to her nose and she blew. Gross. "Calm down." He held her tight, running his hand up and down her back. "Good girl."

"Are you gonna spank me now?"

"We're going to have some lunch then you're going to help me clean this up. Then you can go over my knee for a spanking before I put you to bed for an extra-long nap."

She opened her mouth to protest then saw the stern look on his face.

Well. Darn it.

MARISOL HELPED Linc tidy up all the packaging. He vacuumed up the glitter while she cleaned up her crafting stuff. She felt awful about the mess she'd made as well as disobeying him.

She did deserve her spanking. Even if she wasn't looking forward to it.

Finally, the living room was in some semblance of order.

"Did you put your things in your new purse?" he asked her.

"I haven't moved it all over yet." After seeing how worn her bag was that held her lancing device, insulin and monitor, along with her glucose tabs and a few other things, he'd done some research and bought her a new one. It was made of red leather. She loved it.

"You can do that soon. Where did this car seat come from?" he asked, looking at the over-sized child's car seat with harness. It looked top of the range and expensive.

"I thought you ordered it."

"No," he grunted. "I ordered the booster." He pointed at the half-booster that had no back to it.

"Then who ordered this?"

He sighed. "I have an idea. Zander."

"Why would Zander send a car seat here? Oh no, will he be mad that I opened it?" she asked, worriedly.

"No. Not since I'm certain that it's for you."

"He sent me a harnessed seat for the truck?"

"Yep."

"Why?" she asked.

"Who knows. But the last thing he said to me was that I needed a proper seat for you and then one appears. He's odd like that." He turned to her. "Come here." Linc crooked a finger at her and she walked over to him. Cupping her face, he kissed her lightly. "You're going to spend ten minutes in time-out while I take this stuff into your playroom. Then when I call out to you, you're to come to me and lay yourself across my lap, understand?"

"I understand, Daddy."

"Your naughty girl stool has arrived so you can sit on it." He drew the stool out and set it in the corner of the living room.

She moved towards it, but Linc grabbed hold of her hand gently. "You're going to sit on a bare bottom. You might as well take your pants off entirely. You're not going to need them. You can nap in my T-shirt and I'll put you in one of your outfits after you wake up."

Well. Hell.

She blushed but didn't argue as she pulled off her yoga pants.

Linc ran a finger down her ass once she was bare. "Good to see you can follow some orders. If you'd been wearing panties then your spanking would be twice as long."

He led her to the time-out stool and had her sit with her nose pressed to the wall. "I'll be in and out of the room often. If you feel uncomfortable or ill or off then call out your safeword. Okay?"

"Okay, Daddy."

Time seemed to drift by slowly as she sat there. Tired, she shut her eyes. It had been exhausting, undoing all those packages. Her mind drifted to Caley's book. She hoped she had been helpful with her comments.

"Okay, teeny, it's time to come get your spanking."

"Oh." She sat up and turned towards him, her hand on her chest. "You gave me a fright."

He narrowed his eyes at her. "Were you about to fall asleep?"

"Um. Maybe?"

Sitting back on the sofa, he crossed his arms over his chest. "Teeny, time-out isn't supposed to be sleepy time."

"Sorry?"

He shook his head, looking exasperated and slightly amused. "Most Littles hate time-out. But not my teeny, she enjoys it."

She shrugged. Should she apologize? "I like quiet time to myself."

"Next time, we'll do time-out after your spanking. Sitting on that hard stool with a red bottom might help you focus. Did you even spend the time reflecting on why you were in time-out?"

"Umm." In her defense he hadn't told her to do that.

"Come here. That was my fault. I should have been more specific."

She walked slowly over and took his hand. He gently but firmly drew her over his lap. Because he was sitting on the middle cushion, her legs and torso were supported on the sofa and her middle was over his hard lap.

"Now, tell Daddy why you're being punished," he said as he drew the hoodie up over her ass, baring her completely to his gaze.

"'Cause I was naughty and disobeyed you. And 'cause I made a mess."

"Yes, although I wouldn't punish you for making a mess. I know Little girls get messy sometimes when they're having fun. However, if you're working with glitter, you do need to put a sheet down. That stuff goes everywhere."

"Yes, Daddy," she replied obediently.

"Right, you're getting twenty. Your bottom is going to be nice and red after this. Don't worry, you don't have to count this time."

Lucky her.

"Would you like me to hold your hands for you or are you able to keep them out in front of you?"

"I can do it, Daddy."

"Good girl."

Without warning, he struck. Owie! Once, twice, three times in quick succession. By smack number five, she was wriggling around, attempting to free herself.

"Stay still, little girl," he growled at her.

Oh no. Another five quick spanks warmed her ass. He stopped and rubbed her bottom gently.

"How you doing, teeny? Feel okay?"

"My bottom hurts." She pouted.

"That's the point. I wasn't talking about your naughty bottom, though. Are you all right to continue?"

"I think that's enough, Daddy," she said solemnly.

"Nope, you have another ten. And these ones are going to be harder than the first ten. Learning to obey Daddy, even on what might seem something small, is very important."

Two more smacks landed on her ass. She cried out, kicking her feet. The next two were lower down. He was covering her ass with firm spanks. And the burn in her ass was growing. Two more on the top of her thighs.

Oh shivers. Those hurt.

"Daddy, no more!"

Four more spanks, each in quick succession, landed in the

middle of her ass. When he was finished, she was crying, lying spent over his lap.

"There, there, baby girl. It's all done now. Good girl. Such a good girl."

Gently he turned her then he lay back on the sofa with her on his chest, running his hand up and down her back as he whispered to her, settling her down.

"How are you, teeny?"

"That hurt." Her bottom was still throbbing. She reached down and rubbed at her bottom.

"Uh-uh, no rubbing allowed. I'd make you go sit in time-out again, but it's time for your nap."

Well, she was thankful that at least she didn't have to sit on that hard stool. She didn't think she'd be able to stay still.

"And it was meant to hurt. It was punishment. To make you stop and think before disobeying Daddy again."

She laid her cheek against his chest, listening to his heart beat. "I is sorry, Daddy."

"I know, teeny. And all is forgiven now."

"It is?"

"Yep. A punishment wipes the slate clean."

"Oh, that's good." She yawned, suddenly exhausted.

"You feeling okay? Other than this hot bottom?" He squeezed one cheek, making her squeal.

"Daddy!"

"Well?"

"Yes, I is okay." Another yawn.

"Good girl. Let's get you down for your nap."

He sat them up then stood with her cradled against his chest, her front pressed to his, his arm under her hot ass, supporting her. She wrapped her arms and legs around him with a tired sigh. For once, she didn't feel like protesting taking a nap. She should, out of principle, but the thought of snuggling down in the sheets made her want to purr like a kitten.

He set her down next to the bed and stripped off her hoodie, T-shirt and bra. Then he helped her into one of his T-shirts. Then he drew the covers down as she reached for her bag to test her blood sugar levels. It was part of her routine to test before her nap.

"Go potty, too," Linc told her.

"Don't hafta," she replied as she walked towards the bathroom to wash her hands.

"Marisol, go potty. Or do you need Daddy to take you?"

"I is going. I is going."

She noticed he was fiddling with something on the nightstand but she didn't pay much attention. She walked back into the bedroom, having peed, much to her annoyance. Daddy didn't have to be right all the time. She saw there was a camera on the night-stand aimed her way.

"What's this, Daddy?"

"The baby monitor. It's a camera one so I can watch you on it. Today, I want you to wait in bed until I come get you. I'll see when you wake up so I won't be long. If you need to leave the bed, call out for me. If it's anything to do with your health then that trumps everything and you do what you need to do. That make sense?"

"Yes, Daddy."

He drew back the covers and tucked her firmly into bed. Then he handed her Princess Nana and her snuggly.

"I'm going to get you a bottle of water. Want to try the pacifier we bought? I washed it for you."

"Okay, I'll try it, Daddy."

He brushed a kiss across her forehead. "That's my good girl."

Picking up the monitor, he left. She slipped her thumb into her mouth as she waited, rubbing snuggly back and forth under her nose. By the time he returned, she was half-asleep. He sat next to her, and grabbed another pillow to put under her head so she was slightly raised. The nipple of an oversized baby bottle was pressed to her lips.

She knew he'd bought one, but she hadn't thought about using it yet. But as she opened her mouth and let him feed her, she found herself quite liking it. The water was nice and cool, but the nipple was soft and didn't have that horrid plastic taste.

When she'd had enough, she turned her face away, her eyes closed. She was nearly fully asleep when another nipple was pressed to her mouth. This one she didn't like. She spat it out, replacing it with her thumb.

Ahh. Much better.

"Well, I guess that's the answer to that question," a deep voice said quietly.

Yep. Pacifiers. Yucky.

28

Marisol lay back on the bed naked. Linc was choosing some clothes for her then they were going into the play room. She'd woken up around fifteen minutes ago, groggy and a bit disorientated. Linc hadn't taken long to come into the room. He'd given her some more water with the baby bottle and then when she was more awake, he'd helped her out of bed and pulled off the T-shirt she'd worn for her nap then had her lie back.

It was a good thing he kept his house so warm, considering how often she was naked or half-dressed. She watched as he pulled out a T-shirt with a rainbow on the front.

"Sit up, teeny."

She sat and he put the T-shirt on then added a yellow cardigan. Cute. Next, he drew out a yellow tutu skirt and some striped yellow and green socks. She clapped her hands as he moved to another drawer.

"Did you unpack it all while I slept, Daddy?"

"I did. You were sleeping very soundly. A good spanking will do that."

"Daddy!"

He pulled out some ruffly panties. He slid them over her feet then up her legs.

"Hips up," he commanded.

She put her feet flat on the bed to raise her hips up as he settled the panties, which were more like a diaper cover or shorts. Finally he drew her tutu skirt up her legs and she raised her hips again so he could situate the waistband around her hips. Then he picked up a sock.

"Those are so cute, Daddy," she said with excitement as he put one sock on. It reached right up to mid-thigh. The band around the top was tight enough to keep them up.

"Might have to order you some garter belts and stockings for when you're my big girl. Because that would be sexy as fu...fudge." He caught himself.

"Daddy, were you going to say fuck?"

Quickly he rolled her over and gave her five swats on her backside. They wouldn't have hurt so much if her bottom wasn't already tender. As it was, she barely had time to yelp before she was turned over again.

"Daddy! Why'd you spank me?"

"For swearing."

"I was just repeating what you said," she grumbled as he helped her sit then stand.

"No, Daddy did not say that naughty word."

"Well, fudge," she muttered. "I want it noted that I think that was unfair since you were gonna say that word."

"And I'll note that I didn't say that word and that even if I did accidentally say it, that does not give you permission to use it." He gave her a firm look.

She huffed out a breath, but then forgot all about her irritation as he took her hand and led her to the long mirror that was hanging on the back of the closet door.

Oh man, she was super cute. The whole outfit was adorable.

"Don't you look sweet," Linc crooned.

She swung this way and that, the skirt flying out around her. That was fun. She'd have to do that lots.

"Turn around and bend over for me," he told her. "I want to see the view."

She faced the other way then bent, twisting so she could see into the mirror as well. As she'd thought, the skirt was so short that you got a good view of the ruffly pants underneath when she bent over.

"Now all we need to do is your hair." He disappeared into the bathroom, returning with a wooden hair brush and some hair ties. As she sat between his legs, he tied her hair up into pigtails.

Once finished, he helped her stand then stepped back to take her in. "Adorable."

For the first time in her life, she felt adorable. Cute.

He took her hand and led her to the room that she'd slept in that first night. He'd already dismantled the double bed that had been in there. He'd ordered a princess bed for her but that hadn't arrived yet.

When she walked into the room, she gasped. "Daddy!"

She let him go, moving into the middle of the room and turning around in a circle. She made another circle, then one more.

"Whoa, teeny, you're gonna make yourself dizzy." He grasped hold of her hips as she stumbled.

"Um, whoops. Too late."

He let out a low, growling noise. Uh-oh. Here came overly protective Linc. He set her down on the chair by her desk which he'd somehow found the time to make up. Next to it, in the corner was her beanbag. At the moment, it was empty, the beans still needing to be poured into it. There was also a bookshelf that was still in pieces. A white, fluffy rug was underneath the beanbag, making a cozy reading corner. Her crafting stuff, coloring books and pens and a five-drawer cabinet were set up on the other side of the desk and along the back wall were her other toys. Another corner held her time-out stool which he'd obviously moved in here.

She'd just ignore that corner.

"Are you all right?" He crouched in front of her, placing his hands on her thighs. "Maybe you should lie down. Do you need a drink?"

"I'm fine, Daddy. Just twirled one too many times."

"No more twirling."

She huffed out a sigh. "Daddy, you can't ban twirling."

"Sure can. Just did."

She just shook her head.

"I'm gonna write it on your rules."

"You are not. I like twirling. I do it when I'm happy. Daddy, I can't believe you did all this!" She needed to distract him. Or he really would make it a rule.

"We still need some more cabinets for storage. And I don't think you have nearly enough toys. Although it won't be long until Christmas. You just need to make sure you're on Santa's nice list and not his naughty one."

She gave a shocked gasp. "I is always nice."

He tapped her nose. "No more twirling then."

She pouted. "Daddy, that's silly."

"If I wasn't there, you could have fallen over and hurt yourself. What if you'd done it outside and hit your head on something? Nope. No more twirling."

He was truly insane. She'd just have to save her twirling for when he wasn't around.

"Daddy, can I do some more crafting?"

"Yep. I'm going to get you a snack first, then set up the cabinet with your stuff. I'll find a sheet to put down to save the carpet. You sure you're not dizzy?"

"I'm fine, Daddy." She clasped his face between her hands. "Thank you for doing this for me. Nobody has ever done anything like this for me before."

"You like it then?"

"No." She shook her head. "I love it."

Just like I love you. Surely it was too soon to say it. She bit her lip as he moved back and the moment was gone. It welled inside her. This love for him. It was deep and limitless. It could consume her if she let it. And she wanted that. Wanted him to fill her entire world. And she wanted to be the same for him.

Doubt bubbled in her stomach and she pushed it down.

He's not going to leave you, Marisol.

Trust him.

Linc watched Marisol crafting with an indulgent smile as he set up the rest of her room. He wished he'd had time to put it all together before she woke up. But it needed a few more things anyway, including her bed.

Had anything felt as right as this? Not even leaving his job in the city and coming here had felt this right. Certainly, being with Jess hadn't felt like this. Marisol was a part of him in a way Jess never had been. She fulfilled all parts of him. While Jess had been a Little, she hadn't really embraced it like Marisol did. Now, he was coming to realize that while she'd liked him serving her, she hadn't wanted to give back.

This was it. This was what he'd always wanted.

"Daddy! These scissors aren't sharp enough. I need proper scissors."

"Not sure you're old enough for proper scissors."

"Daddy, of course I am. I need to cut out snowflakes for my picture and these ones keep ripping the paper." She held up the mangled snowflake with a pout.

"Okay, Daddy will get you some proper scissors. But I'm going to supervise to make sure you can use them safely before I leave you to it."

"Yay!"

He returned with a pair of scissors and watched her carefully cutting out a snowflake. Her tongue was poking out as she used them.

Adorable. He left her to start putting together the bookcase.

"Daddy, I've finished it!" Marisol called out about twenty minutes later.

"What is it, teeny?" he asked, looking up from where he'd finished putting up her ball pit. He'd strung some fairy lights he'd ordered around the top. He also had fairy lights to go along the top of the canopy of her princess bed when it arrived. All the ball pit now needed were the balls.

"Ooh, Daddy, that looks great! Can I play in it now?"

"Yep, soon as I get the balls in it. What did you make?"

She held up her creation proudly. She'd made a greeting card and glued the snowflakes on the front then covered it with a sprinkling of blue glitter.

"That's gorgeous, baby. I'm so proud of you."

She lit up. Her smile was beaming. He bet no one had ever really told her that they were proud of her. Leaning down, he kissed her forehead.

"Want to sit in the ball pit while I pour the balls in?"

"Oh yes." She put the card down then scrambled into the ball pit. He poured the balls in as she squealed and picked them up, throwing them around, some landed out of the pit and he grabbed them, throwing them back in and laughing with her.

Happiness filled him. This was definitely everything he'd ever wanted.

29

"Bath time, teeny. Then Daddy has some big girl activities for you."

Big girl activities? Hmm. She wondered what exactly those were. Heat built between her legs. This was the longest she'd spent in Little space and she'd had the best afternoon playing and crafting. She'd even helped Linc pour the beans into the beanbag.

Although she thought maybe she was more of a hindrance than a help, since at least a third of them landed on the carpet of her playroom. But he hadn't growled at her. He'd just patiently scooped them up.

Her beanbag was epic. She wanted another one for his office and for the living room.

"Can I use the bath crayons, Daddy?" she asked. They'd already had dinner and he was tidying up while she colored at the table.

"Of course. I'll go run your bath. You keep coloring."

"Okay, Daddy."

"And drink some water."

With a huff, she reached for her sippy cup. She wasn't going to admit it, but she much preferred the baby bottle.

"Right, the bath is running," he said, walking back into the dining room. "Come on, teeny. Let's get you undressed."

"Can't, Daddy. Not finished."

"You can finish in the morning."

She probably should have heeded the stern note in his voice.

"Nope. Gotta finish now."

Suddenly, her pen was pulled from her hand. "Daddy! I was still using that."

"Does someone need a reminder about listening to Daddy?"

"No." Although she wasn't sure what he meant by reminder. But she figured 'no' was a pretty safe answer.

"Because I could have you write out fifty times, *I will listen to my Daddy.*"

"No, Daddy." She sat up straighter. "I is listening. Listening ears are on." She pretended to switch her ears on.

"That's what I thought." He held out a hand, helping her stand and led her to the bathroom. She looked back at her coloring book with a sigh.

It was such a good picture, too.

When they reached the bathroom, he immediately started stripping her.

The bath was nearly half full and he'd been generous with the bubble bath.

"Ooh, I loves bubble bath," she said excitedly as he stripped off her socks and then dumped all of her clothes in the dirty hamper. All she was dressed in was the ruffly pants.

She went to put her hand in the water but he pulled it back. "Uh-uh, you don't ever touch water until Daddy makes sure it's the right temperature. I don't want my girl getting burned."

"Okay, Daddy, but hurry up. I want in." She didn't even care that she was naked except for the pants.

"So impatient. Somebody does like their baths. Let's get these pants off you." When she was naked, he helped her into the bath, giving her a kiss on the cheek.

As he soaped up a bath sponge, she grabbed the bath crayons and started to draw along the side of the tub. She barely noticed him washing her until he brushed the sponge over her nipples. She gasped.

"My Mari-girl has sensitive nipples."

Her Little side started to fade away as he leaned in and kissed her shoulder. He'd already pinned her hair up high so it wouldn't get wet, giving him access to her neck. He moved the sponge lower.

"Lie back."

As she laid back, he moved the sponge between her legs, cleaning her pussy. Then down her legs. Oh dear Lord. Her breath came in harsh pants with just those brief touches of the sponge against her pussy lips. Putting the sponge aside, he ran his finger along her labia then up to her clit, rubbing it gently.

"Daddy," she moaned.

"I'm going to let some water out then I want you on your hands and knees. Daddy is going to play with your bottom."

Eek.

After he let some water out, she moved onto her hands and knees. Her breasts hung down, the nipples brushing through the water, adding to the sensations.

He disappeared, returning with several items in his hands which he placed on the floor where she couldn't see them. Then he picked them up one by one to show her.

"Lube." He put the bottle down on the lip of the bath. "Remember this heart-shaped paddle?"

She gulped. "But I haven't been naughty."

"Not yet. But just in case you wiggle too much you'll feel this on your bottom."

She bit her lower lip.

"On its own, it wouldn't hurt much." He tapped it against his hand. "It's too small and light. However, with your bottom nice and wet from your bath and still a bit sore from your earlier spanking, it will serve as a small reminder to listen to me." He gave her a pointed look. "Lastly, we have this." He held up a silver anal plug with a rounded end. The end had a pink insert with the words *Daddy's Princess* written on it.

She swallowed heavily.

"Now, if you're a good girl and let me plug you, then you'll get a reward. If you're naughty, you get the heart paddle."

She bit her lip in trepidation, but there was excitement there as well.

"Do you want your special plug? The one you're going to wear for Daddy?"

She didn't say anything and he picked up the small heart paddle and gave her two slaps. He was right, there wasn't much pain. Just a flicker of heat that made her clit throb.

"Answer me."

"Yes, I'll wear the plug."

"I'll wear the plug, Daddy. Or Sir."

"I'll wear the plug for you, Daddy."

"Good girl." He started by washing her bottom then a lubed-up finger entered her hole, slowly but firmly pushing up inside her. Her breath left on a whoosh as he moved his finger around inside her. Ooh. Her clit was begging to be touched by now, her pussy wet with need.

"I've got something very special for you if you're a good girl," he explained to her, moving his other hand down to her pussy to toy with her clit. "That's it. Two fingers now."

She groaned as a second finger entered her back hole. Oh, that stung a bit.

"You're doing so well. Look at you. So pretty. So sexy." He slid his fingers free and then grabbed the plug and lube.

Then the slickened plug pressed against her back hole. "Breathe in. Now out, nice and slow. Relax. That's it. Good. Very good. Such a good girl."

The anal plug wasn't that big, but it still burned slightly. But once it was pushed past her tight ring and settled in her bottom, she felt herself relax. He moved his finger back to her clit and arousal filled her.

"That's it. That's my girl. Come for me."

Oh, she was so close. Her entire body shook with need. Her pussy clenched down, the plug in her bottom only added to her need.

"Come with that plug inside your bottom."

Her head fell forward as she cried out loud, her body shaking as she came. He continued to rub at her clit until a second orgasm quickly followed the first. Her arms collapsed out in front of her and she would have ended up with a face full of bath water if his reflexes were any slower.

He grasped hold of her, picking her up and setting her down on the floor. He kept one arm around her waist as he grabbed a towel. Then once he was certain she could stand on her own, he dried her off and picked her up again, carrying her out to the bedroom where he wrapped her up in a blanket.

"I'm going to have to change. Someone got me all wet."

"Shouldn't that be my line?" She grinned at him.

As he undressed, she quickly took the chance to test her blood sugar levels. But her gaze kept moving to him. When he drew off his shirt, revealing his muscular chest, she licked her lips hungrily. Then he moved to undo his belt and it took her longer than usual to read her monitor.

She put everything away then settled in to enjoy the show. His impressive erection was revealed as he stripped off his jeans and boxers. Marisol stood and moved over to him. Bravely, she reached out and lightly ran her fingers along his shaft.

He closed his eyes with a groan as she pumped his cock. She'd never done this before and she hoped she didn't hurt him. Then he wrapped his hand around hers, squeezing tighter.

"Baby, feels so good."

"Let me help you with this. Please."

He opened his eyes, staring down at her intently. "Can't take you until you're ready to commit to me. No matter how much I want to, I won't claim you until you're ready."

"I know, but does that mean I can't touch you? Taste you?"

"You want to taste me?" he asked huskily.

"So much. Please."

"Go sit on the edge of the bed," he commanded.

She moved back and sat on the bed, her feet resting on the floor.

"Part your legs."

She widened her thighs.

He grabbed hold of his cock, running his hand up and down the shaft. Oh man. Who knew that watching him touch himself could be such a turn-on?

"Offer me your breast."

She cupped her breast, holding it up to him. It seemed crazy to her that she was still a virgin, yet here she was, sitting naked in front of the sexiest man she'd ever met, offering her breast at his command.

He walked over then leaned down and suckled on her nipple.

"Now the other."

She held up her other breast, moaning quietly as he sucked on her nipple then lapped at it. He stood up, staring down at her.

"So pretty."

He grasped his cock around the base. She stared down at the long, thick shaft.

"Sure, baby?"

"Yes. God, yes. Please."

"Open your mouth then. Take me inside you. Good. That's so good."

He thrust shallowly into her mouth. In and out. Not giving her mouth much more than the tip.

"You haven't had a cock in your mouth, have you, my baby?"

"No," she told him as he drew out.

"Then I get to teach you just what I like. I don't know how I was lucky enough to find you. But the more time I spend with you, the more I realize that I wasn't living. I was surviving. Your laughter, your sweet touches, your shy looks. Christ, it's almost more than I can stand."

As he spoke, he continued to thrust into her mouth, giving her more and more of his cock. She sucked as he pulled out.

"That's it, baby. Suck on my cock. Show me how much you want it. You do want it, don't you? You want it inside your pussy."

She moaned her agreement as he thrust in deeper. She drove her mouth forward, gagging slightly as she took him deeper than she was comfortable with. Immediately, he drew out and gave her a concerned look.

"Easy, baby. You're to let me set the pace, understand? Or you won't be allowed my cock."

"I'm sorry. I just wanted more of you."

"And I don't want you hurting yourself. We take this slow."

There he was again.

She let him set the pace and depth again. Sucking on him, licking him when she could but letting him control it.

"Fuck, yes, baby. Your mouth is so good. Too good. It's going to have me coming far too quickly. Reach up with one hand and cup my balls. That's it. Gentle. Yes. Yes. I'm going to give you more. Just relax. That's it."

He pushed more of him inside her and she relaxed her throat, humming in pleasure. He let out a shout. "Do that again. Yes. Hell. I'm going to come, baby. Do you want me to pull out?"

She shook her head as much as she could.

"Sure? Baby, you were made for me. You're going to drink me down, aren't you? That's it. Swallow me down. Good girl."

He gave several fast thrusts then came in her mouth. She swallowed quickly, the taste was different yet not entirely unpleasant. She knew she could get addicted to this, though, the look of pleasure, the way all tension had drained out of him made her feel a sense of pride.

Then he picked her up under the arms and set her back on the bed before kneeling between her legs. "My turn."

Well, who was she to say no?

30

"Ed, that woman from the spa is demanding to see you," Kiesha stated from the doorway, a frown on her face.

For a moment he thought she meant Marisol and his heart skipped a beat. But of course she didn't mean Marisol. She wouldn't be frowning if she did. And he needed to get over this interest in the dark-haired, curvy beauty. She was Linc's.

"Do you mean Rosalind? Marisol's aunt?"

Kiesha snapped her gum and he gave her a disapproving look. She knew he didn't like her chewing that crap at work. She just stared back at him calmly. They'd known each other too long for him to intimidate her much.

"Yeah, she's a real peach."

Ed grimaced. He should have left an hour ago. Right now he could be in his hot tub with a bottle of cold beer. Instead, he was about to deal with a viper. "Fine. Christ. Send her in."

He stood as Rosalind walked in. She was wearing a pair of jeans so tight that it left nothing to the imagination. He grimaced. A blood red see-through shirt displayed her black, lacy bra. And she topped everything off with red stilettos and a black handbag. Currently, she was wiping at her eyes with a tissue.

He raised his eyebrows at the sight. He wondered at the crocodile tears. Any other woman came crying into his office and he'd be all over himself trying to calm her down. Crying women were his kryptonite. But he could smell a rat straight off with this woman.

"Ms. Perez. What can I do for you?"

He sat back and she gave him a startled look. Anger filled her face for just a few seconds. If he hadn't been watching carefully, he'd likely have missed it.

"Sheriff, I've come to report a missing person."

"A missing person?" So that was her angle. "Who is missing? That boyfriend of yours?"

"You don't like Saber much, do you?" She came forward and sat in the chair across from him, even though he hadn't offered her a seat.

"He's a criminal. The leader of a gang. Several, in fact. I'm an officer of the law. So no, I don't."

"That's slander," she spat at him. "You have no proof of any of that."

"Ms. Perez, I have had no less than five call-outs over the last week since the Devil's Sinners moved into my town, including two bar fights. I do not want trouble in my town and that's all someone like Saber brings. Now, what do you want?"

"My niece is missing. I want you to find her."

Shoot. He'd need to at least make this look like he was taking it seriously. He picked up a pad and pen. "You're talking about Marisol?"

"Yes. You've met her?"

"I have. What makes you think she's missing?"

She seemed surprised by that question. "Because she hasn't

come home. She lives with me. Works for me. And I haven't seen her in four days."

"And you're only just reporting her missing now?"

"She has a new boyfriend. I thought she might have gone off with him."

"And not told you? Do you not have a good relationship? Also she is over the age of eighteen, so she can legally leave without your permission."

She stood up. "I know that. Our relationship is just fine. That man has taken her and I want her found and him arrested."

"Who took her?"

"Linc Johnson. He lives on Sanctuary Ranch. I want you to take me there and get her out of his clutches."

"I'm not taking you anywhere," he told her calmly. "Have you tried calling her?"

"Of course I have. I know he has her. He kidnapped her. Aren't you going to do something about that?"

"Have you any proof that he took her?"

"No," she gritted out. "But my niece would not just leave me. She's devoted to me."

Right. This woman was poison. At least Marisol was now safe from her. He wondered at her angle, though. Clearly, she wanted to get onto Sanctuary Ranch. Had Tiger sent her?

"Have you seen Tiger Mason lately?"

She frowned at the change of topic. "I told you the other night, Tiger isn't even in the state."

He just hummed. "Well, if that changes, you let me know. Now, if that's all, my shift should have finished an hour ago."

"Aren't you going to do anything to find Marisol? I need her. She just abandoned her job. Her home. I need her back."

"Because you care about her or you want to continue exploiting her?"

She reeled back. "Excuse me?"

He'd said too much. "Never mind. Have a great night, ma'am."

He backed her out of his office then shut the door in her face. His first instinct was to go straight to Sanctuary. But he had this feeling that maybe that was what she was wanting. Perhaps she didn't know where Marisol was and was fishing for information. If she was watching and waiting, and he went straight out to Sanctuary he could give her the answer she wanted.

So instead, he grabbed his phone.

"Yeah?" Linc sounded slightly breathless.

Ed found himself smiling. "I'm sorry. Did I interrupt something?"

"Yes, you did actually. What can I do for you?"

"Sorry to pull you away from the lovely Marisol. Just thought I'd tell you that her aunt just came in here to report her as missing."

"She did? Marisol decided that she didn't want to call her in the end."

"Yeah, well, my guess is she's fishing for information. Not sure if it's for herself or for Tiger."

"So you think he's around?"

"He might never have left. Or could be close by. If he's here, he's keeping a low profile. Unlike those other bastards."

"Heard they've been causing trouble. Also heard Markovich is pissed off."

"Kent's been talking to him, huh?" Ed said dryly. Markovich wasn't a good guy. He was a loan shark. He owned several bars and ran a number of illegal gambling operations. But he did have his lines and he didn't believe in exploiting or hurting women.

Linc just grunted. "Zander will find Tiger."

"And what is Zander going to do when he finds Tiger?" Ed asked tensely. He was still a cop. Much as he wanted these bastards gone, it had to be aboveboard.

"He's just going to have a small chat with him. I have to go. I'll tell Marisol that her aunt is searching for her."

"Just don't let her cave and call her."

"Of course not." Linc ended the call and Ed stood, stretching. He grabbed his keys and wallet and headed out the door.

"I'm leaving for the night, Kiesha."

"Have fun in the hot tub, boss. Don't stay in so long that you turn into a wrinkly old prune. Actually, on second thought it might be too late."

Ed just shook his head. Brat.

31

L inc headed towards his truck. It was already late afternoon. He hadn't managed to finish by lunchtime today. There had been too many things needing his attention. But now he was eager to get home to Marisol.

Clint and Charlie were due home the day after tomorrow and he had some days off coming to him. He couldn't wait to spend more time with her.

Had he really known her less than three weeks? It seemed like he'd known her forever.

"Linc! Got a minute?"

He turned to find Kent pulling up in his own truck. He walked over to him.

"Hey, man, what's up?" Linc asked.

"I was just headed to your place to talk to you and pick Abby up."

"Abby's at my place?"

"She's been with Ellie, but she said she was just popping in to see Marisol and asked me to pick her up from there. I don't want her out too late, and it's getting cold at night."

Linc nodded. He got it.

"Zander just rang. He ordered me to talk to you in person rather than call you," Kent said dryly.

"Why didn't he call me?"

"Why do you think? Because he's a paranoid bastard. He called on my satellite phone."

"Who does he think is going to be listening in?"

Kent shook his head. "God knows. Anyway, he wanted you to know that they've found where the Devil's Sinners have set up headquarters. It's an old farmstead about a half hour north of here. They've been watching the place for a while now and this morning, they had a positive sighting of Tiger."

Finally, they found the bastard.

"What's he going to do?"

"Told me he wanted to observe a while. But he'll let us know immediately if he makes any move towards the ranch. Did Corbin tell you that we've had a few drive-bys of Devil's Sinners members down past the gate?"

He scowled. "Yeah. Ed said that Rosalind has guessed that she's here. He thinks that's why she reported Marisol missing, she was hoping Ed would bring her out here with him to check."

He'd been furious when Ed had called. He'd also had to convince Marisol that she didn't need to contact her aunt and tell her that she was all right. The bitch was just trying to use her.

"One of Zander's people overheard Tiger going ape-shit because they can't find Marisol."

"Think they'll try to sneak onto the ranch?" he asked.

"If they do, we're ready for them. Don't worry. Nobody will get to your girl."

"I hate that everyone here is in danger and that all the women have been locked down."

"Nobody is complaining, man. We all want Marisol safe and

away from those bastards." Kent grinned at him. "Plus, everyone is happy you've found your Little."

She wasn't quite his yet. But she would be.

"No problem. I'll head to your place now. See you there."

Linc nodded. Kent drove away and he turned, walking towards his own truck. He climbed in and just sat there for a moment, trying to gather his thoughts. He wanted this threat to Marisol gone. He hated that they didn't know what Tiger was up to. At least Zander had his people watching Tiger now. Having eyes on him made Linc feel better.

After a few minutes, he started his truck and headed home. One of the best things about his job was that it didn't take long to get home. As he turned the corner and his cabin came into view, he slammed on his brakes in shock. What the fuck?

OH GOD. Oh God.

What the fuck was she doing? Why had she decided to clean the damn windows? She'd already done all the lower ones. And when she'd found the ladder in the shed out back, she figured she might as well do the gable ones.

Big. Big mistake.

"It's okay, Marisol. Just come back down," Abby called out. "I'm holding the ladder, it won't move on you."

It was a big mistake, because when Marisol had gotten to the top of the ladder, it had started wobbling. In a fright, she'd climbed onto the porch roof, which had thankfully held her weight. And then the ladder had crashed to the ground.

Soon afterward, Abby had arrived and seen the ladder on the ground with Marisol clinging to the roof.

"Do you want me to come up and help you down?" Abby asked.

"No!" she cried out, shivering as a cold breeze whipped through her thin clothing. "No, you might get hurt."

"I'll call Linc then," Abby told her.

"No, please don't. He's busy at work." And her idea to help him had turned into a nightmare. He'd been talking about cleaning these windows yesterday and it had planted the seed about how she could take some pressure off him.

Stupid girl.

"I'm coming up," Abby called out.

"No, Abby. You'll get stuck too." She wouldn't let the other woman get in the same predicament as her.

She saw a truck pull up then Kent climbed out, rushing towards them. "Abby! What the hell is going on?"

"I'm going up the ladder to get Marisol. She's too scared to climb back down."

"No, you're not. You know you're not allowed to climb ladders. What's happened? Marisol? Are you all right?" Kent called out.

She carefully looked over the side to see that Kent now had his arm wrapped around Abby's waist. The other woman was pale as she stared up at Marisol in worry.

"I'm fine," Marisol replied. Another shiver ran through her and her teeth started to chatter.

"Marisol climbed the ladder and then it started wobbling and scared her so she climbed onto the roof of the porch and now she won't get down. And I can see how cold she is from here."

A big red truck pulled up beside Kent's and Linc fairly shot out of the driver's seat. Relief flooded her. She was going to be all right. Linc was here.

Linc wouldn't let anything happen to her.

"What the fuck is going on?"

She winced at his roar. He was yelling and swearing. That wasn't a good combination. "Marisol! What are you doing up there?"

"She climbed up to wash the windows and now she's too scared to climb down. The ladder was on the ground when I got here and she was clinging to the roof. But you have to get her down, she's so cold," Abby said worriedly.

She didn't add that she'd been up here at least an hour before Abby arrived. Her whole body was starting to feel like a popsicle but especially her face and hands. She wished she could move, but she was too scared to.

"I'm coming up the ladder to get you, Mari-girl."

She let out a small whimper but didn't protest. She wanted down from this roof. And she knew now that Linc was here, she was safe.

He soon appeared at the edge of the roof.

"Linc," she gasped out.

"Baby, it's all right. I'm here. I want you to come towards me, though. I'm going to guide you back down the ladder."

She shook her head.

"Come to me, teeny. I don't want to add my extra weight to the roof in case it can't take it."

"I . . . I can't."

"Do you trust me, Mari-girl?" he asked calmly.

"Yes."

"Do you know that I'd never let anything happen to you?"

"Yes."

"Then come here, teeny." His voice was firm. An order that was expected to be obeyed and her body was moving before her brain could even catch up. When she was close to him, he reached up and grabbed hold of her hips gently, drawing her closer to him until she was pressed against him, her legs hanging down, on either side of his torso. She wrapped her arms around his neck as she shook, both from the cold and with relief that she was in his arms.

"I'm going to guide you down, baby."

She shook her head. "I can't do it."

"You can." He took hold of her chin. "You can do this. You will do this. Understand me?"

His command filled her. His confidence calmed her. His presence kept her in the here and now with him.

"I am going to take care of you, teeny. All you have to do is listen to Daddy and do exactly what he tells you to. Understand?"

"Yes, Daddy."

"Good girl. Now, I want you to roll onto your belly. I'm not going to let you go. I promise. I won't let you fall."

She whimpered but rolled onto her belly. He kept his hands on her at all times, guiding her down, keeping her between him and the ladder. When he was on the ground, he grabbed her around the waist and lifted her down, turning her in his arms so she was cradled against his chest.

"She okay? She hurt?" Kent asked from behind her.

She burrowed in closer against Linc, breathing in his scent. He walked inside with her. Her teeth chattered.

"No, I don't think so. Just scared and cold."

"You want me to call Doc?" Kent asked.

"Yeah, thanks."

"No," she said. "N-no, I don't need Doc. I'm just c-cold and tired."

"Linc?" Kent asked.

"Call him," he said grimly. "She's freezing cold and I want to make sure she's all right."

"Linc, I don't need Doc. I'm fine," she protested as he laid her on the sofa with an admonishment to stay there.

Kent, who was on the phone, stepped towards the fireplace, throwing on more wood.

Linc returned seconds later with her bag so she could check her blood sugar.

"Is there something I can do?" Abby asked anxiously, hovering to the side. "A hot drink? Hot water bottle?"

"Actually, sweetheart, could you go into our bedroom, it's just down the hall to the left, and grab Marisol's doll and blanket that are on the bed?"

Abby nodded and took off.

"Linc," she hissed in protest. Now Abby would know she slept with a snuggly and Princess Nana.

"Hush," Linc said firmly. "When was the last time you ate?" She held out her finger for him to prick.

"Umm. Lunch time, I think. What time is it?" If she was honest, she was feeling a bit light-headed and woozy.

"What can I do?" Kent asked just as Abby raced back in and bounced into him. She would have fallen if he hadn't grabbed hold of her.

"Whoops." She handed Marisol her doll and blanket.

"Can you get me some blankets," Linc said to Kent. "Her blood sugar is low." He showed her the number before grabbing a small tube of glucose tabs from her kit. He opened up two and gave them to her.

Kent returned with a handful of blankets and they started piling them over her.

"I don't need blankets," she said irritably, pushing them back. She was sweaty and shaking.

Linc placed his hand over her forehead. "You feel cold to me. You're irritable because your blood sugar is low."

"I am not." She scowled at him.

Linc moved to her feet, removing her shoes and rubbing her feet. She groaned in pleasure.

They heard a door open and close and then Doc strode in, carrying a big black bag. "What's going on? What happened?"

"Marisol climbed up on the roof to clean those top windows and then the ladder fell giving her a fright," Linc told him.

"That sounds like a damn foolish idea," Doc said gruffly, coming over to stand over her. "You've taken your blood sugar levels?"

"We just did it," Linc replied. "It's low. She just had two glucose tabs."

"Good. There a reason you guys are here?" Doc asked Kent as he set his bag down next to the sofa.

"Always nice to see you, Doc," Kent said dryly. "We'll go. Linc, let us know if you need anything."

Linc gave a nod and sent a small smile to a worried Abby. "Thanks. She'll be okay, sweetheart. I'll see to that."

"Take tomorrow off, I'll get everything covered. I think I still remember what to do." Kent winked at Marisol. "Feel better, honey."

Abby gave Marisol a gentle hug on her way past. "Let me know if you need anything."

"Thanks, Abby," she said tiredly.

"Right, how long were you up there for, Marisol?" Doc asked as he took her pulse.

"I don't know, about an hour or more."

"And when did you last eat?"

"Umm, I think about four or five hours ago."

"It will be written in her notebook." Linc disappeared for a moment, returning with the notebook she used to record what she ate and when. "Nearly five hours."

"Right. Let's test you again in five minutes and see how you are. Now I want you to lie on your side away from me and curl your legs up to your chest."

She gave him a suspicious look. "Why?"

"I'm going to take your temperature."

"But why do I need to roll on my side away from you for you to put the thermometer in my ear?"

"Because I'm going to use a rectal thermometer."

"Can't you just use the ear thermometer?" she complained.

"Nope. This is more accurate and since you're chilled, it's what I'll be using. It won't hurt."

"Oh God, I can't believe this is happening," she groaned as she rolled over and curled her legs up.

"Good girl," Doc praised. "Linc, do you want to sit on the sofa with Marisol so you can comfort her?"

Linc didn't say anything as he raised her up then sat with her head in his lap. She tried to look up at him, but the angle wasn't great. She felt Doc raise the blankets then lower her yoga pants.

He parted her bottom cheeks.

She squeaked.

"Relax," Doc told her. "Linc? You still with us?"

"Sorry," Linc muttered, then he glanced down at her, running his fingers over her scalp. "Just relax, Mari-girl. It will be over with quickly."

Something wet and cool was pressed to her back hole, the thermometer was pushed inside her. She shuddered. It didn't hurt, but it was the fact that Doc was doing it.

"Good girl. You're doing well," Doc told her kindly. "Did you go outside just dressed in a hoodie and yoga pants?"

Linc growled as he asked that.

"Yes. I wasn't planning to be out long. I was just going to wash the windows then get down."

"Bet you won't do that again," he replied as he slid out the thermometer. "Linc will see to that. Temperature is fine."

Linc let out a relieved sigh as Doc fixed her pants. She rolled over and Linc slid out from under her.

"I have some good news, your new pump and monitor will be here tomorrow or day after. I'll let you know when and you can come to my clinic. Also, Caley was very happy with your beta reading. I think she's going to ask you if you'll do it for all her books."

"Really?" Happiness filled her and she smiled up at Linc. But he just stared down at her tensely, as though he wasn't listening to them.

She pushed back the blankets, feeling stifled. He reached down and pulled them back up.

"Linc, I'm too hot."

"Leave them. You could have gotten hypothermia. You could have frozen to death up there. Or fallen and broken your neck. You could have had a seizure. Gone into a coma."

Doc sighed then had her check her blood sugar again. "Linc, Marisol could use a warm drink. Maybe a small hot chocolate."

"Shit. Fuck." Linc stomped into the kitchen.

"Hmm, he doesn't usually swear much."

She winced. "He's upset."

"That much is obvious. You're in a world of trouble once you're feeling better, sweetie."

Yeah, that's what she figured too.

"Your blood sugar is better, though. Eat something. And keep a close eye on it, okay?"

Linc returned carrying her baby bottle filled with hot chocolate.

"Linc," she groaned.

He just glared down at Doc who was packing up. "What's going on? Is she okay? Does she need to go to the hospital?"

"Nope. Keep her warm but not too hot. I think six blankets might be overkill. We just tested her blood sugar level and it's gone up. Just keep a bit of an eye on her today but she's going to be fine."

"Really? You're sure I shouldn't do anything else for her?" Linc asked.

"Well, given her behavior, she'd benefit from a hot ass," Doc said dryly.

She gasped and glared up at the doctor.

"Oh, she'll get that. Once she's feeling better," Linc agreed. "I'll walk you out."

He handed her the baby bottle. "Drink, teeny."

32

Marisol waited until they'd both left to take a few sips from the bottle. She hugged Princess Nana tight. It was a relief to be off that roof. Even if she did have a punishment coming to her. She pushed back the blankets with a sigh. She was way too hot.

She heard voices murmuring in the hallway and even though she knew she shouldn't, she found herself tiptoeing out so she could listen in.

"She's going to be fine, Linc. She's been managing her diabetes on her own for a long time. And I know you're helping her even more. This was just a mistake."

"She could have slipped off that roof and died. What if it had been hours more until someone found her. I could have lost her." There was a broken note in his voice and she froze.

"That didn't happen. You didn't lose her."

"But I could have. How am I supposed to fucking close my eyes tonight and not see her falling to her death?"

"Just don't think about it."

"That's great advice, Doc," Linc said sarcastically.

"Archer is the words man. You want flowery advice, go to him. Look, I get it. But you can't spend your life thinking of what ifs. You've got to appreciate what you have right now. Take care of her, but don't smother her. Watch her, but don't obsess over her. Got me?"

"She is everything to me. If I lost her, I don't know what I would do . . ."

The words hit her hard. She could hear the starkness in his voice.

"Because you love her."

"Of course I fucking do. I've never felt like this about anyone."

"Scary fucking thing loving someone. But you can't protect them from everything. Coddle her. Spank her. Make her promise not to climb up on any more roofs. Then keep moving forward. Don't let this eat you up or you'll push her away."

"I thought Archer was the one with the good advice."

"Archer is the one with the flowery fucking advice. You want to talk about your emotions, go to him. Me, I'm the practical one. I'll tell you when to pull your head in and stop being an ass. Go back to her. You need to watch her closely for a few days then that's what you do. But like I said, don't let it consume you. I'll call you tomorrow."

"Thanks, appreciate it."

"I take payment in beer or scotch. None of those froufrou drinks."

She scrambled back to the sofa as she heard the door open. She grabbed a blanket and pulled it over her lap. She was picking up the bottle as Linc walked back in. He frowned as he looked at the drink.

"You haven't drunk any."

"I had a bit."

He had her scoot down so he could sit behind her on the sofa, then he drew her onto his lap and grabbed the bottle. She lay back against his arm as she slowly sipped the warm drink.

Finally, he pulled it away from her and stared down at her. "You scared me today."

"I know. I'm so sorry. I wasn't thinking. I just wanted to help you. I knew you wanted them clean and didn't have time to do it."

"I didn't mean for you to do it."

"I know."

"You broke a rule today, Mari-girl."

"Because I washed the windows? You didn't specifically say I couldn't."

"What's your rule about endangering yourself?"

"I didn't think washing the windows could be dangerous," she explained.

He shook his head. "Why didn't you tell me what you were going to do? Text me to ask me where the cleaning supplies were?"

Oh drat. He had her there.

"Because I knew you wouldn't want me cleaning the windows."

"And you definitely should know I wouldn't want you climbing a ladder without me. Nor would I want you outside without plenty of clothing on. None of that was acceptable, Mari-girl and you know it."

"I know, Daddy. Are you going to spank me?"

"I sure am. And this one is going to be far harsher than the others you've received before."

"I deserve it."

"Why do you think you deserve it?" He tilted her face so she had to look up at him.

"For scaring you. Daddy?" she asked quietly.

"Yes, teeny?"

"You're not ever going to leave me, are you?"

"No, teeny. I'm not. I love you. I can't stand the idea of not having you in my life and I'll do whatever I have to in order to prove that to you. To make you believe it."

"I overheard you and Doc talking."

"Teeny," he growled.

"I know, I know, you can add that to the punishment. But I . . . I realized when I heard you speak to Doc, when I heard how upset you are, it just hit me. Everybody leaves me. But not you. You won't."

He cupped her face between his hands. "I love you, baby. I'd never leave you. Ever. And truth is, I said you had a choice when it was safe, about whether you wanted to stay or leave, but I don't have the strength to let you go."

"That's good then, since I don't want to go. Because I love you too."

"You're sure you can take all of me? I might ask a lot of you sometimes, teeny. Maybe more than you ever thought to give. But I will always take care of you. Can you take all the sides of me? The man who'll treat you like a fucking queen, but then demand you submit to him in the bedroom? The Daddy who will have tea parties with his little princess. Who will make sure she knows that he is always there for her. Who will make the tough calls when she can't or won't. But who won't hesitate to take his naughty princess over his lap when she breaks the rules?"

"Oh yes, yes please. I want it all." Her gaze met his. "I've never had someone at my back, fighting for me."

"I won't fight for you at your back. I'll be in front of you, making sure no one gets through me to you."

"Then how could I say no? How could I say no to someone who wants to give me everything I ever wanted? How could I say no to the man who I haven't been able to get out of my head ever since I met him? Who can make me want him with just one look? Who texts me just to check on how I am? Who puts my needs and desires first. There is no way I couldn't want to be with that man."

"Thank God." He leaned in and took her mouth hard. Hot. She let out a sigh as she wrapped her arms around his neck. When he drew back, he ran a finger over her lips. "I love you so much, Mari-girl. I'm glad you realized how much I need you. That you trust me not to leave you."

"Me too," she told him. "I need you so much, Linc. I'm so sorry I scared you today. I'll try not to do it again."

"I need you to know that you don't have to do things to pay me back for taking care of you. You already do plenty of things for me without even realizing it. When I'm stiff and sore, you rub my shoulders. When I'm doing hated paperwork, you bring me coffee. When I need a taste of your pussy, you open your legs."

"Linc!" she cried as he grinned. "Oh my God, I can't believe you just said that." She giggled. "You're crazy, you know that, right?"

"I know. You make me crazy. I love you. And you don't owe me a thing."

"I'll try to remember that. I can promise you, I'm never going on another ladder. In fact, I don't even think I'll get on a step stool."

"Good," he growled. "You could have gotten dizzy and fallen off and broken your neck. You could have frozen to death up there. You could have had a seizure from low blood sugar."

Whoops. He was off again.

"I know. I promise, I'll be more careful."

"Good. You know I'm still gonna paddle your butt for putting yourself in danger though, right?" he growled at her.

She gulped. "Now?"

"No. Not now. Tomorrow. I'm taking tomorrow off to spend with you. I'm going to want you to be Little all day, do you want that, teeny?"

"Oh yes, please."

"Of course, you're going to be punished as well. My well-spanked precious Little girl."

She whimpered at the thought.

"Tonight, I need to feed you and bathe you, pamper you."

"Fuck me?" she added.

He narrowed his gaze as he studied her. "You want me to fuck you?"

"Well, yeah. You said that once I was yours, that you'd fuck me."

"And I will. When I'm sure you're up to it."

"I am, please, Linc."

He smiled. "Glad to know you need me as much as I do you. If I take you tonight then there will be some punishment involved first."

"Punishment? I thought you were going to spank me?"

"Tomorrow, I'll spank my teeny. Tonight, I'd punish my Mari-girl. You'll have to earn your orgasm. But when it comes it will be that much sweeter. Do I have your agreement?"

"Yes, Sir."

"That's my good girl." He kissed her gently "I'm going to make you so happy, Marisol. You'll never regret being with me."

"I know I won't, Daddy. You're my whole world. I couldn't be without you and remain whole."

"Good. That means you'll never leave me."

"Never," she swore.

He treated her extra gently for the rest of the evening. He had her check her blood sugar levels several times, but it remained in the acceptable range. He made sure she drank plenty of water. All from her bottle. She colored in her book as he cooked them dinner. He watched her like a hawk as she administered her insulin. And when she had to pee, he carried her to the bathroom.

She wasn't able to lift a finger. And honestly, she didn't want to. But she didn't see him doing anything other than putting her to bed and cuddling her tonight. And as much as she loved cuddling, she was also desperately in need of him.

After dinner had settled and she'd checked her blood sugar again, he picked her up off the sofa and carried her into the bathroom off their bedroom.

"What are we doing? I don't have to go to bed now, do I?" She pouted as he set her down on the counter.

"How are you feeling?" He cupped her face, studying her.

"I feel fine. Honestly. I promise."

Heat filled his gaze. "Not going to lie, I want you badly, Mari-girl. But my needs can wait if you need more time."

"I don't. Please. I'm sure."

"At any time, if you feel sick or off or in pain, you'll use your safe word. Promise me."

"I promise. But it's going to hurt a bit, isn't it?" Considering she was a virgin.

"Maybe. But with what I've got planned you'll be so wet and ready for me that maybe you'll barely notice it."

Oh, man. What did he have planned? She remembered his earlier announcement that there would be some punishment involved. He turned on the shower and the heater, getting it nice and warm in here before he stripped off then lifted her down to pull off her clothes. She wasn't allowed to help him.

He tested the temperature of the water. Then picking her up, he carried her into the shower and set her feet down. He washed her hair first, using his fingers to massage her scalp until she was a pile of goo. Then he grabbed some shower gel and washed her arms.

"Put your arms behind your back," he commanded. He washed down her chest, paying a lot of attention to her nipples. She groaned as the sensation of him pulling on the tight nubs sent waves of pleasure through her. He moved down her body, cleaning her thoroughly.

When he was finished with her, he had her sit on the built-in seat while he cleaned himself.

"Can I help?" she asked, desperate to touch him.

He shook his head. "Not this time."

She pouted. That seemed unfair. Reaching out, he tapped her lower lip. "Put that away, this is part of your punishment."

Well, that sucked.

Watching him wash himself without being able to touch was most definitely a kind of torture, especially when he grabbed hold of his cock and ran his hand up and down the long length until it was erect.

Damn, she wanted a taste.

Turning off the shower, he got out and grabbed a towel. He helped her out then dried her off thoroughly before wrapping her hair up in a towel. Only then did he dry himself.

He led her out to the bedroom.

"Kneel on the bed and then lean forward with your arms out in front of you. I'm going to plug you first."

Crap. Crap.

She shifted around carefully, holding the towel around her wet hair as she got into position. She felt him moving behind her before her bottom cheeks were parted and lube was placed over her hole. He proceeded to stretch her with his finger before the plug was pushed inside her. Her bottom contracted around it and a shiver of arousal ran through her.

"Stay like that. I'll be back to get you into your teddy soon."

She heard him running the water in the bathroom. Then he returned and had her roll over onto her back. He drew a yellow, snap-crotch teddy from the dresser. It was basically see-through with lace covering her breasts and pussy. He laid it on the bed.

Then he grabbed something from the closet.

"I bought this the other day." He held up the object. It was black on the bottom and pink on the top and was long and curved. There was a prominent bump at one end on the top.

"This is a clit tickler. It sits in your panties and this bump here tickles your clit. I've got the remote to operate it." He pulled a small remote from his pocket.

He removed the towel from her hair before he dressed her in the lacy teddy. Then he had her lie back while he positioned the clit tickler against her pussy before doing up the snaps on the bottom of the teddy. When she stood, it felt very weird, especially with the plug in her bottom. The tightness of the teddy held the clit tickler against her pussy.

He helped her into a matching dressing gown, then to her surprise he had her sit while he pulled some socks on.

"Um, this doesn't exactly match the lingerie."

He shrugged. "I don't want you getting cold feet."

Damn. He was the sweetest. Even when he was about to punish her.

Linc grabbed her hair brush and a pillow then led her out to the living room. She half-expected him to turn the clit tickler on while she was walking. As though hearing her thoughts, he turned and gave her a wink.

"I thought I better not turn it on when you're moving around. Don't want you walking into any walls or tripping over your own feet."

Considering her legs didn't work properly at the best of times, it was likely a valid concern. She should have known he'd worry about keeping her safe. They walked into the living room. It was toasty warm in there, but he still picked up a blanket from the pile on the sofa. He drew her over to the recliner and sat, placing the pillow between his feet on the floor. "Sit here, Mari-girl and I'll brush your hair for you."

She sat and he placed the blanket over her lap.

"Right, what should we watch? Romantic comedy? This one good?"

"Yep," she replied as he brushed her hair gently and slowly. She relaxed against him, leaning her head on his leg as he started braiding her hair for her.

When her hair was done, he pulled her onto his lap and drew the blanket over her as she snuggled into his chest. Soon, she got caught up in the movie and stopped noticing the plug or tickler.

Then something started vibrating next to her clit and she gave a startled gasp, sitting up straight.

"Easy, Mari-girl," he murmured. "Just let it happen."

She eased back down against him. Her breath came faster, she pressed her thighs together, squirming around on the chair as she tried to gain her release. Then the buzzing stopped and she slumped back against Linc.

"Nooo, not fair. I was so close."

"You didn't think it was going to be that easy, did you?" he murmured. "Next time it comes on, you're going to be a good girl and put your hands behind my neck, okay?"

"Yes, Sir," she replied.

She was just getting back into the movie, when the clit tickler started vibrating again. Damn, just as well she'd already seen this movie, because she was going to be lucky to remember her own name at the end of this torture.

"Good girl, keep your hands there. Move them and I'll have to punish you."

A whimper broke through as he lowered the blanket to her waist and pulled the teddy to one side, baring one breast. He played with her nipple as the tickler buzzed against her hard nub. She turned to look at him, only to see he was staring at the movie.

He wasn't seriously watching it, right?

He squeezed her nipple. "Watch the movie, Mari-girl."

Mierda! She turned her head around. Her body undulated

against him, searching for the edge of the cliff to tumble over. Just as she was almost there, he switched it off again.

This continued on and on. He finally had her drop her arms, worried about her getting tired. But she had to place them on her thighs and not move them. He bared her other breast, played with them both, teased her clit until she was writhing on him, a bundle of nerves. Finally, he reached down and undid the snaps and removed the clit tickler. He ran his finger along her slick lips.

"So wet. Do you want my cock inside you?"

"Yes. Yes."

Suddenly, he stood and turned off the TV before striding into the bedroom. She was held in his arms, bridal style. He laid her down on her back at the edge of the mattress, her legs hanging off the end. He knelt between her legs and spread her lower lips, licking at her. He hummed and she groaned at the sensation.

As he sucked on her clit, he slid the plug from her ass. Then he pressed a finger gently into her passage with shallow thrusts. It felt so good but it wasn't enough. Another finger was added as he continued to ready her for him, stretching her. Her orgasm washed through her, coming in a wave that started off gentle before rapidly growing into something that consumed her. She arched off the bed with a scream.

He lapped at her, removing his fingers. Then he stood and reached into the bedside drawer for a condom. She watched hungrily, her body still throbbing with the aftereffects of her orgasm as he stroked his firm cock.

"Take the teddy off, baby. I want you completely naked."

She wiggled out of the outfit as he sat back on the bed and applied lube to his condom clad dick. Not that she thought he needed lube. But she knew he wanted to make this as easy as possible for her.

When she was naked, he slid down so he was lying on his back on the bed. "Come here."

"You want me on top?" Her eyes went wide. She thought he would guide things. Didn't he know that she had no clue what she was doing?

"It's all right, baby. I'll help you," he soothed, obviously seeing her panic. "But it will be easier for you this way. You can be more in control."

Damn. He was always putting her needs first. She straddled his hips and he pulled her down for a kiss then drew her up his body so her breasts were hanging down over his face. He suckled from one nipple then the other.

Finally, he grabbed his cock with his hand and started guiding it into her.

"You lower yourself down when you're ready, Mari-girl," he murmured to her.

She pushed down with a groan. God, she felt full. Stretched. She pulled up then went lower again. Each time she moved, she took a bit more of his shaft inside her. But it didn't feel right. She hesitated, looking down at him.

"Can we try with you on top?"

"Of course we can. Whatever you need. Remember? All you have to do is ask."

He drew out then rolled them over so she was on her back with him between her open legs and pushed himself gently back inside her.

"How does that feel?" he asked.

"Better," she whispered.

"Put your legs around me. Offer me those breasts."

She held her breast up and he sucked on her as he drove himself in further. He pushed into her, taking her carefully but relentlessly until he was fully immersed in her. He moved to her other breast, laving her nipple with his tongue.

"Ready, baby?" he asked huskily.

"Yes. Yes." Now that she was filled with him, she wanted more.

He drew back, thrust forward. Slow and gentle then gradually faster. Harder. Until he was driving himself inside her.

"Oh. Ohhh." She cried out.

He rolled them again so she was on top. "Ride me again. I want to see you. I want to touch you."

She felt more emboldened now. She drove up and down on his cock as he placed his thumb against her clit, rubbing it. She felt her orgasm build, she clenched down around his shaft.

"That's it. Yes! Come for me. Come on my cock. That's it."

She placed her hands on his chest to steady herself as she moved her hips back and forth, driving herself over his dick until her orgasm rushed through her. He grabbed hold of her hips, pulling her down as he roared his own release.

Slumping forward, she lay on his chest. A whimper escaped as he drew his cock from her. She was sated. Satisfied. And loved.

"That was amazing. You're amazing. My beautiful, darling girl." He murmured words of praise as she lay there, attempting to get her breath back. He ran his hand up and down her back, keeping her close.

When he went to roll her off him, she whimpered a protest, trying to hold onto him.

"Easy, Mari-girl. Just going to run you a bath."

"No. Sleep," she murmured.

"You can sleep. I'll come get you when it's ready."

"No. You stay."

He let out a small chuckle. "I'll be back soon."

She groaned but he slipped out of her hold and she heard water running. Then her legs were parted and a warm cloth was placed on her pussy. She let out a sigh.

"Ooh, that's nice."

"Good. A bath will feel even better."

"No bath. Tired."

"I can tell. I want to test your blood sugars before bed though. And you need a snack."

She grumbled. But in the end, he got his way. She ate a small snack, he bathed her gently, much like one would a precious baby. He even helped her brush her teeth, which was weird.

Finally, he tucked her into bed, with one of his T-shirts on. Princess Nana was held tight in one hand and she was drinking down a bottle of water that he held up to her mouth.

"You finish this while I go quickly shower."

She didn't even have the energy to reply. She swallowed a few more mouthfuls before putting the bottle down. When he climbed back into bed minutes later, he picked it up and held it to her mouth again, having to remove her thumb first.

She complained but she was too tired to really fight. When he removed the bottle, he drew her back into his embrace, so he was spooning around her.

"Mine," he whispered in her ear as she drifted off. "All mine."

She certainly was.

33

"What are we doing today, Daddy?" Marisol swung her feet as she colored at the table. Her picture was nearly finished. She concentrated on carefully coloring in the lines.

This morning, Linc had woken her gently. He'd placed a warm heat pad between her legs to soothe her pussy while he'd given her a bottle of water. When he'd let her out of bed, he'd dressed her up in her princess onesie.

She loved it.

Now, they'd had breakfast and he was cleaning up as usual, while she colored.

"Well, after you've checked your blood sugar, I'm going to have you go get your round paddle and meet me in your playroom. You're going to get your spanking for being naughty yesterday and then you're going into the corner for fifteen minutes."

"Daddy, no!"

Drat. How had she forgotten about the spanking! She looked up at him pleadingly. But he simply gave her a firm look back.

Her shoulders slumped. Darn it. This was gonna suck.

Twenty minutes later, she moved slowly towards the playroom, her paddle in hand. She dragged her feet. Opening the door, she walked into the room with a big sigh. Her bed had arrived a few days ago and Linc had made it up with some soft pink linens. It had a canopy hanging over it with fairy lights. She'd missed her nap yesterday so she hadn't gotten to sleep in it yet.

Linc was sitting in the middle of the bed, watching her. He crooked a finger at her and she made her way slowly over. Grabbing the paddle, he set it on the bed next to him. That's when she saw the anal plug and lube sitting there. Oh no. He drew her between his open legs. He took hold of her hips gently.

"Why are you getting punished, teeny?"

"Because I was naughty and put myself in danger."

"And why is that so bad?"

"I could have gotten hurt and Daddy would have been sad."

"I would be devastated if anything happened to my teeny. She's everything to me." He reached down and undid the snaps at the crotch of her onesie.

"I want you to pull your onesie right up to your waist."

Oh man. This was embarrassing. But she reached down obediently and drew it up so he got a good view of her pussy.

"Good girl. Now lay yourself over Daddy's lap."

He helped her position herself over his lap, with her torso and legs well supported. Then he tucked the bottom of the onesie up out of the way. He rubbed her cheeks.

"It's twenty with my hand followed by ten with the paddle. Can you keep your hands down and out of the way?"

"Yes, Daddy."

"Good girl. Remember you can say red at any time and I will stop. I'll also check in with you. Are you ready?"

Ready? Would she ever be ready? But she knew she wanted to do something to alleviate her guilt over worrying him so much.

"Yes, Daddy."

He started immediately. And it was no warm-up. These spanks were hard and fast. Ten were given in quick succession and she barely managed to catch her breath. By the time he stopped to rub, tears were already coursing down her cheeks.

"How are you doing, baby?"

"H-hurts, Daddy."

"I know, teeny," he said with sympathy. "And we're only part way through, I'm afraid. Is anything else hurting? No numbness? Dizziness?"

"No, Daddy," she replied.

"Next ten."

She was sobbing and kicking her feet as he delivered these next ones. She had to fight hard not to reach back and cover her poor sore bottom cheeks as he whaled into them.

By the time he stopped again, she had soaked the coverlet with her tears. Her sobs filled the room.

"Just ten to go, teeny," he told her with regret.

The smack of the paddle sounded harsh in the room. And she cried with each slap. By the time it had finished, her bottom felt like it was on fire. She wished she could rub away the pain.

"Shh. Shh. Shh."

Linc turned them both so they were lying on the bed. He was on his back with her pressed to his side, her head on his chest.

"Hush, baby. It's all over. You've been punished and forgiven. It's all done. Good girl. Good girl."

He held her until her sobs died and she was relaxed against him.

"How you feeling, baby?"

"Like I've just been spanked and paddled," she replied dryly.

His chest moved as he laughed. "Fair enough. Ready for the rest of your punishment?"

"Daddy, don't you think I've been punished enough? I've learned my lesson. Honest."

"Glad to hear that, teeny. But this will just help solidify it. Come on. Fifteen minutes in time-out then afterwards, Daddy will let you do some crafting."

"Can't Princess Nana do this part?"

"And why should Princess Nana be punished when you were the one who was naughty?"

"'Cause I'm a princess," she explained.

"Do you think that a princess doesn't get punished when she's naughty?" he asked as he helped her sit up. She winced and immediately jumped onto her feet.

"Well, obviously that's not the case," she replied as she rubbed her sore bottom.

"Uh-uh, no rubbing," he said sternly.

"Drat." She crossed her arms over her chest, giving him big eyes. "But Daddy, I don't think a princess should hafta do time-out. She should be able to tag in."

"Tag in?"

"Yeah, like in wrestling."

"You watch wrestling?" He raised his eyebrows.

She blushed. "Sometimes."

"I'm surprised. I didn't think you'd be interested in the sport."

"It's a sport?" she asked with mock-surprise. "I was just there for the muscles and the tight outfits."

He growled. "Brat. Right, bend over the edge of the bed. You're going to be plugged while you're in time-out."

"I say Princess Nana should be plugged."

"Princess Nana doesn't have a bottom hole."

"Lucky Princess Nana."

"Marisol, face the bed, bend over and put your elbows on the mattress."

With a sigh, she did as she was told. She heard him squirting out some lube then felt him part her bottom cheeks and place some lube on her puckered hole.

The cool plug was pressed to her back hole, she relaxed, taking a deep breath in and then letting it out slowly as he situated the plug in her bottom. He helped her stand up and then led her to the naughty corner.

"Right, you can sit on the stool. You might want to rest your thighs on it rather than your bottom then lean forward and place your nose in the corner. That's it."

She ended up with her ass hanging out over the side of the naughty girl stool, which was going to give him a good view of her tender cheeks, with the butt plug poking out between them.

"That's a pretty sight," he said with satisfaction. "I'll start the timer. Fifteen minutes."

She sighed. She really thought Princess Nana was getting out of this on a technicality.

This year, she decided, she was going to ask Santa for a doll with a bottom hole.

34

E d looked up as Kiesha opened the door with a frown. He'd just gotten off the phone with a friend down in Dallas. He was trying to track down who that asshole cop had been years ago who'd scared Marisol.

He groaned. "Please don't tell me Rosalind is back."

She'd been calling constantly and trying to see him since she'd come in the other day to report Marisol missing. He didn't know what her angle was, but she was driving him nuts. Today had been blissfully quiet. Until now.

Kiesha pulled the purple sucker from her mouth. "Nah, it's not her."

"Thank God."

"It's the FBI."

"What? What do you mean, the FBI? There's FBI agents here?" he asked.

"Yeah, well, kind of."

"What?" he asked again, trying to be patient.

"One of them is FBI, another is DEA and I didn't hear what the other one said."

"What do they want?"

"They want to talk to you."

He sighed, striving for patience. "Then send them in."

She turned and strode off. Two men and one woman entered his office soon after. One of the men was big, dark-skinned and serious looking. The other man was smaller with a big smile. The woman between them was tiny. She was dressed in an ugly gray suit with stockings and flat, brown shoes. Her dark hair was pulled back in a braid. Her skin was smooth, her cheekbones high. She was gorgeous.

He turned his gaze from her as the slim-built man held out his hand. "Hi, Sheriff, I'm Jackson Lyle. I'm from the Treasury Department. These are my colleagues, Bronson Clay from the DEA and Georgina James from the FBI."

"Please, call me Ed. Have a seat. What can I do for you all?"

Bronson had closed the door behind them and chose to stand, leaning against the wall. Both Georgina and Jackson sat.

"We've been tasked with investigating Rosalind Perez. I believe you know her?" Jackson asked.

"Of course," Ed replied. "She lives here. Owns a beauty spa. A task force to investigate one woman?"

"I believe you also know about her ties to the Devil's Sinners?" Jackson continued.

"Let's stop beating around the bush, huh? You're obviously trying to get a feel for what I know. I know that Rosalind is dating the head of the Devil's Sinners, Saber Mason. He spends a lot of time at her house. Other night, I went there for a noise complaint. He and a bunch of his gang members were there. They've created a bit of trouble around town. Had a few locked up for drunk and disorderly, that's it."

"And do you know she owns a series of beauty spas across the country? In places where the Devil's Sinners have gangs?" Georgina asked.

She had a firm voice. But quiet. She didn't smile. Didn't show much reaction at all to anything.

"I knew she owned a few across the country. Thought it seemed a bit suspicious."

"It's more than a bit suspicious. We have evidence that she's using those spas to launder money for the Devil's Sinners."

"Not surprising. But if you've got evidence then why are you here and not arresting her?" He looked up at Bronson. "Because you're hoping to use her to get to the Devil's Sinners? What? You want her to become an informant?"

Somehow, he couldn't see that happening.

Georgina frowned slightly, her first show of emotion. "We don't believe Rosalind will work, she's in too deep. Her spas should be failing, but she's got millions in the bank."

Damn. That was really stupid.

"We don't think we can use Rosalind," Jackson said. "But there is someone else close to her and the Devil's Sinners who we think we could convince to help us."

Shit. Fuck.

"Marisol," he said grimly.

"Yes," Jackson told him.

"Marisol is innocent in this." He wouldn't have her taken down with her aunt.

"We thought as much," Georgina said. "But she's ideally placed to help us. She has access to her aunt's business and the Devil's Sinners. One of our informers told us that Tiger is very interested in her. He's had his guys out, searching for her."

"As well as her aunt," Ed said. "She reported her missing. I think she's hoping I'll lead her to Marisol."

"So you do know where she is," Georgina said with a flicker of something in her gaze. "We need to talk to her about helping us."

"Yeah, I know where she is. But her man isn't going to agree to her helping you. I can tell you that much."

"We need to talk to her. Her *man* has no say," Georgina stated.

Ed snorted. "Not the way it works."

"The way what works?" Georgina asked, confused.

"Maybe you could talk to her and her man for us?" Jackson asked.

"That bastard Tiger, wants her. He attempted to sexually violate her," Ed told them grimly.

Georgina blanched. "He what?" She stared over at Jackson. So she didn't know what Tiger had done to Marisol? That made him feel better.

"We'll protect her as best we can," Jackson said. Bronson just frowned.

"No. She's not going back there."

"Can you still ask?" Jackson asked smoothly.

"I suppose I could, but I'm telling you now. Linc's not going to let her be put in danger."

"No fucking way!"

Marisol was so shocked by Linc's angry words that she jolted, spraying small googly eyes in the air.

"Oh shivers," she muttered, looking at the mess that landed off the sheet Linc had put down for her to craft on.

His phone had rung a minute ago and he'd stepped out to take it, although he'd left the door open.

"Not happening, Ed. Tell them no. She's not meeting with them. No way. Fine. Fuck."

She jumped again. Something was seriously wrong if Linc was swearing. She slid completely out of Little headspace as she climbed to her feet. After her time-out, he'd had her lie down on her back on the princess bed, then holding her in the diaper position, he'd removed the butt plug and put some cream on her bottom before doing up her onesie.

But her bottom still reminded her of her earlier spanking as she stood and moved to the door. Just as she reached the door, Linc stepped through. He raised his eyebrows at her.

"What were you doing, teeny?"

She worried at her lip. "I heard you swearing. What's the matter? Is it Tiger?"

He sighed and ran his hand down his face. "Come on, come sit down."

"Oh no. That means it's bad."

He took her hand and led her to the bed. He sat and pulled her onto his lap, her ass hanging over the side of his thigh.

"Ed just called."

"Okay."

"He had three people turn up in his office earlier. From the FBI, the DEA and the Treasury Department."

"Okay." She wasn't sure what else to say.

"They're here about your aunt. And the Devil's Sinners. They have evidence that she's been laundering money for them."

"Oh God."

"Yeah. It wasn't like she hid it well. They have plenty of evidence to arrest her."

"Then why don't they?" she asked.

"They're hoping to get evidence against the Devil's Sinners, in particular Saber. And Tiger."

"And they want to use my aunt."

"Actually, they don't think your aunt will help them. But they want you to."

"They want *me* to help? But I don't know anything."

"They're hoping you can find them information."

Her brain pieced it all together. "They want me to go back to her, right? Back to living with her? Being around Tiger? Do they know what he tried to do to me?"

"Ed told them. They still wanted him to ask you."

She shook in his embrace. "I know I should, but I . . ."

"You're not doing it," he said firmly.

"I'm not?" Relief flooded her even as she told herself not to be a coward. "But I should, shouldn't I?"

"Definitely not." He scowled at her. "Do you seriously think that I would allow you to go anywhere near him? Not just that, but if the Devil's Sinners found out why you were there, what do you think they would do to you?"

She blanched at the thought. "But is it my duty to help?"

"This isn't your problem, baby. This task force can do their job, I'll do mine. Which is to take care of you. I'm in charge when it comes to safety and I've already said no. You can call me bossy and overbearing and domineering, I don't care. As long as you're safe and in my arms, that's what's important. You're not doing this. And you're not to feel guilty. This is all on my shoulders."

Having him take away any choice was actually a relief. That guilt for not helping disappeared.

Because she had no choice. He was in charge of this. It was his decision.

"Okay, Daddy," she told him.

He kissed her. "That's my good girl. Now, you want to explain why there are googly eyes everywhere?"

35

L inc came awake with a start as his shoulder was shaken. There was someone looming over him. He let out a shout and shoved himself up out of bed, ready to defend Marisol.

Tiger.

Tiger had found her.

The person moved back and turned on the light, right as Marisol cried out in fear. Linc dove forward, on the attack, just managing to bring himself to a stop as he saw who was there.

"Fuck! Zander! What the hell! What are you doing in here? It's the fucking middle of the night!"

"I'm well aware," Zander replied calmly. The big man had his arms crossed over his chest. He stared over at Marisol then back to him. "I believe Marisol is scared."

"Jesus, of course she's fucking scared." Linc stormed back to Marisol, who was clutching the sheet to her chest. She was only wearing a see-through nightgown. Her breath was coming in sharp pants and it was easy to see she was on the verge of a panic attack.

He leaned in, kneeling on the bed to cup her face. "It's okay, baby. Just breathe. Breathe in, hold, one, two, three then out, one, two, three. Good girl. And again. For God's sake, Zander, have you ever heard of calling or knocking?"

"It's the middle of the night. I didn't think you'd answer."

"Because we were asleep. Good girl. Just breathe."

"I thought it was T-tiger," she managed to say.

"If it was, Linc would likely be dead," Zander told her.

"Oh God," she moaned.

"Zander! Shit! Shut up. You're scaring her."

"I didn't mean to scare her," Zander said awkwardly. "I was trying not to scare her."

"By breaking in?"

"You have no security on your cabin."

"The door was locked."

Zander snorted. "It was nothing I couldn't easily get through. You need an alarm. Sensors. Cameras."

"I'll get on that tomorrow. It will keep out undesirables." He glared at Zander over his shoulder.

The other man nodded, but showed no sign that he understood that Linc was referring to him. "Better late than never."

"You okay, Mari-girl?" Linc asked her gently.

"Yes, I think so." Her color was coming back. "Why is Zander in our bedroom in the middle of the night?"

"Because I have Tiger. And your aunt. I thought you might want to help me decide what to do with them."

THE WORDS DANCED around in her head. She tried to grasp them, make sense of them but they kept spinning away.

I have Tiger.

Your aunt.

Decide what to do with them.

Linc filled her vision. He gave her a concerned look. "Mari? Marisol, look at me. Good girl. It's okay. You're okay."

She moved her gaze to Zander but Linc gently grasped hold of her chin. "Eyes on mine, teeny. Just listen to me for a moment. You don't have to deal with this."

"D-deal with this?"

Deal with what, exactly?

"If it's what you want, I'll make the decisions that need to be made."

"We will," Zander said with a grunt.

Linc turned to look at him, his shoulders tense. But when he looked back at her, his face was gentle. "It's okay, Mari-girl. Let me take over and deal with it all."

She could give it all to him. What a relief. But at the same time . . . maybe she needed some closure. Maybe she just needed to go see her aunt. To see Tiger.

"What are you planning on doing with them? What do you mean, you have them?" She looked at Zander and this time Linc let her.

"We captured them." Zander gave her a satisfied look.

"You kidnapped them?"

"Nah. Actually, yeah, that's exactly what we did."

"Jesus, Zander, what the hell were you thinking?" Linc asked.

"I was thinking that Tiger and his men were involved in a scuffle with Markovich's men and that gave me the cover I needed to grab an injured Tiger and bring him back to where we've been staying to have a bit of a chat. And some of my guys were watching her aunt's place. Saw the bitch packing up a car to run, so they took her. Now we have both of them. All you have to do is decide whether you want to see them before we take care of them."

"Take care of them?" she whispered.

Zander didn't answer. She looked to Linc who was scowling at Zander. "You can't murder them," she told Zander.

Zander raised his eyebrows. "I can't let them go. Not only are they not good people, but they know my guys and I took them. They'll come for us."

She shook her head. "I don't want them to go free. But I don't want any blood on any of our hands."

"I got no problem getting rid of them, pipsqueak," Zander told her, crossing his arms over his chest. But she didn't care if he did. This was blood he'd spill for her and she couldn't have that on her conscience.

"I . . ." Her mind thought it all through. "That task force has evidence against my aunt, right? They have enough to arrest her, they're just waiting. But maybe we should deliver her to them. Where is Saber?"

"Done a runner. Doubt he'll come back for her. So yeah, might be an idea to land her in their laps." Zander didn't ask who the task force was, so she guessed he already knew about them.

"Shit, Saber got away?" Linc asked.

Zander nodded. "He'll hide away somewhere, regroup. Don't know if he'll come back here, though. Markovich's men ripped his men apart. It was fucking carnage."

"Where did this take place? Does Ed know?" Linc asked.

"I don't work for the sheriff. But guessing he'll know by now. It was out of town, the place where the Devil's Sinners have been staying. Markovich's men snuck in on them. Markovich will be pissed I got to Tiger. Someone must have alerted Saber and Rosalind. Sent them running. He took off on his bike and we missed him, but she was busy trying to stuff shit into her car."

Typical Rosalind.

"I want to see her," she said firmly.

Linc turned to her. "Sure, baby?"

"Yes, not him. I never want to see him again." She shuddered. "But I want to see her before we hand her over. I want to know if she ever cared about me."

"Why would you care about that?" Zander asked.

"She's the only family I have left," Marisol said.

"No, baby, she isn't," Linc told her. "We're your family now. Me and everyone on this ranch."

She blinked back tears then nodded. "Then I just want to see her for closure. Please."

"We can make that happen," Zander said.

"It's safe?" Linc asked.

"Of course." Zander looked affronted. "What about Tiger? Want me to get rid of him?"

"Why don't you hand him back to Markovich?" Linc asked. "Seems only fair."

Zander thought about it then nodded. "Yeah. I've got everything I want from him. Come on then. I don't have all night. And you really need to put some clothes on."

She glanced down her mouth falling open as she noticed that Linc was completely naked.

"Shit!" Linc swore, covering himself with his hands. "Why the fuck didn't you say anything?"

Zander shrugged. "I'm in your home. Figured it was rude to tell you to get dressed."

"Jesus. Since when do you care about being rude?"

Zander scowled. "Since a certain brat came to live with me. You can follow me in your truck. You got that car seat installed for the pipsqueak yet?"

"So it was you who sent it?" Marisol asked.

Zander gave a nod.

"Thank you," she told him.

"You're welcome, pipsqueak. Is it in your truck?" he asked Linc who was busy getting dressed.

"Yes," Linc snapped back. "Now can you please give us some privacy to get dressed."

Zander turned. "Sure, but don't know why you're so shy now. Not like I haven't seen it all."

Linc just growled.

36

Marisol nervously looked out the window at what appeared to be an old, abandoned warehouse. "This is where they've been staying?"

Linc peered out as Zander climbed from his truck in front of them. He held a large flashlight. "I guess so." Linc got out of the truck and came around to get her, pulling her under his arm as they followed Zander into the warehouse. She didn't even know what this could have been used for, it seemed to be in the middle of nowhere.

As he got to the door, he drew it open. The inside was dark and derelict. She shivered.

"You cold?" he asked.

"She shouldn't be with the amount of clothing you put on her," Zander said dryly. He moved to the far end then crouched down and shoved aside a few crates, revealing a trapdoor in the floor. He gave three knocks followed by two then stepped back to wait.

The trapdoor opened and to her shock, a woman poked her head out. She wore a headlamp, adding more light to the dark building. "About time, boss."

Zander shrugged. "They had to get dressed. Linc's shy."

"Huh. Got a small one, does he?"

Linc groaned.

"Nah, average," Zander replied.

Average? She felt herself bristle then to her shock, she saw Zander grin at Linc. Glancing up, she saw Linc shake his head.

"This is Honey. She works for me. We've come to see the woman."

"Webb gagged her after she tried to bite him. Which was actually pretty funny. What about Tiger?"

"We're going to make a gift out of him, deliver him to Markovich."

"Fun," Honey said as she disappeared down the hole. "Want me to get on that?"

"Yep, have Ammo and Webb help you. I called Markovich on the way over. We've arranged a meeting place." He followed Honey into the hole. Marisol gulped as she peered into the darkness. She wasn't keen on climbing down a ladder she couldn't see.

Then light flashed up at her, illuminating the way.

"I'll go first, Mari-girl and guide you down, okay?" Linc soothed.

"Yeah, okay."

He climbed down a few rungs then made space for her to follow. He moved at a slow pace and it felt like forever until they were at the bottom. Zander was waiting there.

"You are afraid of small spaces? The dark? Ladders?" he asked.

"Maybe all of the above?" she half-joked.

"You won't do well down here then."

Right. That was an understatement.

"Let's get this over with," Linc said briskly.

"She's this way."

Zander led them down a hallway, his flashlight bobbing. Then he knocked on a door. It opened, to reveal a dark-skinned, bald man. This room had more light, thanks to the battery-powered lanterns that had been set up. It held two chairs. One close to the door, that the bald guy had likely been sitting in. Then another chair across the far side of the room, which her aunt was currently tied to.

As soon as Rosalind saw her, she started to wiggle, making noises behind the gag. She looked terrible, her hair was wild, her clothes dirty and torn in places. Her mascara was smudged down her cheeks. Marisol didn't like seeing her like this.

"Can we take the gag out please?" she asked. She searched in her bag for some wet wipes, pulling them out as Zander nodded to the guy guarding Rosalind.

He drew out the gag and her aunt scowled up at him. *"Coño de tu Madre!"*

Marisol jolted in surprise as her aunt spat Spanish at Zander.

"Aunt," she said quietly.

"You." Rosalind turned her lethal gaze on Marisol. "Get me out of here. Now."

Zander snorted.

Marisol looked over at Zander. "Can I wipe her face?" she asked, holding up the packet of wet wipes.

Zander reached out a hand to take them. "I'll do it." He moved closer to Rosalind. "Just a warning, you bite me and I'll bite back."

Rosalind spat at him. "Fuck you!"

"Aunt!" Marisol said, shocked by her. She was like a wild animal.

Zander calmly drew out a wet wipe and cleaned her face with measured movements. Then he turned away from Rosalind and gave the packet back to Marisol.

"Marisol. Get. Me. Out. Of. Here."

"I can't, Aunt."

"Can't! After all I've fucking done for you! I should have let them send you back to that she-devil in Venezuela. I gave you everything and this is how you repay me? By letting them treat me like this? You owe me, Marisol. Do you think I wanted to take in a whiny brat? I had a life to live and you held me back, dragging me down."

Marisol flinched, her gaze dropping to the ground. She tightly grasped hold of the pack of wet wipes.

"Why did you take her in?" Linc asked, placing his arm around Marisol's waist. She leaned into him. Was Rosalind right? Did Marisol owe her?

"Because she was my sister's daughter. I loved Gaby. And Gaby would have been devastated if her brat got sent back to our bitch mother."

Marisol took in a shaky breath.

"So it had nothing to do with the money?" Zander asked calmly.

"What money?" Marisol asked.

"How do you know about that?" Rosalind snapped, glaring at Zander.

Zander turned to his man. "Leave us for a moment?"

"Gladly," the other man replied and slipped out of the room, shutting the door behind him.

"Zander?" Linc asked.

"The money Rosalind's husband settled on you, pipsqueak, when he divorced her."

"What?" she whispered. "Harry?"

"Yep. See, I got curious about why someone as selfish as Rosalind would take in a four-year-old kid. So my tech guy did some research. Seems that when he was a teenager, Harry had an accident that left him unable to have children. My guess is that he pressured Rosalind to take custody of you. Or he got wind of you and she didn't want him to think badly of her, so she took you in."

"He was such a do-gooder," Rosalind spat out. "My mistake was introducing you and Gaby to him. I couldn't hide you from him once she died. He insisted that we take you in. He doted on you. Adored you."

"But you said that he divorced you because of me. That he got sick of me."

"I was sick of you!" Rosalind shouted. "I told you that to shut you up. Every night you'd cry for him, you were always asking for him. Christ, I should have left you with him."

"But if you'd done that, you wouldn't have gotten your monthly stipend from him to support Marisol," Zander commented.

"What do you mean? Are you saying that Harry paid her to take care of me?" Marisol asked.

"Yep. Because Harry was smart and had a clause in his pre-nup that if Rosalind cheated on him, she got nothing. He had someone follow her, and Rosalind got caught on camera sucking some guy off in the parking lot of a bar."

Eww.

"Rosalind was out with nothing," Zander continued. "Except for you."

"That asshole wanted me to leave you with him. I wish I had. It wasn't worth the money he paid me to keep you," Rosalind spat out hatefully.

"But you took the money, didn't you, Rosalind? You're still getting paid, aren't you?" Zander asked.

"What?" Marisol gasped.

"What are you telling Harry? That's she's in college and you need it for the fees?" Zander queried.

"None of your fucking business. I am owed that money for taking care of her all these fucking years."

Marisol's mind was reeling. "All these years and I thought he didn't want me. I thought it was my fault. You told me it was my fault."

"You're so gullible. A little mouse scurrying around, scared of your own shadow. It was all too easy to manipulate you into doing what I wanted. Now, get me the fuck out of here!"

"Marisol?" Linc asked quietly. "What do you want to do? We'll let her go if that's what you want." She could tell he didn't want that, though. The way he held himself told her that he'd rather do something much more horrid to Rosalind but was holding back because of Marisol.

Zander made a noise but didn't say anything.

"He would have taken me?" she whispered. "He wanted me?"

"You were all he wanted," Rosalind spat. "It was Marisol this, Marisol that."

"Surprised he didn't try to pay you for her," Zander said.

Rosalind smiled. "He didn't deserve to get what he wanted."

That evil bitch. She'd made them all suffer, while she'd reaped the rewards.

"Take her to Ed or that task force. Drop her off. Tell them I'll tell them whatever I know if they lock her up and throw away the key."

"Gladly." Zander smiled. It wasn't pretty.

She turned away, but Linc paused, looking back. "You never deserved her. You were given her to care for and you neglected her. Abused her. And you're going to hell for it. I hope someone makes you rot in jail and someone makes you their bitch."

She didn't say anything, instead she leaned into Linc as he guided her out. She barely heard Rosalind's screeches. Barely paid attention as Linc led her up the ladder and out into his truck.

Halfway home, she turned to him. "He wanted me."

Linc reached over and grabbed her hand, squeezing it lightly. "Of course he did."

"She kept me from him all these years." Tears dripped down her face.

"I know, Mari-girl. I'm so sorry."

"I wonder why he never tried to contact me."

"Maybe he did. Or maybe he agreed not to contact you. Maybe she told him lies like she told you."

She gasped. "Oh God, maybe he thinks I didn't want to see him." She thought of all those lost years. "I could have had a family."

"You have one now, teeny. You have me and everyone on the ranch. We will always be here for you."

"I know." She smiled at him through her tears. He parked outside their cabin. Their home. She let out a sigh of relief. He turned and undid the clasp of her car seat, pulling off the straps. Then he came around the truck and lifted her down. But instead of letting her walk, he carried her into the cabin.

After he removed their jackets and coats, he led her into the bedroom and sat on the bed with her on his lap.

She looked up at him. "If I'd stayed with Harry, I'd likely have been happier. Taken care of. Loved."

"I know, Mari-girl."

"But I wouldn't have met you," she whispered. "And if going through all of that pain means that I get you at the end, then it's worth it to me. You're worth that to me."

"Teeny." He closed his eyes and kissed her forehead. "Me too. All the pain that Jessica caused me was worth it. Because here I am. With you. Always."

EPILOGUE

"**D**addy! Look at that giant gorilla. It's so cute!"

She kept her voice low so no one would hear her. Although the fair was pretty quiet tonight. In fact, there was hardly anyone around them, other than the game attendant. It was one where you had to get the rings around the tops of bottles.

"Can I play?" She tugged at his arm excitedly.

"Of course you can, Mari-girl." He kissed the top of her head.

It had been over a month since she'd seen Rosalind. Zander had been true to his word. He'd handed Rosalind to the task force on a platter. They hadn't been overly pleased since they'd been hoping to get to Saber and the Devil's Sinners. However, Rosalind had surprised them all by singing like a canary about everything.

Marisol wasn't sure how Zander had gotten her to keep quiet about the role he and his people had played in everything. And she didn't want to know, frankly.

Tiger had disappeared. She guessed Markovich had taken care of him. Sometimes she still felt some guilt over it, but then Linc reminded her of everything Tiger had done. That he likely would have gone on to hurt other women and she didn't feel so bad.

It was less than three weeks until Christmas and Linc had brought her down to Houston for a break from the Montana winter. She loved the snow. But she was struggling with how cold it was. Linc had banned her from leaving the house without him, because she'd gotten a cold a few weeks back when she'd been making snowmen and stayed out too long.

He'd gone into protective overdrive. She'd found herself in bed for a week. And as soon he'd declared her well, she'd ended up over his knee, getting paddled.

Last night they'd gone out for some Venezuelan street food. She hadn't eaten *arepas* since Ana had made them for her. They'd been delicious.

She attempted the ring toss, pouting as most of them missed. "I'm no good at this."

"You can't be good at everything. Let Daddy have a try."

She glanced over at the attendant to see if he was paying attention, but he was more interested in his phone than the two of them.

Linc started tossing out rings, getting each one over the bottles. She clapped her hands and cheered excitedly.

"Well done, sir. You can choose anything from the top row."

"The gorilla! The gorilla!"

"That's going to be interesting to get home on the plane," Linc said dryly as the attendant handed over the pink gorilla which was nearly as big as Marisol was.

"We might have to buy him his own seat," she said with a giggle, hugging him tight. "Can we go have a corn dog, Daddy?"

He grimaced but nodded. "All right."

Linc kept a close eye on her diet, but he wasn't an ogre about it. And she liked that she had freedom, but she still knew he was watching over her. He could be far stricter about other things. Like her walking around while reading. She'd done that just this morning in the hotel suite when she'd thought he was in the shower. She'd just needed to finish beta reading Caley's latest story. She hadn't been looking where she was going and had ended up walking right into Linc.

Then she'd ended up over his knee, getting spanked. Afterwards, she'd had to sit on her hot ass and write fifty times, that she would not walk while reading.

Caley had hired her on as her assistant. She just worked in the mornings for her. Then in the afternoons, she read. Or if Linc was home, she crafted or played. Often times, he'd come home for lunch then put her down for a nap afterwards.

As they walked towards the corn dog stand, she slowed then stopped. There was something about the man ahead of them. He was walking towards them, watching her intently.

His dark hair was sprinkled liberally with gray. He had a handsome face. One of those men that got better looking as they aged. He wore a neatly pressed shirt and slacks. His clothes seemed too formal for a fair. And yet, he wasn't exactly out of place.

As he drew closer, she gasped then looked up at Linc.

"I wasn't sure whether to tell you," Linc said quietly to her. "Don't be mad at me."

"You found him?"

"Yeah, baby. I didn't want to let you know until I'd talked to him."

He meant he'd wanted to make sure that Harry wasn't going to hurt Marisol.

"He wants to see me," she stated.

"Baby, as soon as I told him everything Rosalind revealed to us, he wanted to be on the first plane to Montana. Then when I told him about your life with her, well, he thought that you wouldn't want to see him."

Harry had stopped by now, he was watching them, obviously waiting for her to come to him.

"What?" she gasped. "Of course I want to see him."

"He thinks you might be upset with him. Angry that he didn't fight harder for you. That he took Rosalind's word that you wanted nothing to do with him."

"She told him that?" Pain lashed at her insides.

"Yep. She did her best to keep the two of you apart. But you have the opportunity to be together now. Go to him, baby. He's hurting as much as you. If not more. He has a lot of guilt."

She stepped forward, shaky at first but then as she grew closer to Harry, she gathered up speed and threw herself at him. He opened his arms, catching her, pulling her tight against him and rocking her gently.

"Oh, my girl. My darling girl."

He even smelled the same. Sounded the same. He still had that accent.

She pulled back and looked up at him, tears dripping down her cheeks. "Harry."

He ran his hand over her hair. "Look how beautiful you are. My precious girl. I'm so sorry. So sorry I left you with that viper."

"It wasn't your fault."

"It was," he insisted. "I listened to her lies. I shouldn't have. I thought about finding you so many times. I sent investigators to check on you, but they always said you were fine."

"She never did anything to me in public."

He closed his eyes in pain. "I'm so sorry, banana. So sorry."

She giggled at the old nickname, given to her because she'd gone through a stage of only wanting to eat bananas and nothing else. Harry had had their housekeeper make her all sorts of banana concoctions.

"I should have checked in on you myself. But it hurt too much to see you. I love you so much, banana."

"Love you too, Harry. I've missed you."

"Well, maybe we can make up for lost time, huh?" he asked.

She smiled, tears streaming down her face. "Yeah. I'd like that."

Harry looked over and she turned to see Linc approach with a smile. Harry moved her to his side as he reached out his hand. "You must be Linc."

Linc shook his hand. "Sir."

"None of that. Call me Harry. If you're with my girl then you're part of my family."

She closed her eyes with contentment. The missing part of her heart was here. Maybe she hadn't seen him for years. Maybe he had changed, although it didn't seem that way to her. But even so, she wanted to know him. She wanted him in her life, even if it was just in a small way. She looked from Harry to Linc as they chatted.

Life with Linc was amazing. Not perfect. But pretty damn close.

And she wanted it noted, that staying with him was the best decision she'd ever made.

Printed in Great Britain
by Amazon

25411483R00212